I0669458

# SPACE BRIDES LLC

Edited by Dana Bell

WolfSinger Publications ❧ Brackettville, Texas

# DEDICATION

For God who inspired the idea.
To those brides of yesteryear who traveled west to wed a
complete stranger, the Harvey Girls for their dedication to the
railroad and those children who were shipped out of the cities for
a sometimes brighter future.

# TABLE OF CONTENTS

Introduction -                                                      1
Space Brides LLC Ad -                                               2
The Heist – Jocelyne Gregory -                                      3
Gravity – Sage Kelly -                                             20
The Bad Luck Bride – Kat Farrow -                                  37
Mining the Stars – Hayley Liversidge -                             56
Runaway Bride – Harriet Phoenix -                                  66
Sol Maritus – K.B. Johnson -                                       80
A Spectrum of Secrets – Eric Taveren -                            100
Finding Common Ground – Cecily Winter -                           121
Lapin Chasseur – Jennifer Roberts -                               136
The Titan and the Princess – G.A. Babouche -                      154
Her Big Fat Lunar Wedding – Jean Martin -                         174
Romance of the Algorithm – Laura Hilse -                          183
Hope Among the Stars – Luke T. Barnett -                          201
Had My Reasons – Dana Bell -                                      217
She's a Bit Green – Bogna Jordan -                                235

# INTRODUCTION

When the human race begins to settle other worlds, no doubt it will be like sailing to the new world or journeying to the west on foot, horseback, by stagecoach or via railroad, except spaceships will be used.

With the expansion will come the need for husbands, wives, mates, or partners. As in the old days, no doubt various agencies will step up to fill the gap with rules and regulations on how the matches are to be made.

Thus the theme for this anthology: Space Brides, LLC.

The authors of the various tales come from parts of the United States, Canada, and Great Britian. They are written by a mix of writers.

Most of the stories are male and females matches, but there are a few which use other pairings.

It is the hope of the editor that the readers enjoy the stories. They are varied, full of surprises and end in unexpected ways.

# SPACE BRIDES LLC

Tired of those lonely dark nights? No one in your settlement suitable? We are here to help! We will help you find the bride or husband to keep you company, raise your children, and be your partner building a dream together. Contact us directly and give us your specifications. Success guaranteed.

Looking to settle off world? We have husbands and wives searching for you. Have children who need a second parent? They're more than welcome. Contract signature required and once signed can't be withdrawn.

On site ministers at no charge available for immediate marriage or up to six months after your spouse's arrival. After that there will be an extra fee for our services or you may hold a private ceremony with the official of your choice. Copy of marriage agreement/ document required to be sent directly to us. This is to advertise our success rate and encourage others to use our services.

Any children must be declared before the contract is signed and approved by the potential spouse/partner. This includes those seeking our services off world or anyone traveling. Failure to do so will require the child's travel to be paid for by the party who did not declare the minor before being allowed to meet the contractor of our services. If either party does not approve the child, then another candidate will be sought up to three times.

If the imported spouse is not suitable after a two-week trial period, it is the contractor's responsibility to find another potential candidate and annul the marriage, if there has been one. There will be no refund of the charged fee if this occurs.

Spouses sought for all legal adults and in all age brackets.

Our offices are available on Earth, Mars, the Asteroids, Titan, Io, and Triton. Helpful staff will walk you through the steps and make certain all legalities are conformed to local ordinances.

Contact or walk into any of our offices 24/7. We are here to help you find that special someone and start a new future!

Other conditions apply. Please ask for more information before contract is drawn up and signed.

# THE HEIST

Jocelyne Gregory

## Emma

"Good morning! It's time to wake up, get up, and greet a new day."

"Hannah, our shift doesn't start for three hours," Emma groaned. She pulled her blankets over her head to block the sight of her cheerful roommate and coworker. "Let me sleep for another hour."

"Aw, come on, sleepy head. Today is a very special occasion."

"How?"

"We're skimming the Asteroid belt, and we'll be able to see Saturn's rings from the viewing windows."

"And?"

Hannah pulled back the company issued grey blankets revealing the cramped, cell-like room with pale artificial lights and numerous ferns dangling from the ceiling. Hannah sat on the edge of Emma's bottom bunk bed already dressed in her ankle length black dress, and blindingly white apron. Her curly hair held back with a white headband. Her polished copper nametag shined like the sun.

"And the tourists on board are going to want pictures with us in our uniforms which means more tips!"

"Ah. Capitalism."

Hannah rolled her eyes. "Yes, capitalism. I know you come from one of those utopian," she quoted the word with her fingers, "socialist colonies. But in the rest of the solar system, we use money to buy things."

"Like what?"

"Clothing. Technology. Attractive husbands. I mean, if you didn't have this job, you wouldn't be on your way to meet your future husband."

"Please don't remind me." Emma rubbed her face, her voice muffled as she spoke.

"What's this? Are you regretting it? You have three USB sticks filled with messages from him, you literally said you two have been messaging each other for two years." Hannah leaned closer, her brown eyes filling with raw curiosity. "Tell me."

"I'm not regretting it, I'm just…I don't know. Our beliefs might be too different."

Hannah groaned. "Then just stay on board the Light Train for a few seasons, earn a ton of money, buy a husband to your liking, and go home."

"You can't buy love," Emma pointed out.

"You're starting to sound like one of those Arkavarian aliens. Heart mates this, heart mates that, glowing scales when aroused, blessed are the children, blah blah blah." Hannah waved her hand. "Come on, get up. We're losing tips."

## T'Aner

"General, we're approaching the Asteroid belt."

"Good. M'Ackle, Fu'Shin, ease into the Asteroid's field, slow speed, and get as close to the Light Train's path without triggering their security systems," T'Aner ordered.

He stood on the darkened command deck, the only light came from the various consoles hugging the walls. The ship was small, far smaller than the traditional galleons he led in service to the Arkavarian empire. He wasn't skimming Earth's vast corporate colonies and territory on Empire's orders, he'd come on a personal mission, and he'd sworn he would accomplish his duty.

"Last weapons check before mission start." Su'Sar joined him on deck.

Like him, she was tall with crested black hair and glowing purple eyes. The thick layer of green scales trailing from behind her ear, down her jaw, and to her chin glimmered faintly in the darkness of the command deck. Like him, she wore a maroon-coloured bodysuit. She held out her gloved hands expectantly.

"The others ready?" He glanced at the door separating the deck and the rest of the ship. He handed her his neon yellow rifle. No doubt overkill for what they expected, but experience told him most humans feared their style of weapons.

"All ready, General. I checked their guns, knives, and emergency equipment," she reported. "The Freeson brothers are getting restless. They know the parameters of this mission. No death, capture, retreat."

"Good."

Su'Sar quickly checked his weapon in the dim lights. Her glowing eyes examined every detail before giving him a curt nod and holding out his rifle.

"Weapons checked. We're ready, General. May the Seven Sisters be with us."

"May they bless us," T'Aner agreed.

"General, the Light Train is approaching," Fu'Shin announced. "Ten minutes to contact."

"Maintain course, and be prepared." He reached into the side-pocket of his maroon suit, his fingers tracing the delicate edge of folded paper.

## Emma

"On the lunch menu, we have Martian eggs over Lunar toast," Emma explained. She stood by a table in the crowded dining car, her tablet in hand as she took customer's orders. Roughly eighty people sat in the car. About twenty women like herself dressed in black dresses with white aprons taking orders, bringing coffees, teas, and snacks.

"Sounds good. Please, no paprika," the couple ordered, both wearing brand new corporate mining uniforms.

Emma made the note on the tablet and gave them what she hoped was a smile. "Of course. Your order will be out in a few minutes. Excuse me."

She left the couple, checked on another table packed with soldiers seeking their fortunes among the stars, and made a beeline for the kitchen, filled with hectic activity. Several service robots making food exactly as described on the menu, while a smaller group of human cooks made the meals with the changes in ingredients and flavours. Meal plates were beginning to pile up beneath the long row of heat lights, and she ducked out of the way as several other women swooped in, took the plates, and swooped out of the kitchen.

Hannah swept into the kitchen carrying a tray loaded with dishes. She dumped them in a pile next to the dishwasher and let out a heavy breath.

"You know, I'll never understand why they have can't robots clean up the tables."

"They'd get stuck on a speck of dust, or a stain," Emma mused.

"Probably. Oh, did you hear? There's a train compartment filled with orphan kids," Hannah whispered.

"Orphan kids?" Emma frowned.

Hannah nodded. "Yeah, apparently they're being sent to families who work for the Asmos Corporation."

"The mining company on one of Jupiter's moons?"

"It is. Anyway, could I ask a huge, and I mean, huge favour?"

"Let me guess, you need to take them food and you don't want to?" Emma crossed her arms.

"I'll share half of my days tips, and I'll handle your orders."

"Fine," Emma reluctantly agreed. "What am I taking them?"

Hannah grabbed her sleeve and dragged her to the back of the kitchen. She revealed a trolley lined with sandwiches and juice boxes, and a roll of stickers showing a space train flying past a rainbow with the name Light Train Express written at the bottom.

"Each kid gets a choice of sandwich, juice box, and a sticker," Hannah explained.

Emma's tablet suddenly chirped. "Table nine's lunch is ready."

Hannah plucked the tablet free. "I'll bring it to them. The kids' section is two carriages back, before third class baggage. See you at Saturn's Picture event!"

Hannah ran over to the counter, took the Martian Eggs and toast order, and danced out of the kitchen with a brilliant smile on her face.

Emma shook her head as she pulled out the trolley and pushed it towards the rear door. She waved her wrist band over the door sensor, and it *chirped* as it opened for her revealing the food, extra plates and other items storage section. The room felt cooler, a pleasant escape from the heat of the various stoves and cooktops. She continued towards the next door, and waved her wrist over the sensor again. It opened with another chirp, and again the carriage grew cooler.

Ships and light trains carrying orphans were famous among the many corporate colonies. Death, a common occurrence for many reasons particularly among mining families, industrial accidents at research facilities, and the occasional collapse of non-terraformed planets, encouraged the practice. Emma loathed the idea of moving children out of their communities and the only homes they'd ever known. Her viewpoint came from her own colony. Neighbors and other families took in orphaned children, raising them as their own.

*Would her future husband be willing to accept an orphaned child?*

Emma shook her head. Every time she'd tried to bring up kids in the messages they sent back and forth, Teddy never responded. Maybe another red flag their relationship wouldn't work.

"Come on, Emma. At least meet him in person," she tried to convince herself.

She pushed the trolley down the narrow grey corridor, noting the few viewing windows and the exterior lights illuminating the outside of the train. She stopped in front of the door, willed herself to smile like the training guide taught her, and opened the door.

Rows and rows of makeshift bunk beds lined the right side of the train carriage with kids sitting quietly. A middle-age security guard, wearing black pants and a white shirt, sat on a chair by the door reading on his tablet. He carried a Light Train issued rifle on his side.

"What's this?" He looked up from his tablet.

"Lunch for the children," Emma informed him. "Sandwiches, juices, and stickers."

He set his tablet on the narrow table beside his chair and stood up. He cleared his throat. "All right kids, line up for your lunch. Don't cut in line or you're not eating until supper."

Appalled Emma started at him. "Is that really necessary?"

"Damn kids are feral. You have to be firm with them. Most have no manners." He sniffed.

She clenched her hands and resisted the urge to slap him. The children had gone through a rough time after losing their families. Straightening as she'd been taught, she smiled at the first child in line, a nine-year-old boy with sad brown eyes wearing beige coveralls.

"What would you like, Sir? We have Martian chicken or fresh Phobos chickpea sandwiches." Even though they were young and without money, she would treat them just as if they were a famed scientist or poet, and she ensured they had a choice.

*Probably the first choice they'd had in a long time.*

"Phobos chickpea," he whispered.

"Very good. And choice of drink? We have Orange Manx, and Appalicious Frizz."

"Orange."

"Excellent choice, Sir. We also have a sticker, if you would like one," she offered.

He shook his sandy coloured hair and quietly shuffled back to his bunk with his juice box and sandwich.

Her heart ached. She bit back the words of comfort she wanted to say. She smiled at the next child who shyly approached her, a girl maybe three or four with a bandage on her cheek. She knelt so she was eye-level with the girl, and gave her the biggest smile she could muster.

"Hello, Miss, what would you like?"

She did this with each child until the trolley only held a few items. Last in line, a little girl with her head bowed carried a small, furry rat-like creature with long ears in her hands.

"Oh my," Emma gushed. "May I ask what your companion's name is, miss?"

The little girl glanced up at her.

Emma's mouth parted at the sight of large purple eyes staring back at her with a very thin line of soft pink scales along the girl's jaw and eyebrows.

"She's one of those Arkavarian cross-breeds," the security guard spat. "Ugly things. Stupid to boot."

The little girl quickly looked at her feet.

"She's a child. Don't say such things," Emma snapped.

"Thought they taught you girls to smile and laugh, not talk back. You want me to report you to your superior?"

Emma gritted her teeth. She shut her eyes and silently counted to ten, calming herself before she turned to the guard and flashed him one of the patented Light Rail smiles.

"Oh, I don't think you need to do that, Sir. If you'll excuse me, I'll take the young miss back to her bed with her food. Her hands look full." Emma grabbed the sandwiches, juice box, and stickers, then gestured for the girl to lead her to her bed.

"I'm taking my break," the guard yelled.

Emma glared at his back as he left the train carriage.

The little girl shuffled to the last bunk bed and settled on it. The boy with sad eyes sat on the top bunk, watching them.

"Here we are, isn't this more comfortable? I'm Emma. What's your name, miss?"

"Suzie," she whispered.

"What a lovely name." Emma smiled. "Which sandwich would you like to eat? Martian chicken? Or Phobos Chickpea?"

"Can…An'Ranna eat too?" She held up the long-eared rat.

"Of course. Companions are always welcomed on Light Rail trains."

"Martian Chicken," Suzie decided.

"Good choice. May I help you unwrap it?"

Suzie nodded.

Emma easily unwrapped the sandwich and placed it on the bed beside Suzie. She was just about to ask which juice box she wanted, when the overhead lights suddenly went out.

The room immediately filled with the soft sounds of children panicking and whispering.

"Nobody panic," Emma announced. "I'm sure it's just an electrical issue of being too close to the Asteroid Belt. Everything will be all right."

She felt her way off the bunk bead and hit the top of her head on the metal bunk above. She hissed at the shot of pain.

"Let me help you," Suzie offered. "I can see in the dark."

Suzie took Emma's hand and led her towards the doorway the guard left through.

"Thank you." Emma felt for the control panel, and waved her wrist over the sensor. Suddenly the room flooded with red emergency light. "There we go, see? Nothing wrong."

A sharp hiss came from the overhead speakers, and an electronic voice began to speak.

"*Warning. Train Robbery in process. All civilians return to your rooms. Security report to your stations. Serving staff report to your superiors. Warning. Train Robbery in process.*"

The door to the carriage hissed open. Emma dragged Suzie behind her. The security guard stood there, his eyes wide, his rifle in his arms.

"What's happening?" she asked.

The guard wobbled where he stood before his eyes fell shut and he dropped to the floor. Emma looked past him, and paled at the sight of several men and a woman wearing maroon bodysuits carrying strange, alien, weapons. Their leader, tall, broad shouldered, with crested black hair, large purple eyes, and dark orange scales hugging his jaw line that ran up his temples and disappearing into his hair.

"Arkavarians!" a child screamed.

Without thinking, Emma grabbed the security guards' rifle, switched the safety off, and took aim at the aliens.

"One step closer and I'll shoot!" she snarled.

## T'Aner

*She's beautiful.*

Of all the scenarios T'Aner imagined, all of the life or death events, all the plans of fighting their way through the train to the so-called orphans carriage, in all the back-up plans not once did he ever think he would come across a lone human woman dressed in a strange religious black and white gown aiming a weapon at him and threatening to shoot.

*She's beyond beautiful.*

Her hazel eyes shined with a primal viciousness informing him she would shoot to protect the young behind her. Her brown hair was held back with a narrow white head band, and the way she held the humans rifle told him she knew how to use it.

"General, what are your orders?" Su'Sar hissed beside him. Her own rifle aimed at the human woman.

"Did the Seven Sisters send you?" T'Aner asked suddenly. His heart beating faster, his eyes drinking in her body.

"General?" Su'Sar gaped.

The human woman frowned, her perfect brown brows pulling together across her gorgeous face. "What?"

"Surely the Seven Sisters sent a goddess such as yourself to be here now, as we dance along the edge of time and space, as our paths kiss the Asteroid Belt that divides our lives," T'Aner continued.

"Why is he reciting poetry?" one of the Freeson brothers complained behind him. "We don't have much time!"

T'Aner ignored him. He watched as confusion and bewilderment crossed the human woman's face. Obviously, his words were unexpected, such was common when the Seven Sisters blessed a meeting between fated souls.

"I don't know what you're talking about, but one step closer and I will shoot," the woman threatened.

Oh, how his heart ached at her words. He needed to show her he posed no threat. He raised his hand, and slowly put his rifle on the ground. "See me, goddess of the radiant world, I mean you no harm. Only to speak to you, to hear your voice, to learn your name and etch it across my heart as the Sisters demand."

"For Harker's sake," Su'Sar groaned. "Please tell me what's happening isn't what's happening."

"Quiet, you'll scare her," T'Aner hissed. He focused on her again. "If not a goddess, than a fallen star from the eternal heavens, gifted to take form amongst us of flesh and scale, a light in the darkness depths of space, a siren among broken ships."

He dropped to his knees with his hands held out and his palms turned upward. He would await her words, and if she declined him, he would throw himself out the nearest door and surrender his life to space itself. Better a quick death than to live without her.

"Why is the general reciting poetry to a human?" one of the brothers hissed behind him.

The woman seemed to hesitate at his words. His heart felt like it climbed from his chest to his throat. She glanced behind her, before turning her wide gorgeous gaze on him.

"You think I'm your heart mate?"

## Emma

"Why is he saying weird things?" The children asked as they gathered behind Emma.

After the initial fear, they'd crowded around her to watch the much-feared Arkavarian robbers began to speak.

Suzie tugged on Emma's white apron. "He's saying poetry."

Emma glanced down at her. "Why?"

"Because he thinks you're his heart mate."

Emma paused and slowly let Suzie's words sink in. *Heart mate?* The Arkavarian's were famous for their bloody civil wars and battles against various human corporations. Even she'd heard the rumours of their strange marriage bonds. What Suzie described rarely occurred between humans and Arkavarians, although Emma had a sinking sensation Suzie had been the result of one such bond pairing.

"That's stupid, why would anybody recite poetry?" a boy muttered from somewhere behind Emma.

"Because it means they don't want to attack or kill you," Suzie told him.

A soft chorus of *ohhs* came behind Emma.

Emma turned her attention back to the now kneeling Arkavarian train robber. His expression flickered between desperate hope and terrifying fear.

She cleared her throat, and tightened her grip on her rifle. "You think I'm your heart mate?"

The tall alien woman next to him slammed her hand over her face and let out a loud groan, while the rather ferocious men behind him seemed to be bickering with each other.

The Arkavarian leader nodded, his purple eyes wide. "I do. Allow me to speak my name. I am T'Aner of House Serie, General of the Imperial Arkavarian's Galleon fleet."

Emma wet her lips. T'Aner seemed sincere enough, but it could be a ploy. What exactly was a general of an alien navy doing on a Light Rail Train on the inside of the Asteroid Belt? *Where was security?*

Suzie tugged on her apron again. "He's waiting for your name."

*Well...anything to buy them some time.* Emma cleared her throat, "I'm Emma from the New Earth Collective."

One of the Arkavarian robbers in the back of the group raised his hand. "What's a collective?"

"They fight with words, not weapons," the female alien explained.

"But she knows how to hold a rifle," the male alien pointed out. "What if they can use their words as weapons? What if they have word weapons?"

"That's not important right now," T'Aner interrupted.

"That's right. The mission is what's important, *General,*" the female alien growled.

Emma narrowed her gaze. "Whatever you want, it's not back here. First Class passengers and their freight are the first two carriages at the front of the train."

"We're not here for the freight." T'Aner slowly reached into his side pocket, and withdrew a folded piece of paper. He tossed it across the room so it landed at Emma's feet.

"What's that?" Emma didn't take her eyes off the others.

"What we're looking for." T'Aner seemed to wait for her response.

"General!" the woman alien hissed.

"It's fine," T'Aner assured the female. "Just, look."

Without lowering her rifle, Emma slowly knelt and plucked the piece of paper off the ground. She unfolded it, and pressed it against her apron, quickly glancing at the sheet. She did a double take at the image. The drawing showed the smiling face of a young girl with large purple eyes and pale pink scales on her jawline and eyebrows. A long-eared rat sat atop her head, while a woman with purple eyes and red scales on her jaw smiled at the artist from behind her.

It looked just like Suzie and her companion rat.

"This is…" Emma trailed off.

"I promised her grandmother I would bring her home," T'Aner said slowly. "We mean you, and the occupants of this train no ill will. We just want the girl."

Emma tore her gaze from the image down to Suzie who looked up at her with wide worried eyes.

"They want you." Emma handed her the piece of paper.

Suzie took the drawing with trembling fingers. She cautiously stepped out from behind Emma's broad skirts and swallowed hard.

"My grandmother wants me?"

T'Aner nodded. "She didn't know about your parents' death until a week ago. You need to come with us."

"Is that what you want, Suzie?" Emma asked.

"You too."

"Excuse me?" Emma snapped her head up.

T'aner offered her his hand. "Emma of the New Earth collective, gift of the Seven Sisters, brilliant light of a newly born star, please, share your radiant warmth with my cold, frozen, heart."

"I have a boyfriend."

Abject despair crossed T'aner's handsome face, his purple eyes filling with so much sorrow it made Emma feel guilty about her words. Before she could explain further, the carriage began shaking.

# T'Aner

*"I have a boyfriend."*

Waves of grief washed over T'Aner at his heart mate's proclamation. It took him several seconds to digest her words because Arkavarian's didn't have 'boyfriends,' they had heart mates.

But Emma of the New Earth collective had a 'boyfriend.'

The knowledge drove a dagger through his aching heart. She had given her love to another. If he could learn of her 'boyfriends' name maybe he could find him and they could have a long, thoughtful, conversation with knives, as was the Arkavarian way.

The sudden smack on the back of his head caught him off guard. He jerked his head towards Su'Sar just in time to watch as she started to float. The lights in the carriage cut out. The children started screaming except for little Suzie who clung to the white part of Emma's religious gown.

"What's going on?" Emma yelled. She floated upwards and blindly clawing at the space around her.

The speaker in the ceiling crackled to life. *"Warning. Disengagement of Last Two Carriages. All personal evacuate immediately."*

The screaming transformed into terrified wailing as the children burst into fresh tears. Even T'Aner knew what the warning meant. Such cruelty infuriated him at the thought the human company would willingly endanger the lives of children.

"Harken's Dogs," T'Aner growled. "Su'Sar! Tell M'Ackle and Fu'Shin to ready the emergency evacuation shields!"

"On it, General," Su'Sar acknowledged. She hit the ceiling with her boots and touched her earpiece.

*"Disconnection in ten seconds. Nine…eight…"*

"Kids, Emma of the New Earth Collective, when you see the bright light, hold your breath for ten seconds and think of your favourite sweet!" T'Aner ordered the floating children.

*"Six…five…"*

"Everyone, grab hold of something!" Emma yelled.

"Aim for the children!" T'Aner ordered the Freeson brothers behind him.

*"Three…two…one…Disengagement."*

A bright flash of brilliant light shot through the windows of the train carriage. T'Aner kicked off the floor toward Emma and

Suzie. He grabbed Emma's wrist in one hand, Suzie's wrist in the other. He used the force to drag them both into the children's train compartment. Su'Sar followed behind him, as did the Freeson brothers. The flash of light passed leaving them in complete darkness of open space as the train disconnected the carriages and shot forward along its designated path.

A quick glance showed many of the children kept their eyes squeezed shut. Some were beginning to kick and struggle in the lack of gravity. Little Suzie met his gaze. Of course! She would be able to see in the dark. Her pet rat clung to her hair.

Emma jerked on his wrist. He turned his head towards her only to watch as she stared at the rapidly disappearing Light Rail train. She turned her gaze towards him, squeezed her eyes shut and parted her lips.

Panic swept through him at the sight. He yanked her close and sealed his lips against hers as the warm glow of the emergency shields enveloped the carriage and chased away the freezing cold open space.

## Emma

"Miss Emma, you need to wake up." Suzie shook her.

Emma groaned, and slowly opened her eyes. The lights in the room were thankfully dimmed. It took her several seconds to realize she wasn't in her cabin, but on a firm, broad, bed. She blinked at the ceiling as it swirled with a gentle wave of lights and resembled galaxies and universes, just like when she'd looked through the train's open door and—

*The train.*

She sat straight up and gasped at the resulting pounding headache. She hissed, touching her forehead.

"T'Aner said you would have a headache." The pale pink scales on her jaw glowed faintly in the room's dim light.

"What happened?" Emma shook her head, and groaned as it made the headache worse. "Where did the train go? Where are the children? Where are the Arkavarians?"

"We're all here," T'Aner answered from the doorway.

Emma glanced at him, and at the tray of food he carried. He wore a fitted silver trimmed, maroon suit with an open collar. The orange scales framing his face glowed in the low light, and made his purple eyes appear darker by comparison.

"What's going on? Where are we?"

"You are on one of the Arkavarian Galleon ships," T'Aner answered. He entered the room, the door silently closing behind him. He set the tray on the bed beside Suzie and stepped back. "How's your head?"

"It hurts," Emma confessed. The tray had two tall glasses filled with a strange liquid, and two savory smelling buns.

Suzie picked up a glass of bubbling blue liquid and drank slowly. She licked her lips and smiled at Emma. "It's sweet!"

"I wasn't sure what human women drink, but the kids liked it, so I thought it would be acceptable." T'Aner's look showed his concern for her wellbeing.

"The children?"

"Safe, fed, and currently being entertained by several of my crew," T'Aner explained. "Everybody made it safely, but you've been unconscious for a while. The drink should help with your headache."

Emma reached for the second glass and sniffed the contents. It did smell sweet. She sipped it. It tasted like blueberries, but sweeter. She licked her lips and drank half of the glass before setting it back on the tray with a contented sigh. T'Aner was right, the drink did help her head. The pain quickly faded into a slow throb in the back of her skull.

"Amazing. It tastes like summer," she mused.

"Can I have the bun, too?" Suzie asked T'Aner.

"Of course. Su'Sar is out there if you want another one," T'Aner offered.

Suzie took the bun and raced for the door. It opened, and the sounds of excited, shrieking children drifted in to the room before the door closed again.

"They sound happy," Emma murmured.

T'Aner leaned against a far wall, he crossed his arms over his chest. "We might fight amongst ourselves, but children are precious to our species."

Emma frowned. T'Aner's words tugging at a stray thought in the back of her mind. "What will happen to the kids? Suzie has her grandmother, you said? But what about the other children?"

"From what we've learned with speaking to them, the children don't have families or places to call home," T'Aner started, his words slow and careful.

"They were going to mining families in some of corporate colonies." Emma rubbed the back of her head.

"Some of the children are siblings, and they're terrified they'll be split up or lose their family names," T'Aner continued.

Emma fell silent. He was right. Sometimes all one had in the universe was a brother or sister or just a name to tie a person to a sense of home and family.

"What will you do?" she asked him.

"We'll take them with us. I'll ensure the siblings stick together, and they're paired with capable parents."

"You can do that?" His answer surprised Emma.

T'Aner flashed her a smile, his scales flickering faintly. "I am a general in the Arkavarian Empire, I can do a lot of things."

Emma eyed him, suspicion beginning to curl its way around her mind. "And the heart mate thing?"

Panic quickly replaced his smile, and he coughed into his hand as his orange scales glowed brighter. "Yes. That. What I mean, is, er—"

"I have a boyfriend."

"That's right. You said you have a boyfriend." T'Aner nodded his head. "You must love him dearly to be crossing the Asteroid Belt for him."

Emma brought her knees up to her chin, and bit back the smile at the way T'Aner said the words. He seemed absolutely bitter, almost sulking. A general of the Arkavarian empire pouting she had a boyfriend. What were the odds? In the light of the cabin, he wasn't too bad looking, tall and broad shouldered, with a strong chin and a broad nose. He seemed compassionate about helping the children, and he had hijacked a train to find Suzie and take her home to her people. Plus, the poetry he told her wasn't too bad. A bit saccharine for Emma's liking, but it hadn't been bad.

Her boyfriend, Teddy, had never written her any poetry. Nor had he any interest in having kids. He'd been cold to her. The more she thought about his letters, trapped on USB drives on the train, which had left her in the galactic dust. Did she really love him?

"Not really."

Judging by the way T'Aner's jaw dropped at her words, he looked stunned. "You don't?"

Emma shrugged. "There were a lot of red flags, the closer I travelled to meet him."

"You've never met him?" T'Aner's strangled voice inquired.

"No. Online conversations and letters only. I was on my way to meet him," Emma explained.

T'Aner pushed off the wall and began pacing back and forth. "So, excuse me, you vowed your heart to someone you never met in person, only through letters, you don't love him." He stopped pacing and looked dumbfounded at her. "Your heart mate is standing right in front of you!"

Emma tilted her head. T'Aner seemed close to hysterics or maybe fury. She felt badly for him. Watching a general panic about her dating life almost made her laugh. Almost. He really was a strange person. A strange person Emma wanted to learn more about.

"I didn't know I had a heart mate waiting for me," she mused.

T'Aner froze. He slowly turned his gaze toward her, his eyes wide. "You didn't?"

"As my friend Hannah once commented, what I look for in a man is something Arkavarian's look for too. Besides, I think I'd have to work a million years before I could afford someone like you."

T'Aner sat on the edge of the bed. He grabbed Emma's hands in his, and held them to his heart. "You can't buy love."

Emma bit back a laugh. That was exactly what she had told Hannah. "No. But you can buy attractive husbands."

T'Aner's purple eyes narrowed, his voice lowered. "Who are these 'husbands' you want to buy? Let me talk to them. We Arkavarian's have ceremonies for situations like this."

"And weddings?"

"We live for weddings."

Emma sobered, her gaze flickering between his eyes. "Will we see the universe?"

"We go wherever you want," T'Aner assured her. "The stars are yours."

~ * ~ * ~

**Jocelyne Gregory** lives on the Sunshine Coast of British Columbia, Canada with her cats and various wild creatures. She holds an MFA in Creative Writing from UBC's School of Creative Writing, and a writing certificate from Simon Fraser University's The Writer's Studio. She works as a manuscript consultant. Her work has appeared in 50-Word Stories, Emerge16, The Dancing Plague: A Collection of Utter Speculation, Beach Shorts; Zooscape, and BraveNewGirls: Tales of Girls who Engineer & Explore. Two of her short science fiction stories received honourable mentions for the L. R. Hubbard Writer's of the Future Contest in the 3rd and 4th quarters of 2022.

# GRAVITY

### Sage Kelly

All three kids floated sullenly behind as we made our way through the Enyo Station shuttle dock. Mars shone bright and stark through the viewport on the concourse in contrast to the serene blue-green beauty we were used to. Uncertainty clawed at my belly. It usurped the grinding fear and overwhelming loss of the last few months. Was I doing the right thing?

Life and death choices were a part of my job, a background noise like the ventilation system, a susurration you only noticed by its absence. But I'd never had to make life changing decisions for three other people before.

I felt their invisible tug behind me. We were inexorably caught up in each other's orbits, bound together by love and family. My sister's kids, the only family I had left. I couldn't let them down.

Dammit, Leah, why'd you have to go and get yourself killed?

Then there was Yanina Cooper. She too, got caught up in the spin of our gravity, her and her infant daughter. All because of Space Brides, my last-ditch effort to keep my little family together. By agreeing to marry me, she and her family offered the stability the kids needed. I would do anything for them.

Gabe groaned. "You forgot to lock down the ferret's food again, Becca."

I checked over my shoulder. Eleven-year-old Gabe held the ferret cage in front of him. Willy and Nilly clung to their climbing rope while food pellets floated all around them.

"Don't be mad at me. It's Uncle Jake's fault. He made me rush." Becca kicked at the bulkhead.

Even her Luna-strength kick sent the six-year-old careening into other passengers. After some shuffling and a lot of apologies, I snagged a line from my belt and tethered her to me.

"Uncle Jake, I'm not a baby!"

"No, but you sure are acting like one." Gabe scoffed as he tried to contain the ferret's food.

"Enough, Gabe." I put a hand on his shoulder. "We're all

doing our best, you don't have to be mean."

Motioning for the kids to move out of the pedestrian traffic, I pulled Becca close. "You're not a baby, but you're having a hard time controlling your body right now. And it's my job to keep you safe."

Safe. Hilarious. Their whole world upended when my sister died and here I was, moving them to another planet. Marrying a stranger. So I could keep them safe.

I took a breath and tried to get my bearings. I had only ever used Enyo Station as a transfer point to the Belt and was familiar with the transient sectors. Today, I needed the commercial area. I turned to Zach and motioned him over. "Can you find an information terminal, please? We need a place to store our baggage and find the business offices."

He nodded and handed me the controller for the anti-grav sled holding everything we owned. I watched him gracefully navigate through the other passengers and wondered, again, whether I treated the fourteen-year-old too much like an adult. Zach was quiet, and smart, and so damned capable. I couldn't have managed the last few months without his help. It was hard to remember he wasn't an adult and not ready for the full weight of responsibility. Clipping the controller to my belt, I turned back to Becca. She floated next to me, sniffling.

"What's going on, sunshine? I thought you liked microgravity."

"The seam on my skinsuit is bothering my toes and it's rubbing under my arms and I have itches everywhere and I have to use a hood like a baby when Zach and Gabe get real helmets." She batted at the hood that would engage automatically if it sensed a loss of pressure. "And Gabe yelled at me about Willy and Nilly's food when I forgot because you made me hurry and now I have to wear a tether and I'm not a baby and I want to go home." Floating globules of tears and snot gathered around her face.

I hooked my foot into a bulkhead anchor and used an absorbent pad to sweep up the loose moisture, then wiped her face and helped her blow her nose. I pulled her in for a hug and wished I knew what to say to make it all better. I was clearly not winning any Best Uncle awards. Or Older Brother awards.

As irrational as it felt, I wanted to scream at my sister. How dare she die and leave me with her kids? I could barely manage my own life, how was I supposed to manage theirs? I was an itinerant worker, a space dog who went where a company sent me. That was no life for kids.

Becca had the right idea. I wanted to kick something, too. I huffed in frustration and kissed the top of her head.

Zach came floating back.

"Storage lockers are down that way" He pointed down the corridor. "Gabe and me can handle it so you don't have to bring Becca and the ferrets. Besides, we have to come back this way to the ramp for the next level."

"Good thinking." I handed Zach the controller then grabbed our *yarmulkes* from my duffle on the sled. We would need them for the *chuppa*. Gabe hooked the ferret cage to an anchor near Becca and the two of them headed off. I stared at the slips of fabric in my hand. The last time we wore them was to say *Kaddish* for my sister. I'd almost tossed them into the incinerator after *Shiva* ended. But then, I'd have lost the good memories too, like holiday dinners, and Zach's *Bar Mitzvah*. I shoved them in my vest pocket.

It didn't take the boys long to get our stuff stored. When they got back, Zach handed me the claim chit and led us to the ramp.

Offices lined the upper corridor, some even boasting grav plates. I spotted the Space Brides logo about halfway down. Pulling the kids to a stop, I gathered them into a huddle.

"I know I can count on each of you to be on your best behavior, right?"

Gabe held the ferret cage in front of him like a shield. "We're meeting her now?"

I nodded. "Remember, she's not taking the place of your *Imma*. No one can." I swallowed the lump in my throat. "But I hope we can all be friends."

"And we're going to live on her farm on Mars, right? And I'm going to be a big sister?" Becca grabbed my hand, squeezing tight.

"You'll have another uncle and a grandpa too." I straightened Becca's pigtails and pulled her close. "Do you think you can keep control of your body better?"

She nodded. I unhooked her from my tether and raked my fingers through my close-cropped hair. "How do I look?" I'd never be called handsome with my beak of a nose and long face, yet I cleaned up okay.

"*Imma* was prettier, but you'll do," Zach teased. Gallows humor,

Zach was too much like me to expect much else.

We'd come so far together, the four of us. The kids lost their home when Leah died. Maybe it was selfish of me to keep us together, not let them stay on Luna with a foster family. But they were all I had left of my sister.

"Okay Miller family, let's do this." I hoped the waver in my voice sounded more like excitement than nerves.

I took a breath and palmed open the office door.

"What do you mean you won't refund my credits?" A man with gray hair shouted at the woman holding a pile of flimsies. Behind him hovered a man closer to my age, with auburn hair and a pointy chin. From the way he filled out his skinsuit I could tell he was no stranger to hard work. He tried to calm a crying infant in the pressure bubble hooked to his belt. No one noticed us enter.

"Sir, your signature is on the papers." She tried to hand the man a flimsy. He smacked it away.

The second man waved a toy in front of the baby. "Dad, Nina's been able to forge your signature since she turned ten. And yelling is not helping."

The flimsy drifted past me, caught in the tug from the ventilation system airflow. I noticed my name across the top and grabbed it. "What the hell?" Three sets of eyes turned toward me. "This is my contract with Yanina Cooper."

Everyone went silent, except the baby. Since this was my contract, they might be Yanina's father and brother. What was going on? Had something happened? "Where's Yanina?"

"She's gone and run off," the older man spat. "You're released from the contract. You can go home."

My stomach dropped, like the fluctuation of a grav plate.

"Dad, that's not fair." The younger man juggled the crying baby to take the contract from my numb fingers. "He brought his kids all the way from Luna."

I didn't want his pity. I just wanted to give the kids a home. A chance to work. To not be so desperate. There was nothing left for us on Luna. I'd even sold my hardsuit so I could buy good quality skinsuits for the kids. Without it I couldn't take the better paying jobs on the docks. Without the better paying jobs…I struggled against the freefall of my thoughts.

The children hovered behind me. Had I dragged them all the

way to Mars for nothing? This was supposed to be a chance at a better life, for all of us. I wanted to push them back into the corridor, to protect them from more loss.

The baby's squall reached a crescendo, loud enough to drown out my untethered uncertainties.

"Eli, I can't think with the baby making all that noise," the older man yelled.

"Let me try." Desperate for something to do, something to fix, I motioned for Eli to pass me the baby. He raised an eyebrow at me. The dark circles under his eyes stood out against his pale complexion. "I won't hurt her, I promise. I have a hunch I know what's bothering her."

He unhooked the baby's pressure bubble from his belt and handed her to me. Gently, I unzipped the top and used another absorbent wipe to mop up the mess. I held her tight against me until her sobs finally died down.

"How'd you do that?"

"She's never been weightless before, has she?" He shook his head. "I've worked on Belter miner ships. They travel with their whole families and many of them don't have grav plates, even in their living quarters. They use pressure with the babies. It's not the same as gravity, but swaddling the baby and wrapping it tight against you helps them not feel like they're falling all the time."

His hand gripped my shoulder, strong and warm. Keeping us from drifting apart. He smelled like clean air and growing things, and I felt a tug in my chest that had nothing to do with gravity and everything to do with his proximity. With his other hand, he rubbed a finger against the baby's cheek. "I'm sorry Lily, I've done nothing, but let you down since Nina left."

I knew that tone, that feeling of trying. Trying again. Still not getting it right. It was compassion, not pity, I'd heard in his voice.

The older man shoved his chrono into his vest pocket. "Eli, we've wasted enough time here. And credits, thanks to your sister."

"But what about…" Eli looked at me and the kids quietly waiting behind me.

The woman behind the counter spoke up. "Don't worry Mr. Cooper, we'll take care of Mr. Miller and his kids. He can stay here in Enyo Station on our credit for two weeks while we help him search for another spouse."

Two weeks? It took over a month just to find Yanina. No one wanted a man with three kids. Especially a man with no job, despite my work history and skills.

Eli must have seen the despair on my face. "Dad, his contract says he's a mechanic. He's worked on hydroponic systems and knows plumbing."

"His contract also says he doesn't have the certificates, and we don't have time or space to take on three more kids," Mr. Cooper shouted, frustration rolling off him.

Eli's quiet voice turned sharp. "But the kids were okay when Nina was going to marry him?"

"I thought your sister had finally got her head screwed on right and decided to settle down. Instead," he waved his hand at me and the kids. "She left us with a mess."

Eli squeezed my shoulder, an unspoken apology. "That's not fair, Dad, and you know it."

"Fine," he shouted. "Then you marry him!"

"Dad, that's..." he turned to me, a flush creeping up his cheeks.

The words were meant to be cruel, but it was the most constructive thing the old man had said. I hadn't cared who I had to marry, I just wanted to take care of Leah's kids. I took a long look at Eli. He was easy on the eyes, and seeing him blush... Well, maybe there was a way to save this after all.

I opened my mouth to say something, when Becca shrieked and launched herself at Mr. Cooper.

"You can't yell at Uncle Jake like that! He's the best uncle ever!"

Mr. Cooper wasn't anchored. Becca's inertia pushed both of them across the small office to slam into the far wall. He grabbed an anchor with one hand, bracing so he wouldn't smash her with his own mass. Becca pounded him with her fists, he shifted his hold to the front of her suit and held her at arm's length where her flailing arms and legs couldn't hurt him.

The unanchored ferret cage sailed toward me and Eli. My clue the boys were about to enter the fray. I redirected its flight, knowing I only had a microsecond to intercept them. Handing the baby to Eli, I flung myself across their path. I crashed into them with enough inertia to divert their trajectory and slow our momentum. We drifted to a stop near the wall by the counter.

"Uncle Jake's doing the best he can!" Zach struggled against me as I clipped his belt hook to a wall anchor.

"Let my sister go!" Gabe pushed against my knees clamped around his waist. A moment later I had him hooked to the wall next to Zach.

And of course, Lily started crying again.

"Enough," Mr. Cooper roared.

Eli quieted the baby, holding her like I had shown him. The boys closed their mouths, staring daggers at Mr. Cooper. The Space Brides agent hovered by her console, holding the ferret cage in front of her. Their food floated loose again. Mr. Cooper handed Becca a tissue and brushed her hair out of her face while she wiped her tears. He looked around the room and let out a sigh. Frustration and worry tightened the lines of his face and bracketed his mouth. I knew his look. Same as the one I saw in the mirror when I shaved this morning.

"Maybe we ought to have a conversation," Eli spoke into the silence. He glanced at me, then at his father. "Maybe we can still work something out."

I nodded slowly, not sure of my mooring.

Mr. Cooper gave his son a long look, then turned to me. "Can we buy you folks lunch? The next level has catering, and gravity. It's Mars gravity though, is that going to be okay?" He directed his last question at the kids.

The boys nodded and Becca sniffled. "Uncle Jake has been making us practice for hours in Mars gravity. Every day." She groaned.

Mr. Cooper smiled and gave Becca a slight push in my direction. I untethered the boys and herded the three of them out of the office. Gabe grabbed the ferret cage held out by the agent as we passed.

Mr. Cooper led us up the ramp to the next level. Eli floated along the corridor next to me, little Lily now snugly strapped to his chest instead of floating loose next to him.

"I'm sorry about my dad. Nina's been pushing his buttons for years, and we'd all thought she'd finally pulled herself together when she told us about you."

Lily let out a whimper and I reached over to touch her baby-soft hair. "He's angry. And worried, I think."

"He's definitely worried. Aside from Nina disappearing again, the heating system in our largest tunnel stopped working, and we can't get a mechanic out to look at it for another week. It's put us behind on a few contracts."

I wanted to tell him I could fix it. I wanted to tell him I'd marry him if it meant giving the kids a stable home. Not willing to risk my fragile hope, I stayed quiet as we navigated a turn down another corridor.

"Dad was even okay with the price of the contract with Space Brides since your work record and references were really good."

"And the kids?"

He gave me a wry smile. "He agreed to the kids too. He said Lily deserved to have siblings and, with any luck, the kids were old enough to be more help than hindrance."

We'd reached the entrance to the catering area. Mr. Cooper was showing the kids the handgrab and which way was down. Zach stepped through first, and Gabe followed. Mr. Cooper handed them the ferret cage and offered to help Becca. She refused his hand and leapt after her brothers, smiling proudly when she stood on her own. Mr. Cooper applauded her then pulled himself through the entrance.

"That one," Eli said with a shake of his head, "will have Dad eating out of her hand in no time."

I chuckled. "No doubt. She's something else."

He surprised me by snagging my suit sleeve and pulling us both to the side. He tugged a little too hard and I ended up pressing into him, squeezing Lily between us. I bracketed him between my arms and grabbed handholds on either side, keeping both of us from rebounding into other folks. I was near enough to see the gold flecks in his brown eyes. I should move back, give him room, move away from his radiating warmth, but his hand still gripped my sleeve, keeping me close.

"Listen, I'm sorry about Dad and the way he threw that line about us getting married."

"I'm not."

"You're not?"

Had I read him wrong? What else could his earlier blush have meant? "I'm sorry, I assumed, and I shouldn't have. I mean, you said we should talk, and I thought you meant talk about contracts, because marriage is a contract..." The tenuous hope I still might have a way to take care of Leah's kids drifted out of my grasp again. Bile tickled the back of my throat. It must have shown on my face because his warm calloused hand squeezed mine where it rested on the anchor next to him.

"Looks like you're not the only one who made some assumptions." Our eyes caught and his smile, slow and shy, lit up his face. He blushed and ducked under my arm. "Let's go get some lunch and negotiate a contract."

I grasped at his lifeline and followed him towards the gravity.

Lily perked right up once she could feel her own weight. She looked around, waving her chubby little fists and babbling. I wiggled my fingers at her and she grabbed one, holding it tight.

Eli pointed to a table at the end of a row where the kids sat, the ferret cage perched on the bench next to Gabe. Mr. Cooper set a large tray, piled high with containers, on the table in front of the kids. The boys took some of the boxes, opening them and tasting the different foods. Mr. Cooper, sliding onto the seat next to Becca, offered her forkfuls of each item like she was royalty.

Eli looked at me, grinning. "I'll bet you five credits that he'll have them calling him *Zaidy* by the end of lunch."

"It'll take a little longer, I think. I'm betting on the shuttle downside." I smiled back.

We reached the table and I sat down next to Gabe. Eli slipped in next to me. I held Lily while he rummaged through his belt pouch for her bottle. She reached for it eagerly and a drizzle of milk trickled down her chin as she drank. He tried to take her from me but I pushed a container in front of him. He got the hint. I looked up at the kids to make sure they were doing okay and caught Mr. Cooper's curious glance.

I tilted my head at the kids. "I came home for each of their births and helped my sister for a few weeks. Learned pretty quickly how to take care of a baby."

He gave a thoughtful nod, then helped Becca spear another bite.

"Becca, you can feed yourself."

"But the fork is so heavy, Uncle Jake."

I caught Eli's eye and the two of us grinned at how his dad was already a goner.

Lily finished her bottle, but Eli was still eating so I passed her across the table to Zach. She was a happy little thing and laughed when Zach made faces. I grabbed an unclaimed container and started eating.

"Can I hold her, Uncle Jake?"

"I don't think that's a good idea, Becca. If your arms are too tired to lift your fork then how can you hold a baby that masses so much more?"

Eli leaned into me. "She didn't think that one through, did she?"

I chuckled. "That one never does." I tried to focus on my food and not how good his body felt pressed into mine.

Zach made a face and held Lily away from him. "Eww, she smells."

I took the diaper Eli had set on the table and pushed it in front of Zach. "Finders keepers."

"That's just plain mean, Uncle Jake."

"Your mom used to pull the same shtick on me, kiddo. Payback time." I grinned and went back to eating.

Zach rolled his eyes, but he was a good sport. With a huff he picked up the diaper, put Lily on his hip and headed to the bathrooms.

"As much as I like this game, no one deserves one of her messes. I'll go help him." Eli slid off the bench and followed Zach.

Becca jumped out of her seat with more energy than I expected and chased after them.

Mr. Cooper chuckled and shook his head.

With an eye on Gabe, I reached across the table to pull Becca's half-eaten food in front of me. I didn't want to get caught in Gabe's single-minded eating. I grimaced, remembering what a black hole Zach was at that age. Feeding these boys was expensive.

"If you're still hungry I can get more," Mr. Cooper offered, kindly.

"She's not going to eat any more, but thanks." Conscious of obligation, I didn't want to spend any more of this man's credits.

"I'm sorry for earlier. I was out of line."

"Mr. Cooper—"

"Dan, please."

"Dan, when you've spent as much time as I have in a hardsuit, where one wrong move could kill you, your tether mate, even your whole work crew, you learn to pay attention to a person's actions, not their words. When Becca launched herself at you, your gut reaction protected her from hitting the wall and being smashed by your mass. That told me more about you than a few words said in anger."

He looked away for a moment, like he'd steeled himself for my derision but not gotten what he expected. "I'm still sorry. I forgot that I was not the only wronged party, and I was needlessly cruel."

"Apology accepted. Thank you, sir."

Oblivious to the conversation, Gabe headed to the drink dispenser to refill his cup. Dan leaned forward like he had more to say. I finished the last few bites on Becca's plate and waited him out.

"Did, uh, did you and Eli talk?"

"Sir, while I realize you funded Nina's contract with Space Brides, it was still a contract between me and her. If Eli and I agree for him to take over Nina's contract, then I don't want to have this conversation without him present."

He leaned back in his seat and took a long look at me. Had I upset him by refusing to talk? Eli said we would work something out, but did this man have the final say? My mouth dry, I reached for my drink.

Gabe returned and started rummaging through the containers. "There's nothing left."

I raised an eyebrow at him. "Try again."

"Excuse me, Uncle Jake, but I'm still hungry."

Before I could react, Mr. Cooper handed him a credit chit. Gabe thanked him, and we both watched as he made his way to the food vendors.

"Jacob Miller, those kids are good ones, and you are honorable. You and your family would be an asset to our farm, whatever you and Eli choose to do about the Space Brides contract."

I wasn't sure I'd heard him right. "Sir?"

"Son, I don't want you to feel forced into marrying Eli just to gain security for those kids. I'm offering you a job and a home either way."

My chest grew tight. The last few months had been a whirlwind of taking care of the kids, trying to find a job, applying at Space Brides, interviewing potential spouses, and finally packing all our belongings and moving out to Mars. I'd been holding it together for the kids, but I couldn't any more. The relief of knowing it was going to be okay set free all my previous pain and loss, fear and doubt, and it all came out in a sob. I buried my face in my hands.

Gabe reached me first, all elbows and knees, wrapping his arms around me. Footsteps rushed behind me, accompanied by a baby's babble, and Zach hugged me while holding Lily, who tried to wiggle loose. I looked up to see Eli approaching, Becca riding piggyback, of course. Which made me laugh through my tears. I pulled her off Eli's back and onto my lap.

"It's all going to be okay," I told them. "We're going to be just fine. We have a home. Eli and I don't have to get married if we don't want to."

Eli had taken Lily from Zach and held her close, his nose buried in her hair. His shoulders slumped and I wondered for a minute whether he was disappointed his father had released us from the contract.

I wiped my face on a napkin and gave the boys one more hug before they pulled away. Zach, full of questions about the farm, moved to the other end of the table to talk to Dan, and Gabe sat down next to me. He lifted the ferret cage to the table to check on them. Becca shifted off my lap to help him gather up the ferret food. Willy and Nilly were no worse for wear, despite being tossed around. He took their water bottle to the dispenser to be refilled and Eli sat down in his seat. Lily tried to grab the cage, but Becca pushed it out of her reach. She pulled Willy out and showed him to Lily.

Eli held Lily's hand and helped her gently pat Willy's soft fur. "I'm surprised he's not trying to get away."

"They're actually trained for certain types of tasks." I scratched under Willy's tiny chin. "Leah used them to help with small equipment. I've used them around her house to get inside conduits to help pull wires through and find things the kids dropped into the ventilation."

"So they're not just pets." He looked thoughtful. "We could use them on the farm in areas which are hard to get to."

I nodded. "They can help with pest control, too. They're obligate carnivores so safe around the seeds and seedlings, but yeah, they'd be useful."

Becca put Willy back in the cage and pulled out Nilly so she could get some attention. Lily, tummy full and diaper clean, fell asleep, her tiny lips pursed in a sucking motion. Gabe returned with the water bottle and clipped it to the cage. He moved to the other end of the table with Zach. Dan had pulled out his tablet, showing the boys pictures of the farm and the community, telling them about the school they would go to. Becca closed the ferret cage and climbed onto my lap. She leaned against my shoulder, gravity finally winning.

"I think you should marry him, Uncle Jake." She yawned. "He's a good uncle to Lily. Like you." She too fell asleep.

Eli neatly avoided my look by examining Lily's tiny fingers in his hand, but the tips of his ears reddened. It wouldn't be a hardship to marry this quiet man who stood up for me when he didn't have to.

"It's just a contract, right?" I asked.

The sharp turn of his head jostled Lily on his shoulder. She made a moue, yet stayed asleep.

"What are you saying?"

How could I answer his question when I didn't know what I was asking? We had the same goals, to raise the kids in a safe and stable home, to work to support the family. Did we really need marriage? Couldn't friendship be enough? Friendship wasn't security, it wasn't a contract.

"I'm saying I want to honor the contract I signed with your sister, with you as her substitute."

"But Dad already said you didn't have to." He shook his head. "No, I can't let you do this out of some sense of obligation."

"Are you saying you don't want to marry me?" I swear this man had me so confused. His sweet smiles and blushes tell me he's interested, but then he goes on about obligations.

His blush was back, making the freckles on the bridge of his nose bright enough I could count them. "I'm not saying no. I just think we need more time. Marriage, on paper, may be just a contract, but it's not the same as a work contract." He buried his nose in Lily's hair. "I like to think there's at least friendship in a marriage."

Becca shifted in her sleep and slipped off my shoulder. I was starting to feel her whole mass in Mars gravity. Dan approached and put out his arms for her.

"Let me take her, son. Then you two should talk."

I shifted her into his arms gratefully. He carried her to his seat with the boys. I turned back to Eli to find him studying me, curiosity in his clear brown eyes and maybe a bit of understanding. Then he gave me one of his shy smiles.

"Let's go talk where there's less ears." He tilted his head at his father who had his back to us, but was clearly hanging on our every word.

Together, we headed to a quieter corner of the large concourse. I collapsed into a seat with a sigh.

"Gravity getting to you?" He sat next to me, close enough to feel his warmth.

"I spent more time on Luna than I usually do after my sister died."

"I read your application. Nina shared it with Dad and me." He looked uncomfortable. "You're not what we expected."

"You mean for an itinerant worker?" It wasn't an unfounded stereotype. A lot of the people I worked with were rough around the edges, unpolished, and sometimes unreliable.

He nodded, looking abashed.

"I'm a child of academics. My dad was a biochemist, mom a physicist. Leah followed them into the sciences. I just wanted to know how things worked. By the time I realized that I was good at fixing things, it was a little too late and I was a little too stubborn to take the required courses to earn the certificates needed to get the better jobs." I shrugged and bumped his shoulder. "You're not what I expected, for a farmer."

He held out the hand not supporting Lily, fingernails clean. "Hard to get dirt under your nails when you farm hydroponically." He chuckled. "I actually have advanced degrees in botany and hydroponic agriculture. In the last ten years, I've been able to increase our harvest enough that we could afford to build another growing tunnel, hire regular employees, and increase revenue. The work is still pretty physical, but not as dirty." He squeezed my shoulder. "Why are you being so stubborn about the marriage thing?"

"A gut feeling, I suppose. Maybe because marriage offers a little more permanency for the kids. If I get hurt and can't work your dad could let me go. But if I'm family, and the kids are family…" I shrugged again, not knowing what else to say.

"And you honor your contracts."

"And I honor my contracts."

He turned in his seat to face me, our knees brushing, resolution in his shoulders. The tilt of his lips hinted at humor. "Ya'akov Miller, would you accept me, Eliahu Cooper, as a replacement for Yanina Cooper in your contract with her and Space Brides?"

"Are you sure you're okay with this? I had a few weeks to get used to the idea of marrying a stranger."

"Are you actually questioning me after I've agreed to marry you?"

"No. I just…"

His shoulders shook as he chuckled, and Lily stirred.

For the first time since Leah died, I felt lighter, despite Mars gravity. A weight had been lifted off my shoulders. "It would be my honor, Eliahu Cooper, to accept you instead of Yanina Cooper." My smile stretched across my face easier than it had in the months since my sister died.

He got to his feet and offered me his hand, his grip strong as he helped me up. He stood, looking at me, still holding my hand, and twined his fingers with mine.

"Let's go tell Dad and the kids."

~ * ~

A shuttle headed downside in an hour. Dan booked us seats and made arrangements for our belongings to be loaded. The Space Brides agent met us in the cafeteria with the contract and the marriage documents, agreeing that forcing the baby to tolerate freefall again was not necessary. Eli and I signed everything, while Dan somehow pulled a *minyan* together.

I handed the boys their *yarmulkes* and twenty minutes later, surrounded by family and strangers, Eli and I stood under the *chuppah*. We laughed together as we slid vacuum rated silicone washers onto each other's fingers. Enyo Station didn't have any jewelers, so we made do. Eli held my hand and together we smashed a glass beaker stolen from the labs on the next level with our bootheels. To shouts of *mazel tov* and *congratulations* we made our way to the shuttle.

We settled into our seats as the flight crew were finishing their pre-flight tasks and moments later the shuttle dropped free of Enyo

Station. I watched Mars grow in the viewport. Eli sat next to me.

"Zaidy, is that the farm?" Becca's voice came from the seats in front of us. I burst into laughter when Eli pulled a five credit note from his pocket. Across the aisle Lily let out a shriek of giggles as Zach gave her cheek a raspberry. Gabe slid back into his seat, his hands full of snacks he'd cajoled out of a flight attendant. Next to me, Eli smiled and pulled out a tablet. I watched him work, drifting asleep to the soft click of his stylus against the screen.

"Jake, wake up." Eli's voice was soft in my ear. "It's time to strap down. We're landing soon."

I blinked, then yawned. I'd fallen asleep on his shoulder. I tilted my chin up until I could see his eyes, our noses brushing. His freckles made tiny constellations across his cheeks. I smiled and sat up.

"What's that smile for?"

"I was just wondering how long you're going to make me wait before I can kiss you."

His blush rivaled the brightness of the red planet below us. His hand slipped into mine. I wouldn't have to wait long.

"We're almost home kids," Dan called out.

"Home," Eli whispered as he squeezed my hand.

I felt the tug of Mars's gravity as we dipped into atmosphere.

$$\sim * \sim * \sim$$

**Sage Kelly** writes queer romance, science fiction, and fantasy, sometimes at the same time. She has been telling fantastical tales since she can remember, even chronicling a D&D campaign. Sadly, Hickman and Weis beat her to publishing. After raising five children she decided to pursue writing as a career. As a member of the LGBTQ+ community, Sage strives for representation in her works. Everyone deserves to see themselves in their fiction. Sage lives just outside of DC and can often be found, with her dog Nava, curled up under a handmade quilt, reading. Alas, writing isn't her only vice. She owns more wool, fabric, spinning wheels, and sewing machines than she ought. And books. Lots of books. But that's not really a problem, per se.

To find out more about upcoming releases and appearances go to www.sagekellybooks.com.

# THE BAD LUCK BRIDE

Kat Farrow

## Maradean

I looked past the wiry man in black and gray next to me scanning his visor display, and caught sight of a railgun launch out the Traverse-pod's window. Its long, triangular launch track was not as massive as I'd thought it would be, but Iapetus's gravity is weak enough, and resources held tight enough by the mining Triarchy, I suppose it's the bare minimum needed. The payload should reach the processing facility above Titan in less than a cycle. I suppose I'll be settling into my new home and married life by then.

I shifted back to scrutinizing the man beside me. The Space Bride LLC's appointed minister and acting chaperone was sunk deep in his feed, oblivious to the barren, rocky landscape we raced through. The man, middle-aged with a hooked nose, looked like someone had broken it more than once. He doesn't seem to like his job. Maybe he just doesn't like me. He'd said little on the trip and his last words still sat heavy in my chest.

"It's your last chance, Maradean. You know the consequences if this one fails."

I didn't need to be reminded.

Looking up through the curved, glazed roof, the clear image of Saturn and her rings punctuated the vast speckled darkness of space. Iapetus is her only moon with this view and it was beautiful.

The T-pod is packed with boxy supply containers plus a few other passengers intermittently dispersed along its length. Five people sat across from each other at the back chatting quietly. All wear badges on their sleeves for the Seville mine colony, past the branch line of my destination, the TurgisMal mine colony.

Four Triarchy Techs sit ahead of us toward the front. Only one Tech has paid any attention to us. Well, to me. They glanced at us when we first boarded, then must have recognized the minister's colors and badge and turned to stare straight at me, mouth ajar. They snapped it shut and focused on strapping in with their companions. I've caught them glancing at me a few times. It must just be the Space Bride thing. Nothing about me says 'clone'.

I shifted a little in my seat. The new weighted suit had been surprisingly comfortable despite the heavier micro-layers. Still, it's the only time I hadn't worn some type of wedding gown. I had a triplet-clip of red fiber-flowers pinned to my hair. The most I could do with the suit.

I wondered if it was a good or bad omen? I'd read many Sat-miners had grown superstitious in their isolation and minimal supplies. Will my miner be?

Xander Greaves.

I'd only had two comms with him and the first got cut short from a radiation flare. He seemed...nice? Solid? He hadn't been very talkative and looked distracted and worn during the comm. Kind of friendly. His hair, thick and shaggy brown with a beard to match. Pale eyes of some undetermined color. His skin seemed a similar light brown to mine. He looked broad shouldered, though miner suits are thicker and more padded than the ones I'm used to.

It really doesn't matter. I had to find a way to make it work. I hoped his son liked me at least.

I closed my eyes, concentrating on breathing until the T-pod slowed, and the automated announcement chimed.

"Arrival at Othon Way Station in one hundred twenty seconds and counting. Please remain in restraints until the pod completes dock-lock procedures."

## Xander

Everything always happened all at once.

I expected it to a degree with the colony only getting shipments every tri-cycle, but still...supplies, losing the Haedigs, and dealing with the Triacrhy Techs all at once?

And then there's my bride-to-be.

Maradean. An unusual name. I like it.

I still don't understand why a clone bride was listed in the normal tier of that LLC. I thought they were exclusive. Specially trained. A life like this? I couldn't imagine her being willing to stay long. She must know the condition we're in since the accident.

I paused.

Would she know about it? It'd been four months. The news

must have spread. Unless the Triarchy had tried to downplay it. That wouldn't surprise me.

I drummed my fingers on the stack of empty containers I'd hauled in to exchange. Mostly empty. We hadn't been able to produce any material to refine. Still, recyclables needed to be processed up on Titan Septimus. The behemoth station might be where we end up if I can't pull this together.

I shook my head, trying to dislodge the growing pile of worries from taking hold.

As long as Maradean and Edison got along, that's all I could hope for.

I watched the T-pod glide onto the platform and lock in place. The seals hissed and the clerk-bot opened the doors to start the disembarking procedures. I caught glimpses of passengers as they moved around behind the glazed shielding, weaving around supply containers.

She's in there somewhere. Hope she didn't have to sit with the Techs.

The way station's been less busy than usual for a delivery run. Usually some of the crew would have ridden in with me to make comms and such, or just take a break. There's too few of us now. Hopefully, when this inspection's done, the company will authorize more staff and things will settle down.

There's a commotion on the platform as one of the Techs tried to make demands of the clerk-bot. I chuckled. Good luck with that. Their colleagues grouped up behind them, Triarchy badges prominent on sleeves, chests and backs. Properly tagged in case they got lost, I guess.

They're bunched up and blocking the pod's exit until the deep clearing of a throat behind them caused them to shuffle forward a few steps.

The minister pushed through and waited, dressed in his black with silver trims. Skinny, with a broken nose. Looked unpleasant.

And that must be…*oh*.

She's much prettier in person. Taller than I expected, and her hair's a much richer brown than I'd thought. The flowers went well with the reddish highlights. A nice touch.

My jaw popped open, and my head dropped to stare down at the stains and patch marks running down the front of me. *I forgot to change into my nicer suit.* I fingered the ends of my ragged beard and heaved a sigh.

Roman Gods. She's going to think I'm a cretin.

Way to go, groom. Way to go.

The clerk-bot pinged me and I sent a wait request, took a deep breath and headed over to meet my bride.

## Maradean

The minister cleared his throat. The Techs finally moved out of the way so we could exit the T-pod. I've never been to this type of way station before. It's both smaller and larger than my imaginings. Lots of stacked, aluminum-carbon containers, a cargo-bot standing by, and the clerk-bot who the Techs seemed to have taken issue with.

A wide, arched passageway headed off the platform and I glimpsed an eatery of some sort, and part of another shop that didn't seem open. The five other passengers shuffled past us and headed toward the eatery.

Even though there weren't many people about, the number of towering containers made it feel crowded, almost claustrophobic. The minister moved off to one side. I followed, setting down my kit to wait.

Standing next to a stack of containers several meters away I noticed a dark-haired man, head bent, wearing a scruffy, gray Satminer suit.

When he looked up, I realized it was him. Xander. He tapped his wrist cuff and headed our way.

My foot started to take a step back and I forced myself to freeze. I glanced at the minister, took a determined breath, and plastered a warm smile on my face to greet my husband-to-be.

Xander halted a few steps away and dipped his head before meeting my eyes. "Maradean. I hope the trip wasn't too unpleasant."

His voice was a warm baritone and his eyes a gray-green. Striking against his light brown skin and dark hair. I felt my cheeks grow warm. "It was fine, thank you."

He turned to the minister and held out his hand. "Minister."

The minister rolled his eyes and didn't take the offered greeting. "Not necessary. Will there be witnesses? Are we waiting on anyone? I don't want to miss the departure time."

Xander slowly shook his head, dropping his hand back to his side. He gave the minister a quick once-over before he answered. "Not to worry. It takes a while to exchange the cargo. I can guarantee the pod won't leave without you on it."

My smile felt a little more natural suddenly. I'm not the only one who didn't appreciate my travel companion.

Xander shifted his attention back to me, and my smile froze in place again.

"Shipment deliveries tend to be rather chaotic. We also have someone leaving the colony, and, of course, you've noticed the Techs." Xander nodded toward the four, still in discussion with the clerk-bot. He stared at the continued commotion, then sighed before he returned his attention to me.

"We're not waiting on anyone. The clerk-bot cleared itself to attest to the ceremony, and it can be quick as long as that's agreeable to you, Maradean?"

Well, he didn't seem to have any misgivings at first sight. He did seem a bit harried. I appreciated him speaking to me instead of the minister. "That's fine with me."

"All right. I'll need to deal with a few things before we start. Do you have your things yet? I wouldn't want them to get lost in the shuffle."

I tapped my kit with my foot. "This is it."

He quirked an eyebrow. "That's everything?"

"Yes. It's the half-square meter your company recommended."

The minister cleared his throat again. "I'm sure it's fine. Didn't you say you needed to do something before the ceremony?"

Xander gave him a quick glare before he returned his attention to my kit. Was it too much? I hadn't needed to pare down very much, but still.

His wrist cuff pinged and he headed off to do whatever needed to be done before he became my husband.

## Xander

The clerk-bot pinged me again.

"I'll get a few things settled, then we can do this," I tipped my head toward the minister, and added to Maradean, "then I'll show you where to wait until we're ready to go."

I tried to give her a reassuring smile. Her puzzled expression left me unsure of my effort. I couldn't believe the company would suggest such a small amount of personal items. Even one other suit would take up nearly a third of the space. If she'd brought a bulkier miner's suit? We'll have to see. Maybe we could get a few things in on the next shipment. I exhaled loudly as I headed over to the clerk-bot. By the Roman Gods, I hoped our marriage worked.

I finished signing off on the goods transfer and caught sight of the Haedigs coming toward the dock.

I understood why they're leaving.

Adam losing both wife and husband. Jess expecting their third. My...*wife*? Not such a loss.

The Haedigs were who I'd gone to commiserate with after Calla'd told me about the quit requests. Quitting the colony. Quitting me. Not quitting Braden.

Adam Haedig was my best friend. It took an accident to make me realize how much he really meant. It'll be a much sadder place without him and his kids.

He saw me, waved, and headed over. Five-year-old Nada nestled against his chest, her slightly oversized suit scrunched up under her chin.

"Is she actually asleep?" I asked.

Jansen rolled his eyes. "She fell asleep as soon as we got on the pod." Two-years older than my Edison, Jansen is his close friend.

All the kids had been close.

Adam shifted Nada a little and she let out a muffled grumble. "I thought we'd be on the pod with you. Just how early did you get here?"

"Early. I brought half the containers and sent it back so there'd be plenty of room for you and your things. I also needed to make some comms while the reception was good."

"Huh." Adam gave me a skeptical look. "Not nervous or anything?"

I shook my head. "Techs. Like they're gonna find anything we didn't."

"I didn't mean them." Adam nodded toward the T-pod. "You sure about her? Kinda soon and all."

I turned my head and saw Maradean still stood in the same

spot with the minister, hands clasped and trying not to look at everything.

"You know Calla and I were over long before…" I didn't finish.

The Haedigs had been one of three communal marriages at TurgisMal. Usually, those were good for a colony. More people committed to looking out for each other. It'd never been my thing. Too committed to my job and making sure everyone had everything they needed. I had Calla, and we had Edison.

Apparently, I had no longer been enough for Calla.

I turned back to Adam. "I am surprised the request went through so fast with the Triarchy and the LLC."

He studied Maradean. "Cute. Let me know if it doesn't work out." He quirked a half-smile. The humor wasn't quite there, just a dim glimmer in his eyes. I missed it. I was going to miss him. The corner of my eyes stung.

"Hey! Are you the foreman? Greaves?"

The hail came from one of the Techs. They'd tried to ping me earlier, but I'd ignored it. They were huddled together, one counting their cartons off on a pad. I tried not to glare as I met their eyes and gave a brief nod.

I clasped Adam's hand, and we leaned in to touch foreheads. "Take care."

"We will. Come see us on Titan Septimus."

I tried to pull the corners of my mouth into a grin as we separated. "You take care of your sister, Jansen." I tousled the boy's thick, white hair then nodded at Adam. "And him."

"Tell Ed I'll comm him." Jansen's lip trembled a little, and I gave him a wink before I turned to deal with the Techs.

## Maradean

Xander had given me a quick peck on the cheek at the end of the ceremony. I honestly thought he did it to spite the minister more than anything else. He'd also taken my hand as he led me away from the platform to the eatery, his other hand carrying my kit. His hand felt calloused, yet warm. I found myself not minding as he guided me to the counter through the continued bustle of loading and unloading.

The closed shop I had noticed earlier stocked supplies. All

automated, and only accessible with proper clearance. On the other side of the eatery, stood a fully equipped exercise station. A large storage area at the opposite end of the way station held mined mineral and element containers awaiting transport to the processing facility.

While we waited for the server-bot, Xander suggested, "You might want to use the exercise station before we leave. The one we have at the colony is quite basic."

My body was grown to withstand slightly wider variables of gravity than baseline humans. I still needed to exercise daily to keep in shape on Iapetus.

Xander glanced at the menu. "Feel free to select whatever you'd like to eat." His tone sounded apologetic. "Our diets are a bit restricted depending on what supplies we have." He told the server-bot to put my food on his account then grabbed a large energy drink bag for himself. "I need to finish supervising the supply transfer. I'll be back soon." He hurried off.

Glancing around, I observed the minister sitting at the table closest to the platform, buried in his feeds again. The five Seville Sat-miners sprawled across three tables they had pulled together with what looked like far too much food. The Techs sat bunched up near the exercise station. I settled in the middle and awaited my order.

"Maradean. Mind if we sit next to you?"

Adam and his kids pulled out the stools at the table next to mine. He had wandered over to the wedding ceremony just as the minister pulled up his script pad. Xander had given him a strange look and Adam gave a one-shouldered shrug, saying, "We're already here, Xander. It's fine."

As we ate, he told me, "My family and I are relocating to Titan Septimus." He snagged a few of his son's vegetable crisps and received a grunt of complaint in return. "We've been at Turgis for almost seven years."

His daughter woke up halfway through the meal and wanted to go to the exercise station. She and Jansen ran off as soon as they finished eating. Adam watched them, the corner of his mouth quirking up, then he turned to me. I saw sadness in his warm, brown eyes.

"Xander's a good person. He's…under a lot of stress right now, so you won't see him at his best. He has a kind heart, though most of it belongs to Edison. Keeping the colony together and going means the moons to him. If he seems remote right now." He shrugged and let out a sigh. "I hope you'll still give him a chance."

I didn't know what to say.

Later, Xander sat next to me in the T-pod traveling the dead-end spur of the monorail heading to my new home. The Techs were with their gear in their own compartment behind us. I realized we were alone for the first time.

Our compartment, at the front, offered us the view of the approaching Turgis crater and the towering mountain range beyond. As we entered the Cassini Regio, Xander dimmed the compartment lights and I could see much more detail in the pocked landscape.

They had proven the theory of an asteroid ring collapsing onto Iapetus to create the massive equatorial ridge to be true. It held a wealth of different minerals and elements, and the range was dense enough to allow laser-cut tunneling without issue.

I'd read TurgisMal had been established to test a chain of mining stations going throughout the entire range. The original mining company went under, then the Triarchy scooped them up a few years ago. The project had supposedly gotten back on track. I'd heard something had happened recently.

I felt Xander watching me and turned to meet his eyes. His worn expression looked even more troubled than I'd seen so far.

"Do you know about the Turgis colony? About what happened a few months ago?"

I blinked. He'd been quiet since we'd strapped in for the ride. It wasn't a question I expected. "The Triarchy informed me there had been an accident and some of the crew were killed."

"Some," he muttered under his breath as he nodded and stared up at the towering vertical mass ahead. "Well…you should know what you're in for." He took a deep breath. "TurgisMal had twenty-eight of us living there." His shoulders sagged. "With the Haedigs leaving, that leaves twelve."

Lucky thirteen with me I thought, but didn't interrupt.

"Adam and Rumi, our recycler tech, had taken most of the kids on a way station run." He paused.

I watched his chest expand and contract in two deep, silent

breaths before he continued.

"A few of us were inspecting some of the new mining tunnels in full gear. The tunnels sealed themselves off from the main chamber when a temperature change registered. We worried it was a breach. A crack somewhere in the cavern housing the colony. But it was a simple equipment failure in the heating system." His next words fell to a hoarse whisper. "Everyone in the main cavern froze to death within moments. Those of us who survived we…we moved back into the original base camp. We've lived there ever since."

He motioned back at the compartment behind us. "Hopefully, the Techs will finish their inspection quickly and give us the all clear to officially move back in and get back to work."

The soft whirring of the T-pod as it glided over the rail filled the space between us for a time.

Xander cleared his throat. "There's one other thing you should know."

My stomach clenched as I braced for more misfortune.

"My former wife, Calla. She filed a quit for our marriage, and one with the company, six months before the accident. She, and her lover, Braden, were set to leave Iaputus as soon as the official paperwork came through." He glanced at me. "The Triarchy took its time. The official quit arrived the day after the accident."

My jaw dropped.

He gave me a weak smile. "I'm not sure if I'm a divorcee, or a widower."

## Xander

Well, now she knew. She needed to know. Hopefully, it wouldn't scare her off too quickly.

We were quiet for a while as we passed into the far crater wall tunnel and started up the slight incline.

"You don't seem to like the Triarchy much. Especially the Techs." She sounded curious, not critical.

I chuckled. "Obvious? I signed on with the original company when TurgisMal was first established, long before they got bought out by one of the Triarchy." I shifted in my seat, adjusting the straps. "I guess the theory behind having a principle entity over mining was well intentioned. Some resources are scarce. Overseeing things so no one hoarded was a good idea. So was setting ceiling prices of newly discovered elements. But…they got to policing everything. They have to verify *everything* before any kind of change is made. If the Triarchy doesn't approve of something, it doesn't happen." I took a breath, not used to talking so much. "It surprised me when they passed the request for you so quickly. I thought it would take much longer."

I glanced at her and saw she grimaced slightly as she watched the smooth dark surface of the tunnel lit by the rail light. Enough light reflected off the glazing from the dim interior lights to illuminate her face. She had light-golden brown eyes and flawless skin. Maradean really was quite lovely.

"Sorry," I apologized. "I have to ask. I mean, I'd never heard of a clone bride being listed in the regular tier before. I thought all LLC clones were high tier?"

She hesitated. "There was one other. But yes, clone brides are usually special orders and trained in a specific support role."

"Were you trained in something specific?"

"Bio-Tech assistant. They originally trained me for Enceladus."

"Huh. So why were you in the regular tier? Enceladus Techs are pretty specialized, aren't they?"

"My history would have been listed in the contract specifications."

Her words came out clipped and monotone. I pressed on. "Probably. I've been rather busy, so I'm asking you."

I noticed her fingers worrying at the cuffs of her suit and waited.

"This is my fifth contract."

My neck gave a loud pop as I jerked to look at her. "Fifth?"

I hadn't expected that revelation.

Her shoulders dropped as she sighed. "My first contract was seven years ago. My spousal contractor drowned accidentally just before I arrived on Enceladus. The second contract…Well, there were two children, and they didn't like me, so they annulled it. I heard he ended up marrying his childminder. The third, my spouse died two weeks into the marriage. A freak accident on Titan Quintus. A malfunctioning dock-bot crushed him. My fourth…" She took a slow breath and let it out before continuing. "His coworker declared his undying love for him during our ceremony. The ceremony paused as they discussed things and then they left together.

"There were talks of another contract on Io. After the last eruption the company didn't hear from him again." Her eyes glistened with unshed tears. "I think they were trying to get me out of the Saturnian system."

"Wow." Words failed me as I processed her unfortunate past. "So wait, the company discounted you after that?"

"Clone brides have a ninety-nine percent success rate. I've been bad luck for the company's ratings."

"But it doesn't sound like you caused any of those issues. They just happened."

"The company puts a great deal of emphasis on their success ratings."

"*Hmmm.* Yeah. Companies do tend to do that."

I felt the T-pod level out as we drew closer to the base camp.

"What would have happened if the Io one had gone through but hadn't worked out?"

Maradean fell silent, staring at her hands. I wondered if I'd finally crossed a line.

"I don't want to put any pressure on you." She paused and bit her lip. "If this doesn't work, you're within your contractual rights to annul it. It's fine. But…this contract is my last chance."

"What do you mean, your last chance?"

"I'll be decommissioned."

I stared at her. "You're not an irreparable bot. You're a person. They can't—"

"I'm technically the property of the LLC. They created me for a specific purpose. They don't want my bad luck to rub off on anyone else. I'll be recycled."

## Maradean

I met seven-year-old Edison shortly after I arrived. He had bright, curious, green eyes and similar features to his father, and the same slightly haunted look I'd seen in everyone else here. He quizzed me about meeting Jansen at the way station, and I could tell he already missed his friend terribly.

Edison owned a maradoo, the small, six-legged pets bred to aid against Sat Isolation Syndrome. He currently has three, actually. Dodger belongs to Jansen and is a sibling to Edison's Remmy. The third, Celeste, belonged to Ana, one of the children who was killed in the accident. They are lovely, soft creatures who bound off the walls in the light gravity. Celeste proved skittish after all the changes, but both Dodger and Remmy took to me right away.

Remmy's approval of me went a long way with Edison. I even saw a true smile from him and heard a laugh. He found it funny my name is so similar to the little creatures, though. Hopefully, I don't get a new nickname from him.

Xander had been gone for a few hours getting the Techs situated. He introduced me to a few people before he left, then Adrian took over and showed me around. I've met everyone except Rumi and Vekka, who are still out doing a perimeter check on the mine tunnels.

The bots do most of the mining with humans supervising different aspects. Everyone is cross-trained on at least two other systems other than their specialties. Handy considering what happened. I can tell everyone feels both overworked and underused at the same time.

I found out a little more about the accident and of the condition of the proper TurgisMal colony. A lot of the electronics, from drives to control panels, were damaged since they were designed for livable environments and not exterior extremes. The crew spent most of the past tri-cycle doing salvage and repairs, all the while mourning friends and family.

The extreme temperature change destroyed most of their food production. A few young plants survived. They'd been raised in hyper-insulated hothouses undergoing study. The colonists hoped to use those to propagate from. Unfortunately, the lead herbologist had been one of the casualties. Hopefully, my bio skills will help. I'd love to be useful in other ways, not only tending the few remaining children while the others try to get the mine running again.

With Jansen gone, there are four remaining, counting Edison. I met them briefly. All had the same traumatized look in their eyes. I'm glad I've taken survival recovery modules. The training will be useful, and not just for the kids.

Edison told me I might have some trouble with Shaeda. She's turning thirteen soon and thinks she should help the adults. Not be babysat by some stranger.

No one seems to like the Techs being here. There's an undercurrent of uncertainty that the Triarchy wouldn't mind shutting the mine down, or at least restaffing it completely after shunting the current crew somewhere else for "safety reasons".

Everyone seems to hold Xander in high regard. That's a good sign.

He'd said little after I'd shared my story and my potential fate. His silence had worried me at first.

I kind of have a good feeling about this place. It seems to be on its last chance too. Everyone here seems to be ready to fight for it. Until the end.

## Xander

Damn Triarchy Techs!

We spent the last week packing everyone's living space tight with supplies so the Techs could set up in the storeroom. They took one look at the place and refused. "No." They'd camp in the main cavern in the modules they brought while the inspection commenced.

So I had to spend extra time taking them down the tunnel in the spare Sub-pod. They wanted me to leave the pod! I told *them*, "No." They'd have to wait until Rumi and Vekka were back safely from perimeter check. I'd have the bot take the spare back for them to use.

They had the audacity to argue!

I let slip I needed to get back to help my bride settle in and the looks they gave me.

I swear by the Roman Gods, if they hadn't been wearing their faceplates I would have popped each and every one of them.

Ugh!

I needed to pause the Sub-pod's trek halfway back so I could compose myself. I hadn't felt so angry since I'd been a hot-headed seventeen-year-old. Not even when Calla told me about the quit she'd filed. I mean I'd known about Braden. How could I not? The quit to leave the company entirely, though, had surprised me.

One of my comms at the way station had been with the survivors' councilor. I'd made sure everyone else placed the comm, but I'd kept putting it off. There'd been no time to grieve. I'd known it would be a hard day with the Techs here. Hearing about the LLC contemplating *recycling* a person and then the Techs' comments and attitudes! Any benefit from the comm had evaporated.

If Edison truly hated Maradean, and I couldn't imagine he would, someone with bio-tech skills was valuable here. Even if the marriage turned out to be a pretense, there was no way she would be leaving.

Unless we all do.

I headed back to the base camp and set the Sub-pod to standby before making my way to our quarters. As I approached the door, I heard…laughter?

I slowed and cautiously peered through the sidelight. Edison laughed as Maradean played with the maradoos. It was a full-on laugh. I hadn't heard it since before the accident.

The corners of my eyes prickled watching Edison rock back and forth on his heels, as he continued to giggle. Maradean tried to coax Celeste out from under a blanket with a treat. Remmy draped across her shoulder, nuzzling her hair. Her true smile, warm and broad, graced her features. Not the stiff one she had greeted me with at the way station.

Absolutely beautiful.

"You finally done with them?"

I jumped. The voice came from behind, and I turned to see Adrian standing with hands on hips. He was possibly the only other person here who distrusted the Triarchy more than I did.

I mentally shook myself. "Yeah, I need to send the spare Sub-pod back when Rumi and Vekka get here. They don't seem to want to mix."

"Good. Means more food for us. We're still having the group dinner as soon as the wanderers get back." Adrian nodded at the door. "You going in or just admiring the view?"

I felt my cheeks heat. "First time I've heard Edison laugh in ages."

Adrian grunted and clapped my shoulder. "He seems to like her. That's good. You could use a break. I'll ping you when everything's ready."

I nodded, placed my hand on the control panel and went

inside.

## Maradean

I got to tour the main cavern today. It's odd and a little eerie.

They have stripped down many of the surviving bots and equipment, looking for less obvious damage, some of it done by the crew and some done by the Techs.

It looked skeletal, like a ghost town.

The colony had been thriving with fruit trees and a well-established hydroponic greenhouse. After being flash frozen, even the slightest touch turned the leaves and stems to shards, then dust.

The bio-cleanup had begun. Not the crew's remains. They took care of those in the first few days. They'd spent the first few weeks examining the cavern and ruling things out. Then the work of damage reports, assessing what could and couldn't be fixed.

They had left the greenhouse and hydroponics alone, concentrating their effort on the bots and equipment, since they had been good about keeping foodstuffs stocked at the base camp and other supplies could be shipped in.

The Techs had made progress with the inspection and even allowed me to enter Xander and Edison's home. It's more than double the quarters at the base camp. I thought the three of us could be quite comfortable there.

Vekka had been ecstatic when Adrian told her I'd studied bio-tech. When she saw me in the cavern, she ushered me over to look at some of the hydroponic equipment. Vekka had helped work with the plants, but the system was already set up when she joined the colony. She'd been at a loss. She explained what repairs she thought needed to be done. I thought she was right, but before we could dig into it, one of the Techs angrily shooed us away.

It's true most of my time has been minding the kids, yet the adults circle in and out whenever they're not busy. I don't think it's a trust issue with me. Everyone has been kind and welcoming. I think it's still the shock of losing so many people all at once. They just seem to want to see the kids, and each other, as much as possible.

I asked Shaeda a lot of questions about the colony and about what the other kids liked to do. My questions seemed to have countered any qualms she had about me being in charge. She's turned out to be very helpful. She and her three-year-old sister, Bree, are the only survivors of their family. I just can't imagine what she's going through. I'm hoping I can become someone she feels like she can talk to.

The colony's still small enough that everyone knows each other well. The communal families were especially close to each other, since they all had at least one child. So I know Shaeda has support already.

It makes me wonder about Xander. Adrian told me Xander had been very insistent on everyone scheduling time with a survivors' councilor. He wasn't sure if the foreman had actually done so himself.

I hope the Techs leave soon. More importantly, I truly hope we pass the inspection. The stress level would drop tremendously for everyone.

Maybe less stress would allow the two of us to get to know each other better. Adam was right about Xander being kind. He's a good father to Edison. He's good with the whole crew. Only the Techs continued presence seemed to annoy him.

We're sleeping in separate hammocks right now. He proposed we wait on any physicality until we were settled back in the main cavern. It's true that our small quarters are tight with Edison, the maradoos, and extra supplies. I really think he didn't expect me to arrive so soon. I don't think he was really ready.

He's not sleeping well. I swear if he wasn't zipped into the hammock, he'd fall out. I've even woken up to find him not in the room. Tempting to try and to follow him.

## Xander

We passed! Thank the Roman Gods.

The Techs pinged me while I ate lunch. I almost choked. Won't be official until they relay their report to the Triarchy. They finished in time to catch the next T-pod passing through the Othon Way Station. In less than two cycles, they'd be gone.

Everyone took it well. As in, everyone screamed and bounced around. I felt relief. We'd won.

I'd slept so poorly. I thought the end of not knowing our future would allow me to sleep at least ten hours. No. I slept for a while, but awoke to Edison's snores and Maradean shifting slightly in her webbing.

I turned my head to watch her silhouette in the dim light. Maradean. She'd fit in with the crew well. Everyone seemed to like her, especially Edison. Even Shaeda seemed to like her, and she's hit the age of not really liking anyone. Her bio-tech skills are already coming in handy. She's smart and eager to learn. I've seen her lending an empathetic ear not just to the kids, but Rumi and even Adrian.

When I sent in the request for a new bride, I didn't know what to expect. I didn't really know why I did it. With Calla set on leaving the colony, I started thinking it would be good to have someone else here for Edison. I mean, we were all one big family to an extent. Yet…

Honestly, I guess I really just wanted someone here for me.

I slipped out of the hammock, donned my shoes and left as quietly as I could. Rumi sat in the monitoring room reading and waved when he saw me. I continued on, meandering down the tunnel toward the pod dock. I perched on the rim of the platform, gripping the edge as my feet dangled.

I thumped my heels against the well wall, lost in thought. I didn't hear the approaching footsteps until they were right behind me. I looked up to see Maradean.

"I hope I didn't wake you," I inquired.

"I woke up thirsty and noticed you were gone."

She sat down on the ledge next to me.

"Do we have to wait until the Techs are gone before we start moving to the cavern?"

"There'll be less friction if we do. I doubt most of the crew will wait. It'll take multiple Sub-pod trips and a lot of prep to live there full time again. The Techs started the air filtration system and upped the heating the last few degrees a little after dinner. By lunchtime tomorrow, it should be livable."

I met her golden eyes. She gave me a warm smile. I felt my face relax into a matching one. How could anyone have ever thought of recycling her?

Her cheeks tinged pink, and she glanced away.

"Maradean, I'm sorry. I haven't really paid much attention to you since you arrived."

"Well, you have been rather busy. Seems like the chaos is starting to settle down."

I chuckled. "Well, it will be a much more manageable chaos as we get things up and running again."

I felt her fingers tentatively settled over the top of mine. They were cool and trembled slightly.

I hesitated half a second, before interlacing my fingers with hers. Gently I squeezed until she stopped trembling.

"Nothing about you has been bad luck, Maradean. In fact, I feel incredibly lucky right now."

She met my eyes again. "A time of new beginnings?"

I leaned close and kissed away the tear trailing down on her cheek.

"A time of new beginnings."

~ * ~ * ~

**Kat Farrow** grew up skinning her knees and listening to the wind among the rabbit trails and red rocks of the Four Corners area of the western U.S. A multi-genre author, her works span fantasy, sci-fi, mystery, historical, and children's stories.

Her short stories appear in several anthologies including *The Librarian Reshelved* (Air & Nothingness Press), *Noncorporeal: an Anthology of Ghosts, Haunts, and Spirits* (Inkd Publishing), *Parliament of Wizards* (Hemelein Publications), and *Mistletoe Merriment* (Camden Park Press).

*Bobbin and the Magic Thief,* her children's fairy tale retelling of Rumpelstiltskin, released in 2023.

Kat drinks vast quantities of tea and spends far too much time as cat furniture. When not writing, she is often battling weeds, gaming, or watching anime.

Find out more about Kat and her work at Loreweaver.com.

# MINING IN THE STARS

Hayley Liversidge

WHAT happened? Where was she? Eleanor coughed. Her ears were ringing, her mouth and nose full of dust. She could barely breath. What was that acrid stench? Yes, definitely, burnt galletite.

Slowly Eleanor opened her eyes peering into the lamplit smokey gloom. Above her some kind of curved roof made of jet rock. She must be lying flat. Her arms and whole body felt every sharp stone point on the floor.

Grimacing, she slowly sat up. Her hand lightly touched the back of her head. "Ouch." She could feel a lump right in the middle of her skull. If only she could remember. If only her head wasn't pounding and she didn't feel quite so dizzy.

Gradually she pulled herself to her feet. A huge screeching noise pierced the silence. Something flew past scratching her face with its talons. Ow, that hurt. Her hand slapped to her face. Blood tricked through her fingers. What was it?

Eleanor picked up a jagged rock. If that thing came near her again…

Slowly she turned, forcing herself to peer into the darkness to see what it was.

There, crouched in a corner flapping its wings, squawking and trying to pull out its feathers perched a grey parrot. Eleanor sighed with relief. "Zac, it's me, Mistress E," she whispered. Her throat felt so dry and sore making it difficult to talk. Oh, for a pool of water to moisten her chapped lips.

She sank again to the floor, exhausted. Zac still cowered in the corner. At the sound of her voice he looked up briefly from pulling out his feathers. Already a small pile of them were floating down and landing on the jet surface.

How to calm a frightened parrot? Eleanor desperately tried to remember through the fog of pain. If Zac didn't relax soon he'd do himself and her an injury. She sighed. That was it, don't approach or you may get bitten. Speak in a soothing tone to the bird. Praise him when he tries to calm down and stops harming himself.

"Zac," she croaked. "It's alright, you and me we'll be fine. I never should have taken you down the mine. I'm so sorry."

The bird stopped pulling out feathers and looked up staring at her with his bright black eyes.

"That's it." Eleanore encouraged the parrot, hoping Zac listened. "It was only a nasty bang, we'll be out of here soon. I'll feed you your favourite sunflower seeds and millet."

"Sun flower seeds, millet," squawked Zac.

"Yes," whispered Eleanor, breathing a sigh of relief. "Sun flower seeds and millet. Good boy."

Zac flew carefully to a rock beside Eleanor and started preening himself nuzzling his beak into one of his wings.

"Sunflower seeds and millet," he repeated in a muffled screech.

Eleanor reached out and very gently touched his head. Zac purred.

"That's better," she soothed. "We're in this together eh?"

"In this together," added the parrot giving a quick peck at the outstretched hand offered.

Eleanor closed her eyes trying to ease the pain in her head. At least she wouldn't die alone. No, that wasn't the attitude to take. She needed was to clear her mind, remember what had happened and work out a way out of here. How did it all start? Oh yes, two space years ago September 2450. Her arrival at Triton, on the nicknamed Bridal craft. The time she met the most annoying man it had been her bad luck to bump into.

~ * ~

"Welcome to Triton," the AI voice came over the tannoy system. "Please make your way to the arrivals centre. There you will be decontaminated and checked for infection. Please remember, do not attempt to leave the station at any time without The Board's permission. The outside temperature is minus two hundred and fifty-six degrees Celsius. The air is mainly nitrogen. Breathing equipment is required for life forms that are not human. For those who will be working in the mine, it is encased in an environmental sleeve so no breathing equipment required. An up-to-date survival certificate is a compulsory for permission to go to the surface. Survival suits are available to hire from The Board's Stores. Thank you for flying with SC one. We hope to see you again in future."

"Master, I am a humanoid. Will I require breathing apparatus?"

Grant stared at his companion with a twinkle in his eye and stretched his legs. After the long journey from Earth he needed a bit of light relief. A wash wouldn't come of a miss either. The air in the spacecraft had become distinctly malodorous. Humans smelt badly enough of stale sweat, but the Ontorians emitted hydrogen sulphide. Despite air scrubbers the place reeked like an antique stink bomb. "Well now," he replied scratching his head. "On Earth do you need breathing equipment?"

Cy looked vaguely puzzled. "Why ask? You already know the answer."

Grant laughed and slapped his fellow traveler on the back. "Look, the station has an atmosphere specially designed for humans. You have been built to survive on Earth. So…"

"No need to wear any EPG unless my primary circuits malfunction or the temperature drops below minus fifty degrees Celsius."

"Exactly. Now if you track down the cases, I'll see about getting checked in."

Grant looked around at the small group disembarking through the hatch in the air lock. Doctors in their blue overalls were already waiting to take the new arrivals for a health check. With all the pre-flight injections required the chances of picking up some alien disease were minimal. Still protocol was protocol and had to be followed at all times.

Cy returned carrying two silver chests and a sporran round his waste that seemed to be shaking. Grant stared at him and laughed. "What's that white muck all over your face? I do believe there is a small dent in your cheek bone."

"I had a minor disagreement with one of the passenger's grey parrot. It seemed to take exception to my presence."

Grant laughed even more. "What a bird got the better of you?"

Cy glanced down at the trembling sporran. "Not exactly."

Before any reply could be made he heard a scream. Something hit Grant on the chest. He staggered back as an arm hit his ribs followed by the rest of the body.

True, being squashed by someone falling on you wasn't pleasant, but when the most delectable aroma of fresh spiced lavender filled your nostrils, it was at least some compensation.

"I am so sorry," said a muffled voice. The young woman hastily disentangled herself and stood up. "I hope you're not hurt."

Grant slowly got up looked at his assailant. A smile spread across his face. How could he possibly be hurt by the most beautiful woman he'd ever met crashing into him. Her luscious chestnut hair fell in long wavy curls over her shoulders. The acorn brown eyes that seemed to take in everything and the small pert mouth. This was someone he definitely wanted to get to know.

"No worries." He hastily straightening his cyan jacket. "The name's Grant Shepherd by the way. I've just arrived here, I am taking the role of deputy mining engineer controller."

"I'm Eleanor Wright," she replied holding out her hand. "I was on the same flight as you. I am a geologist, here to work on the galletite deposits."

Cy, humanoid in every possible way, even to the extent of wearing clothes, raised his eyebrows.

"So I'll be seeing you at the speed dating tonight." Grant couldn't be sure if he liked or dreaded the prospect of seeing her later.

Eleanor's cheeks went a dark rosy colour. "I guess so. It's compulsory for new residents. The Board are really keen to get this new colony up and running. In the meantime I'm looking for my pet, a grey parrot. Apparently there is a suitable female grey parrot he might mate with. Have you seen it. Some idiot frightened it, so it flew away."

Cy raised his eyebrows again and looked down at the wriggling sporran. "I must confess, I think that idiot is me." Carefully he opened the sporran and extracted a bird. It hissed pecked the humanoid's hands furiously, ruffling up his feathers squawking in alarm.

"Poor Zac," cried Eleanor holding out her arm so the bird flew to her. "What have you done him?"

Cy stared at the bird, then at his battered hand streaming blue liquid. "Rather, it's what he has done to me. Your pet decided to take exception to my presence and decided to attack me. The only thing I could do was put him in the dark to quieten down. The sporran was the only way I could do that."

Grant slapped his companion on the back. "Quick thinking mate. Now go to cybernetics to get that hand fixed." Cy nodded and walked off.

Eleanor stroked the bird. "You poor thing," she murmured. "Don't worry I'll see you are fine and make sure stupid humanoids don't frighten you in future."

Grant glared at her. "Perhaps you should consider keeping the animal under better control so he doesn't attack anyone else."

The response was exactly what he'd expected. "Perhaps you and your humanoid should be more considerate of others feelings." With those words she turned and walked away. Zac sat on her shoulder happily nibbling her ear.

Grant watched her leave. Infuriating woman, yet what an amazing character. A female geologist with a parrot. How her eyes sparkled when she was annoyed. Grudgingly, he had to admit he was really looking forward to their next encounter. Perhaps he might provoke her even more. There again, perhaps not. One thing was for sure working with her was going to fun. He'd already got a nick name for her, The Comet.

~ * ~

Eleanor dressed in her favourite emerald evening attire. The design was simple and elegant, with a skirt falling to her ankles. Her pearl necklace, a gift from her mum, showed off the modest neckline.

She wasn't into speed dating and wasn't looking forward to it. However, it had to be done, and maybe just maybe she might find the right man for her. She'd been looking for a few years. Somehow, she'd never met anyone she'd be really interested in, let alone marry or spend the rest of her life with; no matter how attractive they were.

Unbidden the face of Grant came into her head. The smell of his pine cologne reminded her so much of her days on Earth. The funny way he had of wrinkling his nose while they talked. His jet-black hair, done in the old-fashioned short back and sides look.

She shook her head. No absolutely not. This had to stop, no way could this man be her soul mate.

"Would all new arrivals not kept in medical please proceed to deck four for the Triton Colony Speed Dating Evening," came the tannoy announcement. "Please bring any pets with you, where possible, so they can be introduced too. At the end of the session put the names of any people you are interested in getting to know straight into the computer data base in your quarters. Within forty-eight Triton hours we will process them and make time for you to meet as a prospective couple."

Hu, fat chance, Eleanor thought putting on a lace shawl.

One thing was certain, she had no intention whatsoever of going out with Grant.

~ * ~

Grant stood nervously with a few other men waiting in what posed as a bar. It was really a sterile white room that held a few amber stone seats and bottled drinks sat on the tables. He had a cocktail in hand. "Triton Blue," the bartender told him with a grin. "Should calm your nerves." He took a sip and frowned. The burning taste of black liquorice and aniseed combined. Food and drink were obviously scarce on this new colony, but this drink was foul.

Better get used to it, he told himself. He took another sip ignoring what the man to his right was saying, something about explosions. Normally he'd look forward to speed dating as a laugh. This time he wasn't. The worrying thing was he knew why.

Eleanor, he couldn't get her out of his head. Somehow, she'd penetrated his armour without even trying. Ever since the death of his beloved wife Jo in an accident, he'd lost interest in life. He'd flirted with a few women. Yet that had been nothing more than harmless banter, to convince himself he was still alive. Never again would he allow himself to love someone. Too risky. He wasn't sure he could go through that pain again. Triton seemed the perfect answer. A new start, a totally different environment where he could concentrate on work. He would do the speed dating to satisfy The Boards requirements. No compulsion to marry or even just have a partner.

Grant took a final sip of his noxious drink. His resolve had lasted right until he'd set eyes on Eleanor. Suddenly he felt alive again. As if the ghost of Jo was finally beginning to be laid to rest. Yet would she be interested? That didn't look promising.

~ * ~

Eleanor's heart jumped as he sat down next to her. Why did he look so confident with that arrogant smile? By contrast she'd arrived with Zac sitting on her shoulder, her hand sweaty, resisting the urge to wipe them on her skirt. She knew her hands trembled. Why couldn't she display such bravado and ease. Instead she felt like a teenager all over again. Infuriating.

"You have five minutes to get to know the person at your table. When the buzzer sounds people in Group A must get up and walk clockwise to the next table. Group B should remain seated the whole time," the compere announced.

~ * ~

A beep signaled the start of the conversation. Grant smiled at her and she couldn't be sure what it meant. He joined her. "We did get off to a bad start earlier today. I hope that can be rectified."

The infuriating man, what if she didn't want it to be rectified? Eleanor shrugged her shoulders dismissively. "I'm not sure. There's a problem."

Grant frowned. "What problem might that be?" his voice like ice. Where had his smile gone?

Eleanor wriggled uncomfortably in her seat. Should she do this? Yes, she must, if only to honour her parents' memory. "It's awkward…"

Grant snorted. "You can't mean the silly incident with your pet parrot? You crashed into me, not the other way round. I didn't get attacked by your bird, Cy did."

Eleanor slammed her fist down on the table. "The bird has a name. It's Zac. A living creature like you."

Zac started at his mistress in bewilderment and chirped.

Grant held up his hands. "Ok, Ok. I'll be more careful what I say."

"It's not that incident, as you call it. It's something else," she paused. "I checked information on the database today." She hated herself for saying it, but she felt it should be done.

"Well?"

"Your father, Captain Shepherd of STI killed my parents."

Grant stared at her in stunned silence. "You mean the STI Intrepid Space crash?"

Eleanor nodded miserably. He laughed nervously. "For goodness sake there was a war going on. The ship got attacked. People were killed. Nothing he could have done to save them."

"He was drunk at the time."

Grant slammed his glass down on the table. "Perhaps," he replied, his expression icy. "You should study history properly, rather than make it up. He wasn't drunk. Being wounded in the battle, he had to have a hand amputated. The doctor decided to use alcohol to numb the pain since they'd run out of regular medication." He rubbed his forehead. "My father needed something to get him through the procedure."

He stood up. "Good day to you." Then stormed out of the room.

Everyone stopped talking and stared. Then quietly got back to the business in hand. Eleanor put her hands on her head and felt hot tears streaming down her face. How could she have made such a fool of herself? Would he ever forgive her?

~ * ~

Time was running out. Wearily Eleanor opened her eyes and wiped the dust off them as best she could. Zac sat on a rock next to her ruffling up his feathers. "Seed" he squawked miserably. "Millet."

Eleanor touched his wings gently. "I know." She'd made her parrot a promise and hoped she could keep it.

Now that she could think a little more clearly she remembered what had happened. They'd been taking some new rock samples for examination. She had gone deeper to find some rarer samples. That was when it happened. An explosion, the buildup of gas and a spark probably. Stones came tumbling down from the roof of the cave. The plain truth, she and Zac were trapped with no way out of the tunnel except for the way they'd come, which had been covered with boulders.

Once the limited air supply in the pocket of the cave was used up, they'd die. Eleanor shivered. The tunnel's environmental jacket still worked. At least they wouldn't freeze to death.

"Sorry," she whispered to Zac. "I should never have taken you here."

Why? Oh why was all that she could think about was Grant's face when she spoke to him that fateful night speed dating?

~ * ~

Grant paced up and down. "What did you say?" he demanded.

Trevor his second in command shifted nervously from foot to foot. "There was a problem, with unforeseen buildup of gas."

"Anyone injured?"

"Thankfully no, but…"

"But what?"

Trevor hesitated. "We have reason to believe one of the workers went deeper into the tunnel. She hasn't been accounted for."

Grant stomach lurched. "Any likelihood of being alive?"

"Well, our geological scans indicate there is a pocket of air at the end of the tunnel where she was last."

Grant gulped. He just had to ask the question. "What's her name?"

Trevor squirmed. "Eleanor Wright."

The name acted like an electrical shock. Grant could feel the blood rushing to his ears. He felt physically sick. "What are we waiting for?" he shouted. "The clock is ticking."

"It's too dangerous, there's nothing we can do," Trevor countered.

Grant hadn't heard, instead he dashed out of the room. He had to find Cy, now.

~ * ~

Eleanor gasped for breath. Zac sat motionless on the rock. The air was getting so thin. Only a short time left. Suddenly she heard scraping on the rocks. A voice shouted dimly in the background. Too late, she thought, closing her eyes as blackness descended. Too late.

~ * ~

A light shone in her eyes. She could breathe. Someone stood over her.

"Just five minutes, no longer," a muffled voice said.

Slowly she opened her eyes. Grant's face staring down at her smiling. This must be some sort of a dream.

"Eleanor," he pleaded.

No this couldn't be a dream, she could feel him touching her, making her spine tingle.

"I'm alive," she could barely whisper her throat felt so sore.

"You're going to be fine," he promised. "Just the effect of the gas."

"Where's Zac?" she rasped. Her bird was sat on Grant's shoulder, nibbling his ear.

"Did you rescue me?"

Grant made a face. "I'd like to say yes, believe me. But that wasn't really the case." He took a deep breath. "You see Cy and I went down on our own. They said it was too unstable to risk a rescue attempt. Cy has great physical strength and removed some boulders to carry you out."

Eleanors heart leapt. So he had risked his life to save her. It didn't matter to her if he wasn't the one who pulled her out. Not at all.

She held out her hand and smiled. "Thank you," she managed. "Would you like to go out on a date?"

~ * ~ * ~

**Hayley** is an independent writer from the UK. Having completed a creative writing course she has had articles published in the local community newspapers, Woman Alive magazine and MIMAzine. Her short stories have been shortlisted in Writing Magazine competitions and in the annual Crossing The Tees short story competition. Her latest crime story was published in the anthology, *A Grave Diagnosis.* More recently her work has appeared in the collection of stories, *When This Is All Over,* in the Czech Slovak Review, and in an Annihilation anthology published by Black Ink Fiction.

When not working with children or tapping on the computer, she loves going for long walks in the countryside. One of her ambitions is to walk the Camino Way, if she ever gets round it.

# RUNAWAY BRIDE

Harriet Phoenix

This is the second-stupidest idea I've ever had.

It's just, I'm out of smart ones.

"Kasih Jaeger?"

I sit up in my waiting room seat as the receptionist calls my name. "Yes?"

"Your agent is ready for you." To her left, a door swooshes open. "Just go right in."

As the door swooshes shut behind me, I find myself in a tastefully-appointed office with a sofa and two armchairs with a coffee table in the middle. All very cosy, as if people will just forget they're here to be paired off with a stranger based on a personality algorithm.

This is stupid. This is crazy! Why am I doing this?

The bag bumps against my hip as if to remind me. Physically it weighs no more than if it held a lunchbox, but psychologically it weighs as much as the Moon itself along with its population of ten million. For the last four days I've felt as if a searchlight has been trained on the holdall swinging from my shoulder.

The thing is, I know if I left it behind, I'd feel worse; sick with worry, imagining I'd return to my hotel room, listed under a fake name, to find the safe broken open, its precious contents replaced with a note saying, "Did you really think that would work?"

It's no safer on my shoulder and I know it. The only safety lies in getting off this damn rock.

I slide it carefully under my armchair, where it can rest against my foot.

"So, Kasih," my agent says. The name on the door was Rachel Salinas. She seems my age or a little older, but more polished in a business-casual jumpsuit and updo. "Welcome to Space Brides, LLC! I understand this is a daunting step to take, so let me just run you through how this'll work. First, I'll ask you some questions to establish exactly what you're looking for in a partner, what kind of destination you'd enjoy and what you hope to get out of marriage generally. I'll also establish your skillset to determine where you might be a good fit. Then there'll be a psychological assessment and some personality tests to ensure a suitable match. I see you've submitted your medical certificate, so…before we begin, can I get you anything? Tea, coffee, bulb of water?"

"No, no thank you." I don't mean to be rude, I'm just nervous.

"Alright then, straight in." she turns her attention to the pad on her lap. "So, you're twenty-four Earth years old, biologically and socially female, and a lifelong resident of Lunar City?"

"That's correct."

She looks up at me and smiles. "I'm from Mars, myself. You know, it's funny, I keep expecting people from Luna to be rich? It's silly, I've been here for years now, I know perfectly well Luna needs all the same infrastructure and support as any other place, but it's hard to get rid of those stereotypes, isn't it?"

"I'm sure." There's no way she's still so clueless. The super-rich don't use services like this. Desperate people from all social strata must pass through here all the time. It's just something she says to make herself appear vulnerable to get me to relax.

"Actually, it's not so surprising," I expand. Things will probably go faster if I play her game. "Most people do live in one estate or another. Each one has thousands of support and technical staff. I grew up on the Maddox estate, myself. My mother was a software security specialist and my father worked in one of the agri domes. I learned both trades, growing up, plus the same educational rotations everyone does."

"Wonderful. Now, it says here you're interested in either male or female partners, and you have no children but are interested in having them?"

"That's correct." I know the bag didn't *really* nudge my foot.

"In terms of skillset, you're an environmental engineer. You also have a decent range of maintenance skills. You're also a Level Three Medic, a Level Two Shuttle Pilot and you're qualified for spacewalks. Under 'Other,' it also says you like to cook."

"Also correct."

"Lovely. Well, we can certainly find you a placement with your skillset. Now, if you'll come with me to the next room, we'll run your assessments to see if we can find you somewhere to really thrive. It's alright," she adds as I reach for my bag. "Your belongings will be quite safe here."

I hate leaving the bag. I hate it. I hate it. I hate it! Yet insisting on taking it would only create interest, so I have to bite my lip and do as she says.

The assessments take about an hour. I sit under a medical scanner, which records Deity-knows-what while Rachel asks me a barrage of questions, ranging from sensible ones about my expectations to logic puzzles. If a fish has sixty-six scales on its left side and sixty-six scales on its right, on which side does it have the most? Answer: the outside. Then there's technical questions about my areas of expertise, and sprinkled in are odd questions about my feelings on anything from song lyrics to the extinct bumblebee. At random, faces of people of every gender, body type, age and nationality flash up for my viewing pleasure.

And, all the time, I feel the bag's absence like a constant ache at my side.

Finally, it's all over and we return to the office. I run a hand over the bag as discreetly as possible. The three hairs I stuck into the zip are still there. Of course, they are. Why wouldn't they be?

"So, Kasih," Rachel says, taking her seat opposite me. "I have a question, and I invite you to consider carefully before answering. Have you given any thought to the possibility of group marriages?"

I blink. "Um…wow. No, I hadn't, really."

"The reason I bring this up is that some of your responses suggest you find traditional family models restrictive, and there are plenty of societies out there founded by others who feel the same way. If you're willing to explore those possibilities, then your options can obviously widen enormously."

"I like options." And it's true I haven't had the most success with traditional family models. Again, the bag seems to nudge my foot, as if its contents are reaching out to tap me.

Her smile widening, Rachel places her pad on the coffee table and activates the holo feature. A model of the solar system appears between us. The planets are, as with all such models, disproportionate so they can all fit and be a useful size.

"Well, then," she says. "Let's see what we've got."

She uses hand movements to zoom in on Mercury, where a green tag indicates a point near the pole.

"Here we have the MacGregor settlement," she suggests. "Mining and manufacture. They also make a decent sideline as a recharge point for various kinds of ship, what with all that lovely solar energy, meaning they see a fair amount of traffic, which keeps the social scene fresh. They *are* hoping to expand and improve their facilities, so an Environmental Engineer would definitely be welcome.

"They practice a system of four-way marriage between two women and two men, all of whom couple as they see fit. There are currently two such foursomes at the settlement seeking a woman to complete their set. You could try both out for a few weeks before making your decision."

"Hmm." I pinch my chin, staring at the model settlement. It doesn't *seem* like anyone would look for me there. I imagine someone squinting into the sun's glare, hoping to spot me on the tiny dot of Mercury. If anyone *did* think to look in that direction the same sun feels like a wall I'd be backed against. Which I know is *stupid*, you can't be boxed in in *space*, by definition. I feel how I feel. "Maybe we can come back to this later."

"Of course." She zooms the holo back out again and zooms in on Venus. "Here we have a space station dedicated to scientific research, with the ultimate goal of successfully terraforming Venus into a new Earth. Members of the Gemini Institute engage in a flexible arrangement of plural marriages."

"Ngh." I've heard of the Gemini Institute. Notoriety is not my friend. "Is there anywhere else? Maybe…further out?"

"Further out, hmm?" Her face looks thoughtful. "Have you considered Titan? That's pretty far out."

The moon is marked with a green tag as it orbits Saturn. I lean forward, pinching my chin. The settlement is made up of domes embedded in the rock across the moon. Depending on the atmosphere, the views must be spectacular.

"The Soun estate," Rachel continues. "Population stands at seventy, of whom forty-one are adults. They're always looking for people with technical skills, with a special interest in Environmental Engineers and agriculture, so in terms of skills you'd fit right in. As for family models…that's somewhat singular."

"Tell me about it."

"Well, this is unusual. It seems, were you to select Soun as your destination, upon arrival you would be welcomed with a ceremony where you would be officially married to each member of the adult population. Every. Single. One."

I feel my jaw drop. "The *whole*…"

"I should elaborate," she hastily adds. "That no one is under obligation to…well, although polyamory is encouraged, everyone's living and coupling arrangements are at their own discretion. All adults are inducted into the group marriage, with the exception of children who grew up there, who are of course only married to those who are not biological relatives."

"That, uh…well, good."

"The idea seems to be everyone is considered equally responsible for everyone else, just as every child of the colony is considered equally the responsibility of every adult there. Equally family, and equally dear. I don't quite know how that *works* in reality, but…"

"But it's a nice idea." I stare at the network of domes. It's definitely an overwhelming idea. Still, having so many people in my corner…well, it's more appealing than the rows and rows of turned backs I encountered when Lakshmi threw me out.

The bag, once again, seems to nudge against my foot. "Forty-one husbands and wives…"

~ * ~

Saturn is eight months away by cargo shuttle, the standard way to get around the solar system. Passenger liners are prohibitively expensive for most people, and at least as a crew member I have something useful to do on the journey, a way to keep my skills sharp.

Of course, a passenger liner wouldn't be prohibitively expensive for Lakshmi. Actually, she wouldn't need one.

I push the thought away and run my thumb over the zip of my bag as the golden swirls of Saturn grow bigger and bigger on the viewer. Lakshmi's in the past.

"Jaeger!" My head snaps around as Reggie, my supervisor, approaches. "Your shuttle will be docking in five minutes! As well as your fine self, they will be taking on some cargo and then you will depart, unless you come to your senses and allow me to make an honest woman of you instead."

He's made the odd joke like this since we left. At least, I think they're jokes. They'd better be. I'm engaged, after all.

I wait next to the pallet of cargo marked "Soun," counting down the seconds. Is the shaking in my belly from excitement or fear? Finally, the airlock door engages with a deep metallic *thunk* and the decompression indicator changes from red to green.

This is my ride.

"Seriously, though," Reggie adds as the magnetic grappler locks with the cargo pallet and manoeuvres it through the airlock. "We've dropped people off here before. And, often as not, we've picked them back up again not so long later. Whatever the *deal* is down there, it's not natural."

I want to point out he works on a spaceship. My throat isn't working. All those doubts I laid aside in Rachel's office all those months ago threaten to bubble back up. Am I making a terrible mistake?

"Well, that's you, if you still want to go," Reggie teases as the grappler reappears from the shuttle's hold. "See you in a couple of months," he adds as I pick up my holdall and head for the door.

I wave at him as the airlock door cycles shut. The *Elgin* will be passing this way again in a few weeks, once it's completed its round of the inhabited moons of Saturn, and it costs nothing to be friendly. Just in case.

"Hello?" I call into the cargo hold of the Soun settlement's shuttle, cramped between the pallet and the bulkhead. The lights are low. I see a ladder leading up. Getting up it and through the small hole to a different level is tricky, even in the low gravity, with my holdall trailing me. I manage.

"Hello?" I call out again. "Is anyone there?"

They do know I'm coming, right?

"Hi!" The woman's voice drifts from an open door at the end of the corridor. "Cockpit, this way!"

Following the voice, I come to, as she said, a cockpit. Three seats are arranged in a triangle, with a pilot and co-pilot's seat in front and a passenger seat on the back wall. Only the right-hand pilot's seat is occupied, with a woman a few years older than me, grinning like a lunatic.

"Hi!" she repeats. "You must be Kasih! Sorry no one was at the airlock to greet you."

"Don't you have a co-pilot?" There definitely should be one. Pilot and co-pilot will spell each other over long stretches. Both should be present for docking with another vessel.

"That's the thing." Her blazing smile becomes a wan grin. "He got sick, last minute, so I just nipped out myself. It was that or make you wait a few more weeks."

"You're flying *solo*?" The ingrained training kicks in, moving my legs of their own accord to the empty seat.

"Yeah. So, that's why I wasn't there. Had to co-ordinate the delivery." She watches me strap into the co-pilot's seat, her grin widening. "Gosh, you're pretty! The Space Brides folks sent over your vital stats, and there was a picture, but those things never do you justice, do they? I mean…*gosh*, you're pretty!"

"Thanks."

"So, my name is Lena Porter. I go by Lee. I'm your primary contact, which means I'll be secondary officiant for your ceremony."

"That's my wedding ceremony, right?" I try not to sound trepidatious. This all seemed like such a neat idea back on Luna. A marriage of many partners, all looking out for each other! How can it work when those partners are people? "To…everyone?"

She beams. "That's right! Did they tell you how the ceremony works?"

"Not in detail."

"Well, the good news is we've got a couple of hours until we reach Titan, so I'll explain everything and answer all your questions. Don't be shy, you can ask me *anything*. Don't worry about offending me, either. I grew up in Soun, then I moved to Mars for a year when I turned eighteen. I wanted to transition. We don't have the facilities for that here and I wanted to see the system anyway, so off I went."

"Oh, wow." That's certainly a lot of information to get at once. "Then you moved back?"

"Yeah. I'd been gone nearly three years, travel time included. When I returned, we held my wedding so everyone could welcome the new me. It was like I'd never left. Mars, though! Talk about staid! Their idea of marriage is so narrow I couldn't even comprehend it! And the *jealousy*! People get jealous here, obviously, we're still human, yet they talk it out with someone and it gets worked out. On Mars, though, the way treating someone like property just seemed to be *normal*…I couldn't believe it. When I mentioned I was from a settlement that practices plural marriage, they obviously thought I meant three or four people, and they were *scandalised*.

"So, in short, ask away. Because however stupid you think your questions are, *believe* me I've heard worse."

~ 71 ~

~ * ~

Lee guides the shuttle expertly into the dock. Metallic noises sound throughout the ship as docking clamps engage and the cargo bay airlock decompresses for unloading. I turn towards the door. Lee shakes her head and points to a smaller airlock that leads directly from the cockpit.

"We take *this* door," she tells me. "This leads to guest quarters where you can freshen up, get changed if you want. Traditionally, your primary contact is the only person you see before the wedding. Nervous?"

"Yeah, a little." I'm about to marry forty strangers. Plus one recent acquaintance who, okay, I can definitely see getting to know a little better. "Do I have to wear anything in particular?"

"Whatever you want! One guy did it in the nude a few years back."

"For real?"

"Yeah. He didn't stay, though. I guess he heard 'group marriage' and thought 'sex cult,' and then it was nothing like he'd imagined. One mass divorce later, off he goes. Good thing too; that guy turned out to be a creep." She grins. "You can wear what you want."

~ * ~

An hour later, I leave the guest quarters in a plum-coloured tunic and legging set. My outfit emphasises my small waist and brings out the gold tones in my complexion. Lakshmi always hated it.

I follow Lee through an archway onto a raised dais at the end of a hall carved into the rock of Titan. Forty people mill around the space in front of me. When Lee claps her hands three times, everyone falls silent and turns to look at me.

"Wives and husbands! Partners of Soun! Tonight our family grows. Let me introduce you to our newest member, Kasih Jaeger who joins us from Luna!"

Applause from the crowd. Some of them smile at me. One or two wave. Someone at the back cheers. Lee waves me towards a chair near the front of the dais. I take my seat, trying to ignore the lurching feeling in my stomach.

A man, the oldest in the room, stands to my left holding a pad. The crowd falls silent.

Lee kneels on the dais in front of me and reaches out to take my hands. She explained this part. As my primary contact, she will be the first one I marry.

"Kasih Jaeger," she raises her voice to be heard. "I, Lena Porter, welcome you to hearth and home. For as long as you are mine, I am yours."

"Lena Porter," I reply. Earlier, she told me to say whatever seemed right. "I, Kasih Jaeger, thank you for welcoming me. For as long as you are mine, I am yours."

The older man holds out his pad to us, and we disengage our nearest hands to press our palms onto the screen. The machine chimes, and he steps back. Our marriage is now legal.

Lee leans in towards me. The height of my chair puts her face on a level with mine and she whispers, "You look wonderful." I find myself smiling, and when I look into her sparkling hazel eyes, I think *what the hell.*

Her lips feel like butter and they taste like honey. My hands find her waist and rest there until she moves away, winking at me, and moves to stand behind my chair.

After that it goes quite smoothly. The crowd of people comes forward, one at a time, to kneel before me and welcome me to their family. Most of them kiss me on the lips, although one or two go for a cheek peck or even a hug. Finally, the older man is the only one left. He steps in front of me and kneels, taking my hands as Lee takes his place with the pad.

"Kasih Jaeger." His voice is a deep bass and easy on my ears. "I, Rahim Tamm, Elder and Founder of the settlement of Soun, welcome you to hearth and home. For as long as you are mine, I am yours."

Lee told me about this man. He's one of the settlement's original founders, the only one still alive in fact. I'm not sure of his age. His eyes are clear and blue, his hair still mostly dark, and the only lines are laughter lines.

"Rahim Tamm, Elder and Founder. I, Kasih Jaeger, thank you for welcoming me. For as long as you are mine, I am yours."

We scan our prints, and he leans in for a brief kiss. We both stand to face the hall, which erupts into cheers and applause. The crowd parts as we pass hand in hand to the other end of the hall and through a door into a well-furnished room.

"Well," I say as the door closes behind us. The room is comfortable looking, with an upholstered conversation pit of the kind which goes in and out of style every century or so. "So this is the, uh…"

"The consummation room," Mr Tamm, Rahim, I suppose I should call him, given he's my husband, explains, releasing my hand and stepping away. "Don't worry, we don't have to do anything. This isn't one of those demented old cultures where someone had to actually watch and certify the deed was done. This is more of a symbolic thing. We spend a little time in here, playing scrabble, if you like, and then leave and everyone *considers* the marriage act complete. That takes pressure off others, you see, so no one feels self-conscious about approaching you first."

"Okay, that makes sense, I think." I slide down into the conversation pit. This place is reassuringly more a den than what my imagination supplied. "So, I have to ask. How did this all start? This 'everyone marries everyone else' idea."

"When we first settled this planet, there were seven of us." He settles into the pit across from me. "The journey back then took over a year, a dangerous year. We relied on each other for everything. Drove each other crazy. Pulled each other out of trouble. By the time we'd reached Titan, it had become an in joke that the seven of us were like a big couple. By the time we'd built the first dome I think we'd realised it was never a joke, and so we marked our first anniversary by making it official. We all married each other."

"And everyone else?"

"Well, when the first new colonists started arriving, it wasn't the same for them. They'd often been shunted into the colonial life by one circumstance or another. They were dispossessed, without family, and when they saw what we had, they were often lonely. We didn't want anyone to join our settlement only to feel left out. We experimented with letting others into our partnership, and so our marriage grew. Inevitably, of course, we had to work out a system for eventualities such as our children growing up. The Space Brides people did explain?" He let his questions hang, waiting for me to answer.

"Yes, they did."

"Good. Of course, most of them head out when they turn eighteen to see the system, or to attend university. A good number of them come back after a while."

"Like Lee."

"Like Lee." He settles on his section of cushion and brushes the knee of his jumpsuit. "Now, Kasih, may I call you Kasih?"

"I don't see why not. We *are* married."

"Indeed. Now, Kasih, I have some questions for you. What we've found is people join our settlement for one of two reasons. Either they've got some strange idea in their head about how things work here, those people usually don't stay very long, with one or two exceptions, or, like those other colonists, it's because they have nowhere else to go. They're *missing* something they hope to find here. Now, after watching you during the ceremony, I don't think you're the first kind."

He leans in gently. "Your profile said you were recently divorced? No living relatives?"

"That's right." I've never discussed this with anyone. This man just let me into his family. I owe him honesty. "My parents died a few years ago. Spacewalking accident."

"I'm sorry."

"Thanks. They both worked for the Maddox estate, where I grew up. When a member of the estate's staff dies, members of the ruling family attend the funeral." I blink back tears at the memory. "I met Lakshmi Maddox there."

"She was a member of the family who employed your parents?"

I nod. My arms come up of their own accord to curl around my chest. "After that, she started contacting me. Checking in, inviting me places. I couldn't believe my luck. She was beautiful, glamorous." I take a deep breath at the memory. "She could have anyone. She wanted *me*. It was like being wooed by a goddess."

"She took advantage of your grief," Rahim says gently, seeming to understand.

"I know that *now*. It's been over a year since we broke up. I've had some time to sort this all out. Back then, though, I was just miserable and she showed me a way out. Everything looked bleak and grey. With Lakshmi all became light and colour again. Of course I reached for her." I paused, collecting my thoughts. "Only …it took me a while to notice. We always did whatever *she* wanted. I'd have a preference, yet we ended up doing her thing. Then suddenly we were married, and I couldn't quite remember how it had happened."

I took a deep breath, steadying myself. "But our relationship didn't really go to hell until I started talking about kids."

"You had children with that woman?"

"Not…exactly." He blinks at my words and I press on. "I can't remember why I thought having a baby would be such a good idea. I knew I did *want* children. I think I started noticing I never got what I wanted. Lakshmi resisted for a while. Then suddenly, for some reason, decided it was a terrific idea. We called up geneticists. Talked about names. I didn't realise at first what I'd done, by making her realise how much I wanted a child.

"I told her what I wanted. I told her how to control me."

"But you divorced?"

"She threw me out. Weeks of doctor appointments. One day she said, 'Never mind, get out.'"

Rahim sits forward, his blue eyes piercing. "*Did* you conceive a child?"

I can't hold it in. This poison has been churning inside me for so long his question just forces the truth out.

"Yes," I whisper.

He sits back, his face stony. "I'm so sorry. I can't imagine she gave you custody. In fact…yes, I see what you're saying. The embryo is the lead she used to control you. She didn't want you anymore, but she wanted to keep control."

I nod. "The baby should have been *mine*. She suggested we have a boy, and even had the idea to use my father's stem cells. Two women can't have a son by themselves, because you need a Y chromosome, which has to come from somewhere else. She suggested using my father's DNA, 'a lovely tribute to him,' she called it. We even used my ovum! So you see, the baby is genetically a little more mine than hers, and if she weren't a Maddox, custody would have been awarded to me. Oh, she knew how to twist the knife. I tried petition after petition, to the Lunar government and to the doctor who created the embryo, all rejected. Not for any legal grounds, just because of who the other party was."

"I notice your use of the past tense there," Rahim's eyes have never left my face. "I know your profile says you have no children, but that specifically refers to children who have been born. And, somehow, I cannot imagine this person I see before me leaving

Luna without her child."

His lips quirk into a smile. "Where is the embryo now?"

"In my holdall," I tell him. "In an urn that appears to contain my parents' ashes. And it does, but only about half, enough to make room for the cryo-canister. I scattered the rest in the Maddox estate. I knew they'd like that."

He chuckles, shaking his head.

"My mother was a security expert, and she taught me a lot," I explain. "Though if she knew I used her expertise against a Maddox, she'd have slapped me silly and thrown me out of an airlock." I took a deep breath, feeling free for the first time in a long while. "Yes, that's what I did. I went there under pretence of pleading with the doctor, planted a trojan on the clinic's systems and came back during the night to get my son. I swapped him for a tissue sample from one of their labs. I went to Space Brides, LLC and asked them to get me the hell out of Luna."

"A bold plan," Rahim compliments. "Simple, but effective. Because Space Brides are proud of their security, aren't they? And, as they're a system-wide organisation, the name Maddox won't mean to them what it means to a Lunar judge. She can't use her identity to batter down the door and find out where you've gone."

"Assuming she even learns what I did." I find a smile creeping across my face. Rahim's grin is infectiously conspiratorial. "She only wanted the baby to control me. When she realises I've left Luna, she *might* check on our son and realise what I did, or she might forget he exists altogether, or even order him destroyed out of spite, in which case she'll *never* know."

My voice shakes a little over that last part. I take a deep breath.

"Rahim," I begin. "I know *technically* I told the truth in my application, but what I said was still…misleading. I've brought a child here you didn't count on, and possibly a lot of trouble too. Lakshmi probably won't find out what I did and she probably won't come looking for me, although she might. She has the resources to cause a lot of trouble. If my problems *do* follow me, if your family…"

"Kasih." He leans forward and takes my hand. "That's *your* family as well as mine, and there are forty people nearby who'll tell you the same. I have fifty children, by blood and by choice, here on Titan and spread out across the system. What's one more?

"You are my wife," he reassures me. "Your problems are my

problems. Your fight is my fight, and your son is my son."

He grips my hand and I grip back, returning his warm smile. I have only just met this man, and we've done nothing more than hold hands, yet I feel closer to him than I ever did to Lakshmi. In a way, it's as if we did consummate this, after all.

My son is going to have a wonderful father.

~ * ~ * ~

Harriet's brain has a habit of doing odd things, and sometimes she's able to write them down in a way that other people find entertaining. Given that she's wanted to be a writer since she was old enough to understand that books are written by people, this all worked out pretty well. She studied Creative Writing and English at Aberystwyth University. She now lives in Wiltshire, UK, where she reads a lot, bakes terrifyingly large cakes whenever she can get away with it, grows oddly-coloured things on her allotment and watches entirely too much TV.

Harriet's short fiction has appeared in numerous odd little places, including The Screw Turn Flash Fiction Competition 2020, the *Riptide Journal* and in *Swindon Writing*. She's also appeared in a previous WolfSinger anthology, *Never Cheat a Witch*. In addition to *Space Brides, LLC,* she will soon be appearing in the Phobica anthology *Terrors from the Toybox*. Find her at harrietphoenix.com.

# SOL MARITUS

K.B. Johnson

## RIGEL

*"Do you have it?"*

Rigel imagined the breath of the question in his ear, warming him from the breeze of his pace through conditioned air. The chill throughout the aerospace drome was unnoticeable until the inquiry fired him up and tingled his skin. The question having tugged at his conscience, he ducked into one of several nooks along the corridor. The innocent tone of her voice could have also filled him with self-doubt, with his sneaking around. Her eagerness and hopefulness needed an answer. The right answer, he sighed, for the wrong answer would be an undesired conversation.

Rigel firmed his arm around an elongated box at his side. "I have it." His voice hushed before he made a quick peek up and down the corridor's length. "Ordered as specified. Or as I ordered, to your specifications."

*"Good."* Her relaxed tone eased Rigel. *"Is it pretty?"*

Rigel uncurled a broad smile as he leaned against the nook's inner wall and held the box before himself. Even in the nook's shade, the corridor's dim lighting shone its ribbon's satin sheen and loopy bow. "That remains to be seen." A haphazard glimpse of the nook's sealed entry to the farer's lounge reminded him he was about to infuriate his father. "Where are you?"

*"I can't believe this is really happening."*

Rigel pushed himself off the wall by his back and stood as straight as his face had become. Another peek down the corridor, to the hangar's main entrance. "I'm about eighty meters from changing my life forever." Rigel tucked inside the nook again. "Our lives. As planned. After four years of virtual dates and video chats, it's now or never."

*"I know."*

Rigel pressed the box at his side, looking to the window wall opposite the nook, questioning himself. His shadow faint on the glass, and it obscured his desire and anticipation to deliver the box

~ 79 ~

in person. "Are you still up for this?"

*"I am. I'll be waiting for you at Daphnis. As planned."*

"I'm on the way, then." Rigel strode on. "I'll check in once I'm in Jovian space."

*"Okay. Keep to this network link. Relays will redirect it to Daphnis."*

Rigel grinned in admiration of her tech savvy skills, which enabled them to connect outside of normal channels, unmonitored and without a record for his father to discover. "I won't ask how, but may—"

*"Maybe when I am seen."*

Rigel chuckled. "Okay. I'm looking forward to doing so."

*"Be safe, Rigel."*

"I will."

*"I love you."*

Rigel halted a few meters from the hangar. "I love you, too, Carina. See you soon."

*"En."*

Rigel tapped at his right ear, ending the communication.

Staring at the double doors of the hangar, it was now or never. His father, a shrewd businessman, would realize what had happened after the fact, for as many times as they had fought about Rigel's future. Rigel just hoped *borrowing* his father's prized asset would be valuable enough to spare him. His father would destroy the flier with him in it and write the incident off as an accident, and buy a new one, if he refused to return with it.

~ * ~

"Notify the Skipper."

In Rigel's ear, Paul's breath had been heavy, but his voice subdued and carried an ambient echo. Such was helmet speak. Rigel squatted at a small, squared opening in the bulkhead to the warp drive compartment. By the brightness of light waving and flickering inside the compartment's dimness, Paul made his way out. Surprised by the hurling of a tool kit through the opening, Rigel had fallen back onto his hands and buttocks. He had been quick to his feet as the senior engineer crawled out.

"The collider is secured."

Rigel, wide eyed, received Paul's displeasure with his rise before him. He would rather face an actual desert bear disturbed from its slumber than be scolded by disappointment, or to be reprimanded by the captain. "Must I be the one to tell her?"

"Your father's weight had you assigned to this ship." Paul glanced at the tool kit at their feet. "As an ensign at that. Taking responsibility will go a long way toward you captaining a ship of your own, which is what he desires for you."

"I know." Rigel sighed, squatting to pick up the kit. "I'd rather pilot a flier than a ship this big," he said, standing. "This is too much, for me."

Paul rested a hand on Rigel's shoulder. "A flier would be a prudent way to become a farer. As it is, you performed the maintenance inspection. While I should have followed up, I trusted you did proper and thorough job."

"I'm sorry."

"It's okay."

Rigel observed his shoulder after Paul removed his hand. His suit now just as smudged and grimy, as if he had brushed up against the ring accelerators a few times or balanced himself against the Elemental Separation Unit. Given the tightness of the compartment.

"It's not like the antimatter containment had failed and blew us all to Kingdom Come. Or caught the Skipper or XO on the head, if we would've lost gravity."

Rigel grinned at Paul's more humorous disposition. "Fortunately." There was sense of comfort exhibited by most farers, with the realities of space travel or warp technology. "The AG generators are on reserve supply."

"Well, do me a favor?" Paul's smirk disguised his seriousness. "Don't kill me over your bleeding heart. Torque the collider to spec next time. Before you rush off for some virtual meet up."

Embarrassment warmed Rigel's face, and he turned away from Paul while handing over the tool kit. "Yes, sir."

"What service are you dating on, by the way?" Paul took hold of the kit.

"Space Brides."

"Oh, that serious, huh? I guess if I didn't like my father arranging my marriage, an antimatter failure would definitely get me out of it."

Now Paul was just being cheeky, as Rigel stared at him in frustration.

"But running away from someone chosen for you, I'm not so sure about."

"My father wants to keep the business in the family, and I'm not interested in marrying a third cousin."

"Think about your practicality." Paul walked past Rigel. "It does come from him. Besides, cousin marriages are commonplace. That's why laws exist for it. Human beings have to survive in space some kind of way." Paul had paused at the egress of the engine room. "Before you commit to anything virtually, just think about if you're being selfish or not. I hear those sun-boats races on Earth are quite the ceremony."

Rigel turned to Paul. "They are. At least mine will be, with the one I truly love."

The discomfort of Paul's scoff and scrutiny and his mocking smile made Rigel shrink inside his spacesuit. "Well, while you're dreaming, report to the Skipper the cause of *Sumra Solstice* stalling out of hyperspace. It's lucky she was on the bridge to keep us from running into an asteroid. So soon after leaving Earth, too."

Rigel hated being reminded of the consequences of his neglect.

"Be sure to tell her why, too. She might sympathize with you. Might. Then as the XO directed during our briefing, be sure to check the hold, to make sure our passengers are…comfortable. Do I need to come behind you with that? Or maybe Knight should escort you?"

"No, no." Rigel released a breath after his fervent rejection of the master-at-arms. "I can manage the passengers."

"Okay. The Skipper will be furious if they awake before we arrive at Saturn."

"Yes, sir."

The egress whisked open with a hiss. Rigel nodded to Paul's lasting stare, before he had stepped over the knee-knockers of the threshold and disappeared beyond it.

Paul's exit from the primary engine room prompted Rigel to squat at the warp drive compartment, and tapping on the side of his helmet, he poked its beam and head inside the space. Perhaps he had looked for courage from the imagined lair of the desert bear, to help him face the Skipper. Seeing the illumination of the collider and hearing the hum of the accelerator rings assured him Paul had addressed the system's malfunction. That withdrew his inspection, and he closed up the compartment and secured its entry with a few touches to a panel adjacent to the opening.

Around the corner of the bulkhead, from the warp drive compartment, Rigel approached the circumference of the engine room's main system, the torus rings. From the main level, he observed each of the other eight levels which enveloped and nestled the three-ring structure in the middle of the ship. The collider and ring accelerators were much smaller than the actual rings, and even compared to the components output of power, too. Though the structure's initial spins were slow from the antimatter feeding into it.

The whomping of each ring across his presence took Rigel's breath. If there were any one part about the size of the *Sumra Solstice* which frightened him most, it was the massiveness of the rings. If the torus ever failed while in motion, the outcome would be more catastrophic than the chain reaction of escaping antimatter. No way he could phantom the responsibility of commanding such a sizable piece of technology.

It would be a matter of a few minutes before the quantum computer optimized the spinning of the Solstice's rings. Then an opening in space-time would be created at their center. The negative pressure inside the spinning would pull on and widen the warp field around the opening, and when the distortion in space-time expanded beyond the rings to encompass the entire ship, the *Sumra Solstice* would resume its voyage to Saturn.

The warp drives of star fliers, on the other hand, were less intimidating. Fliers also kept Rigel's fascination with faster-than-light travel. It just seemed better to tear a small hole into space-time and zip through it rather than an obtrusive, large one.

The Solstice lurched and Rigel was quick to catch the handrail, adjusting his footing for balance. Activity at the engine room station, a level below him, suggested the bridge had been informed of the warp drive's restoration. The Skipper had ordered the ship's acceleration with its conventional thrusters, as managed from the secondary aft engine room. The *Sumra Solstice* needed to achieve terminal velocity in order to travel hyperspace and slingshot passed light speed.

Rigel carried on as well, exercising the option to check on the ship's passengers before reporting to Skipper. Besides, as he exited the main engine room, the hold was on the way to the bridge. It would be good to report a positive status on the passengers, to offset his mistake, and perhaps appease his father, he had hoped. The Skipper would have to report the incident to his father, the shiplord, who owned the ship after all. He and the crew were just all on the payroll of the family business. It was what paid for the *Sumra Solstice*.

Though unparticular about the practice of the business, Rigel only fancied the nepotism for it allowing him to become a farer. He had determined to earn his place in sailing the stars. Despite his rank giving him quite the advantage over the other fifteen farers aboard. Shipmates whose sightings in passageways became infrequent with his transition to the lowest deck.

Crossing the last hatch to the hold, Rigel saw Knight. He had postured with an inflated chest after pushing from a slouch against the bulkhead. A real desert bear if there were ever one aboard. Paul must have notified him. Rigel sensed he was always being tested in some way by the senior officers.

Rigel inflated his chest as he approached the master-at-arms. "Chief." His voice carried through the long passageway, leading him to stand squarely before Knight. "I have to check on the passengers."

"I just did."

"Good. When I report to the Skipper, I can validate your inspection. With mine."

Knight's narrowing eyes reminded Rigel of the two's precarious relationship. It was one thing to be an ensign of equal rank to the lowest ranking executive officer, but after Knight had professed his opinion about him and started a brawl between them during a return trip to Earth from the outer region, his defeat by Rigel had left him sour. On many levels, especially as the *Sumra Solstice*'s security officer.

Knight insisted his drunken stupor at the time had been to his disadvantage. His intoxication, however, proved irrelevant. Rigel had been justified in defending himself. Having held his own against Knight's fury and skills, most of the crew now gave thought to any idea of confronting or taunting Rigel over his familial connection.

Locking eyes with Knight, all Rigel could think about was a flier's crew accommodation. Two people, the most required to fly one. Unlike a ship.

"Stand down," he said with quiet insistence. "I need to report to the Skipper."

"Tell the Skipper—"

"I will tell the Skipper only what I have inspected, Chief, or would you like to accompany me, and we both can report to the Skipper?" Rigel suspected Knight had more routine matters to tend to other than harassing him over the passengers.

"Right." Knight stepped aside to Rigel's relief. "You'll find the passengers secure then. I'm going to inspect the launch bay."

Passing Knight, Rigel envied his inspection tour. The *Sumra Solstice* carried two fliers in its launch bay. "Have fun."

"I shall. Care to join me in the gym when you're done?"

Rigel halted at the hold's entryway and turned his head to his right shoulder, with a slight pivot of his body, and he side-eyed the Chief. "Maybe. Let's talk over lunch, after we make good on our delivery."

Knight chuckled. "Sounds fine." The Chief stomped off, the clanging of the grated floor fading with each step.

Rigel sighed, deflating his posture after Knight left the corridor silent. He placed his right hand on the biometric panel next to the hold's entryway, and once the instrument beeped and the door clanked and hissed open, a rush of frigid air spilled over him. A chill ran up his legs and across his spine to which a shiver had shaken off. With the air, the hold cast its bluish-green lighting upon him. The clubs at home were more inviting, he thought with crossing the threshold.

The meager lighting darkened with the hold closing after him. By the illumination of faces and data displays lining the walls of the rectangular space, he was able to see his way to the AI station in the opposite corner. The station monitored and regulated the stats of all the pod occupants. Procedure required him to first check on the twenty-five passengers from it, particularly their stasis.

The manifest of the station and the numbered pods helped him identify which person was consuming too much of their oxygen supply, perhaps stuck in a nightmare, and required neural sedation. They all needed to remain relaxed while in hypersleep. From the ages of the people, though, Rigel disliked the thought of children being regarded as adults. Even though that's what they would become. Adults. Eventually. To serve Earth's colonies in Jovian space.

Except for the one passenger who was a year away from becoming of age. Pod twenty-one. He took note of her name. According to her information, she was a few years younger than him. Rare for a passenger to be older than fifteen.

Alas, the family business. All the passengers checked out at the station. Rigel began his visual inspection of Earth's most valuable commodities. Children. Sometimes the seeds of distant worlds. Often the replenishment and expansion for colonies. So precious were they, Earth had decided they must be preserved from time itself, no matter how much time warp drive technology shaved off planetary trips. Migrants had to arrive at their destination as young as possible, grow and acclimate to their new environment, and ensure Earth's prosperity. Someone had to transport them. Though, the current task had made Rigel less proud. Still, he was a farer. While he could argue the pros and cons of transporting children, it was widely understood from his father to the lowliest farer knowing too much about passengers was bad for business.

Circling the room, ten pods against the left wall, five along the back, he came to pod twenty-one, and a breath escaped him. Amazed by the beauty of passenger twenty-one's sleeping, with a thin, dark bang crossing the length of her oval face, her ivory complexion most reflective of the pod's interior red lighting, Rigel stepped toward the chamber and rested his forehead against it.

Closing his eyes, he ignored reason, ignored the odds of an actual connection being slim to none, and even ignored the coldness of the glass nipping his forehead. For the moment, he listened to the pattering of his heart. Its beat filled his imagination with the inspiration enclosed inside the pod. In his mind, he spoke her name to begin their first conversation. After introductions, they took a walk. A walk along a beach, at sunset. Just him and her under the vastness of a purple sky and the warm glow of Sol glimmering across a calm sea. Their holding hands would lead to her hugging on his arm as she snuggled close.

~ * ~

"Hey! Wake up. We're here."

However, it was the clack of the driver's door which snapped Rigel awake, to the incessant bustle of people about the square. The noise, an unobtrusive alarm of sorts, with people chattering over shopping, clinking utensils and dishes over meals, and the resonance of solar vehicles all roused him from his nap. The baking of breads, the spicy aroma of stir fry, and the fragrance of flora aided in his awakening. Rigel yawned and stretched in his seat. He preferred to stay put and bask in the afternoon sun. Its warmth urged him to ignore everything and remain comfortable in his recline.

"Hey, Rigel. Come on. I found her."

Rigel raised his seat to his friend's arduous excitement, squinting and scowling at the same time. "Pleiades." He yawned again. "If I were interested in a Gaean, I'd just marry Sirius."

"Your cousin isn't a bad choice, but don't worry. This one, she isn't Gaean."

Rigel raised an eyebrow at Pleiades.

"Come on." Pleiades opened the passenger door. "She'll be waiting to meet you in less than five minutes."

"What? She who? Here where? On Earth?"

"No. Will you just come on?"

Rigel was unprepared for Pleiades to seize and pull him by the wrist. Stumbling out of the vehicle and even before he could close the car door and recover his balance, Pleiades sprinted him through the busy sidewalk, weaving them through, around people and the outdoor seats of restaurants.

"No more moping around. You've been a drag, since your grounding."

Rigel thought to stop, hold his ground and correct Pleiades. He'd been placed on probation. His father's *recommendation* for almost destroying the *Sumra Solstice*, and the Skipper had only followed his decision. Paul had been right. The Skipper had been lenient; she sympathized with his bleeding heart and only dry docked him, as it was called, for a year. Now, seven months in, he was subject to his friend's will. A glance skyward carried a longing to be off world and among the stars.

"I know this will cheer you up."

Rigel almost missed the sign, Space Brides, LLC. "I'm already registered here."

"That's not why we're here." Pleiades led Rigel through the agency's sliding doors.

The transition from the bright and warm outdoors to the shaded and artificial lighting indoors had refreshed Rigel as chewing a mint leaf after dinner, by the sight of an avatar chatting with an attendant on duty.

"She is."

Rigel slipped his arm from Pleiades grip to step forward, awed but unsure about the avatar. When it faced him, its hand wiping a long strand of hair from its face while blinking, the microsecond of its amethyst eyes closing and opening to gaze upon him pattered Rigel's heart and took his breath. He had remembered *her*. The passenger…his inspiration which had been sealed in pod twenty-one.

"Carina." Her name barely a whisper off his lips.

"Oh." The attendant's tone graceful, it veiled her surprise. "Have you two met before?"

Rigel sighed with embarrassment, stammering with his words. "Uh, no."

"What do you mean?" Pleiades stepped up beside Rigel. "All you did your first month back was talk about *Carina*."

## CARINA

"How does it feel?"

"How does what feel?"

Carina had noted Rigel's disregard to what was obvious to her, as his full lips wrapped around the mahi-mahi burger. As good as the sandwich looked, ensnared in the claws of his lean and brown fingers, virtual reality for her only offered a faint trace of its smell. Mostly the scent of cayenne and grilled onions. Aside from the pungent freshness of a kale leaf which accented the burger.

Though sharing a bistro which had franchised from Earth to Colony 35 and allowed them to eat together, their impromptu and very first virtual date, so soon after meeting, had been both an opportunity and a precursor for Carina. An interview of sorts. The most pressing question she had for Rigel needed to be direct, if she expected an honest answer.

"How does it feel being a transporter? With placing children into an uncertain life?"

Carina met Rigel's eyes. He paused mid-bite into the burger. An index finger had risen to ask for her patience, at least until after he chewed and swallowed his first take of the food.

While Carina waited, her server brought and placed before her a bowl of mushroom bisque and buttered garlic bread. The meal quaint compared to Rigel's, but then resources were limited in colonies. Between the variety of mushrooms making up the soup and its mint leaf decoration, all from hydroponics and flavored by the salt of Saturn's rings, it was a staple.

Carina picked her spoon and swirled the ring design of sesame crème into the bisque, around the mint leaf. "You placed me into the hands of a souteneur."

Carina glanced at the shock of Rigel's wide eyes and bulging cheek of unchewed food. As she sipped her first spooning of the bisque, he mumbled, "I'm sorry."

The sincerity of his apology veiled Carina with a comfort that raised her skin. No one had ever apologized for her experience, let alone a transporter.

"I didn't know." With the sense of a *but* coming on as he resumed chewing and then swallowing while resting the remaining portion of his burger, Carina hoped Rigel let it stop there. "My father's business," he continued, both his hands clenched into fists on the table, glowering over the burger. "Most employees don't question what it is we do. Or why. Not beyond transporting *passengers* to the outer planets. As contracted."

Carina smiled. Rigel managed to keep her skin from crawling in frustration with a weak excuse. His honesty and passion were appealing. "I understand," she said, picking up her bread and tearing a piece from it. "It is fortunate for me that I...*exited* the cybersex trade."

"Oh?" Carina met Rigel's eyes and curious stare. "Exited?"

"I am a smart girl. With skills. My tech literacy allowed me to hack the Planetary Com Network and contact a prohibitionist couple. They helped me escape. Before I was in too deep."

"Is that why you registered with Space Brides?"

Carina studied Rigel, after dipping the piece of bread. "Partly." She fed on the bread and its flavor melted her face as much as it had in her mouth.

"Is it that good?"

Carina grinned through her chewing. "It is. You should try it."

"Perhaps I will. When I visit."

Carina gave Rigel a shrewd stare. Despite the bistro's namesake and shared tech between Earth and Saturn's colony, the limited menu on Carina's side was arguably a good reason to visit. None of her food choices were available on Earth. Though, she would love it if she could return there. Earth did have the better food. Still, giving Rigel the benefit of doubt, she liked that he wanted to come to Saturn, even if for just the food. Unlike others who were much older and all too often with ulterior motives, he was the first to propose visiting her in person. "Why are you registered with them?"

Carina noted Rigel's sigh and his following hesitation. His sitting back from the table to contemplate a response could be a merit, or a demerit.

"It's complicated," he said, picking up his strawberry blue lemonade, its salted brim sparkling under sunlight.

The observation caused Carina to glimpse the time and the simulated sky. Time passed quicker for her. The colony's days were fourteen hours shorter than Earth's, with the sun growing dimmer on her side. The time made her look Rigel over and wonder, just how much older would he be if she were to return to Earth at that very moment.

"It's okay." She offered a reassuring smile. "You can tell me. If we're going to commit to a relationship, I would prefer us to be honest about our motivations."

Carina was flattered by Rigel's boyish smile, by his seeming comfort with her.

"When I first saw you, in that pod, I thought I would never meet you after…" He took another sip of his drink, before resting it. "I had wondered how you became a passenger. At first. Then I dreamed of us walking together, on a beach. Holding hands."

Carina, intrigued by his dream, slid the bisque aside to rest her elbows on the table, placing her chin atop interlocked fingers.

"It was the ideal beginning. To the life I want for myself."

"For yourself? A marriage has been arranged for you, huh?"

Rigel grinned to her deduction. "You are a smart one."

Carina chuckled.

"You seem wise beyond your years, too."

Giggling louder to Rigel's compliment and him having similar thoughts about her age, Carina countered, "Now you're just stroking my ego."

Rigel chuckled. "Is it working?"

The way Rigel lit up to Carina's broad smile, she was uncertain who smote who. "Well, I understand your situation. I think, we're off to a...ideal beginning."

Carina had placed an open hand on the table, and she was pleased by Rigel taking and squeezing it with a warm touch.

~ * ~

"Will the sun-boat race be all that we miss?" Carina enjoyed walking the delta of the Susquehanna River. The virtual deck of the *Sumra Solstice* did well to replicate the squishiness of wet sand squeezing through her toes. Coupled with snuggling on Rigel's arm and a light breeze of a long afternoon, she relished the peace of their date. It had made her relaxed enough to talk about their realities.

"It will. If we're serious."

"It's okay. We can have a virtual race. But..."

"I have a plan about work."

"You do?"

"Mmm-huh." Rigel's hum was melodic and comforting. "We'll start our own business. Rescuing and shuttling passengers back home."

"Easier said than done."

It had been a couple of years since Rigel had returned to the stars, and though Carina disliked his occupation, he was her best chance of leaving Colony 35. She tightened her hold on his arm, leaning her head on his shoulder. He had become more than a solution.

Perhaps she fell for him when they had gone camping in Sproul Forest and shared a sleeping bag under a starry sky. With only the glow of the campfire's simmer and their BTUs keeping them warm. If Rigel had indulged in temptation, in her willingness to share herself that night, she would have permitted it just to ensure their union. Even if coitus would have been a placebo experience.

Carina had realized early on after arriving at Colony 35 how a life of cybersex would affect her, and in adverse ways. In anticipation of it with Rigel, she had been nervous and decided detachment would help her. It's what she had learned to do from virtual hookups. Though, she would have hated detaching from Rigel in such an instance.

She recalled exhaling a deep breath to his choosing to talk

about the stars instead. In that moment, she had made the right choice in selecting him. The same night she also learned from him their very names were those of stars.

Hers, Eta Carinae, was a nebula some eighty-five thousand light years from Earth, in the neighborhood of the Milky Way; and his, the giant blue star in the Orion constellation, was closer to Earth, some nine hundred light years. Carina had commented on how their companionship was swirling them to become a binary star. As accepting as they had been of one another. With a hand under his shirt and on his abdomen, the notion had waved a warm tingle of goosebumps from Rigel's body to her. It caused Carina to snuggle and purr into him. At least she had called it purring. Rigel called it snoring.

As peaceful as camping had been, it was also much quieter than the ocean's imbibing of the river, with its low tide whooshing over the beach, and the squawking of frigate birds.

The dowdiness of Colony 35 paled in comparison to the virtual representation of Earth being so full of life. All Carina had shared of any real adventure with Rigel was a simulated flight across Saturn's rings. The farer that he was, he had fun, too. More than she would have thought possible. Seeing him pilot, darting in and out of the fairy dust, as Saturnians called the rings, she had adopted some of his passion for the stars.

"I'm sure my prohibitionist contacts would be willing to help us." She wanted to keep both of them encouraged about his plan; it was a good idea. "But, we'll need a ship."

"I think I can get us one. If I *acquire* one, can you make it go dark, so it's not traceable? Or detectable?"

The idea became at least feasible now. Carina liked the challenge of making a flier stealth. "I'm sure I can handle that." A firm squeeze of Rigel's hand reassured him. "By the sound of it, you're really coming to try some bread."

Rigel chuckled.

"And your father?"

The question had waned Rigel's joy, and Carina squeezed on his arm to offer a comforting apology. He surprised her by kissing her head.

"Let me be the only one of us concerned about him."

"En."

From all their virtual dates, Carina had observed how Rigel never talked about his father. Of course, she had foregone talking about her past experiences as a passenger, and even of her feeling stranded or isolated on Colony 35. Their time together, she realized, was about them bonding, and she fancied both Rigel and their courtship for it. Carina's optimism would carry over after marriage, especially as partners helping others out of forced servitude.

"If you're coming out all this way for me, for us…" Carina reached into her pants pocket. "Then I'll make the arrangements for our ceremony." She presented Rigel with a piece of paper, folded. "I'll also need you to bring me something for the occasion. It may make up for the sun-boat race?"

"Maybe. I guess."

Carina smiled at Rigel's confusion, from his reading of the note. She was confident he would figure out the simplicity of *175 centimeters* and *33-30-36*. He was smart, too.

Chiming enveloped them, and after looking about, Rigel said, "Duty waits."

Carina had stepped away from him. "Call me tomorrow? I may see you then. It'll depend on my station control shift and possibly my cat sitting for a neighbor, while they are out mining."

"I will call, but I want to see you tomorrow. And every day after that."

"Soon, you shall. I promise." Carina smiled and waved as Rigel's image faded to him dressed in his spacesuit, before they both became a distorted assembly of light and pixels and disappeared from the virtual deck.

~ * ~

The spacesuit was a cumbersome thing for Carina. She panted under its helmet to ease her nerves. Between structural beams and a view of Daphnis's landing deck, she floated in the shadows of its processing facility. Having transferred from Colony 35 under the pretense of covering for a friend's lunar duties, she anticipated a matter of minutes to go by before someone realized she'd gone AWOL. Carina tapped the side of her helmet. "Are you there?"

*"About fifteen minutes out."* Rigel's voice garbled, Carina exhaled with relief, turning to the window and smiling to Saturn's rings beyond the deck. The Keeler gap between Daphnis and the rings

appeared a short distance. *"Approaching rings now."*

Excitement coursed through Carina. "Remember, jettison your fuel. Radiate the flier. Let inertia carry you through. All at the moment you enter the fairy dust. Collect and convert as much of it as possible. The rings are an ideal point to throw off anyone that comes looking for the flier."

*"Radiating. Jettisoning fuel. Cutting power."*

"Bear with the cold." Carina took pleasure in Rigel's chuckle.

*"You're the engineer. I trust you. Besides, piloting on momentum is fun."*

Carina was flattered by the declaration of trust. "Glad you're enjoying yourself."

*"Elemental Separation Unit is liquefying the fairy dust and refueling the flier. Ten minutes to touch down."*

The vote of confidence and Rigel's success with navigating the rings warmed Carina. She exhaled some of her nerves with a breath. "Does the flier have a name?"

*"No. It's just a shuttle."*

"Just as well. Small warp signatures are unnoticeable by Colony 35, but if people come looking for it—"

*"Oh, they will, knowing my father."*

"They'll likely track its chem burn to the rings. Because the fairy dust's elemental composition is unique from Gaean fuel but ubiquitous to space, they'll hit a dead end—"

*"In the rings. Deceptive,"* Rigel said. *"ESU done. Refueling complete."*

"I was thinking, Orphanus Licht."

*"Say again?"*

"Orphanus Licht." Carina propelled off a beam, out of the shadows to a nearby airlock. "We could name the flier, Orphanus Licht. Orphan's Light."

*"Sounds nice. Exiting fairy dust. ETA five minutes."*

"I see you. Approach is good."

As expected, the flier's exit from the rings was unexciting. From Carina's vantage view, as she glided to her feet, *Orphanus Licht* appeared as an unassuming and tiny mass adrift in the Keeler gap, heading for Saturn's atmosphere.

"The moment I exit the airlock, Daphnis will go on alert. Colony 35, too."

*"Depressurizing the flier. Opening outer hatch."*

"Glide all the way in. By the time Daphnis realizes the flier, we'll be taking off."

*"Roger that. I have the landing deck in sight."*

Activating the magnetism of her suit's boots, as to remain affixed to the deck without floating off into to space, Carina paused and said, "By the way—"

*"Of course!"* Rigel laughed. *"It's strapped in your seat, waiting for you."*

"Good." Carina smiled, and then she fingered the airlock's keypad. "It's now or never."

*"Now or never. Warp drive on standby."*

"Exiting airlock." Carina depressed the keypad's green button.

An alarm sounded and the grounds of the facility turned red. Carina hurtled the landing deck. Having treaded by the unloading of a ship, its crew had stood about, confused, until someone pointed upward. They noticed her approach to the flier's displacement of a few thruster bursts, as it squeezed and set down between two other cargo vessels. Boarding steps extended, Carina strode up into the flier, and it lifted off just as quick as it had landed, with the boarding steps folding inward and the hatch closing after her.

"Pressurizing the cabin." Rigel's voice feverish over his control of the flier, steering it clear of Daphnis as Carina floated to just over his shoulder. "Preparing to warp."

"This thing doesn't have artificial gravity?"

"Ah!" A quick flick of a switch rested Carina on her feet.

"Thanks."

The box seated next to Rigel had drawn a smile from her. In haste, she removed it from her place and set it aside. "Give me access to the flier's mainframe."

"That switch there." Rigel pointed over her lap before punching a couple center console keys. "Going full burn to jump."

Carina strapped herself in as the flier's acceleration pressed her with gravity, and as she strained for the dash, through tight lips, she said, "As long as you get us out of here."

Then Saturn, its rings, and the stars were all gone. There was only blackness beyond the flier's windows and bow. Having warped to relatively safety, gravity had eased and Carina slid her chair to the dash and began working over a keyboard, a display, and a few dials and buttons.

"What are you doing?"

"Fulfilling my part of the plan. Transponder and remote access, disabled. Christening the flier as Orphanus Licht." With a final key-stroke, Carina continued, "And just like that, we have our very own ship. Hidden from all."

Carina smiled at Rigel's grin as he pulled up a map. "I've a course for home."

"We're not going back so soon." Now receiving Rigel's curious look, Carina's smile widened. "Our destination is the Kuiper belt. We'll wait on Namaka for a while. Until Earth's perihelion."

"After winter solstice?"

"Yes."

"That's quite the wait."

"It is." Carina slid her seat back, unstrapping herself from it. She ungloved her hands and removed her helmet and set the gear left of her seat. Retrieving the box from her right, she met Rigel's attention with a bewitching smile. "Perfect for a nice, long honeymoon."

Rigel chuckled with a few nods, as he re-plotted *Orphanus Licht's* trajectory.

Carina stood from her seat and headed for the rear compartment. Placing the box on a protrusion of the bulkhead, she unstrapped and unzipped her boots. The composite floor was warm to her feet, as she unlatched, pulled on a few buttons, and unzipped and peeled off her spacesuit.

Rigel had glimpsed her from over his shoulder before he turned in his seat. "Is that all you wore? Under your suit?"

Her back to him, Carina had hooked the hems of her panty to adjust its comfort. "Also why we're going to Pluto. For clothes. And supplies."

"Have you thought of everything?" Rigel ungloved his hands.

"Just about." Carina winked from over her shoulder, reaching behind her to undo her brassier. Letting it slip to the floor, Carina moved the box. "Let's see what kind of taste you have, shall we?"

Rigel's smile broadened as Carina first glided her hands along the length of the box. Her eyes were closed to the tactile feel of the gift, and she inhaled as a wave of goosebumps rose across her skin. Its eggshell ribbon soft, and she opened her eyes as a palm guided her fingertips to trace the bow's tie to one end. "You tied this?"

"I did." Having removed his helmet, Rigel left it in his seat after standing.

"I guessed right. Farers are crafters." Carina pulled the ribbon.

The ribbon's weight slipped it from the box, and Carina separated its cover with eagerness. Her smile widened to the wrapping paper, its flora-folding protecting the content of the gift. The shuffle and ruffle of the paper preceded the brightening of Carina's eyes. A hand then caught her breath, covering her mouth and nose. Lifting her endowment from the box, Carina spun with it, its silkiness and lace softer and lighter against her chest than the spacesuit.

She faced Rigel. "Rigel Tahtinen, it's beautiful."

He leaned against the protrusion, next to the empty box. "Try it on."

The simplicity of the mermaid dress permitted Carina to slide, jiggle, and shimmy her hips through its narrow waist, marveling at it for fitting her tall and slender frame. She turned her back to Rigel. "If you would, please."

Even though Rigel was insulated by his spacesuit, Carina's face reddened with him being so close. The reality of his quickened breath across her neck and down her spine raised her skin. He electrified her when the warmth of his hands rested on her hips and turned her a bit, to align his access to the dress's zipper. In the stillness of the compartment, her pulse amplified her racing heart, over the slow rise and clicking of the zipper's teeth, with the brush of Rigel's knuckles against her back, guiding the closure of the dress around her. After the last click mid back, Carina drew a sharp breath from Rigel placing his palms against her bare arms. Gliding his hands up while stepping and pressing into her backside, she brought her jaw to meet a hand, as he caressed and gripped her shoulders.

The ports, buttons, and pockets of Rigel's spacesuit were cold and heavy against Carina's back, but the warmth of his cheek to her right ear was comforting, and desirable.

"What about—"

"Already forwarded." Carina's breath matched Rigel's. "An officiate with Space Brides, they've received our documents. They are awaiting us to contact them, at their Neptunian branch."

"Well, Carina Steorra..." Rigel's touch slipped away from her. "Seems there's just one more thing. Something of tradition."

Perplexed by Rigel's withdrawal, Carina turned about to find him kneeling with a small box he'd opened to her. She covered most of her surprise with one hand.

The silver band, as modest in design as her dress and with such luster, outshone a star.

"Will you marry me?"

Brought to tears, Carina took Rigel by the wrist and tugged him to stand, stepping into him. She met his forehead with hers, nodding while searching and penetrating his eyes. Delightfully and with a breath of assertiveness to suppress a giggle, taking his face into her hands, she said, "Yes."

~ * ~ * ~

**K. B. Johnson** is an independent author and publisher of science fiction and romance. He often combines the two. As Principal Director of Chaos Studio Seven—his platform—he writes short stories and novels by which he provides literary and visual experiences.

A native of Atlanta, Georgia, K.B. received his formal education in art & design and the humanities from Georgia State University, and through his writings, illustrations, and stories, he promotes the liberal arts, social tolerance, and intellectual freedom.

His science fiction collection, *Skies Over Tomorrow: Constellation (SOTC)*, earned a bronze medal in the 2018 eLit Book Awards. He has also been published online by 365tomorrows, Reedsy, and commuterlit.com. Once a month he volunteers an article for his local newspaper.

K.B. writes with the purpose of engaging one's imagination, and he is thankful WolfSinger Publications accepted *Sol Maritus* and hopes readers enjoy and are inspired by it.

# A SPECTRUM OF SECRETS

Eric Taveren

Alice Harris shoved her anxiety down again. More aptly, she smashed it down with logic, determination, and her inner mama-bear's unyielding rage. It wasn't just that she disliked space travel. She had always felt if humans were meant to travel at near light speeds, they'd have evolved internal cold fusion reactors instead of the appendix. Hurtling through space at 600 million miles an hour meant it took longer to get from her run-down Martian duplex to the spaceport than it did to fly from Bradbury City to Europa. Her anxiety today was a mashup of stressors. Space travel? Check. Meeting a stranger who thinks she was going to marry him? Double check. Leaving her dying son in the care of her floundering employer? Triple check.

She'd started working for GeneTech five years ago shortly after her son Sammy fell ill. She'd hoped between their research and their health plan she'd be able to find a cure, or find someone who could cure him. After five years of continual experimental treatments and a slow, but inevitable decline in health, she was running out of options and sanity. That's when she stumbled across Jacob Headly.

A lone GeneTech scientist in the middle of nowhere, his was one of GeneTech's more far-flung and questionable investments. When she saw his reports, saw the similarity between his research and what GeneTech was working on for cancer treatment, she knew, somehow, that he held the key. He would be the one to save Sammy.

The company had tried many times to squeeze more research out of him, convinced he withheld research data. Each time they sent "routine inspectors" everything was on the level. She needed to try a different approach. So she looked up dating profiles. She tried all the services she could think of. No luck.

Then, out of sheer desperation, she checked Space Brides LLC. She nearly collapsed at her standing desk when she saw his profile. Her knees buckled and her throat ached from the happy crying that would start any second. Jacob was looking for a wife. Putting her communication minor to good use, she convinced the GeneTech higher-ups to approve her request. She was their last resort. Well, their second to last resort.

So now she hurtled through space, the light from distant stars through the window stretched and discolored, approaching a frozen moon and a man with expectations she wouldn't live up to. She almost felt sorry for him. He seemed normal enough on his profile, though she could just imagine what seven years of isolation would do to a man. The seven-year-old company photo showed a scrawny man, and the Space Brides pic showed him a bit thicker in the face. She pictured a ratty beard and a swelling gut, a nervous stutter, and someone who designed homemade board games. She wouldn't have to try hard to stay detached. Not all Space Bride connections worked, happiness wasn't guaranteed. For him this would just be one of those times.

As the dropship landed she climbed awkwardly into her thermoseal surface suit, Europa's reduced gravity messing with her balance. The rear door opened and she jumped back as a grey-clad figure stood waiting.

"I hope I won't always make you run away," he, who she could only assume to be Jacob, said, voice a little staticky through the coms.

"Sorry," she said, taken aback. She absentmindedly moved to straighten hair that wasn't there as her fight or flight reflex dissipated. "I wasn't expecting you. I mean, not right here."

"No need to apologize." He stepped into the ship and past her. "I'll lead the way. Let's get out of this cold." He grabbed her bags and began a bouncing walk out of the ship to a small building.

She didn't follow, irritation starting to boil up inside her. For a person hoping to find a wife that wasn't the warmest greeting. She'd flown across the galaxy for him and he couldn't even introduce himself? She took a deep breath and tried to see things from his point of view, something she'd have to try and do often for her ruse to work. For someone living alone for seven years his manners could have been worse. Plus, the environment didn't seem to be particularly conducive to *warm* greetings.

She stopped just off the ship when her breath escaped her. She'd expected a barren wasteland, frozen death and flat desolation. Instead she saw a majestic landscape of jutting ice and filtered color.

Where she'd pictured a desert like much of Mars, instead sheets of ice stuck out of the ground at random angles, thick pieces casting shadows from the faint sunlight and thin ones colored by the planet engulfing the horizon beyond. A smile broke on her face, and though no one could see it, she felt a joy that'd been absent since before Sammy's diagnosis, a joy she hadn't known she'd feel again.

Glowing brightly, Jupiter filled much of the horizon. The sun shone distantly from behind Alice and lit up the gas giant, big red spot nestled between two particularly large chunks of ice. She'd seen close-up pictures of the planet before, but nothing compared to this. She felt she could almost reach out and touch it, swirl the ancient storm with her index finger. The wonder of this sight told her hope wasn't a wasted emotion, that perhaps this subterfuge of hers would in fact work and in a few short months she'd be sharing this joyful feeling with her son.

She realized Jacob was waiting for her. He didn't seem impatient. She appreciated he wasn't blowing up her coms with enthusiastic chatter. He too turned to take in the sight, keeping her in his field of vision, watching for when she was done. She gave him a wave and bounded toward him and the metal building where she knew an elevator would take them below.

They spent the first couple minutes of their ride down in silence. Part of her wanted to start with a joke or something to break the ice like, "sure is cold here," but decided to let him start the conversation. She wanted to see who she was dealing with.

"How was your trip?" he asked. His voice still staticky because of the suit and the tint of the visor obstructed her view. Without decontamination they couldn't remove their suits yet.

"Short," she replied.

He nodded. "Yeah. Though sometimes I wish they'd slow down. Give you a chance to take everything in. People forget to look for the beauty in things. I get that time is a resource, but sometimes I wish we had more of a choice on how to spend it."

Well, color her surprised. That was not at all what she was expecting. She knew he was smart, though she'd figured book smart, not a philosopher. Maybe he wanted to impress her. "I don't know," she said. "If we're talking about our view of space on carefully delineated flight paths, after one or two times flying you've seen everything you can. I'd rather miss out on watching from a distance and have more time experiencing the here and now." There. See what he had to say about that.

He nodded again. Perhaps a habit? Hopefully it wouldn't get on her nerves. "Who's to say you can't do both?" he asked. "It's not possible to experience everything at once. I'd argue the beauty of the immediate colors the interpretation of the beauty of the distant, and vice versa."

"Do you find much beauty under miles and miles of ice?" Alice asked.

He cocked his helmet and she could imagine a sly grin on his greasy, zit-covered face. "You'd be surprised."

Woah, pump the brakes, mister. He didn't need to get any ideas just because they were a few feet apart. "Before I get settled in, I just want to make sure we're on the same page."

"Sounds reasonable," Jacob agreed.

"Just because I'm here, and I know this arrangement is meant to lead to marriage, doesn't mean I'm ready for full blown commitment on day one. It'll take time to get to know each other and I don't want you to have any unrealistic expectations."

"Completely understandable," he said calmly, as if he'd been listening to a presentation of research and found the data compelling. "This is an unusual situation, in an unusual location. While I hope things will become amicable and more between us, I have no illusions it will be instantaneous. We'll need to get to know each other before any level of emotional or physical intimacy should be expected."

Again he surprised her. After seven years without seeing a woman he should be bursting with hormones and desires. Technically he hadn't seen her yet, not in the flesh. That he was so calm and to the point spoke of his restraint. Or perhaps his overly logical mind. Or both. Maybe it wouldn't be so hard to live with him while she snooped through his research. She knew if it came down to it, she'd do everything expected of a spouse if it meant getting a cure for Sammy. If she didn't have to debase herself she'd be very grateful.

He seemed content to leave her with her thoughts and she started when the elevator dinged and slowed. The door led into a decontamination room and she mimicked Jacob as he positioned himself near a UV emitter, arms extended, and rotating. Once the sensor indicated the all-clear, they began taking off the thermosuits.

Taking the headpiece off proved trickier than putting it on. Alice's wavy long blond hair kept getting caught, the volume of it much more of a hindrance than anticipated. The lack of normal gravity caused it not to behave as it did on Mars. By the time she eventually ripped it off she was panting.

She looked up at Jacob and inhaled sharply. He stood in profile hanging up his suit and the snug compression undershirt left little to the imagination. The cotton rippled up his abdomen as it contoured to his body, his ribs slightly shadowed by his pecs. Just the simple act of bending his arms stretched the sleeves around his biceps and those pants hugged very nicely to his backside. The firmness of his body seemed to fit right in with the landscape above.

Jacob turned to her and damn it if his face wasn't something to behold as well. Clean-shaven with a square jaw. She wondered if he'd ever eaten a carb in his life. His eyes completed the package. Deep blue with green flecks, they were kind and inviting and piercing all at once. The pictures had definitely done him a disservice.

"Is something wrong?" he asked. Alice knew there was no way to pretend she had been doing anything but staring. Her cheeks burned. She hoped he would think her blush came from the exertion.

"No," she stammered, averting her gaze and suppressing a small smile. Yes, something was wrong. She had to spend up to six months with this insightful and beautiful man, remain emotionally detached while pretending otherwise. She had to discreetly sift through his research. Something was definitely wrong.

~ * ~

Jacob glanced over his shoulder from his work. Alice worked in the cold storage preparing tomorrow's specimens. She hummed softly to herself, one of the eight songs she rotated through. Jacob had quickly cataloged them and could predict with a reasonable success rate what song she'd hum at any given time. It wasn't her humming that tried his patience, it was the space she kept between them.

When she arrived almost a month ago, he'd expected a period of awkwardness between them, planned for it even. He'd prepared her own quarters and made every effort to give her time to settle in.

He knew the reality of their seclusion would hit her at some point. He understood the trials of solitude and how to combat it. But he'd expected some measure of progress by now.

Sure, he'd noticed the furtive glances here and there. Whenever he thought to reciprocate those looks, or tried to overcome his shyness and suggest an activity that would lead to intimacy, she shut down faster than potassium oxidizes. Something was going on with her other than simple relationship-building hurdles. He just needed to figure out what.

"After supper would you care to join me in the gym?" he called out to her. Her presence had changed up his routine. At first it had been a bit jarring, but he'd gotten used to it as time passed. He found of all the activities available in the habitat, the gym yielded the highest success rate of interpersonal interaction.

"Sure, hun," she called back.

Almost as confusing as his extremophile experiments, her selection of what relationship staples to adhere to kept him endlessly calculating. She'd use terms of endearment, but only during inane conversations. She showed physical affection, but only in the form of a kiss on the cheek as he donned his scuba gear, telling him to be careful. She intellectually engaged, but only while actively engaged with separate task.

Throughout his life he'd been able to label and categorize, to extrapolate and solve, to rationalize or synthesize a solution to any problem he faced. Data never lied. With Alice he'd hit a brick wall. No amount of computing or defining or troubleshooting seemed to present a solution. She shared responsibilities with cooking and cleaning. She learned his organizational methods and helped with his experiments. She joined him in recreational activities. As much as she did everything he'd hoped, there were still some things missing.

After supper he was reminded of one of those things. After clearing and washing his dishes, he walked into the gym to find Alice using the tungsten alloy weight machine. As usual she wore the GeneTech supplied workout clothes, and as usual she looked very good. As with the spacesuit, and every branded item they produced, the workout clothes were a steel grey with white contour lines directing the eyes as they navigated their way around Alice's body. The shorts went from mid-thigh to just above the hip, snug and showing enough leg to prove she never skipped leg day. The top was a sports bra, supported chest forming a right angle with her trim midsection. Her skin tone hinted at old-Earth Middle Eastern ancestry and paired well with the grey fabric.

She smiled as he entered, bright green eyes squinting as she pulled the bar down in front of her, lifting the 1000 pounds she'd hooked up to the machine. Jacob guided himself as he almost floated to the machine opposite her, knowing her appearance would only frustrate him more, also knowing it'd be rude not to.

"You get it figured out after I left?" she asked. "Those surface cells still being a bunch of bullies?"

He grunted as he extended his legs, ankles hooked under the padded bar. "Same as usual. I hoped by inserting another new set of variables I could elicit a different reaction." He breathed deep and did another rep. "So far no luck."

"That's too bad. I wouldn't worry about it though. You're a smart cookie, you'll figure it out. *We'll* get it figured out." Her smile rang of polite civility. Why was this taking so long between them? They got on fine, sometimes swimmingly. Yet he sensed a palpable distance he just couldn't navigate. She continued, "Maybe you need a catalyst or something. Maybe an environmental shift, or chemical or thermal."

He'd been going at this particular experiment for over a year now, and catalysts were definitely a consideration of his. The problem: figuring it out. He could only change so many variables at a time, which meant until he found a solution there were an incredibly large amount of tests to run. He appreciated her input and her effort. She'd done a remarkable job learning about his research since arriving, so much so that he wondered if she had any scientific background.

"That's a good idea," he said, thinking about the different ones he'd already tested. Maybe if he picked a new one, directed his research and incorporating her thoughts, it might bring them closer together. At this point there was a lot that he'd be willing to try. But his experiment could wait. "So, is this feeling more like home? I mean, as much as an evil supervillain underwater laboratory can?" he said, giving her a grin.

"You're hardly what I'd call evil. Although…" she said, giving him an appraising look, "with the right wardrobe choices we could easily do supervillain."

Jacob gave his best maniacal laugh and they both laughed, dropping their weights as their concentration broke. "You know," Jacob said, trying to think of the right way to phrase his words, "we've been going at these experiments hard since you arrived. I'm grateful for all your assistance." He smiled at her. "You've done admirably. Maybe," he took a deep breath, "maybe we could take a day off tomorrow and relax. Get a nice mental reset. I downloaded the new *Andromeda's Legacy* movie. Maybe we could watch that together?"

A series of micro-expressions flickered across her face as she wrestled with whatever was going on in her head. They switched too fast to process in real-time, so he'd have to analyze them later. He watched as her jaw clenched and loosened over and over, as she struggled with her response. After only a couple of seconds her face relaxed and she smiled.

"You know what, that sounds like a great idea. It'd probably do us both some good."

Seemed like a win to Jacob and he didn't press his luck further. Their workout continued as normal with mostly surface-level conversation. Hopefully by tomorrow they'd be able to go a little deeper.

~ * ~

Alice cursed herself for agreeing a day off. It'd been a week since then, and while she'd thought it'd be a good strategy to get him to open up and divulge his secret research, instead she'd only ended up liking him more. Her plan revolved around staying detached so she wouldn't feel bad leaving Jake high and dry once she found the cure. Guilt wormed its way into her thoughts. If she was being honest with herself, it'd started well before movie day. Before she'd had one of her best days in a long while. Before she'd fallen asleep on his shoulder and woken up tucked nicely in her bed. Jake was a nice man, and she was using him.

She pulled her goggles up and turned to Jake. She realized the adoption of that nickname made matters worse. "Results are inconclusive," she said, removing the slide and placing it in a dish to be cataloged later.

"Crap," he said, looking up from his own microscope. "It was a good idea, a latticed molecular bondage. You come up with a few more like that and we'll have this cracked."

She smiled at his praise, then chastised herself. She could not get attached. She was here for Sammy. It'd been over a month since she'd seen her son and it broke her heart being away for so long. So long as she found a cure, the time away would be worth it. Her gaze lingered on Jake as emotions battled within. As nice as he was, other priorities took precedence. "Don't put all that on my shoulders," she said, forcing a smile and giving him a playful jab with her elbow. "Besides, you've been working on this for over a year. Imagine how embarrassing it'd be for me to swoop in and solve it in a month."

He laughed and shook his head. "Regardless of who figures this out, both our names are going on the paper. I wasn't joking before, you have been invaluable. Now," he gestured to his notes, "perhaps we could incorporate a third party, something to engage with the extremophiles on their level. I found some cancerous cells the other day underwater…"

She watched his face turn from confused to concerned. She knew she'd done a poor job of hiding her reaction.

"What?" Jacob rested his hand on hers. "What's wrong?"

"I…I don't feel well," she managed to choke out, removing her gloves and standing up. Her thoughts of Sammy had shifted from simply missing him, to worrying about his cancer, about his slow, inevitable march toward death. She started to the door but Jake jumped in her way.

"Alice, please," he pleaded. "Tell me what's wrong. I want to help."

She knew he did. Earnest and honest, she knew he'd be there for her. Or he would until she told him she'd been lying to him, playing him for a fool. How much would he want to help once her secret came out?

"Jake, I can't. Please let me through." Alice bounced on her heels impatiently, wanting, needing to leave this room. Sammy's cancer pounded at her feelings for Jake and she couldn't be in his presence right now, not if she wanted to stay sane.

"It's been over a month, Alice. If we're not able to talk about what's bothering us by now, when will we?"

"Maybe we won't Jake!" she snapped. "Maybe this isn't work-ing. Maybe we're wasting time playing foolish games thinking we can make our lives better." Jacob took half a step back at the outburst. She was wasting time though, wasting time with movie days, wasting time thinking about what could be with Jake when all that mattered was what needed to be for Sammy.

"Just because something hasn't worked yet, doesn't mean it can't," Jake said. "You might have misgivings, but I still believe this can work, we can work. I don't know what's going on in your head, but you're important enough to me that I will wait for you to figure it out, even if you need to keep things from me."

She knew it hurt him to tell her. He'd been alone seven years, and while he was no longer by definition alone, emotionally he may as well have been. She'd brought him badly needed companionship and he needed more. She couldn't give it to him. Hurt as he may be, he did just give her the opening she needed. It pained her to take it, but it would pain her more not to.

"Keep things from you?! How about what you keep from me?"

"I don't know what you mean."

"Oh come on. You go on your dives and are gone for hours. You come back with a dozen samples. A dozen? It takes hours to harvest a dozen samples? I never said anything because everyone needs their alone time. I thought maybe you needed a break from me. Maybe you had the same misgivings I did." She knew he didn't. She needed to dig.

"I don't." Jacob rocked back in his seat as if he'd been punched. "There is nothing wrong with you, nothing wrong with what could be us. I just..." he trailed off.

Her repressed feelings for him buoyed by his words and she fought to push them back down.

"That's what I thought." Her voice became stern, her eyes turning hard with resolve. "If you really think this can work, if you really want me to trust you, you need to trust me. Until then, this whole relationship is a sham with us going through the motions."

Alice pushed her way past him and he didn't try and stop her. She barely shut the door to her room before the tears spilled out. Angry tears for taking so long, happy tears for Jake audibly caring for her, resentful tears for letting that eat at her.

She'd been here for five weeks and what had she to show for it? Images of Sammy dominated her thoughts. She missed him. Worried about him. Hoped he'd survive. Tears flowed anew. For every smiling face she saw, every vibrant happy memory, there was another plagued by sickness, his already sepia-toned life slowly losing all its color. She ached to hold him. To comfort him, even a million miles away. To reassure him that everything would be okay. But she couldn't promise that. She couldn't even talk to him all the way out on this godforsaken frozen moon and that killed her all the more. All she could do was cling to the hope that Jake's secret research would save her boy.

Her mind replayed the harsh words she'd thrown at Jake. He'd tried to understand, to help. She'd attacked him. She'd tried to build walls, Jake had been trying to break them down. He didn't deserve her deceit. He deserved what he had asked for, the same thing anyone wanted, someone who could truly be there for him, in mind, body, and spirit. Not a desperate mother willing to destroy him out of love for her child.

And she would destroy him. She knew when it came down to it she would. Unfortunately for him, that when was now. Wiping the tears from her cheeks she made her way to her desk, unlocking the top drawer. Alice pulled out a data card, the information inside filling her with hope and dread at the same time.

She'd found his hidden specimen a couple of weeks ago. Not, however, his data. So she'd been painstakingly studying it while Jake went out on his dives. She didn't know what the specimen was exactly, she didn't have the same expertise as Jake. The traits she had observed were promising. Since she couldn't send the sample itself to GeneCorp, she needed her own data to transmit. She'd been trying to get a more complete report to send. As Jake had unwittingly reminded her, she was running out of time. She knew Sammy didn't have much time. Perhaps this partial data would be enough for GeneCorp to retain its grant funding.

Transmitting it though would mean the end of her time here. Her time with Jake. Jake would know what she'd been up to. He'd never trust her, especially after her rant a couple of minutes ago. With her actions she'd ensure his research could continue. She'd also alienate herself, a fact that hurt more than it should. Would his research be enough to save Sammy? She could only hope. Any risk, no matter what it cost herself, even her unexpected desires, she hoped had been worth taking.

She inserted the card into her computer, watching in her mind as her possible reality crumbled. She'd come to appreciate Jake's methodical nature. His silly but endearing habit of colloquially defining random bits of their lives. She still found joy bouncing in low gravity from room to room. With a few clicks, all she'd experienced would disappear.

She opened her pre-composed message and attached the data.

~ * ~

Jacob knocked on Alice's door.

"Go away," came the immediate response.

"I need to show you something." Jacob waited in silence. "It…it's important." He held his breath, waiting for her to explode at him again. Instead he heard shuffling followed by the door opening a crack. Alice looked at him, her eyes red from crying.

Part of him wanted to end this fledgling relationship. Whatever she was going through was breaking her, and even though she hadn't explicitly laid blame directly at his feet, he couldn't help but think that if she weren't here she wouldn't be dealing with whatever it was that haunted her. If he sent her away now she'd be gone from this situation, gone from whatever hurt lay within these walls.

Or he could show her his secret, let her in and hope sharing would be enough for her to share her pain. He knew the risk. Beyond great. His Space Brides experiment was close to success. He'd examined Alice and himself, identified the variables, accounted for everything in his power. There was one last variable, one last component to this experiment that couldn't be avoided if he wanted success. If he wanted to keep her. He held out his hand, and to his surprise and relief, she took it.

He led her to the hydrolock chamber and they suited up in silence. The silence relaxed him. He wouldn't have to explain anything to her. He hoped her coming along hinted at least at the beginnings of trust. She'd never gone into the ocean with him, though her profile said she'd been scuba certified. Her slow pulling up of the suit seemed to suggest it'd been a long while since she'd dived. He moved to help her, watching for any sign his assistance wasn't wanted.

Even the casual brushing of his fingers on her body as he adjusted straps and checked seals increased the pounding in his chest. Seven years without intimacy heightened every physical contact, and something about helping her now, about her finally joining him in the ocean, resonated more than he could have hypothesized.

Once they were both fully suited up, Jacob pulled the lever to suck out the air, then a second lever to let in the water. What weightlessness they felt in the lab shifted as the water enveloped them. The suits had bladders to adjust their buoyancy. They'd been designed with Europa in mind. With less gravity to pull them down, their natural buoyancy wanted them to rise, even with the suits. So, in addition to an open helmet to allow for verbal communication, each scuba suit had small propellers to direct them in the ocean.

Jacob took her hand once more and together they floated into Europa's vast subterranean ocean.

As the lights from the lab dimmed behind them, Jacob switched on their helmets' floodlights, illuminating the path. As they went, he began to point out different species he'd discovered and natural habitats he'd spoken of. He knew she'd never actually seen them. The dark water filtered their light, amoebas and tiny fish casting rippling shadows as they floated and flitted about.

"I've only seen one species larger than my hand," he told her, "and none of them have shown any sign of aggression." When he first began his exploration the dark waters had scared him, the mystery of the unknown alluring and terrifying all at once. Nightmares of giant whale-sized carnivores tearing him to shreds had plagued him. Those had faded quickly, the ocean instead calming him somehow. Alice had not had that time and he wanted to assure her there was nothing to fear out here.

"It's amazing." He heard wonder in her voice.

Those were the first words she'd spoken since she'd stormed out of the gym. He counted that as a win. The winning wasn't over yet. They swam for almost an hour and he watched as the awe on her face grew and grew until finally they reached their destination. He stopped her just in front of a large jut of ice.

"I'm going to show you something, something you can't tell anyone. Can I trust you with this?" He watched as an odd expression passed over her face, something both weighty and freeing. Her eyes, which had been staring intently into his through the dark water, softened.

"Of course," she promised. "And thank you. For trusting me."

Together they rounded the icy protrusion and he heard her

breath catch as a rainbow of shimmering light reached them. Floating in the distance were hundreds of creatures Jacob had refused to officially name, even to himself. They floated in an intricate dance of movement, their directions not restricted to mundane horizontal movement. As the marine beings swirled and moved through the water, their colors changed, rippling chromatic patterns choreographing their movements.

"They're beautiful," Alice whispered, the speaker in his helmet keeping her voice at normal volume. Her tone held all the awe. "What are they?"

"Aside from immortal? They haven't told me yet," Jacob wait for her reaction.

She turned sharply toward him. "They speak?! Wait, back up. Immortal?"

"Yes. Near as I can tell, they don't age. Once they reach maturation, there is no senescence. And talking? Not exactly." He pointed to a few of them who'd strayed from the dance. "You see the color variations between them? Near as I can tell, that's how they communicate. It might be as simple as emotion or as complex as "words." I think I've figured out what some of it means. I don't know how they self-identify, or even if they do for that matter. I don't want to give them a name in case they already have a name for themselves."

"I don't think it's fair to simplify emotion, but I understand." Her eyes followed the shifting colors.

Jacob had meant base instincts and amygdalic responses, but looking at her wonderment and feeling the pulsing in his own chest he couldn't discount emotional entanglement. Indeed the swirling of colors as the creatures passed each other seemed to create their own shimmer of light and movement. Jacob proceeded to explain the colors he had worked out and his suppositions on what the various shades indicated.

"There is one I'm completely baffled by," he admitted. "None are exhibiting the color pattern now—"

"Pattern?" Alice interrupted.

"Yes. Every once in a while I will see a singular creature shining with a myriad of colors all at once, shifting and changing position on their body."

"Kind of like what we're seeing here," Alice said. Jacob looked back and tried to take in the whole picture, something he'd not done for a while. And wouldn't you know, Alice was right. The dancing pattern here did bear a striking resemblance to the individual projections he'd seen before.

His train of thought broke as he felt her take his hand. "It must be hard, living with your emotions on display, unable to choose what you let the world see. Emotions can be…tricky. Often they contradict each other and never do they come as you want when you want. Everything is just so…tangled." She turned to face him and she could see her pulse pounding through the mask. "Just for once I'd like everything to simplify, to just be one of those colors." She gave him a wry grin. "I'm tired of being a rainbow."

Jacob reached out and held the side of her mask, thumb brushing inches from her cheek.

"Rainbows are how our eyes interpret beauty."

~ * ~

Alice woke in a dreamy haze, weighted blanket covering just up to her collarbone. Jacob's weighted blanket. She turned to see him sleeping soundly, his side of the blanket barely covering his waist. Not that she minded of course. After last night's activities she couldn't rightly call stealing glances a guilty pleasure. She'd been surprised by reduced gravity intimacy, surprised by exactly how much she'd wanted her and Jacob to happen, but above all, she'd been surprised by the creatures.

She turned and looked out the window. Like many of the rooms, Jacob's room had windows allowing an underwater view. Lack of sunlight usually left little to see. After their rendezvous last night a handful of the color-emitting creatures had appeared, shining a deep red. They'd both been taken aback, but their passions had gotten the better of them and it wasn't until they'd finished together they noticed the creatures had turned from red to that rainbow pattern and had danced wildly. As her and Jacob's heartbeats had slowed, so too had the creatures, shifting from their multicolored spectrum to a soft blue.

She could have sworn she'd felt something prick her mind, a soft probe curious and open. That feeling, foreign at first, immediately became familiar, then faded into the background. In the moment she'd chalked it up to her raging emotions. But now she wasn't so sure. Had the creatures been watching and cheering for them or had her hormones tricked her? It'd been a long time since she'd been with a man. Had her mind and body betrayed all rational thought? On one thing in particular her mind was clear about.

Alice reached over and nudged Jacob awake, hand gripping his bicep. She had to suppress the instant pounding in her chest. His eyes opened and when he saw her he gave the dumbest grin she'd ever seen. It was adorable. "Jake," she said, tone serious, "we need to talk."

Alice told him everything. She told him about her son, about working at GeneTech and finding his research. She confessed her plan to betray him and how he'd interrupted her sending the data. Her face burning, she shared her goal hadn't been to become attached to him.

Through it all he listened and didn't interrupt once. When she finished she sat back, feeling more exposed from her admissions than from the blanket that had fallen to her lap. The silence ate at her as she watched him process the information, knowing he'd be analyzing and categorizing and rationalizing all the new data. It was his way. After agonizing minutes or hours or days he spoke.

"Do you have feelings for me?" he asked. The softness with which he spoke showed a vulnerability she'd never seen from him, and if her answer had been teetering at all before it was now cemented.

"Yes," Alice admitted. A weight she hadn't fully realized seemed to roll off her shoulders. She leaned forward, held his face in her hands, and kissed him hard. "Yes." Then she took him into her arms and buried her face in the crook of his neck. "Yes."

When he hugged her back she knew everything would be okay. She didn't know how, but she knew it would. She lingered in his embrace, in his scent. When he released her and gently pushed her back she hated and loved the immediate sense of loss she felt. He stared directly into her eyes.

"I have a plan."

~ * ~

Jacob had barely pulled his pants up when the alarm rang. Alice had mentioned GeneTech's recent use of mercenaries to clean up defunct sites and she wasn't exaggerating. With no grant renewal they were taking no chances in profiting in any way they could. He watched on his tablet as a squad of five in heavy gear and some large firearms he couldn't identify came down the elevator. He was fairly certain they thought they'd been undetected. A GeneCorp security override code had been used. GeneCorp hadn't known Jacob had written in his own code to ignore such action. Unfortunately for Jacob and Alice, that elevator was their only way out.

"Was this part of your plan?" Alice gave him a grin. He was glad she could keep her sense of humor in this situation. He knew he couldn't.

"Sort of. When I set up the alarms years ago, the idea at the time had been to destroy anything pertaining to the creatures by the time anyone arrived. I didn't have a solid escape plan for myself per se, and I hadn't altered the plans yet to account for you."

"Hardly the proper consideration for a future wife." When he glanced at her she raised an eyebrow and gave a slight shrug. He couldn't be sure how much of her behavior was coping with the situation or if she finally felt more open with him. He appreciated the effort either way.

"I will endeavor to include you in the plans and the planning," he told her. "But for the time being, our next step is hiding in the ocean."

"Can't they just wait us out?" Alice asked.

"Yes, but only if they know we're there. I don't think they will wait that long. We'll take my research with us. If for some reason this doesn't work, we trust the ocean to protect its own."

"What exactly are you going to do though?"

"I'm going to get my hands dirty."

They spent the next five minutes gathering the hidden data in the lab and getting their scuba suits on. She'd been surprised at the hiding place for his data, a place he knew she'd never think to look. It'd been in her room, stuffed in the hollow of her metal bed frame. "Looking for an excuse to come into my room?" She'd teased, to which he had to force a grin. He'd smile for real once the danger had passed.

His mind considered what might happen once they left the station. He'd engineered a biohazard to be released throughout the lab. Safe in the ocean, the lab would run its sterilization procedures to remove the pathogen. Not before it took out their armed guests.

He didn't relish the idea of killing anyone. With the fate of an entire species on the line, he would do what he must. He had no delusions whatsoever about what GeneCorp would do to those poor creatures to fully exploit their unique genetics and make a profit in the process. He'd made this plan before Alice had arrived. He only hoped she wouldn't look at him differently once the deed had been completed.

Fully suited, he was just about to pull the lever when the click of a gun and a man's voice froze him in place.

"Don't move Mr. Headly," the deep, authoritative voice ordered. Jacob and Alice both turned slowly to find the five armed intruders filing into the room.

"Hi," Jacob greeted, trying to sound surprised and just the right amount of alarmed. "Did I miss an inspection schedule?" One of the agents snorted. Jacob tried to maintain his demeanor. "We were just on our way out to collect samples." He hoisted the case with all his data. "Can I point you in the right direction before I go?"

"Cut the crap, Headly," the man barked. "We're here for the research. The research you *haven't* sent in."

"I don't know what you're talking about," Jacob said.

The man pointed the gun right at him. Jacob raised both his hands slowly, but didn't say anything. After a few seconds the gun shifted toward Alice. His mind raced. How could he stop them? How could he save her? Maybe if he distracted them, Alice could get in the water and he'd trigger the biohazard then. He wouldn't make it, but she would, and the creatures would be safe. Perhaps if he was lucky his scuba suit would protect him. He hadn't considered the possibility in his plans.

"Okay! Okay! It's back in the specimen room, I can take you. Just leave her out…" Jacob trailed off as something in his head shifted, softened. The edginess he felt from the situation seemed to vanish. He felt calm. Reassured. He looked at Alice and she too seemed somehow unworried.

"Whatever you're thinking, Headly, unthink it. There's no way…" he too trailed off. Though it wasn't calm Jacob saw in his eyes. It was fear verging on terror. Jacob saw then all the intruders were beginning to look unhinged. Without warning the lead man swiveled and fired two rounds into the person to their left. Then the dam broke and all of them began shooting at each other. Jacob tackled Alice to the ground, trying to protect her with his body. In moments the gunfire ceased. Jacob looked up at the mess of bodies before them. When he turned back to Alice he noticed something else, something through the viewport into the ocean.

Lights shined in, two blue and a dozen fading maroon, shifting to blue themselves. Suddenly everything clicked. The urge he'd felt to protect the creatures, the kinship that made no rational sense. Even last night, the ecstasy had been beyond anything he'd experienced before. He thought it'd just been because of how long he'd been alone, but remembering the rainbow outside the window he knew it had been more. Now, in the face of certain death he'd felt calm, and the calm killers who came for him had lost it on each other.

"They saved us," Alice whispered, following his gaze into the ocean. "They knew we were trying to protect them so they protected us." Immediately the colors shifted to a bright yellow and he felt—he knew—Alice was right.

~ * ~

Alice stared at the data stick in her gloved hand, knowing everything rode on her convincing explanation to the authorities. Jake's plan seemed straightforward enough. The doctored video showed him sabotaging the lab when the mercenaries arrived, triggering explosions, killing himself and the team. She'd only escaped because he'd cared for her and let her go. The sabotage included a reaction with the extremophiles he'd already given them damning reports about, promising future catastrophes should any company rebuild. The part she'd have to really sell was why he'd done it. The simplest explanation seemed the best. After seven years in isolation, he'd gone crazy. That was why the reports had been weird lately. That's why she'd never found anything. There was nothing *to* find. Nothing but a crazed, self-proclaimed extremophile.

GeneTech itself was finished. If their plummeting value and loss of contracts hadn't been enough, the scandal of a destroyed research station after employing mercenaries would certainly do the trick.

In her other hand rested her motivation for this whole endeavor. A small set of vials, doses of a treatment to cure her son using the unique genetics of the underwater glowing creatures. In the same way Jake had been able to make that one specimen she'd found live longer, he'd been able to use them to make a cure for Sammy. It hadn't been the solution she'd envisioned. It had been better.

Behind her Jake loaded her luggage in the ship. She could have carried it, especially with how little it weighed. He'd grumbled something and insisted. She didn't want to make a big deal of it. Although he said he'd accepted their arrangement, she knew, like this moon, there was more beneath the surface.

A hiss of compression sealed the door and she turned to find Jake removing his helmet. She did the same and they stood facing each other, the only sounds the faint hum of the engine and their own unsteady breathing.

"Jake, I…" she started, but trailed off, not knowing the right words. Were there right words? What did one say to someone who not only cured her son's terminal illness, but also trusted her enough to leave his fate in her hands? Thank you? No. Just one thing that needed to be said. One thing, until this very moment, looking into his eyes, she knew to be true. "I love you."

He smiled a smile both relieved and smug and reached out, taking her face in both his hands. "I love you too." Then he pulled her toward him and kissed her, first tenderly, then harder. She imagined him trying to stockpile intimacy with no real guarantee he'd ever see her again.

She returned the kiss, tempering the firm passion with a softer, yet insistent embrace, willing their bodies to become one despite the inch thickness of their suits and the soon-to-be millions of miles of space between them. Her heart pounded and she swore she could see rainbows in her periphery.

She pulled back with a shudder, knowing she had to leave now. The longer she waited the less convincing her story would be. "I'll come back," she promised. Once she informed the authorities and dealt with GeneCorp. Once she helped her son. "I'll be back."

"I know," Jake rubbed his thumb one more time across her cheek, then put his helmet on and exited through the airlock. She watched him walk back to the elevator, watched as the elevator and the moon itself shrunk with the departure of her ship. Only then did she realize he'd left a note on one of her bags. Her eyes moistened read as she it.

"You swooped in and solved *me* in a month. I patiently, painfully, await the return of my heart."

~ * ~ * ~

**Eric Taveren** writes and lives in Minneapolis. He is in the tail end of his MFA program at Hamline University and his work appears in Great Weather for Media, F(r)iction, and Avalon Literary Review. One of the small percentage of people with aphantasia, he writes to create the worlds he cannot see.

# FINDING COMMON GROUND

### Cecily Winter

FROM: SPACE BRIDES LLC on behalf of Contractor K-three-five-nine
TO: Bridal Candidate LUCE-EUS-seven-eight

Thank you for your candidate registration with Space Brides, LLC, Houston Street, New York, America, Earth.

The notary's certification of your facial configuration, physique, and medical condition places you in the high-acceptable range of candidates.

Aged point zero six Kepler cycles and never married, the contractor seeks lawful marriage with a genetically certified human female.

His goal is:

"To *find lifelong love and create a family of three boys and a girl, number and gender subject to negotiation and chance.*"

His occupation is:

"*Robotics engineer with Kepler Mineral Extraction.*"

His hobby is:

"*Breeding heirloom llamas on a family ranch operational since the planet's settlement.*"

To advance your candidacy, contact the contractor at our memo exchange, code GRIKA K-three-five-nine.

We wish you the fulfillment of your every dream!

MANAGING DIRECTOR, SPACE BRIDES, LLC

~ * ~

From: LUCE-EUS-seven-eight
To: GRIKA K-three five-nine

Dear Grika:

Thank you for including me in your candidate pool. As my profile indicates, I am a single human female who anticipates finding happiness in the bosom of a traditional family.

I admire your frontier charisma and have to say your stamina and agility ratings are impressive. I find it quite charming you have only a tiny percentage of Neanderthal genes. As a homo sapiens cheerleader, this is a definite plus. I take an active interest in our species' continuing vigor.

Though many of my off-world friends and colleagues are as cute and brilliant as we are, their hybrid offspring rarely match the vitality and intelligence of a human child. I may be a curmudgeon but guess we share the ideal of same-species marriage.

If you wish to pursue my candidacy, please clarify your views on this topic and discuss your guiding principle.

With best wishes, Luce

~ * ~

Dear Luce,

You guess rightly I share your concern about species' integrity. In fact, my guiding principle is to fulfill our manifest destiny, to spread our example of good works and industrial zeal to every habitable solar zone.

Like you, I celebrate the qualities of our exotic neighbors and acknowledge our great debt to them when we arrived on the frontier in our rag-tag convoys. Whatever our species, I believe intelligent beings will always thrive by upholding traditional values. I admit my experience with off-worlders is limited. On Kepler-Nine, we have more robots than humans and far more humans and llamas than off-worlders.

My contribution to humanity's manifest destiny is the improvement of my llama herd whose ancestors voyaged with mine from the Americas. The mountains here are mossy barrens, nothing like the grandeur of the Andes. Llamas are highly adaptable and can contribute significantly to our success in taming the galaxy.

They are the perfect settler resource. They adapt to low oxygen levels, extreme weather conditions, and sparse fodder, all the while keeping families in milk, meat, wool, transportation, and companionship. In short, they ensure settlers' survival while they perfect their exploitation of local resources.

When you meet my champion macho, Jorge, you will understand my admiration for these amazing creatures.

I must ask, have you ever been in love, Luce?

Yours, Grika

~ * ~

Dear Grika:

As a resident of the cement jungle, I hardly know what to make of your llama enthusiasm. I'm sure colonists know best.

If we prove compatible, I would be delighted to meet Jorge. I imagine him as a tall, aloof character with soft, ivory wool. Please don't contradict me. Shh!

When I was considering off-world migration a few years ago, I studied home arts and food science at New York's Emigration Institute. Toward the end of my studies, faults arose in the artificial intelligence apps aboard many space transports. The kinks were ironed out and travel from Earth resumed. By then I'd found a career in scarce-resource cookery.

It now claims so much of my time, I haven't dated since high school, the lowlight of which was a roller coaster ride with a date who hurled in my lap. So much for my experience of love. I confess to being a hopeless romantic when it comes to fiction dot-files and virtual reality.

Who in real life compares to the sultry Adam Perfect or the gruff and burly Captain Gregor Seafarer? Well, perhaps you do. I look forward to finding out.

Is romance to be found in mining? I recall brave Allan Quartermain in *King Solomon's Mines* and the lovers Raphael Santana and Lisbet Woo in *The Dragon Emeralds of Triton*. I can picture you now hacking at a rockface with a pick, your hard hat tilted rakishly, and your biceps gleaming. Please don't disappoint me.

Affectionately, Luce

~ * ~

Dearest Luce,

Because I terminated my other Space Bride candidacies, I can freely admit your memos fill me with delight. If you are weighing the qualities of several contractors, I beg you to consider me your sole focus. I feel we already know each other so well.

My work is AI design for Kepler Metallica's excavation robots. In modeling those systems, I have gone short distances underground, armed with only a flashlight and an oxygen tank. If my muscles gleamed, my robotic amigos did not swoon.

Robot excavators are typically immune from romance. They do manage to surface intact from our deeper mines, however, which feat is almost impossible for a human. More on that later.

As for Adam Perfect, my palms were exceptionally sweaty whenever I dated and I certainly never met my soul mate. Did I mention you remind me of Lisbet Woo in *Dragon Emeralds of Triton*?

On the subject of rare minerals, my company sells components for computing, industrial machinery, and spaceships. The excavated matrix is pulverized for brick-making, cement, and other building materials. I attach our capital city's Chamber of Commerce dot-file designed to attract immigrants and investors.

At present, we are primarily rural. New Cusco recently added several housing estates on the perimeter. These developments have access to mock forests and salt lakes, and I understand an urban life might suit you best. I admit right upfront I would never sell my family's ranch. I'm not sure how we could resolve this dilemma. Your thoughts would be welcome.

I never had an opportunity to stroll under a canopy of leafy hybrid trees. Have you romped through woodland to hear the chirping of songbirds or run along the shore to the crash of incoming waves?

I await your reply anxiously. Now I must attend to a llama dam having difficulty delivering her cria. Shepherds are on call for lambing in one season. Llamas are more like people than sheep, solidly individualist.

I applaud your pioneering skills and wonder about the career that drove migration from your thoughts.

Your Grika

~ * ~

Dearest Grika:

I responded only to your Space Brides invitation and am happy to continue our correspondence.

My career? I compose and illustrate recipes for home cooks and survivalists. My dot-file recipe sales provide sufficient income for a single woman. I doubt any of them appear on the tables of a

10-star restaurant.

I cram my days with experiments, foraging, and composing text. While I enjoy city amenities, I prefer to be outdoors. I have strolled in woodland, smelled the soil's perfume after a rain shower, and listened in delight to natural birdsong. This paradise is one of several zoological arboretums scattered across the Earth. All are seeded with local fauna and flora and attract many tourists. Tourists give me a headache.

My favorite activity is searching for new ingredients in distant fish and farm markets or along rugged Atlantic beaches. From your comment on crashing waves, I assume Kepler seas are static?

My best food find was a vividly-colored, salt-water crustacean whose tender flesh carries the tang of grapefruit. It is sublime in sushi, and the crushed exoskeleton adds a nice crunch to cereals and candy. Unfortunately, my recipe set off a harvesting boom. Within a season the species, as yet unnamed, had disappeared. Our carelessness about the welfare of our local fauna and flora saddens me. I gladly pulled the tasty treat from my dot-file.

I attach the revised dot-file of *Even Scarce Resources Can Feed Hearty Appetites*. I think you'll appreciate my illustration of a proud llama doing the splits on a banana peel. Did you ever imagine the taste and texture of this extinct fruit? It haunts me. I'm constantly on the lookout for its cousin.

I hope you have a ticklish sense of humor. I love a good laugh.

Affectionately, Luce

~ * ~

My Sweet Luce,

Here on the foothills of commitment, I will be frank about the drawbacks of Kepler-Nine.

We have no amusement parks. On the upside, you can forget your roller coaster date. When our population warrants the expense, I'm sure we'll commercialize the idea of family fun.

Our long-time settlers are well-rooted. Most off-world humans or hybrids are contract workers whose families remain aboard their transit ships. We are actively recruiting immigrants and, hopefully, we will see an uptick in new faces soon.

My reaching out to a "mail-order" bride is partly a consequence of our closely-knit community and relative isolation. Rest assured, I have a wide circle of friends to welcome you into their hearts and homes.

We improvise concerts and theatricals, which always turn into rowdy knee-slappers. Music and dance are our favorite pastimes. May I wean you from square dancing and teach you Kepler-Nine's traditional fandango known to roast your bones?

From this high note, I'll switch Kepler-Nine's wildlife. Your crustacean triumph leads me to believe you would easily adapt to our arthropods. Most resemble your spiders, flies, lobsters, crabs, and so on. We don't interfere with them, and they rarely interfere with us. In high summer, a fever bug bite may raise a small localized swelling.

On the darker side, we harbor a toxic species we call rock spiders. Geologists and zoologists who rubbed up against them in mines or mountain crevices have been killed on contact. Scientists have yet to identify the toxin's composition.

Rock spiders are not the eight-legged, bald or hairy creatures familiar to Earth inhabitants. With no sign of legs, they appear to relocate in large groups from time to time. We don't know how. My engineering superior is convinced rock spiders are invasive robots gone feral.

They are shaped like boxes, cubes, or parallelograms, often with several smaller attachments. Perhaps each unit is a colony. Biologists theorize their origins off-world, probably carried here by crashed meteors. It would be a true blessing for the entire colony if you discovered a way for us to eat our way clear of them and detoxify our mines.

One surprising feature is their striking luminescence. They are most vivid at dusk. A huddle, as we call their gatherings, migrates through the rock to the surface where it radiates every color in our spectrum. Perhaps the closest scientific phenomenon and visual comparison would be Earth's aurora borealis.

At this point, you're probably bolting for your woodland sanctuary while I'm ready to book your passage and pre-paid return ticket this instant. Our meeting here on Kepler-Nine involves no risk on your part. If you join me, I promise to fill your hours, days, and cycles with boundless affection. Send word instantly.

With all my love, your devoted Grika

~ * ~

Grika—Yes, my love. You are truly the man of my dreams. Besides, I'm hooked on every facet of your amazing planet.

Please send an open ticket so I can arrange the sale of my apartment and large possessions. I would prefer to arrive in autumn, which your Chamber of Commerce assures me is Kepler's most attractive season and the perfect time for a wedding.

I hope you can make the arrangements. I'll bring my wedding gown and a foolproof cake recipe if my syrups make it through Customs.

I have never been so giddy.

Kisses, Luce.

~ * ~

Luce took in stride her economy berth. She'd not expected Grika to be stingy. If he turned out to be a miser, at least her return voyage was guaranteed.

Once aboard *Spaceship Bowie*, she wanted to stay awake through the wormhole. The captain mocked her resolve until she showed herself immune to the skeletal warping and mind fog afflicting most humans during a voyage.

She had given something away by her resistance to the ship's pressures. Luckily, the Captain and his crew spent most of the time slumbering in their quarters while passengers enjoyed induced dreams in theirs. She studied Kepler's geology in library dot-files or devoured romance dot-files featuring Venus, her species' ancestral planet and fount of female eroticism. For exercise, she strolled the decks before plonking herself beside the robot pilot to enjoy her passage through the eerily sparking wormhole.

As she traveled, she put the finishing touches to her mother's wedding gown with new lace on the cuffs and a collar of bluish river pearls at the throat. The garment was nearly weightless, a cloud imparting an air of divinity, which was a look every bride deserved.

When she finished, she folded the gown over her lap thinking about what she might borrow to complete the tradition of 'something' old, new, borrowed, blue.

Her thoughts scattered when the ship slid into planetary orbit.

Almost in a trance, she gazed at Kepler-Nine growing ever more detailed topographically, a scattering of thumbnail seas and craggy mountains at the poles.

A light show raged across the peaks of the northern mountain. Hauntingly beautiful. Was this a phenomenon of the solar wind or a massive congregation of dusk-worshiping rock spiders?

Her stomach lurched when the ship docked. The cabin went dark and Luce shivered. Had she lied herself into a nightmare?

~ * ~

Shaved, bathed, and dressed in llama-leather trousers and matching vest, Grika paced his hacienda. For the first time, he noticed the shabby furnishings, the worn rugs, and the trite Inca cosmology carvings.

Luce would be unimpressed. He had no funds for home improvements; he was only an apprentice engineer and her tickets cost a season's salary. Raising llamas was a labor of love more than an income stream.

He had one treasure to impress her. The robot with him hadn't recorded the theft. If Grika were caught selling it, the colony might expel him. He believed it would be safest on Luce's ring finger and couldn't wait to surprise her with it. A mineral so many eons in the making. He longed to gallop to the spaceport on Jorge and fetch his bride home in the way of his ancestors.

Romance gave way to practicality, and soon his truck rattled along the unlit, rutted roads. With every bump, he prayed to the old Inca gods to hide his falsity from Luce. Their exchange of memos barely touched the surface of what a marriage partnership ought to be, and he'd wasted too much time daydreaming about kissing and walking hand-in-hand on silver beaches instead of exploring her heart and mind.

~ * ~

Luce emerged from Customs, breathing shallowly. She expanded the surface area of her lungs. The officer with a surprisingly feathered scalp had confiscated her syrups and nixed a traditional wedding cake. Shaken by the confrontation, she lingered in the caustic, eye-tearing light of the receiving area. Her head ached and she considered turning tail. It would do no good. On Earth, she would only dead-end again.

She scanned the people behind the gate. Dressed in a kind of gaucho outfit, Grika waved madly. He was cute. Also, at least six inches shorter than his profile indicated. She would be a fool to trust his 'one hundred percent homo sapiens' certification too. She caught her breath and stepped forward. He looked human enough for her purposes.

The species-purity gambit in her first memo had been pure theater to flex her muscles and ensure she couldn't go far wrong with her marital partner. Besides, shipping home unmarried and unfertilized would scotch her last chance of becoming the mother of divinities. She squared her shoulders and shrank her thigh bones by five inches. Her skirt swept the floor.

At the gate, she narrowed the contours of her eyelids and restored the color of her irises to their original purple. Hacking Lisbet Woo's romantic allure and DNA had gained her a prospective husband. Now she had to make reality work for her.

She was a Venus witch mongrel with a destiny to fulfill.

~ * ~

Grika clasped his beloved in his arms. He didn't dare kiss her on the lips. When he released her, he squeezed her cold hands. Her chill was a response to oxygen depletion. Her lungs would adjust, and, anyway, he planned to keep her warm for all eternity.

Her hesitation at the gate had almost broken his heart. Still, she'd walked through. The ice-cold diamond burned a hole in his pocket.

On the homeward drive, his truck headlights cast faint beams over the empty road. He hoped the house oxygen supply was set at max. He held Luce's hand in his, his palm already sweaty, while she stared through the window in a state of extreme fatigue.

She gradually turned her lovely face to his. "Are there rock spiders in the valley? I'm really curious about them."

Relief roiled up his spine like a homecoming.

~ * ~

The next morning, Grika walked onto the kitchen deck and watched the pallid arc of the sun brighten on the horizon. His service robots prepped the wedding feast. He inhaled the fragrance of yeast bread, spicy marinade, and citrus fruit. Primarily a celebration of love, the wedding was also a rare opportunity to impress New Cusco society. The guest list was huge. What had he been thinking, getting into debt for a party?

~ * ~

When Luce appeared at midday with her pant legs rolled up and ankles goose-bumped, she tucked her face into Grika's neck and rocked him gently side to side. She'd slept well in a spacious room with pretty hangings and a big brick hearth burning an herb akin to sage.

Before rising, she'd listed Grika's plusses: he was young, strong, good-looking, propertied, and blessed with a pleasantly musky smell. Her mind was made up. She played the romance card and smooched his lips, his breath as sweet as mown grass.

With her future settled, Luce sent a robot to fetch her gown and sewing box. She had to take up the hem by five inches. While she hemmed, she ate her cereal, dried berries, and cold llama milk in the kitchen, almost delirious from the aromas driving every thought of cake from her head.

~ * ~

When Luce put her sewing aside, Grika dropped to one knee and urged a diamond set in silver onto her ring finger. His mouth was dry. If only he could drink the milk left in Luce's bowl. He cleared his throat to make his pitch, his best chance to win the beautiful bride he'd loved with all his heart since the beginning of their correspondence.

She was radiant. She'd been working on her gown. They would make a perfect couple.

"Will you marry me, Luce?"

"Yes, I will."

He rose and kissed her full on her trembling mouth.

~ * ~

In her room, Luce traced the contours of the gem with a fingernail, cherishing its coldness while triumph heated her cheeks. Kissing Grika would always be a pleasant task. Kepler-Nine's Health Ministry had certified him as fertile. Their needs and ambitions would mesh in the family they would raise. What else mattered?

She trusted his generosity if he ever discovered how he'd forfeited the chance to find his soul mate. Her soul, perhaps half her genes, and her first loyalty belonged to the planet Venus.

~ * ~

Guests were already arriving when Grika changed into a black tuxedo, a white shirt, and a bola hung with golden teardrops. He grew light-headed watching the women gush over Luce's gown and ring. They whispered about her calm and ethereal beauty. Meeting Luce in person had banished his delusion she resembled Lisbet Woo. Luce was a solitary star in winter's indigo sky.

The priest in his cassock stood facing Grika under a fragrant umma trellis. Grika resolved to wait there until Luce took his hand even if she delayed for all eternity.

He knew he should have confessed about his low-level job, the diamond theft, and the mortgage threatening his ranch. His refusal to sacrifice her was set in stone.

His knees nearly gave way when she grasped his hand and the service in a mix of Incan and Christian belief began.

In a daze of ecstasy, he passively absorbed the familiar promises he'd already vowed to uphold a thousand times while his brimming eyes fixed on the upper meadow burning autumnal in the sun's residual glow.

The crowd cheered at a skyline huddle of rock spiders flaring like celebration fireworks. A good omen.

The ceremony concluded with the exchange of gold rings and the traditional kiss. Her soft, eager lips eased his soul and persuaded him to become the man she could love forever.

After the guests toasted the bride and groom, Grika led the party through the house where they gushed over the authentic carvings, hand-woven rugs, and hammered Spanish-silver goblets. Selling some antiques would pay off a large part of his mortgage. He refused to think of his debts.

The band began playing when the guests sat to dine in the courtyard under an array of heating lamps.

When the after-dinner dancing grew lively, the service robots removed the lamps and tables. The newlyweds and their guests twirled, stamped their feet, and sang along.

A community was another kind of paradise.

~ * ~

After the guests left at dawn, Luce napped on the couch. Grika watched her, his treasure gifted by all the gods. He would be a better man. He would deserve her love.

As if Luce were his good luck charm, his prospects improved dramatically. He was hired to advise ranchers in reestablishing llama herds on their properties, and a trio of entrepreneurs invited him to partner in a housing project, ballpark, and home décor emporium respectively. He also got promoted to chief engineer at Kepler Metallica.

His days grew busier and his nights more blissful. Luce remained the fixed star in his sky. When she shared the news he had waited long months to hear, he fell to his knees and wept at her feet like a child.

~ * ~

Luce joined him for their celebration meal and immediately went into seclusion. In the room she'd preferred since her arrival, she ate her meals alone and meditated. Reflexively, she rolled a marble Venus figurine between her palms.

In the hush, she assured her unborn brood Venus would summon them home by a celestial sign. It had never materialized for Luce, stained by her mother's commercial witchcraft and a nameless human father who'd abandoned them. Her children would be untainted.

It had been a ploy to offset her disadvantage Luce married a foolish, gentle man whose great joy was nurturing llamas, the supreme symbol of fertility. Whether Venus or the Inca gods were best pleased with Luce and Grika's union, they blessed them with six identical girls who were largely human though not certifiably so.

From their first panting breaths as their tiny lungs adjusted to Kepler's oxygen scarcity, these precious infants had one foot on Kepler-Nine and the other on Venus.

~ * ~

Grika never regretted his mail-order bride, though he didn't approve of her preparing their daughters for a 'Venus rapture,' whatever it was. His wife led prayers to Venus each morning and during any twilight brightened by a huddle of rock spiders.

For sixteen years, Luce and the girls periodically held night vigils, searching the sky for Venus' fugitive sign. She had to swallow her disappointment when the girls finished school and took jobs in Grika's various enterprises. They were good and lovely girls, yet none had demonstrated the slightest talent in bodily transformation or worthiness to be recalled to Venus. Their mother's prayers, instruction, and example had flopped. She suspected she'd injected too much homo sapiens into their genes.

She found solace riding on the wooly back of Jorge's son, Raphael. When she stayed out late one evening, Raphael stumbled over unlit rock spiders and bucked her out of her saddle. She landed with her face in the huddle. Where she learned she did fear death.

Sobbing, she'd sleeved her hands but couldn't cover her legs as she crawled across the alien forms.

When she sat up, she wasn't dead nor even bruised where she'd slammed down. Contrary to the images her eyes conveyed to her brain, the spiders she'd landed on were bouncy. They were blocky yet puffy, more like mushrooms than rocks, as much organic as mineral, which put paid to the feral robot theory.

Fascinated by this insight, she embarked on a study, ravenously digesting dot-files and consulting zoologists on Kepler-Nine and Earth. She tried to contact Venusian biologists. Venus was incommunicado. Once upon a time, Luce would have taken their silence as a sign of imminent rapture.

Her immunity to the toxin suggested the rock spider's Venusian origin, its forebear evolving perhaps in Venus' volcano chimneys and cast out across the solar system to seed the more advanced arthropods of life-supporting worlds. Shared Venusian origins would explain both Luce's immunity and her ability to adjust or bend her bones. She didn't doubt the rock spiders were also related to Earth's tasty and still un-named crustaceans which disappeared so suddenly.

Tracing the diaspora of this creature became her goal. It took the sting out of her disappointments. She rode out at dusk seeking huddles. Sometimes, she sat on the perimeter and scooped up a small one to cuddle in her lap. Her nerves thrilled under the same deep bond she'd shared with her infants.

~ * ~

Her face once glowed as softly as sunrise and had recently taken on the weary mantle of an unlit dusk. In the process of aging, her leg bones regained their lost five inches while Grika shrank. His arthritic spine curved cruelly and some of his fingers were stiff as rocks.

They didn't talk much. Wherever their days had taken them in triumph, happiness, or disappointment, they clasped hands, hers cold and supple and his warm and stiff. They remained bonded through the flurry of starry and starless nights. If neither found a soul mate, Luce had found her purpose and they'd built a paradise in their family.

~ * ~

## TESTIMONIAL: SPACE BRIDES, LLC

Do not hesitate to seek love across the galaxy. Space Brides, LLC operates in all habitable worlds. We succeed in bringing happiness to billions of lonely hearts.

Today we highlight the testimonial of Grika from Kepler-Nine who wrote to us shortly after the death of his beloved Earth-born wife, Luce.

*We recently celebrated a wedding anniversary of point-two-five of a Kepler cycle (one hundred Earth years) after Luce and I began a Space Brides, LLC correspondence that blossomed into a partnership and grew into a family. We worked, laughed, wept, and danced while raising six daughters now themselves happy mothers who, inexplicably, gave birth to thirty-six infants born at the same hour. I bless my wife for her role in furthering humanity's manifest destiny and for acquitting me of error through her simple love.*

Phenomenal, right, folks?

Remember, we now offer inter-species introductions in all our primary locations.

Contractors and bridal candidates may contact us in person at any office or through our exchange.

Never lose faith in true love.

~ * ~ * ~

**Cecily Winter** is a former college teacher writing juvenile and adult fiction. Her published academic work and short fiction are listed on her website http://Cecilywinter.com.

She is only now considering a return to the convention circuit. Cecily is the group leader of the Orleans SCBWI chapter and, until the pandemic, was also a member of Sisters in Crime, Mystery Writers of America, and Cape Cod Writers.

# LAPIN CHASSEUR

Jennifer M. Roberts

## Clarissa

Pluto glittered white out the window, icy peaks making Clarissa shiver at the sight of them. She would love to don a space suit and walk those peaks, but unfortunately the Pluto surface wasn't open for exploration. The spaceship aimed its docking clamp at a pit that went deep under the Plutonian surface to the farming colonies below. As the surface vanished into rock, Clarissa called up her latest messages on her data pad. It would take half an hour to complete the pressurization and security cycle for docking. She had time to kill.

Another message from Vincent. Clarissa smiled and hit play, grateful the ship did not have a real-time communication relay. Her dark hair had matted from three full days spent in this narrow seat. Clarissa wasn't one of those girls who needed every detail to be pixel-perfect, but she still wanted to look presentable.

Vincent came into frame, broad shoulders, simple flannel shirt, and thick brown hair Clarissa had once longed to run her hands through. He held a fat rabbit in his hands with a white face flecked with black spots.

"Greetings, intrepid traveler!" Vincent waved at the camera. "Here's your daily update from Luna III. Freckles has almost mastered the ring toss." His voice crackled through the tiny speakers, the data having been corrupted during transit. The image wavered yet, could not hide the warmth and excitement in Vincent's eyes. He set the white-and-black flecked rabbit aside and lifted a fat brown one into view of the camera. "Porkchop here is going to be a dad again! He still can't hop a double hurdle, but Porky the second just cleared three." Vincent stroked Porkchop between the ears and then set him aside. In the background, more rabbits hopped across the lawn, nibbling on grass in stark contrast to the rocky gray lunar surface beyond the window behind them.

Clarissa hadn't known it was possible to cultivate grass on the moon before she met Vincent. Nor had she known there were so many varieties of rabbit.

"We'll have a whole new show worked out by the time you get back." Vincent grinned, showing wide white teeth. That had been the start of all this, Clarissa falling for a handsome grin. She hadn't realized about the rabbits back then, among other things. So when Vincent had posted a job, she had taken it.

"Can't wait to hear all about your trip, and we all miss you." Vincent leaned closer to the camera. "Alexis isn't nearly as good at sweeping out the hutches."

Alexis? Clarissa leaned closer to the screen, backing up the recording. Yes. Alexis. Shit. Clarissa should have known her sister would use this chance to steal her man.

Vincent gestured to something offscreen and Alexis came into frame. They were identical twins, Clarissa and Alexis, both with long dark hair, sharp noses, and dark eyes. Alexis had her hair pulled back and wore gray coveralls, rubber gloves, and a perpetually pissed-off expression.

"Hurry back sis!" She sounded less-than-happy to be cleaning out rabbit hutches. Ha.

Vincent reclaimed center frame and made his fingers into bunny ears, his own version of a wave. "Enjoy the solar system!"

Clarissa's seat mate leaned over, staring curiously at the screen. The spaceship wasn't roomy, and they were squished elbow-to-elbow in the narrow chairs. Meaning Clarissa had no privacy. The woman wore a white dress, which didn't look comfortable for travel at all. Clarissa much preferred her coveralls, pink and covered with velcro squares meant for patches from all of the places she would travel to. So far, she had filled six out of ten squares.

"Is that your future husband?" the woman asked.

"None of your business." Clarissa scowled and turned off the device. Everyone on the tour had been extremely nosy the entire trip. They were all intent on talking about future weddings and setting up new homes. Clarissa knew when Vincent handed her the ticket as a gift this trip would be with a cheaper company. Training rabbits didn't bring in much money. She had at least expected some level of customer service. They hadn't provided any sort of history or guided tour at any of the stops yet, just a curt reminder about the departure time before they were turned loose for their layover. It was a wonder she had managed to find the gift shops to collect any patches at all.

Worst tour company ever. Clarissa planned to leave a negative star review when this was over and she returned safely back home to Lunar Colony III.

"I can't believe we have to go all the way out to Pluto." Clarissa's seat mate craned her neck to look out the window at the tunnel as they descended deep under the planet's surface. "I mean, is anyone actually stopping here?"

Pluto. Dark, cold, and on the very edge of the human solar system, Clarissa looked forward to this stop more than any other. She wanted to stare into the vastness of unknown space, and then return home to tell everyone about it. Which sounded too melodramatic, so she said, "Pluto mushrooms are the best. Don't you want to try one?"

"Ugh." The woman made a face. "No. I want to get back to sun and civilization, meet my husband, and hope his apartment is decent. You can never tell with these videos they send. He could be a slob who borrowed a friend's place to film."

"Yeah, ok." Clarissa bobbed her head, even though she had no idea what the other woman was talking about. Most of the people who had started this trip had left at different ports, acting as if they were moving to a new place instead of coming home. Others had joined, with so much luggage it surprised Clarissa it had been allowed. She only carried a small backpack.

Clarissa looked down at the itinerary on her screen. Moon, Mars, Ion, Titan, all were crossed off except Pluto. She had thought it odd there was no return list, and assumed the return ticket would be issued once they arrived at the last stop.

The docking light above the seat flashed red and the ship gave a familiar jerk as the docking clamps locked. Tucking her device in her pocket, Clarissa waited for the passengers to file through the narrow rows and descended the docking tube to fetch her bag and find out about the return itinerary. The docking tube ran longer than at any other stop, taking a full five minutes for the elevator to descend all the way to the cavern below.

Flood lights lit the stone cavern, about three times the size of the spaceship passenger bay. Several shops lined the walls and a handful of tunnels branched in different directions. The flight manager, a thin woman in a blue pantsuit with the HEAE logo on the chest, handed out boarding time slips to the rest of the passengers as they dispersed for a few hours to stretch their legs. She shook her head as Clarissa approached and pointed to a space beside her. Confused, Clarissa waited until everyone else had departed, most clustering at the small cafe built into the rock face a few feet away.

"Have you got my return itinerary?" Clarissa asked.

"Return?" The woman blinked, her expression turning brittle. "They should have made it clear this trip was one-way. There are no return voyages on the Happily Ever After Express. Ah! There he is." The flight manager beckoned to a man waiting at the docking terminal. "Mr. Arnold! May I introduce Clarissa. Clarissa, this is Doug."

Doug was a squat man with a receding hairline, and what little hair he had remaining thin and greasy brown. He had small eyes, a long nose, and a weak chin. His palm felt clammy, but his grip firm as he shook Clarissa's hand. He seemed nervous, and his words came out in a rush. "So happy to meet you! I've got everything ready, just like we talked about. Please—let me." He reached for the bag as the flight manager handed it over, then frowned. "Is this everything?"

"I—yes." Then Clarissa shook her head, determined not to be distracted from her main question. "No. What about my ticket?"

"Read your contract, dear." The manager retreated into the tunnel and shut the door firmly.

Clarissa stared at the door. Vincent wasn't the brightest. Had he really bought a one-way package on accident? Or was this some sort of a joke? If so, it wasn't funny. Yes, Clarissa wanted to explore Pluto. After, she wanted to go home. Only Alexis would find something like this funny. Her sister had a warped sense of humor. Clarissa remembered Alexis cleaning out rabbit hutches, something Alexis who loved fancy champagne and high fashion would never enjoy. This entire mix-up felt like her doing, and the thought made Clarissa shiver.

No. Ridiculous. No way could Alexis mess with her ticket all the way back on Lunar Colony III. Clarissa needed to find a communication port and talk to the company about her ticket.

"Please, this way." Doug gestured to a small, open vehicle with large rubber tires parked near the elevator doors. He loaded her bag into the back seat. Was there actually going to be a tour at this stop?

Beside her bag sat two crates of flat round, organic discs with mottled brown-and-beige skin.

"Mushrooms." Clarissa's eyes lit up at the sight of them, momentarily forgetting about the lack of return ticket and the angry call she needed to make to customer service to get it sorted out. "You just drive around with them sitting out? These are worth five thousand each back home."

Doug shrugged. "Nobody is going to steal them. We're all mushroom farmers here. I don't know why people in the inner system think they're so special."

"No sun, ever," Clarissa explained, recalling her reading. "Plutonian deep surface minerals and the imported worms." Clarissa took another look at the mushroom farmer in front of her. "So, are you my tour guide or something?"

Doug laughed. "I can be. But I thought you'd want to see your new house first. Get settled. Maybe go see the minister?" His face turned red. Nerves?

"Why would we see a minister?" Clarissa asked, suddenly wary of climbing into a vehicle with this man. She needed to find a communication terminal and call the tour company. Thinking about it now, Happily Ever After Express didn't sound like a tour company. It sounded like a honeymoon thing.

"To get married!" Doug beamed, his smile displaying surprisingly straight teeth. "I know your last video said you wanted to tie the knot right away, but I thought you might want to wait a week and see how we settle in." He paused, expression falling. "Or have you decided to leave already? I know the tunnels can be strange at first. Please give it a chance."

"Married?" Clarissa repeated, a cold shiver running through her. This whole trip had felt odd from the start, and if Alexis had given her the tickets, Clarissa would have been asking questions from day one. They'd been a gift from Vincent, and she trusted him. He wouldn't team up with Alexis against her. Would he? Clarissa turned away from the vehicle, heart hammering, hoping her suspicion wasn't true, and scanned the rock cavern. "Do you have a real-time Earth capable relay?"

"There's one back at the docking station." Doug paused, his expression both sad and resigned. "This way." Doug led her to a black terminal built into the rock wall between the cafe and booth selling apparel that consisted mostly of coveralls and goggles. "It isn't much, but it works great. Our technology is top notch."

"Yeah, yeah." Clarissa scanned the controls, quickly figuring out the dialing system, and put in Vincent's number. The screen swirled with colors for a full five minutes before his face appeared, smiling as always, with an orange rabbit in hand.

"Hey! Didn't expect a real-time call. How is it going? Taste a Pluto mushroom yet?"

"Hey, Vin, not yet. Soon. I think I'm gonna get my chance real soon." Clarissa paused, searching for the right way to ask her question without throwing around premature accusations. "Silly question, where did you get my ticket?"

"Ah, that." Vincent's expression fell and his face turned nearly as red as Doug's. "If there's any trouble, you'll have to go through Alexis to sort it out. She bought it, said you'd never accept from her, but you might from me. I can get her—"

"Don't bother." Clarissa cut the screen, not ready to say anything more to Vincent. Alexis was an expert manipulator. No doubt the story had been convincing and Vincent had believed every word. This wasn't his fault, and he didn't deserve to be yelled at. Her hand curled into a fist, wishing she had something softer than a brick wall to slam it into. Preferably, Alexis' face.

## Doug

"You ok in there?" Doug called through the bathroom door. It had been an hour, and the woman had alternated between sobbing, screaming, and laughing several times as she showered. "We've got water rationing here. Can't get a new supply for two weeks."

The water shut off. The woman did not emerge.

"Right." Doug sighed and returned to the dinner table where he had set out the porcelain plates and real bread with mushroom soup for a welcome dinner. The soup had gone cold, and the sign hung across the kitchen entryway seemed to be mocking him. Doug and Clarissa Forever, surrounded by blue hearts. It had been her idea. The other one, the twin sister to the woman currently hiding in the bathroom, who had set this up as an elaborate plot to—what? Play a practical joke, or get rid of her sister for good?

Only this morning, Doug thought he'd fallen in love with Alexis. He had played her videos on repeat for the past week. He had cleaned up his small home, he had made mushroom soup, he had even hoped they might be married by now. Every part of this life for the past six months had been built around the hope Alexis would be his bride. Now, he had to face the reality she had never cared at all. Every word had been a lie, every video part of a scheme in which Doug was just collateral damage.

No sense wasting good soup, even if he had nothing to celebrate. Doug tapped the handle of his spoon, waited a moment until the wide end glowed yellow, and dunked it in his soup, stirring to spread out the heat. The musky scent of mushroom filled the room, something far too familiar. Doug had made the soup for his bride-to-be. Like most farmers here on Pluto, he barely touched the stuff. The inner system folk who ate Pluto mushrooms were too obsessed with its rarity to know it tasted like dirt.

Doug called up an image on his data pad, a portly woman with short, steel-gray hair dressed in dark coveralls, mushrooming goggles pulled up onto her forehead. "What do I do now, Ma?" he asked the image. "I know you built this business for the family, but if I haven't got any family to leave it to, then what's the point?"

Doug scrolled through the list of recordings on the side of the screen. A laugh, a song, a recorded conversation from dinner one night when the mushroom haul had been particularly low. "Now son, hard times will come." Doug mouthed the words with the recording, sipping at his soup. "That's the life we chose out here. We don't give up, we wait and see what tomorrow will bring."

The bathroom door opened and Dough spilled his spoonful of soup across the table in his haste to shut down the recording. Clarissa's eyes were red, her hair a mess. She didn't look at Doug with the same level of rage she had before.

Doug rose to his feet and gestured to the empty place. "Soup's on."

Clarissa sniffed at the brown concoction, and Doug had to show her how to ignite her spoon so it could heat things up for her. She tasted the soup warily, then frowned. "Tastes like dirt. Are these Pluto mushrooms?"

"What other kind would we have on Pluto?" Doug pushed his soup aside and handed Clarissa a slice of bread.

"Ok, that's not so bad," Clarissa complimented after tasting the bread. "Is this what you usually eat out here?"

"No, this was my…my wedding feast. We usually eat ration bars, dried fruits shipped in from Io and Titan when we can get them. Life on Pluto is simple."

"Simple." Clarissa nodded, setting her bread aside. "How does someone find a job out here?"

He should have expected this. He knew she wanted to leave. Still, some part of Doug had wished she would give this place a chance. Maybe they could get along and make a home together. No. She had been tricked. She needed to get home to her man with the rabbits.

"I have no idea, I've worked the family farm all my life. There's only five hundred people in this colony, and most of them own their own business. If we married, then you'd own this farm with me and work it with me."

"Mushroom farming." Clarissa shivered. "In the dark. I mean, how do you get sunlight here?"

"We don't. I've never seen the sun, or the surface." Doug only knew the floodlights of the caves or the dark infrared of his mushroom goggles. "You get used to it," he offered.

"Who chooses this life?" Clarissa immediately shook her head. "Sorry. Clearly you chose this."

"My Ma chose it," Doug corrected her. "I was born here, and it's been difficult to find anyone willing to come this far, well…" he trailed off. Great way to make things more awkward.

"Sorry." Clarissa looked up, over Doug's head at the banner hanging across the ceiling. Her eyebrows rose and she looked back at him, actually seeing Doug for what felt like the first time. "Alexis did a number on you too, huh?"

Doug shrugged. "Is your sister always such a good liar?"

"You have no idea." Clarissa played with her soup. "You know how some twins are so close and do everything together? Well, Alexis has been acting like I stole her face since we were born. She hates it when I have anything she doesn't. She broke my doll when we were five, she broke my data pad when I got into accelerated classes and she didn't. When I got a boyfriend, she pretended to be me and now he's never speaking to me again."

"What about that man you called with the rabbits, Vincent?"

Clarissa gave a half-smile. "He's a good guy. I wanted to get back at Alexis and he was willing to play along. We're not together. He's not into girls as far as I know. As long as I helped with his rabbits, he didn't mind playing boyfriend for me. I thought Alexis would try to steal him and then be super embarrassed when she realized he couldn't care less. I never thought…" Clarissa gestured at the tiny kitchen around them, as if that explained everything.

"Ever think Pluto could be home?" Doug asked. He had been in love with her face for so long, it was hard to let go of his feelings.

"I'm amazed I haven't had a panic attack yet, honestly. No windows," she shivered. "This place freaks me out. At least in the spaceship we could see the outside."

A message alert interrupted them, a cheerful tune Doug hadn't heard before. Clarissa darted across the room to fetch her pad from her bag and called up the video message. The dark-haired man, Vincent, filled the screen. His eyes were moist, his expression firm. This time there were no rabbits in the grass behind him. "I've got an offer," Vincent informed her, voice trembling. "Freckles, Porky the second, everyone. It's only half the ticket price." He wiped his eyes. "Maybe the bank can lend you the rest?"

"No." Clarissa stared at the screen in shock. "Why would he—" She dropped the data pad and shook her head. Somehow, she looked even more upset than when she realized she had been tricked into taking a one-way ticket to Pluto.

"Who is Freckles?" Doug asked.

"His rabbit. Vincent trains rabbits. I know, stupid, right?" She shook her head. "He can't sell them. He loves those little fluff balls." Clarissa's fist pounded the table. "It's enough for me to qualify for a loan for the rest. I can be out of here as soon as another ship arrives."

"That'll still be three weeks." Doug realized he was already mentally preparing himself to have Clarissa around for the next month, with no romantic expectations attached. He nodded to the data pad. Very rarely had Doug seen anyone show the level of kindness Vincent had shown to Clarissa. Doug didn't know much about rabbits, yet the look on the other man's face had told the story. Those rabbits were as important to Vincent as Pluto mushrooms were to most other people. "It seems Vincent might like you more than you think."

"No, he's just like that. Too kind for his own good." Clarissa put her hands on her head pulling at her hair. "If he sells all his rabbits for this, I am going to hate myself for it for the rest of my life. Ugh! I can't—" She paused. "How else do I get home?" She looked up at Doug, sudden hope in her red-rimmed eyes, and he knew before she asked exactly what she wanted. "You paid for my ticket here. You make five thousand apiece on those mushrooms. Can't you send me home? Then you can sue the company or Alexis to make up the cost."

"It'll take three years to save up enough for another ticket." Doug didn't have to do the math, he'd already done it when he bought Clarissa's ticket. Mushrooms were valuable, but fuel, fertilizer, and living expenses added up. Doug didn't have any savings left. Silence fell between them, awkward and heavy. Clarissa dabbed at her eyes to prevent fresh tears.

"Can you tell me what it's like on Lunar Colony?" Doug asked. Was it a good idea to ask her to talk about home? Maybe not, but her expression cleared as if having anything to talk about was helpful.

"Lunar Colony III." Clarissa keyed up another video on her data pad and slid it across the table. "Here, the videos Vincent made me for the trip here. Reminders of Luna, sunrises, stuff like that."

Sunrises. Doug cradled the data pad as it showed a recording of Vincent with three rabbits in his lap watching as the sun rose out a wide window. He'd never seen a sunrise, never even seen the stars. In all his life, Doug had never seen the outside of a Plutonian cave. He played the next video, and the next, drinking in the sights of a different world. He had hoped his new bride would bring something of her world to him. It seemed that wasn't going to happen. If Doug wanted to see the rest of the solar system, he'd have to get off this rock.

When Clarissa finally went off to curl up on the small couch, Doug retreated to his room. He called up the image of Ma on his own data pad again.

"Grandbabies." Ma's tone, warm and hopeful, surrounded him. Doug could still remember her smile as she thought of being a grandmother. "Five or six of them running around, helping with the harvest, creating new breeds, tunneling out further so we will have the largest farm here. Put old Porter to shame."

"I can't build the life you wanted Ma." Doug had allowed himself to fall for Alexis' lies because he wanted to please Ma. Truth was, he had never been happy on Pluto. He had hoped a spouse would change things. Maybe part of the reason he had bought into the lies was because he wasn't doing what he really wanted. Besides, Vincent had done nothing wrong. He shouldn't have to sell his rabbits. The look on the other man's face had gotten Doug thinking, and now he knew what he had to do. Doug closed out the image and called up his real-time communicator instead. Two clicks and he made his call. A man appeared on screen, dark hair disheveled, wearing red pajamas instead of his usual coveralls. Kyle Porter, Ma's nemesis. "Doug! What's wrong?"

"Wrong?" Doug repeated, confused.

"I assume you wouldn't call this late unless you had a bad cave in or outage."

Doug checked his chrono. He'd lost track of time and woke Porter more than halfway through sleep cycle. Nobody called at this time of night unless it was an emergency. He should have waited a few hours. Too late now. Porter was awake and curious why he called. Might as well ask. "I'm selling. You still buying?"

Porter's eyes grew wide and he licked his lips. "If you are pulling my leg—"

"No. I'm selling." Doug waited for the rush of nerves or regret. Neither came. He felt only anticipation. He had always wanted to see the sun.

## Clarissa

The bubble of champaign and the clink of silverware on porcelain underscored the sounds of chatter filling the restaurant. A view of distant Earth's blue oceans filled one window, stars filled the other. The view was what brought some Earther's here just for dinner. It was the perfect kind of place to show off your money, or your new boyfriend. Made sense Aexis had picked it.

Clarissa scanned the crowd, looking for her sister. Per Vincent's message, they should be here by now. Once he realized how Alexis had tricked them both, Vincent had wanted to stop any communication with Alexis. Clarissa had reminded him they had good reason to be worried Alexis would retaliate if she didn't get what she wanted from him.

So Clarissa had offered to finish things, if Vincent could keep up appearances until she got back. Apparently, keeping up appearances meant letting Alexis think the relationship was moving forward.

"This is incredible." Doug stood beside Clarissa, looking out-of-place among the wealthy, classy clientele. He still smelled like mushrooms and didn't own any clothes other than jumpsuits. The wait staff would not have let him in the door, if not for the law keepers in tow. A visit to the local law keeper office, a succinct telling of the story with Doug to back her up. The law keepers agreed Alexis would go to prison for kidnapping. If the story proved true.

They needed a statement from Vincent and verification the two women looked identical. Both of which Clarissa could get here. The fact the arrest would make a scene bad enough to embarrass Alexis for the rest of her life gave Clarissa a great deal of satisfaction.

"Rabbit farming must make more money than I thought," Doug surveyed the room, sounding impressed.

"No," Clarissa shook her head. "Alexis works here. She earns points toward a free meal every year. She uses it to show off."

"Ah." Doug nodded, then pointed to the back. "There."

Alexis and Vincent sat at a small table by the far window, the view of Earth visible behind them, toasting with champagne. Vincent looked stiff and uncomfortable in a black suit jacket while Alexis looked gorgeous in a strapless, sparkly dress Clarissa would never dare wear. Alexis' dark hair fell nearly to her waist, twice as long as Clarissa's, and there was a smug look on her face as she posed cheek-to-cheek with Vincent for a photo with Earth in the background. Then she pecked Vincent on the cheek and sauntered toward the bathroom.

"Suspect spotted," one of the black-uniformed law keepers pointed after Alexis.

"You wanna scare half a dozen women, be my guest," his companion shook her head. "We can wait until she comes out."

"What if she spots us and runs?" Doug asked. Vincent had already spotted them and was picking his way through tables toward them.

"I've got this." Clarissa peeled away from the group, following her sister into the bathroom. They could not look less alike today, Carissa with her hair matted and sweaty from the long trip. She hadn't bothered to shower or change after disembarking. Still, as she entered the bathroom and approached the mirror, the second face reflected there looked more like her than she wanted it to. They were such different people it didn't seem fair they didn't get their own faces. Alexis held a stick to her eye, repairing her make-up, so absorbed in the task she didn't notice the second face in the mirror until she put the tube away.

Her sister's look of surprise made Clarissa smile. Alexis stumbled backwards at seeing a second face like her own. She spun around, eyes wide, her expression quickly turning to happiness. "Sweetie! Oh my gosh, you made it back!" Alexis' tone sounded convincing. After all, she'd had years of practice. Clarissa had listened to her sister's lies grow better and better every year. For a moment, she almost wanted to accept the hug, almost wanted to believe Alexis was relieved to see her.

Clarissa had accepted apologies too many times before. On the long trip home, she had had plenty of time to think, to steel herself for this moment. Alexis would get no sympathy today, no traction for her lies and manipulations.

"Yes, I did." Clarissa kept her voice cold. Alexis' expression foundered briefly before she found her footing and smiled again.

"You got to see the entire solar system! That was your dream, and you made it home so Vincent's little mix-up wasn't a big deal."

Her play acting so light, as if they could brush the entire incident off as a happy accident. Although it made Clarissa's blood boil, she didn't let her anger show. Alexis would feed off of any emotional response, either blaming, shaming, or cajoling, so Clarissa gave her sister nothing to work with.

"Well," Alexis continued, brushing an invisible speck off of Clarissa's shoulder. "You should know while you were away, Vincent and I made a connection. I was going to break it to you gently, but we're here together."

Clarissa had several things she wanted to say. *I know, Vincent told me.* Or, *you didn't connect in the way you think you did.* Or, *it doesn't matter because the law keepers are waiting outside this door to take you to prison.* There were too many options, none seemed right. For Alexis, words were weapons. She would turn them and twist them around.

Clarissa's hand clenched into a fist. She knew how to make her point.

The law keepers wouldn't like it. Clarissa might have to spend a night in jail or pay a fine. She didn't care. Her fist connected with Alexis' nose, sending her sister staggering backwards into the sink, hands clasped over her face with a shrill gasp. A woman exiting a stall stared at them for a moment, then ducked back behind her door.

"Sorry!" Clarissa called. She turned away from Alexis, opening the doors for the law keepers who were waiting anxiously, hands resting on the butts of their stun weapons. Doug stood beside them, staring out the window at Earth. Because of the lack of windows on their return ship, Doug had yet to see his coveted sunrise. On the other side of the law keepers, Vincent watched the bathroom door anxiously. His eyes widened and he gestured urgently to Clarissa.

"You didn't!" Alexis sharp fingernails dug into Clarissa's scalp as she pulled her sister back by the hair. Clarissa gasped, flailing under the ferocity of Alexis' attack. The law keepers jumped into motion, pulling the two sisters apart. In seconds it was over, Alexis cuffed and unable to lash out despite the murder in her eyes. Her stance deflated as she saw Doug and heard his statement, and then Vincent gave his. The law keepers took everyone's information for trial subpoenas, and escorted Alexis away while the entire restaurant watched in shock.

"Thanks." Clarissa held out her hand to Doug. "I don't know if they would have taken my word alone."

Doug shrugged and nodded to Vincent. "They would have taken his word too."

"No, they needed all of us." Vincent looked at Clarissa. "Do you want your old job back?"

"I think it's time for me to move on." Clarissa looked from Doug to Vincent, noting how both men were shyly not looking directly at each other. "But Doug here needs a job. I'm going home for a proper shower, which I haven't had in two months. You two should talk."

## Vincent

She's gone. The thought held two meanings for Vinent. On the one hand, he was relieved to see Alexis taken away in cuffs. She would not be able to exact revenge on him or his rabbits. On the other hand, Clarissa had just left him here with the mushroom farmer, a small man with soft hair, smooth skin, and kind eyes. His clothes were out-of-place in a restaurant like this. Vincent felt they were practical and comfortable. Besides that, this man brought Clarissa back. He hadn't owed her anything, yet he had done the right thing.

That meant the mushroom farmer was a good guy. There was no reason for Vincent's cheeks to heat or for his palms to sweat with nerves. He had nothing to fear.

"You must be Vincent." The Plutonian held out his hand and Vincent shook it firmly. The skin felt soft and musty, probably due to the mushrooms.

"You must be Doug. It's nice to meet you in person. Thank you for getting Clarissa back here and calling before I sold Freckles and Porky and the rest."

"It wasn't your problem to fix," Doug replied simply.

Vincent shrugged. "It wasn't yours either. Clarissa said you had to sell some land to pay for the ticket." Vincent could imagine how hard that must have been, just as hard as it had been to make the decision to give up Freckles and the rest. He owed Doug for saving them.

"Yes." Doug shrugged. "Mushroom farming wasn't my dream, it was Ma's. Selling the farm gave me enough to do whatever I want. I've always wanted to travel and see the sun." Doug looked toward the Earth-side window. "When is sunrise?"

"In about an hour," Vincent stammered as he realized what Doug had said. "Did you sell the entire farm?"

Doug nodded. "One-way ticket. I realized no one would come join me on Pluto and if I wanted a different life, I had to find it somewhere else."

"Oh." Vincent could not imagine changing his life overnight, but this man didn't give off the impression of being reckless. He seemed more determined and somehow happy as he stared out the window at Earth's blue ocean. "What's next on your plan? Find a wife?"

Doug shrugged. "Wife or—someone. I'm open to possibilities. My only plan was to see the sunrise."

"You could watch it here." Vincent gestured to the empty table Alexis had reserved for them. She wasn't going to be using it tonight. "Would you like to join me? The mushroom soup here is excellent."

Doug shuddered. "No thank you. I will be happy if I never eat another mushroom again. They taste like dirt."

Vincent pressed his hand to his chest in mock horror. Mushrooms featured in all his favorite dishes. "That's only because you don't cook them right."

Doug's eyebrows raised in curiosity. "Really?"

"Really." Vincent nodded. "I can show you. It's the least I can do after you saved Freckles and everyone."

"How is Porky the second's leg doing?"

"Much better." Vincent paused, realizing what had just happened. Someone had asked about his rabbits, someone who actually seemed interested in the answer. "I've got him on a spinach diet and he'll need therapy for a few more weeks. Did Clarissa tell you?"

"She showed me your videos. I know about Freckles and Porkchop and all of them. I'd love to meet them. Clarissa said you have grass. I didn't know you could grow that under the Lunar domes." Doug talked about sun and grass the way a hungry man talked about food.

"Everyone says that, but most people just aren't willing to do the work it takes. I have to have it for the rabbits." Vincent paused, heart hammering. Most people didn't like it when he talked so much about the rabbits. Doug kept asking questions and actually listened to the answers. Not even Clarissa had done that. She would ask, then tune him out halfway through. "Do you really want to meet them? I can introduce you, and make you rabbit stew. Lapin Chassuer, it's an Earth recipe."

"You eat them?" Doug looked horrified, as if he'd just lost a friend.

"No, not the live ones!" Vincent shook his head forcefully; he didn't want Doug to get the wrong impression. "I mean, not the ones that have brains and stuff. I grow vat-meat from their cells. Just muscle, never been alive."

"That sounds…I'm not sure how that sounds." Doug gestured to the door. "If you're willing to show me, I'm willing to give it a try."

An hour later, Vincent sat on his patch of grass, belly full of rabbit and mushroom stew, surrounded by rabbits as Doug witnessed his first sunrise.

## Six months later.

## Clarissa

"You're cutting it close. This expires today." The minister looked at the marriage license and then up at Clarissa, an irritated expression on her face. She had a stern face and short cropped hair, wearing black robes that looked more like they belonged at a funeral. Maybe this woman did both. With five minutes until closing time, she probably thought she'd completed her work for the day. "One of the names on this has been crossed out."

"I looked it up," Clarissa informed her. "Substitutions aren't illegal. Besides, she's in jail." Clarissa felt free. At least for the next five years until Alexis got parole. Finally, she could live her life without her sister interfering.

"True." The minister picked up an official looking book and flipped to a well-worn bookmark. "Traditional ceremony? Religious preference?"

"Anything to make it legal." Clarissa held up her pen. "Where do I sign?"

"You sign after the ceremony. Where's your spouse-to-be?" The minister made a point of looking around her tiny office to show no one else was there.

"Oh, I'm not getting married. I'm here to witness. They wanted to walk in together."

The minister rolled her eyes. "I expect they want music too?" She tapped a button on the data pad on her desk and a wedding march filled the room. Clarissa smiled. Perfect.

On cue, a white-and-black flecked rabbit hopped through the door, a mushroom tied to its back serving as the cushion that carried two golden rings. Behind Freckles came Doug and Vincent hand in hand. They had never looked so happy. Clarissa clapped her hands until the minister glared her into silence so she could begin the ceremony.

~ * ~ * ~

**Jennifer M Roberts** earned her BA in History, but prefers to dream of how things might have been rather than focusing on how things really were. She hails from the Midwest and enjoys cooking, contra dancing, and historical re-enactment. Her fiction ranges from sci-fi adventures to epic fantasy to historical romance. An ordained minister, Jennifer has performed over 50 wedding ceremonies. She enjoys helping real-life couples find the right words to express their vows, and helping fictional couples find their way to a happily ever after. You can learn more at www.jmroberts.com.

# THE TITAN & THE PRINCESS

G.A. Babouche

## Titan Moon - 2579

### El-An

El-An flinched, his Earth Ambassador had just given him the news his bride-to-be's shuttle had been knocked out of the sky.

"What the hell do you mean?" El-An demanded. "Is she alive? Who did this? Where is the ship?"

"My liege, we are unsure at present as to what transpired. We are scrambling a team to intercept the last known location and search for survivors." The ambassador's body shook as he relayed the news.

"We are supposed to be forging an alliance with the humans. How do you think this looks? The whole point of me taking an Earth bride is to show them we are not barbarians. And yet, I must now tell them we have lost their Princess and she could, potentially be dead?" The King huffed.

"I am sorry, my liege, I have no other information. General Ty sent me to update you. We will let you know as soon as we have more intel on the situation."

"You had better find my bride!"

He had not even met her yet and he'd already lost her. That would not do. He didn't even know what she looked like. El-An had chosen not to look at her image as he didn't want a reason to decline. Once she arrived, he would have no choice except to proceed whether he liked her or not. His choice was political, not personal. A sadness erupted in his heart. His new bride may already be dead. He may never look upon her face now.

He looked out of the expansive window in his chambers. Suddenly, something punched through the sky and El-An's heart almost stopped.

### Leila

The Space Brides LLC representative had been rambling on

for the past half hour. Leila wasn't sure what she had been rambling on about as she'd stopped listening around five minutes in. She let out a long sigh. What had she got herself into? Looking around at the metallic shell she was encompassed in presently, made her heart beat faster. They had pounded through the atmosphere of Titan, Saturn's largest moon. No one had thought this moon would have been capable of sustaining life. Well, it hadn't been, not until the Titans arrived and terra-formed it to imitate an actual planet.

The people of Earth knew very little about this new world and it was with bitter-sweet trepidation Leila now arrived upon it. There was no going back now. She had been tasked with carrying the weight of her world and forging a path to this unknown nation. The Titan's real home seemed even more of a mystery, unchartered territory in every respect. Leila wanted to see this new land and angled her head to look out of the window nearest to her. Inadvertently moving closer to the Space Brides rep whose droning continued.

An explosion hit. Their shuttle rocked with a mighty jolt. Everyone shook like ragdolls. The rep screamed. The other two women shrieked. The pilot fought to keep control. The three soldiers accompanying Leila and the royal ambassador, assembled into action. Battling to secure everyone in their seats and trying to assist the pilot. That was, until the right side of the hull blew out and the three soldiers were sucked out into the atmosphere.

Leila went into battle-mode. She unbuckled herself and flew out of her seat. Running to the women first, she pulled them to the escape pods. Securing them in two of the pods, she pressed the release buttons and watched them disappear down to the ground. The ambassador approached, holding on for dear life.

"Get into the pod, Leila!" He demanded.

"You first, I have my suit on. You must hurry, I'll be right behind you."

The ambassador grimaced and tried to push Leila in. He stumbled. Leila took the brief opportunity to push him into the pod. She intended to follow. She did not have a death wish. Another explosion told her time was running out. Her attention turned towards the pilot. When her eyes tracked back to the ambassador, he sensed what she meant to do.

"Leila, no!" But Leila slammed the pod door shut and pressed the release button. The ambassador looked on with shock and sadness as he also tumbled downwards. Leila pushed on to reach the pilot. Fate was not good to him however and he suffered a hit by some errant shrapnel as the shuttle began to crumple and break apart with the oncoming g-forces. Leila pressed into the neck of her jumpsuit and a helmet appeared over her head.

The last pod had also been destroyed with the ships crumpling. The pilot had managed to stabilise the shuttle as best as he could but as the ground neared, Leila knew it wasn't enough to escape an extremely hard landing. Her suit could save her from extreme pressures and weapons, but she was not sure that it would be enough to save her from the crash. She braced herself for impact.

## El-An

Ever since his people had terraformed the moon Titan and made it their home, they had little interaction with the humans. He had sought to change that. He had only been crowned King a few months ago and his reign had already suffered a rocky start. The incident at hand was not going to help. This was a PR disaster of the highest calibre.

He watched as the battered shuttle hurtled downwards. Something inside him made him turn to his power. The power had been lacking so far. An El was chosen as King since they were descended from a lineage of beings who held great supernatural abilities. Unfortunately, aside from some parlour tricks, El-An's magik had not yet asserted itself within him. He knew his court grew restless and would usurp him if it did not emerge.

The King watched helplessly as the shuttle bounded closer. A sense of ownership mounting. That was his bride. *His.* He felt a burning rise inside his chest, and he outstretched his arms to channel the energy rumbling inside him. He directed the energy out towards the shuttle. For a moment, the shuttle froze in place, shuddering. Then it began to fall once more, only slower than it had been. El-An looked on in shock. Had *he* done that? His surprise caused him to lose his concentration and his attempt to freeze the vehicle again failed.

He prayed the impact would be lessened by this miracle. Had anyone else seen it though? El-An looked over his shoulder. Rex, the Earth Ambassador had stopped short, and it seemed he had witnessed what had happened. He looked on open-mouthed.

"Are my men enroute to the ship?"

"Ye…yes, my King," Rex stuttered out.

"I'm going down there. I will find her."

# Leila

What was left of the shuttle, lay sprawled out on a lush bed of verdant grass. The sensors on Leila's suit flashed and then emitted a low-level electric shock to entice her back into the living. As her body shuddered, she gasped and sat up ram-rod straight. Looking around her, eyes blurry, desperately trying to gain focus, it dawned on her what had just transpired. She had been in a monumental crash and yet, she'd survived.

She looked down at herself in sheer surprise, inspecting her body. She did not seem to have any major injuries, unless she was in shock and wasn't registering them yet. Her head throbbed and part of the blurriness of her eyes was blood trickling down inside her helmet. Leila was no doubt concussed but glad to be alive. She gingerly got to her feet and surveyed the scene around her. *How was she alive?*

She looked out of the fragmented shuttle and saw she was in the midst of a forest or jungle. She couldn't be sure which. It was beautiful, nonetheless. Vibrant colours hit her vision with such intensity. The brightest green grass and flora that almost sparkled like colourful gems. It was breathtaking. She took a step. A wave of dizziness and nausea enveloped her. Stumbling, she grabbed onto what was left of a console to steady herself.

It was then that she heard a low, rumbling growl. Leila froze in place. That was the sound of an animal, she was sure of it. Faint rustling reached her ears just outside the slab of metal concealing her. Then scratching against the hull. Leila looked around for a weapon. The best she could find was a twisted metallic piece of a chair leg. Leila squatted, keeping watch, and eased the chair leg up trying not to make any noise. As the animal rounded the corner and appeared before Leila, she gave a gasp. It was a beast! A thing that looked like a panther but was twice as big with elongated silver talons on its paws.

As she waved her pathetic weapon in the air, the beast let out an almighty roar and pounced. Flying towards her, fangs dripping saliva in a twisted display. Leila managed to strike it on its chest and then flipped to the side in a swift movement. Adrenaline ensuring, she kept moving. As she tried to twist away again from the incoming monster, its paw managed to strike out and ripped her across the side of her abdomen. She fell, bleeding. Then all went dark.

## El-An

The search party had reached a clearing where the potential escape pods had landed. It did not take the King's soldiers long to locate the fallen travellers. As the first pod was spotted, El-An quickened his pace until he was standing in front of it in record time. He peered into the reinforced glass and saw it was occupied by two older women, perhaps of forty to fifty Earth years. His soldier's yells pulled his attention away. Another pod had landed nearby, and they'd located it. He ran to join them, hoping it contained his bride. He found another woman of about thirty Earth years he'd say. This was his bride. She had flowing blonde hair. Aside from that, she was, as he'd expected—average.

He sighed as he contemplated this. At least she wasn't completely unattractive. She was alive, that was what mattered. El-An had one of his soldiers unlock the pod and revive the princess. She stirred, then her eyes flew open. A terrifying scream followed as she flapped about, trying to escape the pod. One of the soldiers grabbed her arms, trying to pacify her. The woman stilled when her eyes locked onto El-An.

"King El-An," she whimpered.

The King rushed forward. "You know who I am?"

"Of course, I do. I've come here for you."

"It is alright Princess. We will look after you now."

The woman looked at him strangely and opened her mouth to respond, when another of El-An's soldiers interrupted. They'd found the shuttle's crash site.

"Secure the princess and get her safely to the palace. I will go on to the ship," El-An announced to his first-in-command, Ty. The general gave a nod and El-An stormed past, into the jungle.

~ * ~

The King took in a sharp intake of air as his eyes fell on the shattered remains of the shuttle. It was truly a miracle anyone had survived at all. His musing was interrupted when he spied a dark mass within the vehicle, hovering over something. El-An gave a roar as his men circled the ship. He unsheathed his silver sword and ran forward, much to the disappointment of his soldiers. They fanned out, making space for him. The panther turned its head, tensing for attack. Before it could make a move, El-An leaped into the air, landing inches from the animal and swiped his mighty sword across its throat. It fell in two pieces. It's head landing with a dull thud.

The grimace on El-An's face turned to concern when he noticed the injured woman on the floor. He knelt down immediately, checking the stranger's injuries. The woman had a huge slash on her side, lacerations to her arms, yet it seemed her jumpsuit had properties aiding her. It dawned on him that she must have come down with the shuttle. *Impossible.* She shouldn't be alive. He felt her pulse as his soldiers gathered around, two were carrying a gurney. This woman's lifeforce was draining, he sensed it. He may not have his powers fully yet but there was one thing he could do. *Heal.*

He laid his hand on the woman, surprised when a shock emitted from her to him. *Must be the suit.* He ignored the sensation and concentrated, his hand began to glow gold. His essence flew into her, healing her major wounds. The woman's head was turned away from him and he grew curious to see her face. When he felt enough energy has been released for her to live, he slowly removed his hand. His soldiers moved into place, to secure her for transport. El-An's eyes fell on the remains of a console before him. Perhaps he would be able to see what had occurred on the ship.

He advanced to it and prayed it would be intact enough to relay images from the trip. Pressing a few buttons, which lit up, demonstrating still enough power remained. El-An motioned to one of his soldiers who he knew was good with tech, to access the database archives and playback what had happened. The soldier took a short moment to work his expertise before the images began to play before them in a holographic state.

"Forward to the point it went down," El-An ordered.

The soldier obliged and they looked on in concern as they witnessed the explosion. El-An's face contorted in disgust then it turned to amazement as they all watched what the woman had done.

"She saved them," the soldier observed.

"Extraordinary." El-An said with awe. "The woman must be the princess's guard."

That would explain the suit, he thought to himself. "You must find the missing pod, there's a man still out there, probably the ambassador."

A couple of his men nodded and departed to find the missing royal escort. El-An's gaze turned to the woman strapped to the gurney. A soldier was trying to remove her helmet, to no avail. The King burst forward with an unknown sense of ownership. He pushed the man aside and stared down at the unconscious body. He had seen a suit like this before. If he remembered correctly, the mechanism for the helmet should be located on the suit itself. He swiped on the neck of the suit and the helmet dematerialised before their very eyes. El-An almost jolted when he looked upon the woman's face.

She was beautiful. He had never felt anything like he did at that moment, looking down on this stranger. He could not look away. His hand raised to reach for her cheek. He stopped himself. *What was he doing?* El-An composed himself and addressed his men.

"Get her to the Doctor immediately. I want her looked after as if she were of royal blood," he commanded. The soldiers nodded and wheeled her away as he looked on in wonder.

## Leila

She awoke with a start. As if emerging from a nightmare. Then it dawned on her that the nightmare had been real. *Was she dead?* Leila looked down at herself, patting over her body. Her hands encountered soft, smooth fabric, like silk. A silken sheath-like dress. *Not dead.*

Looking around the surroundings, her eyebrows raised. She seemed to be in some kind of elaborate bed chamber, not a hospital as she would have expected. Leila was surrounded in decadent extravagance. The bed she was on was huge. Bed covers an exotic satin or silk, spun like gold. Much of the room was glass and seemingly high up. *Maybe she was dead?*

Leila felt her head. It had been bandaged. Perhaps she was just concussed or worse, hallucinating? She felt her body but did not seem to have any other injuries. *Hadn't she been hurt?* She remembered the panther, or whatever it was, and a quiver ran through her. Before she could ponder more, the doors to the chamber swished open. Her head darted abruptly to the person entering.

"Ah, you're awake," the pretty woman said with a smile.

Leila looked at her blankly. Then her eyes travelled to her rather revealing outfit. A small crop top of shimmering silver accompanied with a figure-hugging skirt with two slits on either side, revealing her legs. Her figure was to die for.

"How silly of me, I haven't introduced myself. I am Eve. I am part of the royal court. I serve the King."

"I see," Leila said softly, uncertain what had happened while she'd been unconscious.

"The King is very glad you are alive and has made a decree that you are to remain in the royal household. He is very impressed with your actions on the ship, as are we all. You are to be his guest."

Leila continued to stare at Eve in a lost fashion.

"I'm rambling, I'm sure. Here, I have brought you some clothes, as instructed by the King," Eve continued as she held out the bundle of clothing in her arms.

"Thank you," Leila responded, still awfully confused.

"Rest up now. I'll check up on you later and escort you to dinner."

Before Leila could respond, the spritely Eve had bounded out of the chamber and the doors hissed closed.

*What was going on?*

## El-An

He was flummoxed. As El-An sat in his throne room, pondering the events of the day, he found his mind wandering back to the mysterious woman. It was not his style to fixate on a female, so this was highly disturbing to him.

His Earth Ambassador entered the room.

"What wonderful news the princess has been found. Crisis averted. We can now ensure that the wedding festivities can begin."

El-An tilted his head up. "Is it wise to have the wedding so soon, the princess may need some time to get over the trauma of the crash." *Was he stalling?*

"Yes, of course my King. As you wish. I was just thinking it would be a good way to solidify your reign."

The ambassador was right of course but El-An needed some time. *Definitely stalling!* He was just about to make another suggestion when his brother came barrelling into the throne room.

"So, the princess has been found, no intergalactic incident then!" The King's unruly brother, El-De, stated. Slyly he asked, "but who is the woman in the other royal suite? I heard only the princess was travelling from Earth—Valencia?"

"That is none of your concern, brother." A visibly agitated El-An responded.

"It is my concern when a commoner is in a royal suite. I'd like to know what is going on. Also, I hear she is quite beautiful, unlike your princess!" El-De said with a sardonic grin. "Perhaps I will go see for myself."

"You will do no such thing! She is not your concern. And you should not be so derogatory towards your soon to be sister-in-law."

"Oh, you just want them all, don't you? Interesting. I told you before it was a bad idea to be making alliances with the humans. We do not need them. They are inferior to us."

The ambassador, who had been silently observing the conversation, now coughed uncomfortably. El-An glanced at him. "Has the royal ambassador been found?"

"He has, my liege. Your general, Ty, should be bringing him to you shortly."

El-An nodded. "As you can see, I have many matters to contend with at present. We will meet at dinner." His silent command to his brother to leave.

"But of course." El-De gave an exaggerated bow and then left the room.

The King sighed heavily. He did not trust his brother. Ensuring the humans were safe was paramount. As if on cue, the royal ambassador appeared, escorted by Ty. He gave a bow and the King waved a hand to show it was not necessary.

"Is the princess safe? Did she survive? Your soldiers wouldn't tell me anything."

El-An approached the royal ambassador. "Your name is Aaron, correct?" He asked as he placed a hand on his shoulder.

Aaron nodded in return. "Aaron, your princess is safe, and I am very glad that you are too."

"Oh, thank God, I was so worried. I need to see her. I thought she was dead!" He said frantically.

El-An nodded and removed his hand from Aaron's shoulder. "The princess is in the West Wing with the Space Brides representatives and another of the survivors is in the East. I felt it better for her to remain there as she was injured."

"I'm very sorry to hear that, do you know which of the women it was?" Aaron asked but then his head tilted in thought, "but the princess isn't hurt? I'm so surprised about that. You see she…"

"I assure you, she is fine. You may see her as soon as you have rested," El-An interjected.

Aaron nodded and left with Rex.

It was time to see how the woman was doing and finally get her name.

## Leila

She was still in bed as she couldn't muster facing what was ahead. Leila thought she heard footsteps approaching and so straightened up a little. Expecting it to be Eve again, she barely turned her head, until a towering figure stood at the foot of her bed. Leila gasped and scrambled for the bed sheets, pulling them up close to her neck.

The man regarded her for a moment, eyes trailing over her. She returned the favour. Whoever this man was, he was gorgeous. Built like a warrior, muscles rippling, strips of gold criss-crossing his chest in place of a shirt. He had to be around six foot three, no hair but he carried it well and did not make him any less handsome.

"I'm sorry I startled you. I came to see how you are. I am the King of Titan, El-An," said the man in a rumbling, deep voice.

*Oh, this was the King! Uh oh!*

"You will be glad to hear that your companions from the ship are safe and well. The princess made it to us in one piece and all thanks to you."

Leila looked on, blankly. *Did she hear that right, the princess?* The King must have taken her silence as proof that she was still unwell.

"I'm sorry, when I healed you, you had your helmet on, so the effects did not reach your head."

"You…healed me?"

"I did. Magik exists in our culture unlike on Earth. Here, I will show you."

He crouched down beside her and placed a hand over her bandage. A light glowed where he touched her. She felt a warmth and then the pain she had felt—stopped. As their eyes met, something passed between them. It was fleeting but there all the same. El-An quickly rose. He cleared his throat as he stood.

"I would like you to stay on, as a royal guard. I saw what you did on the ship, it was astonishing, what bravery."

Leila's face once again twisted in confusion. The King tilted his head, his expression thoughtful. He turned to leave but the doors opened, and Aaron strode in. He balked at seeing the King there but then his eyes landed on Leila, and he ran to her, embracing her warmly. El-An frowned.

"Thank God you are alright. I feared the worst!" Aaron lamented.

"I'm so glad to see you, Aaron." Leila exclaimed, clinging to him.

El-An coughed. Aaron finally seemed to realise the King was still in the room, he looked between him and Leila. "Your highness, there has been some kind of a misunderstanding…" Before he could continue, Leila had grabbed his face, turning him to her and signalled to him to keep quiet. Aaron was bemused but conceded.

"What Aaron means is we need time to de-brief after the crash and look into what happened."

The King did not look convinced, in fact, he looked all together furious. He inclined his head, "I shall see you at dinner. Please, treat the palace as your own." He spun on his heel and stormed out of the room.

"Mind filling me in on what's going on? They think the Space Brides rep is the princess! What the hell is happening?!"

"I wasn't too sure either but it's beginning to make perfect sense."

It still wasn't making any sense to Aaron if his face was anything to go by.

"This is ideal. It's my chance to be free! Don't you see, I don't have to get married or be a Queen. I can let that, Stacey, I think it was—take the mantle."

Aaron's mouth flew open, "you're serious about this. Have you lost your mind? You signed a contract! We could get into a lot of trouble. The game will be up as soon as he hears your name!"

"He doesn't know my name. The contract merely stated *Princess of Valencia*, not any name. The princess could be anyone."

Leila had chosen not to look at the photo of the King, his appearance had thrown her but if there was a chance she could be free of royal life, she'd take it.

"You know I've always wanted to be a soldier. This is my opportunity."

"But you can't leave here and what of the contract? Also, do you really think that Stacey can be a Queen? She seems like a complete half-wit!"

"I can coach her. The King has already offered me a job as a royal guard, it fits perfectly."

Aaron huffed. "This is too risky," he warned her. What if the agency finds out?"

"They won't. I'll figure it out. Why were there two other reps on the shuttle anyway?"

"Well, they hitched a ride back to the Titan head office of Space Brides LLC. Actually, they've already left to re-join their office."

"Meaning, no one will know who I really am, right?"

"Correct." He didn't look happy.

"We need to find out what happened to the shuttle. That was no accident. Something is afoot."

"I agree. I will start looking into it."

## El-An

He left that room in a foul mood. Why had it irked him so much to see Aaron embracing the woman like that. *Woman. Damn it.* He hadn't got her name yet again. As he raced through the passageway that led to his chambers, he bumped into Ty. His general looked surprised to see the anger in his face.

"My King, we need to talk."

El-An snapped out of his brooding and finally looked at Ty.

They made their way to El-An's study, just off from his bed

chamber. A rustic, antiquated space which was in stark contrast to the rest of the palace. El-An bristled, *was he jealous? Were Aaron and the woman together? Why couldn't he shake the image of her striking green eyes?* El-An looked up and saw Ty regarding him curiously.

"What is it, Ty? Did you find any evidence and play-back the rest of the holo images?"

"I did and it's a tad worrying. The explosion wasn't organic, it was man-made. A bomb."

"You're saying this was deliberate? As in, sabotage?"

"Looks like it. I did warn you that there are many not happy about an El marrying a human."

El-An nodded thoughtfully. He knew many thought humans were an inferior species. But to be so callous? "Make sure there is extra protection around the princess and the other humans."

Ty inclined his head in consent. "If I may be so bold?"

"Speak freely, you are my closest confidante."

"Well, my King, you seem quite taken by the guard woman it seems?"

"How did you—"

"I was watching the holo images remember, I saw what happened before *and after* the crash." Ty responded with a wink.

"I'm drawn to her."

Ty had not expected El-An to be so frank. "Oh hell!"

"My sentiments exactly. I did not envisage this turn of events."

"I think Space Brides LLC may have been in on this ruse. It's the only thing which makes sense. Either knowingly or not, they have helped in some manner."

"You think they would put their own people in jeopardy?"

Ty shrugged. "If the price was right? Perhaps the woman guard was assigned to ensure the reps would survive?"

"They would not have risked the princess? There's a lot of money tied up in this contract. Furthermore, the guard saved the princess."

"Unless someone else wanted the princess dealt with? Like your brother?"

"You think the woman guard has something to do with it?" El-An thought back to what transpired in her chamber, something had not been right about the situation when Aaron had appeared.

"I want you at the dinner, let's see if you pick anything up from the humans' interactions." El-An did not want to believe the woman was involved. Ty had a hidden gift of noticing what others did not.

# Leila

After Aaron left, the first thing Leila did was storm over to Stacey's room. *What was this chick playing at?* As the doors swished open, Stacey, who had been languishing luxuriously on a chaise longue, abruptly stood.

"I can explain…I tried to tell them. But then I thought you were dead, and they were being so nice—"

"So, you thought you'd just take my place and be Queen?"

"I…I…I'm really sorry. But you're back now, I can just leave the palace quietly, no one has to know. We can say I was just filling in for you, right?"

"Wrong. Do you know what the punishment is for impersonating a royal personage?"

Stacey shook her head solemnly.

"Certain death."

Complete shock rolled over Stacey's face. The poor girl looked like she was going to keel over right there. Leila almost felt bad about winding her up. *Almost.*

"Please help me. I'll do anything."

"I was counting on that. You see, you're going to have to see this through till the end."

"Uh, what do you mean?" She asked suspiciously.

"You're going to carry on impersonating me and marry the King."

Stacey's jaw dropped. "But—but—they'll know. What if they find out?"

"They won't. I'll help you."

"Why would you do this? Why would you give up being the Queen?"

"I have my reasons which you don't need to know. Now, are you in or do I call the guards?"

"I'm in, I'm in." Stacey stuttered out.

"Great, let's get ready for dinner then."

Leila went back to her room and not long after, Eve came by

to 'dress' her for the dinner. Again, one of those tiny outfits, silk crop top and long skirt with a large slit up the side. Her brown hair adorned with curls and a fancy gold chain rested through her hair and forehead. *Uh, she looked like a princess!*

"I was surprised when the King instructed me to give you a gold dress." Eve shared.

"Why's that?"

"Well, gold is reserved for royalty. No one else is allowed to wear the colour."

"Oh." Leila whispered. *But why had he let her wear gold?*

"He probably knew you'd look so good in it." Eve added. "You're rather beautiful for a royal guard."

Eve dropped Leila to the banquet hall, where several guests were already seated. Leila spotted a nervous-looking Stacey and took the seat next to her. Aaron sat across from her. To his right sat another handsome man who looked a lot like El-An but with a mop of dark hair. Brother perhaps? As she sat, he stared a tad too long at her. The other guests must have been courtiers or something, they whispered to themselves, staring at her and Stacey. The King's general, sat towards the middle of the table.

A hush fell as El-An entered the room. He certainly made an entrance. Dressed in his gold criss-cross armour thing and a Trojan-like gold skirt? He looked straight at her as he walked over to the banquet table. Taking a seat at the head, with Stacey to the right and Aaron to the left of him. His eyes remained on her. She felt uncomfortable and averted her gaze as a heat had risen in her.

As she looked up and to the right, she noticed the brother regarding her curiously.

"I am El-De, El-An's brother. It's good to see you are all well after that nasty crash," he said through tight lips. "I don't think I have had the pleasure of your name?"

"I'm Leila," she answered with a careful glance at the King. He was still looking at her. In fact, he didn't just look. He smouldered. A small, sexy smile twitched at his lips.

"Leila," he tested the name on his tongue. *Why did he sound so good when he said it?* "I hope you are well now?"

"I am, thanks to you." Leila said meekly and the King inclined his head to her. *Meekly? Since when was she meek?*

The attendants ascended and filled the table with all sorts of strange dishes. Everything was muti-coloured. The food looked like dessert. When she bit into it, savoury flavours hit her mouth. Hues of pinks, turquoise, and even gold adorned the table. There was even something that looked like chicken but on a much larger scale.

Leila happily tucked in and relished the explosions of tastes on her palate. She bit into a bright pink macaron-like appetiser and smiled. It tasted like shepherd's pie! Her eyes went to El-An and he seemed to be happy at her delight. He bit his lip as he watched her and she almost choked. Aaron glared at her. *Why?* Leila decided she was done with her food. Her gaze swept over the grand banquet hall. She hadn't had much time to soak in the palace. She realised now that much of the building was glass, or something akin to glass. Given how high up they were, it must have been reinforced somehow. The glass was all gilded. Decadently opulent.

"How do you like the food, Stacey?" The King asked.

"It's alright I suppose."

"You have not sampled much. You must try this dish." He said as he held out a platter to her.

"I'm not really used to this kind of food or treatment, it's really a little over the top—"

Leila kicked Stacey under the table and the latter stilled.

The King cocked his head in contemplation.

"What the princess means is she tends to lead a rather simple life and is very down-to-earth compared to other royals," Leila explained.

"I see," El-An said as he gave his general a pointed look.

The dinner continued without any upset. Leila felt relieved when the final dishes were served. Then what looked like cocktails were wheeled out. There was an elaborate balcony on one side of the banquet hall. Curiosity got to Leila, and she rose to inspect it. She felt eyes on her but dared not turn to see. As she looked out over the vast expanse of the royal city. She marvelled at the shimmering glass buildings that twinkled in the twilight. The wind out on the balcony should have been enough to blow her away, given how high up they were. And yet, there was a stillness and barely a breeze that simmered around her. *Amazing.*

Leila became aware of someone approaching behind her. She stiffened involuntarily, knowing it could only be the King. The weight of his presence could be felt like a void that sucked all energy within it. He was all-consuming. Even the air grew heavy with his breath. She turned to look at him and their eyes met. Energy seemed to fizzle around them. She pulled her gaze away.

"Tell me, Leila, how did you wind up being a royal guard?"

Leila trembled a little, not wanting to say the wrong thing but in front of him, the truth seemed to fall so easily. "I always wanted to be a soldier, Aaron and I grew up in the royal household. I always wanted to do what he did. So, I followed when he trained to be a royal officer."

"The royal ambassador is also a soldier? Interesting."

Leila almost kicked herself. She'd said too much and the tension between them was a little stifling. He made her dizzy.

"I think it's time for me to retire."

## El-An

He watched as Leila sashayed away. How could he be so enchanted by her in a single day? During the dinner, she had such fresh-faced wonder, unlike his bride who had picked and prodded at everything with a scowl on her face. He shook his head to clear it. El-An had noticed quite a bit, as had Ty. They'd had brief words before he'd made his way over to Leila. Drawn to her, like a magnet. All on the table must have noticed as he'd made no effort to hide it. Even her outfit would not have gone unnoticed. Was he just trying to rub it into the stuffy courtiers' noses?

But as much as he wanted Leila, he still needed to get the truth. For one thing was clear, she was hiding something. He waited perhaps fifteen minutes, then followed after her, picking up a little something on the way. The look of shock on Leila's face as he stood at her door, gave him a little thrill.

"I have brought something for you," he said with casual charm. Leila looked frantic and then she froze in place when he offered her a golden bracelet.

"What's this for?"

"A gift. For having saved the life of the princess."

"You really didn't have to—" El-An did not wait to snap the bracelet onto Leila's wrist.

She looked down at her arm, stunned.

"Now, you will tell me all I need to know. That bracelet is

charmed with the power to compel the truth from anyone."

Leila tried in vain to pull the bracelet off but it was of no use. It only tightened in its place. "Why are you doing this?" She wailed.

"Because I need the truth. Do not struggle, it will tighten with every lie you tell me, and will begin to crush your wrist."

She looked at him in horror. He almost went to hold her but stopped himself. Leila gave up and plonked herself down on the side of the bed. A tear trickled down her face.

"I'm sorry. I have no other way to get answers." He sat down facing her and wiped away her tear. He felt her shiver at his touch. "You act more royal than anyone who was present at the dinner earlier. Forgive me."

Leila seemed to implore him with her eyes. He held strong.

"You aren't human, are you?"

Leila's eyes went wide but she was compelled to answer. "I'm half human."

"I suspected as much when I saw your speed and strength fighting the beast and how you managed to survive the crash. No normal human could have done that. It does not matter to me where you are from. But I need to know who you are." He could see her trying to withhold the truth and not reply but the bracelet tightened until she finally burst out,

"I am Leila, Princess of Valencia."

El-An visibly recoiled. He had not been expecting that. "You did not wish to marry me?"

"I had no choice. My family hate me, presumably because they know I'm only half human and therefore not pure blood. You were the one that assumed I was something which I was not. I merely went along with it, thinking that it would buy me my freedom."

Leila took a deep breath before continuing. "I thought you wanted Stacey because you had seen her and assumed she was the princess. Plus, you offered me something I had always wanted, to be a soldier."

El-An was stunned into silence. But he had to ask.

"Do you find me attractive?"

She answered without hesitation, "yes."

"And do you want to marry me now?"

El-An watched her war with herself. She pursed her lips, trying to seal them from the truth. The bracelet tightened, and she winced in pain.

"No!" She cried out, but the bracelet continued to tighten. "No." She implored but the bracelet squeezed further, cutting into her. Leila's eyes were fresh with new tears.

El-An could not take anymore.

# Leila

She watched as he ripped the bracelet off her. Her wrist was bleeding and marked by the savage tentacles of the bracelet. He tenderly took her hand and raised it to his lips. She watched in alarm as he licked across the length of her wrist. Leila felt warmth and then her wound disappeared. She snatched her arm back and paced to the window, looking out so she wouldn't have to look at him.

He approached her, turning her toward him.

"It's alright. I want you too."

"El-An," she pleaded.

He leaned into her.

"It is cute how you attempt to say my name. Say it again."

"El-An," she purred.

He could not resist any further, he grabbed her waist and pulled her close, crushing her lips with his. He heard her moan into the kiss and his body responded. Their tongues entwined passionately. Until he withdrew from her, cursing under his breath.

"What are you doing to me?" He hissed.

This was her chance to be free and yet, she did not want to be free of El-An.

"Why does it feel like this?"

"In our culture, we believe in 'fated mates'. I always thought it was a fairy story. That is, until I laid eyes on you. In fact, even before I did, when you were on that ship, plummeting to your doom, I knew you were there, and I had to help. You're the reason my powers manifested. To save you, my magik came alive. To save my mate."

Leila gasped. Is that why she had signed that contract, without even knowing what he looked like, because really, her soul knew?

"I do not care if I sound insane but you, Leila, will be my Queen."

~ * ~ * ~

**G.A. Babouche** is a multi-genre writer, encompassing elements of sci-fi, fantasy and historical fiction.

Born and brought up in London, she first began writing as a teenager, focussing on poetry and dark fantasy. She graduated with an LLB Law degree and worked in Finance. Finally putting pen to paper again when the pandemic hit. She is currently working on a series of books, debuting with: Aurora Warrior Princess—Emissary of Justice.

When not writing, you can find her indulging in horror, sci-fi or superhero flicks, armed with a cola and plenty of sweet treats!

Short stories:

"Revelations of a Space Rebel" is featured in a 'Cloaked Press' sci-fi anthology entitled "Spring into Sci-fi" 2023 edition.

"Paralysed" is featured in 'SFWG & Cloaked Press' anthology entitled "Nightmare Fuel—Mind Terrors" 2023 edition.

Twitter: @bubbleguzz

Instagram: @G.A.Babouche

# HER BIG FAT LUNAR WEDDING

Jean Martin

"Where are you getting married?"

"It's called LunarSpace," Blythe sounded genuinely excited. That was something of a rarity. She had her sweet sixteen party in Paris, celebrated her high school graduation at The Four Seasons, and made her debut in Dallas, New York and London. It took a lot to excite Blythe.

"LunarSpace is on the Moon, right on the Sea of Tranquility, which isn't really a sea, you know. It's like way cool. Kleo Klaussan, on *The Klaussans,* is getting married there too, but not until August. I'll be there before her."

"You're getting married on the Moon?"

"Yeah," Blythe enthused. "It's the coming thing. There's a hotel there now, with a caterer, a videographer, a priest, a minister, a rabbi, a justice of the peace."

I wondered where the justice of the peace was from, and how you would get a license to get married on the moon. I figured that wasn't really my problem.

Space weddings had been a thing for the ultra-wealthy for a few years now. The couple would book a spaceship, and you'd see them on the news, floating in their wedding spacesuits, saying their vows in zero gravity.

The guest list was always small. There's only so much room on a spaceship, and not everyone is cut out for space travel.

The ceremony would, of course, be live streamed on a big screen TV, for those who remained earthbound. Then there would be a big reception when the happy pair landed.

That way the couple would get lots of wedding presents.

I presumed Blythe's lunar wedding would be much the same.

I knew there were companies trying to promote lunar tourism. The chief appeal was the novelty and the expense. I did not know a hotel had been built on the Moon, let alone a wedding venue.

"LunarSpace just opened six months ago," Blythe explained.

She showed me pictures of the first lunar hotel on her phone.

I wasn't impressed. The furniture looked cheap and sparsely set, the lighting dim and it was difficult to see details. The staff looked somewhat dispirited.

"We'll say our vows in the Lunardome." A picture of a pair of models, one in a gown, one in a tuxedo, standing before a huge window with a view of the rising earth. "Isn't the view incredible!"

I agreed, it was incredible.

"It's expensive, of course."

For Blythe Corrigan, expensive wasn't simply an adjective, it was more of a virtue.

"They've got everything. We can get our hair and nails done, get massages, before the wedding. Of course we're going to live stream it."

I wasn't surprised. Blythe's first word was "selfie".

"Daddy says we should get like ten million views. So that will pay for everything. Then I'll get all that loot from people."

Blythe's second word was "mine".

"So, you'll be my maid of honor?"

That came as a shock. I wondered if I'd been her first choice, or the others had turned her down. I wondered if I could afford the trip. "Uh, what's it going to cost, traveling to the Moon?"

"Daddy's chartering a ship for the bridal party. So, it won't cost that much."

Blythe's definition of that much was probably higher than mine. Her father is one of the one percent of the one percent. The onesies she wore as an infant had designer labels.

The figure she gave—surprised me. Even with the dress it would actually be affordable; if I worked a little overtime, and spent Thanksgiving at home.

"It's going to cost," she agreed. "Means, Uncle Glen and Aunt Tonya won't be able to afford the trip, and neither will Darby's trailer trash cousins. They're family and all, yet they're tacky."

Blythe shook her carefully highlighted curls. She looked down at the pair of models on the phone screen.

"We'll be married like this," she enthused. "It'll be incredible, and we'll get like two hundred million views, easy."

I wondered what her fiancé, Darby, thought about it all.

I had been surprised when they got engaged. Darb's attractive, of course, someone as lovely as Blythe, wouldn't be seen with a man who looked ordinary. Still, I wouldn't have thought he was her type.

His people were well off. That was how they put it. His uncle a celebrity doctor. His father a producer. Darby Fisher grew up among the rich and famous.

He had a doctorate in psychology. He worked for his father's company, in public relations. He was very patient with the great and powerful, including his future bride, and her family. Having lived among the one percent all his life, he wasn't impressed by them. More the opposite I would have said.

How he had fallen in love with a luxury loving pseudo princess like Blythe Corrigan was a mystery to anyone who knew either of them. Rumor had it they'd met through Space Brides LLC and agreed to get married. The heart wants what the heart wants I guess.

Assuming Blythe had a heart, and it wanted something besides spa treatments and designer jewelry.

She planned on having ten bridesmaids. She ended with four of us, willing to pay for the dress, the shoes, and of course the trip to the first lunar resort.

It would take us three days to get there. The ship Blythe's father booked was equipped with a bar and a restaurant serving real food, not stuff in tubes. Even a movie theater and a small club, with a disc jockey and dancing.

For those of us who didn't get sick from space travel, and didn't mind paying what they charged for meals, drinks and entertainment, it was fun.

Two of her bridesmaids spent most of the trip lying in their bunks, feeling miserable. Darby's best friend, Jim, could afford meals, but nothing else, and spent the three days either in his cabin, or looking out a porthole watching the stars and space debris.

They had a special lunar all-terrain vehicle to pick us up at the station, and take us to the resort, through a massive dust storm. The advertisement didn't mention dust storms. They're fairly common on the moon.

Blythe was not pleased. "How long is this going to last?" she demanded of the driver.

"I can't say." he tried to explain. "They come up sometimes. They can last for a couple hours, or a couple days. Though it's hard to tell time up here."

Dust swirled around us. The vehicle shook, ominously. Blythe whined to her father. Mr. Corrigan looked at his phone and glared. Darby swallowed as if uncertain. His mother looked like she might faint. I understood how she felt. I kind of felt the same way.

The exterior of LunarSpace was anything but palatial. It looked like the larva of some giant insect, a long, grayish brown tube, sitting amid the lunar dust.

"It's on account of the radiation." the driver explained. "Moon's bombarded with radiation from space, all the time. So, we got to have the shell over everything."

"But the pictures!" Blythe whined. "With Earth in the background and all the stars!"

"Uh yeah, we have that. If the dust storm's over and we can get things cleared off in time, you'll have your wedding in the dome. Otherwise, you'll have it in the ballroom. The ballroom's real nice. You'll like it."

"But we're live streaming!" Blythe shrieked.

"I'm paying a lot for this," Mr. Corrigan growled ominously.

"We were promised a wedding with earth in the background and stars." Mrs. Corrigan added.

"If the dust storm ends in time, you'll…" the driver began.

"Nothing in the stuff you sent us said anything about dust storms," Mr. Corrigan barked.

"They happen all the time here," the driver informed them again.

Blythe began to cry.

She is not the kind of person to sniff, apologetically, into a tissue. The sound she makes when she is not happy is somewhere between a wail, a howl and a whine. It's kind of like a smoke alarm, only not as melodious.

Darby put his arm around her to comfort her. For some reason this made her howl louder. Jim, Darby's best man, seemed to have an endless supply of tissues, he kept passing along to Darby, while the rest of us waited for the storms to end and wished we'd brought earplugs.

LunarSpace was kind of a dump. The furnishings were molded plastic, trimmed with chrome plated metal. The color scheme was institutional green, with gray carpets and drapes.

No natural light. There were some obviously fake plants, blooming in corners around the lobby and the hallways.

A few cheap, resin statues of cupids and Greek women in draperies, holding vases, stood by doorways. The ballroom was draped with some discouraged looking gauzy fabric, and lit by clear plastic chandeliers.

The water in the bathrooms smelled strange. We were supplied with scented soap, bath salts, bath oil and shower gel, to cover it.

Bottled water imported in bottles supplied from various springs on Earth. For the most part, complimentary.

Alcohol. No. Mr. Corrigan ran up his bill, as the dust storm continued, his wife whined and Blythe wailed.

Darby tried being there for his bride. He couldn't make the dust storm stop, so she could have her perfect wedding. Blythe was used to having what she wanted, and very disagreeable when she didn't have it. In the end, the bridegroom took refuge in the hotel bar, and sipped Pellegrino water, sometimes spiked with gin.

The resort offered us a complimentary spa day. That had a calming effect of sorts.

It was the best spa on the moon.

It was the only spa on the moon.

On Earth, you could find places like it in most of the finer strip malls.

Blythe's cousin, Alice, and I spent most of our time trying to keep her from having yet another meltdown and screaming at the woman who did her facial.

The hotel had been well enough insulated we couldn't hear the dust particles outside. In fact, we couldn't hear the storm at all. Windows were few, so couldn't see the storm. We felt like we inhabited a giant, furnished box, shut off from everything and everyone, except each other, and a somewhat harried staff. The Birnbaum Bar Mitzvah party, who were put out their celebration would be taking place in the ballroom, not the Lunardome with a view of the rising Earth.

I began making plans for what I would do when I arrived home, and the wedding was over. I had taken two weeks off from work. Ten days off for the wedding, and four days off to recover from it. Though I had thought it would be space travel I would find exhausting, not Blythe.

I found myself looking forward to four days of binge-watching historical romances and crocheting.

The storm ended sometime after the Birnbaum's reception.

The Lunardome was covered in dust, of course. We were told the cleaning crew would start immediately.

The Birnbaum party packed to return to Earth. Blythe had us all at the hairdresser's, sipping nonfat lattes, while we were coiffed, and made up almost, but not quite, to her standards.

We managed to get our own dresses on, while helping Blythe into her elaborate gown and tiara.

I paid three times what I would have paid on Earth, to supply Blythe with a strawberry daiquiri, in the hopes it would calm her down. She complained she'd smear her lipstick, and worried about spilling on her dress, as she sipped it. After a few sips she quieted.

The skies were clear as we stepped into the Lundardome.

Remember the glass bell your grandma had over her favorite figurine? That's what the Lunardome looked like. It wasn't glass, of course. The material it had been constructed from was much thicker and stronger. Made to repel solar radiation and stand up to lunar dust storms.

We could look out onto the Sea of Tranquility, and beyond to the rising earth among glittering stars. Almost made the trip worth it.

An usher escorted Mrs. Corrigan to the front pew, magnificent in peacock blue raw silk, with a huge orchid corsage on her well-maintained bosom.

Another usher showed Mrs. Fisher her seat, her dress equally elegant in gray satin crepe with cream colored lace.

The groomsmen were arranged in front of the altar. Blythe's brother, Jarrott, tall, thin and pimply, her cousin Gary, husky and just a little hung over, her sister's boyfriend Greg, looking worried. I thought it might have something to do with what the trip cost him.

Darby stood by the altar in his morning coat and ascot, with his best man,

Jim, standing beside him.

A short fanfare played before the processional. I started up the aisle, followed by my three fellow sufferers, and then the bride, Blythe, in all her carefully coiffed and made-up magnificence.

She glided down the aisle on her father's arm, with every eye upon her and her expensive gown.

Darby looked apprehensive.

His parents looked apprehensive.

The justice of the peace entered in a handsome blue tuxedo with a ruffled shirt.

The music played softly, as the couple recited their vows.

They kissed, and the guests applauded, as though they had just seen a theatrical performance.

The recessional played. Blythe and Darby walked down the aisle. Jim, the best man, took my arm, and we followed, then the rest of the bridesmaids and groomsmen.

We waited in the hall, until all the guests went to the banquet room, before we went back into the Lunardome, to be photographed, and photographed, and photographed again.

For a climax, Blythe and Darby were filmed waltzing in front of the giant glass window.

Then we adjourned to the reception, where the guests enjoyed their cocktails and *amuse bouches*, and the DJ set up for dancing.

The food tasted flat. The champagne tingly like it should. I've had better cocktails. They were equal to what you'd find in a mid-priced Earth Hotel.

We kept telling each other, we were on the moon and on a grand adventure.

All the toasts had a lunar theme.

The bride danced with her father, then danced with the groom, then the groomsmen all got up and did the Moon Walk.

After that, the reception proceeded like any other I'd attended in any other ballroom,

The cake tasted stale and I didn't finish my piece, dumping it in the trash.

In due time the bride and groom went off to do what they'd been doing since they moved in together, two years before. People still made jokes about it.

They spent the next twenty-four hours in their room, doing I don't know what.

I spent a little extra money to take the Moon tour, in the Moon Wagon. Might as well see the sights while I'm there.

I slept through most of the trip home. I was exhausted from space travel, and wrangling Blythe through one of the first lunar weddings.

I only had to talk to a few reporters. I'd only been the maid of honor. Blythe was the star as one of the first lunar brides.

Featured on all the major news networks, web sites, and late-night talk shows Blythe played the role of celebrity. She could crank out cute sound bites on cue, and smile winningly when necessary.

In a few weeks, she was well on her way to being famous for being famous.

Darby preferred to remain in the background.

The second reception at the Corrigan's home celebrated the nuptials. So, I had to have my bridesmaid's dress cleaned, and wear it again.

The food, a selection of dishes I could dream about, tasted better, as did the booze. I drank a little more than I should have, but not as much as Darby.

They moved into the handsome townhome Blythe's father had bought for them and settled down to open wedding presents and live happily ever after.

He'd lived with Blythe for two years. They hadn't been married before so it made a difference in their relationship. She whined about the problems they had. Darby didn't understand her and wouldn't let her have any fun. I hadn't thought about living with her tantrums and crying to get her way.

I came to dinner six weeks after the wedding. Blythe pouted because the caterer ran out of her favorite pate'.

Darby invited the people Blythe called his trailer trash cousins for a cookout on the Fourth of July.

Blythe spent the day in their living room, and insisted her friends stay there with her, and missed the fireworks.

I missed the party, when Blythe pushed Darby into her parents' swimming pool, because he called their wedding loony, instead of lunar.

I advised counseling. Darby thought it a good idea. Blythe had never been a great one for taking advice.

Anyway, she was busy. Besides her regular job, she still stood in the limelight, making the rounds, talking about her lunar wedding, consulting for a movie, working with someone on a line of moon modes.

She found it all very stressful.

Her father sent her to a spa in Colorado, where she spent two weeks being wrapped in Kelp, scrubbed with Himalayan pink salt, soaking in mineral water and designer mud.

While she was being pampered, Darby packed his things. He'd had enough of his wife's antics and desire for stardom. He moved out of their handsome townhome.

He left his job with his father's company, and moved to Ohio, where he found a position teaching at a university.

Blythe filed for divorce. Darby did not contest it. He let his former wife keep the handsome town home, the furniture and all the wedding gifts. He had had enough of the rich and famous.

A year after the divorce finalized, he met a graduate student, from a family of modest means. They were married, in a small ceremony in the university chapel.

By then, no small thanks to her wedding, Blythe had become a major influencer.

Now, of course, she has her own podcast and a bestselling book she didn't actually write. She is bringing out a line of beauty products at the end of the year.

She met the new love of her life at the Cannes Film Festival, promoting the film "Lunar Brides".

Her current fiancée is considerably more attractive than Darby, and every bit as patient. He is also richer than God.

I think her father was somewhat relieved when he heard LunarSpace had closed. The rich were reluctant to spend large sums for third rate accommodations, even on the moon.

He has promised the couple a villa in Tuscany, if they get married at his yacht club. The club has a beautiful picture window in the ballroom, with a magnificent view of the beach at Big Sur.

They are never troubled by dust storms, and there is no concern about radiation.

I have, again, been offered the position of maid of honor. It would mean I could wear my bridesmaid's dress a second time, which, considering what I paid for the thing, is an incentive of sorts.

I declined. I have had enough wedding lunacy for one lifetime.

~ * ~ * ~

**Jean Martin** has a BS degree in Journalism from Ohio University and has been laughing about it for longer than she cares to admit. She lives, at present, in McKeesport, Pennsylvania, with an orange tabby cat named Samwise, who likes bagpipe music.

# ROMANCE OF THE ALGORITHM

Laura Hilse

## On Earth...

The last woman sitting in the waiting room, Judith forced herself to remain positive. This had to work. She focused on projecting calm, competence, and sex appeal. The first two came naturally, but the last one had proved elusive in the past. Finally, the Space Brides Minneapolis manager called her name.

Once they were both seated, the interviewer began looking over the application details on her computer screen. Judith took time to study the woman, Pamela James, who was stick-thin with short brown hair, and a no-nonsense demeanor.

"Cutting it a little close on the quarterly deadline application, Ms. Sutherland. I see yours came in just before midnight last night. Are you a procrastinator by nature?" she asked. "And your photos look like selfies, not the professional headshots we encourage."

"I've been contemplating my decision for several months, actually. You can appreciate, I'm sure, one shouldn't rush into such important life decisions. So, no, I am not a procrastinator." Judith smiled brightly and hoped she'd rehearsed her lies enough to be convincing. She knew how things worked, as she usually asked the provocative questions to shock people. "I chose selfies because I find they represent the real me." That part was true. She liked the photos she'd used showing her dark brown curly hair framing her face with a summer tan accenting her blue eyes. The angle softened her long face. She knew she wasn't a stunning beauty, but she looked happy in those photos and it made her more attractive.

"What is your main reason for signing up with Space Brides, LLC?"

"It's hard to pick just one. I'm looking for some adventure in my life. I'd like to do it with a compatible life partner. I understand your company prides itself on having a match-making algorithm with a ninety percent success rate on the first try, which is an amazing accomplishment." Determined to show she'd done her homework, Judith hid the fact she'd only researched Space Brides a few hours ago.

Pamela relaxed for the first time and leaned back in her chair. "That's correct. No other companies even come close to our numbers." She leaned forward again and concentrated on the screen. "One lack I see with your application is you haven't any of the background or experience we often look for. You have a degree in journalism and grew up in a suburban setting. You don't have any military, trade school, or agricultural background indicating you can handle tools or deal with tough situations, either physical or mental."

Judith herself leaned forward. "I do have physical and mental toughness. Journalism has shown me I learn quickly and I'm not afraid to ask the difficult questions of important people." Judith forced another smile as she thought about certain questions she'd asked a few weeks ago, causing her to run for her life. "I fully expect, whatever situation I land in, I'll be able to master the details within a short time. Who knows, maybe my new community would appreciate a journalist to help record their struggles and accomplishments. As time permits."

"Well, I must say I was skeptical about your application before meeting you. Let's see if the program thinks there are any possible matches." She tapped her screen a few times and scanned the results, while Judith kept an eager, hopeful expression plastered on her face.

Finally, Pamela looked up and said in a puzzled tone, "Yes, there are some possibilities, but the algorithm is withholding details pending your test results. If you pass the testing phase, you will have prospective husband profiles to view." She paused and shook off her uncertainty. "I'm confident you'll find one of them to be a wonderful life companion. Welcome to Space Brides, Ms. Sutherland. You'll be helping to build the future of humanity in space."

Three hours later, Judith found herself on a jet with about thirty other women heading to Houston, Texas, where Space Brides, LLC had the nearest intake center. The shuttle up to the interplanetary ship would leave from there. Judith settled into a window seat. The woman behind her sat down next to her and promptly introduced herself.

"Hi, I'm Kaj Vang." She had Asian features, shoulder-length black hair, and a friendly grin.

They shook hands. "I'm Judith Sutherland. Nice to meet you."

Kaj made small talk as they sat waiting for everyone to find a seat and strap in. Half listening, Judith offered short responses as she watched the line of women file in. When the flight attendant closed and latched the cabin door, she couldn't help but let out a sigh of relief.

Kaj looked at her and nodded. "Me, too. I half expected my father to track me down and drag me off the plane."

Judith wondered if she needed more of a backstory than just wanting some adventure in her life. She started by asking Kaj, "I take it your family wasn't thrilled with you wanting to do this?"

"No. I mentioned I was looking into it to my mother, and she went into hysterics. They've had their eye on a 'nice Hmong boy' I went to school with. I really don't want to marry him. They think I'm visiting a friend in another state. I'm going to wait to make sure I pass all the tests. If I do and I like one of my candidates, then I'll email them just before we leave. I can't stand the drama in my family. How about you?"

"Not having any luck with relationships here. I think the change will do me good." Judith tried to hide a yawn without luck and then apologized, "Sorry, it's not you. I'm just wrung out. I'm going to take a little nap. Wake me when we get to Houston?"

"Will do."

An hour later, Kaj woke Judith by shaking her shoulder. "We're about to land in Houston."

"Thanks," Judith responded. An hour hadn't been enough to make up for not sleeping at all last night. She forced herself to sit up and stretch. Soon they were wheels down. Instead of parking at a terminal gate, the plane taxied to a building off by itself on the edge of the airport.

The flight attendant announced, "Ladies, as you get ready to exit the jet, check your area and make sure you have all your personal belongings. At the bottom of the stairs, walk between the yellow lines and go into the Space Brides facility. Wishing you all lots of luck on your adventure helping to build the future of humanity in space."

The group of women deplaned and entered a large steel-framed building. The facility had a simple, almost spartan, feel to it. A map in the lobby showed a complex which included small dormitory rooms, a cafeteria, an auditorium, classrooms, and a gymnasium. Judith, Kaj and the others spent the rest of their day with official registration, room assignments, and looking over the packed schedule. Two more groups joined theirs, bringing the total number of women to around a hundred.

After dinner in the cafeteria, everyone gathered in the auditorium.

A Space Brides VP, Linda McLaren, stepped up to the podium to welcome them. A statuesque redhead, she wore jeans, a sequined top that sparkled under the lights, and a cowboy hat. She had a native-Texan voice.

"Ladies, right about now y'all are asking yourselves—" she paused dramatically. "What the hell am I doing?!"

Most everyone laughed, as intended.

"I'll tell you what you're doing." On the large screen behind her appeared the company's slogan. "Read it with me!"

The crowd responded with enthusiasm, "Helping to build the future of humanity in space!"

"That's right! Consider yourselves pioneers, just like some of your maternal ancestors might have been here in North America. There're lonely men out there on the Moon, on Mars, in the asteroid mining camps and beyond. They want love and companionship. Quite a few even want to start a family. The next few days are to make sure you are up to the challenges of space travel and living in unique environments. If you pass your tests, then comes the fun part of looking through your potential spouse profiles, viewing their videos, and making your own acceptance videos to send. Then you will be on your way!"

The room full of women burst into applause and excited chatter. Linda gave them a minute to settle down.

"I know you gals have had an exhausting day, so I'm not going to stand up here and blather at you. I have a short video for you to watch. Afterward, we'll send you off to bed so you can dream about the new lives awaiting you."

She tapped a button on her console controls and the video started. The eager group watched a photo montage of happy couples interspersed with short clips of women talking about how they loved their new married lives and how fulfilling it felt to build businesses and families on this new frontier. The whole show ran for about ten minutes and when it ended, the group applauded again.

Linda stepped back up to the podium, "I wish you all the best luck on your testing. Good night and sweet dreams!"

## On Mars….

Carson Landry tried to minimize what was on the computer screen as his brother Glenn barged in unannounced.

"Carson, did you finish—what are you viewing on the screen?"

Sighing, Carson pulled up the screen again. "I told you, I don't plan to remain a bachelor who sits around staring at you every night."

"Yeah, but I thought you meant to find somebody from around here." Glenn scratched his beard.

While they shared the same dark blond hair and gray-green eyes, Carson knew he and his brother were very different. Short, muscular, and the elder, by two years Glenn rarely stopped talking. Taller and leaner, Carson had heard their mother describe him with the old phrase: still waters run deep.

"The women around here are too young, too old, or too married already," Carson retorted. "I looked into Space Brides. They have a great reputation and they guarantee success. You fill out a questionnaire. They show you women their computer algorithm says will be compatible with you." On the screen a gallery displayed a half dozen women's photos. As they watched, one more popped into the line-up.

Glenn came over and put a hand on Carson's shoulder. "Are you sure this is a good idea? I mean, is it fair to the woman you pick, with your situation and all? Say, that one's cute. I've always been partial to redheads."

"Glenn, what was it you came to ask?"

"Hmm? Oh, did you finish cleaning all the filters on the nutrient pumps?"

"Yes, I did."

Glenn continued to scan the photos and short bios.

Carson waited for a few minutes, before losing patience with his nosey brother. "If you don't have any other objections, I'm going to pay the credits and find a wife. Are we good on that?"

Although Glenn was technically in charge of the family business they had inherited, he didn't usually try to boss Carson around. He shook his head, a look of concern on his face. "I've got my doubts about how smart a mail order bride is, but I understand." He grinned. "I'm going to be your best man, right?"

Once Glenn left, Carson went back to considering all the bios. Strangely enough, he felt most drawn to the newest candidate named Judith. Her photos showed her in a lush, green outdoor setting. No wonder she looked so happy. Her profession as a journalist concerned him. She had indicated on her application she was open to new jobs and helping existing businesses grow. His finger hovered over the screen before he ranked her number one. He pondered how to rank the others.

## On Earth...

By seven the next morning, the women had filed into the auditorium again, eager and nervous for the testing to begin. Linda McClaren and three others stood on the stage holding tablets and discussing arrangements. Once all the potential brides took a seat, Linda began speaking.

"Good morning. Here with me are your guides for the next few days. They will take you through the stages of testing and, if you pass, will help you with the rest of the process. Good luck!"

They divided the candidates into groups of thirty to thirty-five and assigned each group a guide. Deena Langley, a tall brunette who gave off a drill sergeant vibe, quickly had Judith's group lined up and focused.

She had a deep voice and a matter-of-fact manner. "Good morning. Our group is going to start with the actual physical. Follow me to the med labs. None of this should be new. I'm sure you've all have physicals before."

Sure, Judith had been through physicals before, but none this thorough. The med staff weighed and measured, poked and prodded. The lab techs took biological samples to check for genetic defects, pregnancy, and STDs. As they each completed the process, Deena escorted them to benches in the hallway to sit until the entire group finished.

Judith's group waited patiently with some whispered conversations. When the group finished their physicals, Deena checked the time and told them, "Next is the psych evaluation." She led them into a room with enough computer stations for all. They put on special headsets with built-in stress sensors and began answering question after question on the computer screen.

They got a break for lunch and an hour to relax. Deena collected her group and took them to the gym. The huge space contained numerous exercise machines and weight stations, along with an apparatus for testing g-forces.

"We need to know your bodies can handle the stress of space travel. We will work our way through these exercises and scan stations. If you make it through these tests successfully, you'll be on to the next stage of looking at prospective husbands. So hang tough and show me what you've got!"

Judith liked to think she was in pretty good shape. By the time she got to the g-force machine, perspiration covered her body and her muscles trembled from fatigue. A tech strapped her into the seat, and the machine began whirling around, faster and faster. She remembered the advice to clench her lower body and managed to make it to the end without passing out. She got a thumbs up from Deena as she climbed out and tottered over to a bench.

That evening, the women were quiet and subdued during dinner. The various tests had eliminated about twenty percent of them. Those who were left, Judith could tell, were exhausted. When the meal ended, Linda McLaren came into the room.

"Congratulations, Ladies. You have passed all your tests. Tomorrow, you'll meet the video versions of your prospective bridegrooms. Next, we'll have a day of space travel training and then you'll be on your way to a new, exciting life you've been dreaming about.

~ * ~

"The moment you've all been waiting for has arrived. Please find a seat at one of the computer stations. Use the log-in information we gave you and meet your potential mates," Deena instructed. The second round of women to cycle through the computer lab, Judith's group had waited with giddy excitement.

Once everyone claimed a computer, Deena continued, "There is a great deal of information about to come your way. The one thing Space Brides, LLC doesn't want you to think about when selecting a husband is financial status. We verify each potential husband has gainful employment. Other than that, we don't ask how much they have in a bank or what's in an average paycheck. I want to emphasize again, you should go into these relationships expecting to do some type of productive work. Out on the space frontier, every person needs to contribute. If you have questions or need help, let me know. Go ahead and put on the headsets."

Judith took a deep breath and let it out slowly, adjusted the headset, and then logged in. Within moments, two folders popped up on the screen, quickly followed by a third. Each folder contained a photo with some basic facts: height, weight, hair and eye color, age, and location. She studied just the photos to start with. She found all the men attractive. The first two were similar in appearance with short dark hair, average builds, and pleasant faces. The third man was tall, had long hair, and a lean face.

She clicked on the first candidate. Jacob Dunlap. In a professionally done video, Jacob walked through his living quarters talking about himself, then at his jobsite as supervisor at a nuclear power facility, and finally through a concourse in Mars' largest city. He seemed nice. An information file provided lots of other details, including: he would like to have children and had a passing grade on the genetic defects scan.

She tried the next person, Yoshi Takeda. He worked as a maintenance supervisor at one of the bases on the Moon. She watched his video all the way through, but knew she should get farther away from Earth if possible.

Judith clicked on the last folder. She met Carson Landry. He had the most intense gray-green eyes she'd even seen. Six foot and change, he had straight, dark blond hair pulled back into a tail, and a wiry physique. She smiled as his video started and he said, "Sorry, I know they recommend having a professional do this, but it's easier doing it on my phone." She liked his voice, not too high, not too low, but very masculine. She could listen to him talk all day. His video showed him mostly with a backdrop of green, growing things in his family's aquaponics business. He came across as intelligent, hard-working, and maybe a little shy. His video, much shorter than the others, seemed to her more natural. She immediately liked him.

She sat musing for a few minutes. Something about Carson pulled her back to his details, time and again. She felt a tap on her shoulder and found Deena standing there. She pulled off the headset.

"Any conclusions?" Deena asked.

Judith nodded. "This is the one, Carson Landry."

~ * ~

Fortunately, space travel agreed with Judith. She didn't experience any stomach problems. She took to the grav boots easily, and found plenty to do during the three-week trip to Mars. As she regained her sense of safety, she also fell back into her natural routine of talking to people and drawing out their stories. She wandered the ship, asking questions about how the crew handled their jobs and getting to know the other women. She wrote a dozen stories in her head, repeatedly realizing she no longer had a news organization to submit them to.

Judith also spent time reading everything in the ship's computer library about aquaponics. She gained some knowledge, yet knew it probably just scratched the surface. Once a day she took time to rewatch Carson's video. She definitely found him attractive. The thin scar that ran down the left side of his face didn't bother her, but did make her curious about how he'd gotten it.

Her conflicting emotions chased each other around in a catfight. She felt hopefulness for the future, panic at leaving behind all she knew, amazement he'd chosen her. Also guilt. To escape a serious problem Judith knew she was using this man. She planned to put a strong effort into making the relationship work. She wanted adventure in her life and a man to share it with. She knew half a dozen people who had met their spouses through a website. Using Space Brides wasn't much different. Was it?

She and Kaj spent lots of time together. Kaj had found her match on Mars as well, but not in the same city. They started making plans to be in each other's weddings, and to visit afterward.

"I don't want to jinx this. We really should give ourselves the full two weeks they suggest for meeting and getting to know these guys, before we start making real plans," Kaj commented as they sat in a lounge looking over an array of wedding dresses on the large computer screen.

"Yeah. It's more fun to look with a friend. How can we not look at dresses during this trip? Oh, that one's gorgeous!" Judith paused on a knee-length dress in a tight white material with some sparkly bits arranged in a swirling pattern. "It comes in lots of colors, too, if you don't like white."

"Yep, that's a nice one. Let's bookmark it for you. I think I want something a little more traditional. You realize we've only got two more days until we get there. I'm having trouble sleeping at night, I'm so excited. I hope he's as nice as he sounds in his video."

"We all do, Kaj. Like you said, we'll have some time to find out." *Because heaven knows we aren't all honest about everything. Just look at me,* Judith thought uneasily.

## On Mars...

Carson found himself waiting in a private lounge at the shuttleport with eleven other guys. Every one of them chewed gum, tapped toes, or paced while they watched the airlock lights. Carson opted to lean against a wall and tap his foot. Finally, the indicators turned green and the doors hissed open. A short, matronly-looking woman with a data pad shepherded a dozen women through and into the room. The men all came forward, staring intently to spot a familiar face. The women began looking through the group of men as well. Some gave a shy wave when they recognized their match from the video.

"I'm Madeline Brown of Space Brides, LLC. This is such an exciting day, one I know all of you have been looking forward to with eagerness and a touch of nerves. We're going to start with a group luncheon and then a tour of Cassini City. For dinner tonight, you'll dine alone with your prospective spouse. We have other activities planned for the next few days to give everyone time to get acquainted and comfortable. Please remember, it will take time. It's not a race."

She paused to consult her datapad. "I'm going to say the name of one of these fine women and her prospective husband. When I call your names, please come introduce yourselves. Sit and talk for a few minutes until everyone has been paired up. Kaj Vang and Johnny Bowman."

Kaj stepped forward with a big smile on her face and sparkling eyes to meet her guy. Johnny was only a couple inches taller than Kaj, with short sandy hair and even some freckles. He came up and gave her a chaste kiss on the cheek and took her by the hand to go find some seats. Kaj looked back at Judith and grinned.

Madeline kept calling names and matching people up. She called Judith's name last along with Carson's. He came forward tentatively and put out his hand to shake. "Hi, I'm Carson. I'm really glad to meet you."

Judith shook his hand and smiled. "I'm excited to be here and to meet you."

He hung onto her hand and guided her to a seat as far from the other couples as he could. They sat and he shifted as if uneasy. "How was the trip? Was it your first time in space?"

"Yes, my first time off planet Earth and the trip went fine. Very interesting too. Nice to be out of grav boots. How about you? Have you been off Mars?"

Carson hesitated, taking a deep breath. "I spent some time out in the asteroid belt when I was younger. I much prefer it here on Mars." His mind raced trying to find a question. "What's your favorite food? We've got all kinds of restaurants to pick from. Italian. Thai. Chinese. There's even an Ethiopian place."

"I like a variety, but the Italian sounds good," Judith responded. "If you mean for tonight?"

"Yes, tonight."

The awkward conversation continued as Carson forgot all the things he had rehearsed to talk about. Fortunately, Judith asked lots of questions. He knew he wasn't holding up his side very well. When the Space Brides chaperone finally announced time for lunch, he felt relieved.

He continued to hold her hand as they walked with the group to a nearby catering center.

"It's interesting what the algorithm finds in people's backgrounds," Judith observed. "It surprised me to read in your bio you'd lost your parents in your twenties. Is that one of the reasons the algorithm thinks we're compatible?"

"It is a bit unusual, isn't it?" Carson agreed. "It's not something I talk about much. They died in a rare shuttle accident. How about yours? If it's not too painful?"

"Similar, a car accident, an AI glitch. Still makes me sad at times." She glanced his way. "Knowing you've been through the same thing makes it easier to talk about."

He gave her a rueful smile and squeezed her hand gently.

~ * ~

After the long, exciting day, Judith relaxed when Madeline finally took them to their lodging, the Cassini City Grand Hotel. Judith realized it was people like Madeline who made Space Brides successful. The woman helped ease them into their new relationships, smooth over rough patches, and organize the actual weddings. Even before landing, her main advice had been, "Do not feel under any obligation to fall into bed on the first night with your prospective husband. Take all the time you need to get to know him. Make sure you feel comfortable with him. You are all going to have private rooms for when the time is right."

Judith just wanted to fall into bed and sleep. Kaj insisted they go to the group meeting with Madeline in the hotel bar. Judith and Kaj entered the dimly lit space and joined the others at their table.

Madeline raised the fancy drink in her hand to salute them, "Good, now that just leaves Erica."

Someone snickered. "She and Roy really hit it off, if you get my drift. She said not to wait on her."

Madeline sighed and smiled. "Well, I hope the rest of you feel just as excited about your matches. It's such a relief to get the first day over with. It's usually the most awkward. In my experience, things get better and better from here. Obviously, for Erica, things are already 'better'. If you're honest with the computer, the algorithm does a wonderful job." She paused to sip her drink. "Alright, any concerns? Anything you want advice on?"

The women looked around the table happily with shrugs and smiles. They shared with each other compliments about the men they'd met earlier.

Judith raised her hand and Madeline nodded at her. "I think Carson's the quiet type. I feel like I did most of the talking today. If I was interviewing someone, I could badger him for answers by restating the question over and over. In a budding romantic situation, I need a better strategy."

Madeline took another sip and replied, "Focus on open-ended questions and be patient. I will send all of you my list of the fifty best questions to start a conversation." Madeline fussed on her phone for a minute and sent off the list.

"Thanks, I'll look these over for ideas."

Madeline continued, "The other thing to consider, though, is sometimes the computer detects patterns we don't. The algorithm may have figured out a particular person doesn't talk much, but does enjoy the comforting hum of conversation from a partner. I've known couples like this. One enjoys talking and the other enjoys listening."

Madeline paused to see if there were other questions. "So, you had your dinner dates solo this evening. Tomorrow morning, we'll all meet at the Mars History Museum for a tour. Your matches have been encouraged to plan the rest of the day for you. Might include more sightseeing or be a time they arrange to meet the family. It could be anything. I'll be here every night if you want to stop in and get advice or share how things are going. I always enjoy hearing about your progress. And of course, I'm available by phone at any time."

A few minutes later, the group broke up. As she headed to her room, Judith puzzled over what she hadn't felt comfortable telling Madeline. She'd noticed Carson carried a concealed weapon.

~ * ~

Carson thought their first few days had gone well. Judith showed enthusiasm for everything about Mars. She'd loved the museum and the restaurants. She especially liked their group trip in the rovers out to the site of an early scientific expedition. Somehow, she had helped him come out of his shell. He couldn't quite put his finger on it. He found it got easier to have real conversations as the days went by.

He finally felt ready to introduce her to Glenn and show her the business. They were on the tram out to the company his parents had built, Aquarius Aquaponics. They got off the tram and he guided her to the right slide-walk.

"I told Glenn we'd be coming today. He'll probably try to put me to work. He grumbled a bit when I told him I was taking time off."

"If he needs you today, I don't mind. I could watch or maybe even start learning how to help," Judith told him.

"We'll see," Carson hedged. "Neither one of us has taken a vacation in the last few years. Maybe he'd like to take a few days off once you and I get settled. I know I hadn't been to the museum or on a rover trip since I was in school. It's been lots of fun, especially having you to do it with." He smiled and they held each other's eyes for a long moment before he bent down and kissed her lightly.

The slide-walk brought them to a large concourse where they stepped off. Carson guided her down a tunnel and into a smaller concourse. "Our business is this way." He headed to a set of large double doors with a video sign proclaiming: Aquarius Aquaponics. He waved an id card at the wall scanner and the doors opened.

They entered a small office area with desks, computers and a few chairs. "Most of our business is done by computer, but occasionally a new customer wants to come see the product before ordering. Through here takes us right into the heart of our operations." He headed for another door on the other side of the room.

Carson swiped his id card again and they went through. He paused there for Judith to take in the size of the operation. They had entered a large room filled with vats, grow beds and towers, a variety of pumps, and kilometers of color-coded tubing running in all directions. A catwalk ran around the room halfway up the walls with more grow towers. Control panels blinked in a complex display of colored lights. Above the mechanical noises, a faint strain of music played over speakers.

"Wow! This is like entering your own mini jungle. How do you have room to move around?"

"On Mars, you're paying for the cubic meters, not just the square meters. We have to make use of every last bit of space we've got. You get the hang of it."

"I thought it would smell bad, you know, very fishy." He watched her take a sniff. "I can smell soil and scents I can't even identify." She paused. "What's the music?"

"Oh, something my mom always did. She played old Earth classical music for the plants. Claimed it helped them grow better. We keep doing it to honor her memory. Honestly, I don't know if it does anything, but our customers love our produce."

Still holding her hand, he began leading her down a row of grow beds. "Let's see if we can find Glenn. He's supposed to be here. Glenn?"

They were halfway down the row, when something zipped by Carson's head. It impacted a grow tower of tomatoes causing bits of plastic and almost-ripe tomatoes to explode next to them. He jerked them both to the floor and cursed.

As he reached for the gun he kept in an ankle holster, Judith grabbed his hand and whispered, "I'm so sorry! I didn't think they'd find me. Maybe if I leave, they'll follow me and you'll be safe!"

Carson looked at her in stunned confusion then commanded, "Crawl under that grow bed and stay quiet." He pulled out his handgun. Still crouching, he moved down the aisle.

He'd gone a cautious ten meters, when another shot rang out, deliberately hitting a fish vat. Water began leaking out onto the floor. The voice he'd been expecting called out, "Show yourself Carson Landry! Or I'll put some more holes in your stupid fish tanks. Or better yet, maybe I'll put some holes in your brother. After all, you killed my brother. Why shouldn't I kill yours?"

Carson peered over the top of a grow bed full of pepper plants. At the far end of the room, Richie Maguire climbed up a metal staircase to the catwalk. He'd always been a short, scruffy man, yet, deadly. Carson watched as his brother, bound and bleeding from a head wound, got forced up the steps.

"I killed your brother in self-defense, Maguire. A court ruled it was justifiable. You were trying to hijack my load of ore." As he finished talking, Carson scuttled over a couple of rows. Sure enough, Maguire drilled a shot into where he'd been crouching, using some fancy gun with a laser sight.

"I don't give a damn what some court said. You killed him and you've been a dead man walking ever since."

Carson called, "How did you get out of prison so soon? I thought you were locked up for ten years?" Again, he moved quickly, crawling forward under the tables.

"Got out early on account of good behavior. Took me a little time to find the credits to get here. I've been looking forward to killing you for a long time. It's going to feel so good putting a bullet in your knee, and then your belly, and finally your head." Maguire shot several more rounds into the fish tanks.

Carson risked another peek over a grow table. Glenn still served as a human shield. On the far right side of the room, a supply rack fell over. Maguire swiveled and shot in that direction.

He could only assume Judith had toppled it on purpose. Next, he heard a pump alarm begin wailing. He could see Maguire frantically searching the room and getting off a couple more random shots. He tried not to worry about what she must think of him right now. They needed to survive. He could deal with the fall-out later. However painful.

Carson took advantage of her distractions to angle himself more to the left. He could hear Maguire yell about something. He couldn't figure out the words over the noise. He had moved far enough now to have a clear line of sight at him. Maguire held Glenn incredibly close. Could he make the shot? He hesitated.

As he waited, half-ripe tomatoes started sailing through the air.

In his efforts to dodge the hard green fruits, Maguire lost hold of Glenn. His brother did the smart thing and dropped to the floor of the catwalk. Carson finally had a clear shot.

His three bullets all took Maguire through the chest, sending him tumbling down the stairs. Carson stood up and ran over to the body oozing blood. He kicked the gun away and looked up at Glenn. "Are you okay?"

Glenn managed to sit up and lean against the railing, his hands still bound behind him. "I'm okay. Is he dead?"

"We'll let the first responders figure that out." He turned and yelled, "Judith! Judith, it's safe to come out." He ran up the steps to help Glenn. Pulling out a pocketknife, Carson cut through the bindings. Next, he pulled out his phone and called emergency services. It suddenly dawned on him; he hadn't seen Judith.

"Judith! Where are you? Are you okay?" He left Glenn rubbing his wrists and started searching for her.

~ * ~

As Judith armed herself with more tomatoes, she heard three quick shots. The shots seemed different somehow and they hadn't come anywhere near her. She stayed crouched down, holding her breath in dread.

Carson yelled her name.

Relief and despair coursed through her. She'd heard Carson and the man talking. The confrontation hadn't been about her at all. Carson knew, from what she'd said earlier, she'd run from something. She doubted he'd want her problems, too.

She heard him start calling her name again, more frantically. Taking a deep breath, she willed herself to her feet and opened her mouth to answer, when he appeared.

"Judith! Are you all right? Are you hurt?" He ran his hands all over her to make sure she wasn't hit. He took her in his arms and kissed her with the passion that comes with facing death and surviving. She couldn't help responding to him. With her response came the bittersweet realization that she had fallen in love with him.

"I'm so glad you're alive, Carson!"

"You were amazing!" He kissed her again. "Your distractions helped me save Glenn. I hate to think what would have happened if you hadn't been here. Oh! You're shaking! I know the adrenaline rush is great while it lasts, then you crash." He tightened his arms around her.

"Is your brother okay?" she managed to ask.

"Yes, he's a little banged up, but otherwise all in one piece. Emergency services will be here soon. They can check us all out."

She started to pull away, looking everywhere but his face.

Suddenly, he held her at arm's length and fearfully asked, "Are you mad at me?"

She looked up briefly, "No, but you must be mad at me. Carson, I lied about why I wanted to join Space Brides. I'm running away from a serious problem back on Earth." She took a breath before continuing. "I thought that first bullet was meant for me. I used Space Brides as a quick way to escape. I wrote about a politician and his brother and all the corruption in his administration. My editor refused to run the story. I snuck it into an email blast we used to supply story updates. I was fired and had some suspicious close calls. I knew I needed to get as far away from Earth as possible, and as quietly as possible. This seemed like the best bet. I'm sorry. I came to you under false pretenses. It's not fair to expect you to go through with this. I'd better go."

She tried to move. He gently held on. "Wait, Judith. Listen to me. I'm the one who should be apologizing. Look around us! Your life was in danger because of me! I knew Richie Maguire wanted me dead because of what happened out in the mining camps. I thought I had many years before he'd be out of prison. I foolishly hoped he'd cool off by then and realize he was in the wrong. We can see how that worked out. Please don't go!"

"Are you sure?" she asked, finally holding his gaze.

He gripped her shoulders more firmly. "I'm very sure. After

just seven days, it's hard to imagine my life without you. I love you, Judith. I want to marry you and have you by my side. Please stay and be my wife."

Judith felt her eyes welling up. "The most I thought I could hope for was to like the man the algorithm picked. I'm happy to say I'm in love with you, too. If you're sure, I want to stay."

"I'm sure. Let's get married as soon as we can!" He pulled her back into his arms.

Glenn limped up to them and clapped a hand on his brother's shoulder, "Aren't you going to introduce me to my new sister-in-law? After all, I am going to be the best man at the wedding, right?"

~ * ~

Somewhere in the heart of a quantum computing farm, the algorithm gave the equivalent of an electronic chuckle.

~ * ~ * ~

**Laura Hilse** has enjoyed writing since her distant youth. She has a Bachelor's degree in Communication Studies from Northwestern University and a Master's degree in Montessori Education from Xavier University (Cincinnati). She has worked as a public relations assistant, a copywriter, and a Montessori teacher. Currently, she is self-employed as an Orton-Gillingham tutor for dyslexic children. Part-time work and an empty nest leaves her time to get back to writing fiction and the occasional haiku.

She had an idyllic childhood growing up in a small northwestern Pennsylvania town. A resident of the upper midwest for many years, she misses the rolling hills of her home state. Visits back to her hometown inspired the setting for her current work in progress. This story is an urban fantasy about a tattoo artist who, in delving into her past, discovers magical abilities, dangerous enemies, and a long-buried mystery she is destined to solve.

The author is a devoted reader of many genres, most especially fantasy and science fiction. Some of the authors who have entertained and influenced her the most are Elizabeth Peters, Barbara Hambly, Wen Spencer, and Lois Bujold. In her free time she likes to garden, read, birdwatch, and knit. She lives in northwestern Wisconsin with her husband.

# HOPE AMONG THE STARS

Luke T. Barnett

## Paterae City, Ganymede, Feb 27, 2372, Earth calendar

To Mr. William P. Denefore

My name is Agnes Julia Walshire. I am writing to you in response to your advertisement seeking a proper young lady to wed. Your post requested the lady be of refinement, not older than twenty-four, and of healthy mind and body. I meet these requirements and so am writing to offer my hand in marriage.

Strange though it may sound, I do not have the means of attaining a current photograph, so I will attempt an adequate description. I am twenty-three Earth years old, one-hundred, sixty-four centimeters tall, weighing fifty-two kilograms and of healthy constitution. I have blue eyes and bright, red hair that would put starship thrusters to shame. However, I do not attain to the level of temper with which so many women with my shade of hair are stereotyped.

I am the only child of Ander M. Walshire. My father was a wealthy businessman here in Paterae City. Unfortunately, he lost his life during the riots which plagued this city last year. Data thieves swindled away his fortunes which were to be mine, leaving me nearly creditless. I retained some of the wealth, enough to live for the past year on meager means. That is coming to an end, however, as my funds have already been depleted. I have been forced to scrounge for the past month, working where I may in order to earn enough to live by. Even still, work is scarce. I happened across your advertisement and saw an opportunity. I am of marrying age and, though not seeking a husband, am in a unique situation as to need one with suitable means to support himself and I.

I do not write this to arouse your sympathy. I wanted you to know the state of the woman who solicits you. My father raised me as a proper young lady. I will be both obedient and submissive. I am not afraid of hard work and, though not the best of cooks, will endeavor to fill any role you have of me for a proper young wife of a Marsian nobleman, including the bearing of children.

Please send correspondence if this arrangement is to your liking.

Sincerely,
Agnes Julia Walshire

## Mars City, Mars, Feb 29, 2372, Earth calendar

Dear Ms. Walshire,

First, allow me to offer my condolences on the loss of your father and your fortune. You may not have sought my sympathies, but you have them nonetheless. I saw the news of the riots when they occurred, truly a tragedy. I find it remarkable you survived at all, as I heard many aristocrats were killed in those awful dealings. Let me assure you, no such instability exists here on Mars.

I have looked up your father's estate as it was before the riots. While I cannot pretend to his level of fortune, I am a successful business owner. My investments are not locked in to one place, but widely diversified with different levels of security and in different holdings so bankruptcy by a single individual or group would be quite a task. What I mean to say is I would be able to provide a stable home and lifestyle for you, were we to mutually agree on our matrimony.

I am including a picture of myself, but as pictures can often deceive and you have so generously described yourself, I shall do the same. I am thirty-one Earth years old, one-hundred, seventy-two centimeters tall, and sixty-four kilograms in weight. I have short, brown hair and a mustache that elicits many a jibe and jest from my contemporaries, often in reference to something for a woman to grab hold of so she may "lay one on me."

My mother said I should seek a lady of refinement for a wife. Of course, mother knows best and she insists I find a woman not constantly smattered in dirt or in a tattered state of dress. She is forever concerned she will not live to see her grandchildren, though she is in fine health. Do not let her presence in my life deter you. She is opinionated, but by no means does she decide my life, nor my choices. Those are solely mine. And on that note, I find your proposal, thus far, most agreeable.

However, there is an absence which I would like to address: you have made no conditions for yourself upon our matrimony beyond my provision for your well-being. Do you require no further assurances?

I prefer all pretense dispensed with so there may be as little contradiction in our marriage as possible upon commencement. Please speak plainly. I should like to know the woman I am to marry.

Sincerely yours,
William Paul Denefore
[visual data available for download]

## Paterae City, Ganymede, Mar 1, 2372, Earth calendar

Mr. Denefore,

I thank you much for your kind words concerning my late father. He was a good man, though he could be cold at times. He would not so readily jump to humorous descriptions of himself as you have so done. I must admit, I laughed when I read your mustache comment, which received to me an odd look from the other data station patrons. And your desire to know my wishes, not just immediately accept my proposal, is most honorable and straightforward. That is something rarely seen in men today and I commend you for it. It commends me all the more toward you as well.

As for my own desires, I ask only you treat me as a lady. I will not stand for abuse, physical or otherwise. Please understand I say this with the most humble of hearts. Bullying and strong-arming are things I cannot abide. If you would know my desires further, let us call them requests. I shall abide happily in your home even if they are not met.

There are times when I have...urges to act rather un-ladylike. Oh, nothing scandalous. However, taking action is not something foreign to me, especially when there is no one else to do so. If I see a need, I act on it, heedless of my own well-being or reputation. I have been reprimanded by my father time and again for this and have mostly learned to tame this desire except in the most dire of circumstances, in which case I would not suppress it for all the gold in the asteroid belt. I will attempt to restrain this impulse, but do not think less of me if I am given to it now and again.

Also, though I am not boisterous, neither am I content to sit quietly while things happen around me. I love to be engaged in the goings-on of my world, tempered of course by manners, kindness, and all, well, *most* behavior becoming a lady of my former stature.

I should like the ability and opportunity to learn, to better myself. My mind can become somewhat restless and must find things to occupy it. I would prefer this to be open and free, but if not, I may still find small ways in which to satisfy this compulsion within me. I dare say it is necessary for my mental health to have an active mind. I will, of course, temper this as much as possible so as not to interfere with our marriage or your daily life and business dealings. I can keep it quiet, if need be.

Lastly, I would ask that I be allowed to speak my opinion and you would consider it as counsel to your dealings, be they business, social, or otherwise. Please understand, I do not seek to impress my will upon you, only to be considered an equal with as sound a mind as yourself.

Once again, if I am relegated to a quiet housewife, I will take such duty with thankfulness and without complaint so long as the first condition is met.

My thanks for your request and your indulgence. I await your reply.

Sincerely,
Agnes Walshire

## Mars City, Mars, Jingzhe 11, 2372

Ms. Walshire,

I thought it best to start using Martian reckoning of dates and time if we are to proceed with our matrimony. Yes, I intend to move forward with our arrangement. Do not fear your requests. They have not rebuffed me, but endeared you to me all the more. A wife is surely a good thing to have, as the Lord has said. But to have an equal, a partner, a friend, that is truly my heart's desire. Never would I have imagined having found such a one as you in such a cold business as a bride service. It may indeed come to that our personalities do not connect, regardless of your tendencies, but if so, we will make the best of it. And what I have read thus far encourages me greatly.

I am a man of passion myself. I have desires I too have learned to control for the sake of my station and propriety. Conscience must always temper these desires to be sure. But know I will never stifle you in your pursuits. Rather, I will encourage them. Come alongside me in mine and I will gladly come alongside you in yours.

As for that which you cannot abide, you need not fear. I have laid a violent hand on an individual only once. The incident was against a man double my size who attempted to lay his hands on a woman. You will be a lady and treated as such in my—*our* household.

I have purchased a cabin for you on the next transport bound for Mars City. The ship is called the *Persephone* and leaves port in seven Earth days. That should be sufficient time for you to gather any necessities and prepare for the trip. It is long, so please avail yourself of all you need. I have transmitted funds for you to do so as well as to sustain you while you wait to leave Ganymede. Please let me know if there is anything else you need. I look forward to meeting you in person.

Sincerely yours,
William Paul Denefore

P.S. If you would, from this time forth, please refer to me as William.

## Paterae City, Ganymede, Jingzhe 14 (?), 2372.

William,

It is very strange and feels somewhat scandalous calling you by your first name. I am happy to oblige, however. Thank you for your encouraging words. I must admit to some apprehension as to their believability. You know what they say about things being too good to be true. Nevertheless, I thank you and will take you at your word until you prove it false.

I thank you as well for the funds you transmitted. They have been an immense help. I used a portion to obtain a personal datapad, nothing fancy or expensive, just a simple device with a com identifier so I may write to you while I am in transit. I have been using a public data station up to this point.

I purchased food and other necessities I lacked as of late, a change of clothes, and a suitcase. I also purchased a tranquilizer round for a rifle. I heard these trips can be dangerous and wanted some protection, just in case. A gun will not be permitted and deterrent spray might not be effective if I am attacked. Hopefully, I will not need it.

The most expensive of my purchases was a dress. There was plenty of money for it and I still have plenty left over. I did my best to be frugal while purchasing a dress, which would be appealing to your eye. Not knowing your tastes, I went with what matched my skin, hair, and eyes. I want to be beautiful for you when first we meet in person.

Oh, but I felt so lovely when I put it on and looked in the mirror, I nearly burst into tears! You don't know what it means to me to wear such niceties. I sold all that was in my father's house to survive this past year and I have not known such things in some time.

Thank you again. Here is a photo of me taken with the datapad your funds have provided. I do hope you see the sincerity of my smile. It is because of you. You have given me hope and a future again. Thank you.

Yours sincerely,
Agnes
[visual data available for download]

## Mars City, Mars, Jingzhe 15, 2372

Agnes,

I do hope I am not being presumptuous in using your first name. If I am, I beg your forgiveness and assure you I will do it no further. Please inform me which is the case.

Your frugality impresses me as your desire to please me makes my heart glad. I am happier still you found something pleasing to you. I noticed you did not include a picture of the dress. I suspect it is to show me when you arrive. I must say, you have the most stunning blue eyes. Your face is quite lovely and your hair! My, but the brightest meteorite could not outshine your locks!

Yes, I neglected to mention anything about me. Let me see. Red and white are my favorite colors, especially when combined, though I do not include those in my clothing choices. Floral patterns are nice on a lady, but not necessary. Short hair is not unbecoming of a lady, though I rather prefer long hair. I prefer organically grown foods rather than those made in genetic assemblers, though the former is scarce here on Mars. I like a good play as opposed to a digital production. In fact, many of my tastes harken to humanity's past rather than her present or future. I invest in the future, but I indulge in the past, if that makes sense.

But what of your tastes? What do you like to see on a man? And what do you prefer for yourself? I should like to know you more.

Sincerely,
William

## Paterae City, Ganymede, Jingzhe 17, 2372

William,

I am positively bursting with excitement! The transport leaves tomorrow and I cannot sleep. I am in a temporary shelter near the starport. I wish to board as soon as possible. I have confirmed my cabin (oh, bless you, you got me a private one!) and where I am to be when the boarding commences.

I am not at all scandalized by your use of my first name. Are we not to be husband and wife? That sounds so strange. I can scarcely believe this is real. I used the datapad to look up the Martian calendar and believe I have the date right. I have also looked up Mars City. Can you tell me where our residence will be? I should like to learn as much about the city as I can before I arrive. It appears the starport is on the outskirts. I hope you do not have to drive too far.

I love old-world things. I used to own a few of them. I had an analog telescope made of brass and real glass. Oh, it broke my heart to part with it! I even had some physical data streams once called books. Have you heard of them? It amazes me humanity used so much paper and ink. Where did we get it all?

On a man, my tastes are not so much in looks, but in heart. I like bravery and control in a man. If one cannot control his own spirit, he cannot order his life. Likewise, he must have the courage to do what is right, even if it scares him. From your correspondence, you seem to be of that temperament.

It is strange. One side of me feels like I know you already. But the logic side tells me you are still a stranger. I suppose both are true. I am rambling now. Boarding is in a few hours and I must sleep. I will write again when I am settled on board. Goodnight, Dear William.

Sincerely,
Agnes.

## Transport ship *Persephone*, in transit from Paterae City, Ganymede to Mars City, Mars, Jingzhe 19, 2372 [Transmitted Jingzhe 23, 2372, Mars calendar]

William,

My apologies for not writing to you the next day. I was exhausted and after receiving orientation with the other guests, meal, and settling my cabin, I collapsed onto my bunk. I do not know when this will reach you. The captain says this will be a three-week journey and correspondence can only be sent when we pass near a relay satellite. Until then, any outgoing messages will be in the ship's que. Any incoming messages will likewise have to wait until we pass by. The other passengers and I were told to inform anyone writing to us to be sure to address any correspondence to us with the prefix of *Persephone Transport*. Our ship will upload and distribute any message waiting for us at the nearest satellite to our current position toward which we are bound whenever we pass close enough to receive the signal.

To answer your question, I enjoy astronomy and hunting if you can believe it. My father instructed me well in the latter and I found a natural aptitude for it, though I insisted we give away the meat from anything we killed to those less fortunate. I even became proficient in tranquilizer rounds and learned how much to use for what size of a beast, though I didn't see much point to it.

I grew up on finer foods, of course, but have since become accustomed to eating more meager meals. The food on the *Persephone* is a grand feast compared to what I have eaten lately. I have taken to hoarding some away for later. A foolish habit I am attempting to overcome. I am not a glutton, I assure you. I love cheeses and am used to Ganymede cuisine. I am open to other types of food, however. I am sure whatever is within our household, I will become accustomed to. I hope to make you some meals you will truly enjoy.

My, but all this talk of food has made me hungry. I really shouldn't skimp on the meals while I have opportunity. I shall end this letter here and fetch more food. It is free within limits and I have certainly not exhausted my daily provisions. I will write to you again soon.

Sincerely yours,
Agnes.

## [*Persephone Transport*] Mars City, Mars, Jingzhe 18, 2372 [Received Jingzhe 23, 2372, Mars calendar]

Agnes,

I am happy to hear you are prepared to board and are so excited. I find myself rather the same. I must admit to a bit of nervousness. I have included a map with location markers signifying our home and the starport. It is a bit of a drive, but one I will happily make. In addition, the scenery is nice if one takes the long way around. Mars has terraformed nicely. Even those parts with little or none are stunning to behold.

If you like physical books, then you are in luck. I have a small collection gathering dust as none, but myself have been interested in them until now. I must keep this short. There are some major financial goings-on I must attend to. I do desire to share more. Know if I do not respond right away, it is only due to this and not because my desire is not there. I will endeavor to keep writing to you, if only to let you know I am here.

I must away from this letter, but I confess to struggle with it. The more I read your words and look at your smiling face, the more I believe I am falling in love with you. I desire to hear your voice. Write back swiftly, my love. I eagerly await your correspondence.

With a full heart,
William.
[visual data available for download]

## Transport ship *Persephone*, in transit from Paterae City, Ganymede to Mars City, Mars, Jingzhe 24, 2372 [Transmitted Chunfen 1, 2372, Mars calendar]

William,

My heart is full as well and my eyes are filled with tears as I write this. But fear not. These are happy tears. I am of the same mind, falling for a man I have never met. Oh, don't be so eager to hear my voice. It is a timid, soft thing. My father would say if I spoke low enough, not even a sub-sonic microphone could pick up my voice. I miss him.

Please, do not worry about me. Respond when you can. I am bound for you, my love, and shall see you soon. Despite my claim, I have included a voice recording. It must be brief, as there are data limitations aboard this vessel. However, I wanted to send you something. I hope this warms your heart. Take care, my love. I look forward to your reply.

With love,
Agnes.
[Voice message available for download]

## Transport ship *Persephone*, in transit from Paterae City, Ganymede to Mars City, Mars, Chunfen 7, 2372 [Transmitted Chunfen 8, 2372, Mars calendar]

William,

How are you, my love? I am sure you are busy with your business endeavor. It has been thirteen days since your last correspondence, and I miss you. I have attempted patience and to keep busy by getting to know some of the other passengers. Did you know there are two other brides-to-be on board? They seem as nervous as I, but lacking that joy I feel, and they are not in regular correspondence with their to-be husbands. Are they not in love with their betrothed? It would seem more likely than our situation. I am truly blessed to have found you. Write back soon. I love you.

Agnes.

## Transport ship *Persephone*, in transit from Paterae City, Ganymede to Mars City, Mars, Chunfen 8, 2372 [Transmitted Chunfen 14, 2372, Mars calendar]

William,

You have not written me. We have passed two satellites and still no word from you. Are you well? Have I said something to offend you? Please know whatever it was, I did not mean it. Please write me back.

With love,
Agnes.

## Transport ship *Persephone*, in transit from Paterae City, Ganymede to Mars City, Mars, Chunfen 15, 2372

William,

I miss you. I cannot imagine what is keeping you from writing me. Just a simple note to let me know you are all right, that you are there. It would only take a moment, would it not? It is lonely here and I am getting cabin fever. The other passengers and crew seem nervous about something and are mostly keeping to themselves. I have tried to question the crew, but they will say nothing.

I feel some sense of madness creeping up on me, being locked in by these metal walls and this metal floor. I long to hear from you. Please write to me so I may know I have not imagined you. That I have not gone mad with grief and longing over the loss of my father and spent the last of my money on a fantasy made up by a distraught mind. Please write me. I love you.

I love you.
Agnes.

## Transport ship *Persephone*, in transit from Paterae City, Ganymede to Mars City, Mars, Qingming 1, 2372.

Dearest William,

As I write this, I am sitting in one of the many piloting chairs on the bridge of the *Persephone*. I must relate to you what happened with what little time I have.

On Chunfen 19 pirates attacked us. They hacked one of the transmission satellites to know our location and set an ambush for us when we passed by. They attacked and boarded with such swiftness, they completely overwhelmed the crew. All us passengers were robbed and sealed in our cabins. The one who sealed me in took away all my possessions, save my dress which he ordered me to wear after he'd torn my clothes. I had no choice. I had to comply. The disgusting smirk on his face as he watched me left little doubt in my mind as to his intentions. After I changed, he left. For an entire day, I was locked in my cabin, not knowing what was happening.

My bad habit of hoarding food worked to my advantage, for I did not go hungry while waiting. I think it was their strategy to weaken us through lack of nutrition. I heard some women screaming. It still makes me shudder what those women had to endure. I knew they would come for me next. Then I remembered the tranquilizer round. I'd hid it beneath my mattress where I could get to it in case of an emergency.

When the brute returned…oh, William, do not think less of me for this. I laid back on my mattress in a feigned invitation, my hand gripping the tranq round beneath my pillow. When he was on top of me, I tried to stab him. But he was too quick and caught my arm. Fortunately, my legs were still between his and I hit him there with my shin over and over until he collapsed and I had to push him off me. *Then* I tranqed him. I took his gun and a wicked blade he carried and left him in my room.

I didn't know where the crew were being held, so I wandered the corridors, trying to unlock doors and free other passengers. I managed to save one woman who was being set upon. She wouldn't come with me. I took the rifle of the man I killed. Yes, I killed a man. It fills me with such sickness even now. Later, when I am alone, I will break down, if there is a later. For now, I must write.

I freed another passenger from his cabin who walked me through unlocking his door. Thankfully, he had a better head than I. Together, we found the crew locked in the brig and freed them. I was forced to kill more men, which I do not relish.

From there, it was chaos. The crew and the pirates fought a pitched battle. The man who had joined me and I were sent with some crew to the engine room while the rest fought their way to the bridge. The pirates tried to seal us out. We slipped in, the door closing on my hair. I am sorry, William. I had to chop it off.

I won't go into details. Suffice it to say, we took the engine compartment. The pirates left us no choice. We had to kill every last one of them. We received word the crew re-took the bridge and killed the pirates, at the cost of many crew members. They needed any passengers able to keep their wits to help in the piloting. They chose me in light of my participation in the fight and freeing the crew.

Before they died, the pirates sabotaged our systems and knocked out most of our navigation. We were able to ping a distant satellite and so get back on course. At least we managed that much. So many systems are inoperable. The three remaining crew tell me it will be a crash landing on Mars.

I found my datapad cracked and lying in a dead pirate's belt. And now here I sit, about to do what I can to help us not crash into anything habitable as Mars draws ever closer.

I do not know if you will ever read this. I want you to know I love you. I do not regret my choice to come to you. I am happy, happy I could know you and am only sorry I could not fulfill the role of a wife for you. I think I would have been happy with you. Take care of yourself, my love. Thank you for all your kindness to a woman you have never met. I wish you all the best.

We are about to enter the atmosphere. I must go. I will send this out when we are close enough for the signal to get through.

Love with all my heart,
Agnes.

~ * ~

William's datapad chirped just as the small dot in the sky turned into a blazing fireball. It angled away from the starport and William ordered his driver to follow the emergency vehicles chasing after it.

A terrible boom vibrated his chest as the ship slammed and skidded into the undeveloped, red soil. They stopped half a kilometer away and William hopped out, getting as close as the emergency workers allowed him.

It took some time for the dust to settle. He saw ghostly phantoms through its misty presence as emergency workers rushed in. He read as he waited, pacing back and forth and looking eagerly to the settling cloud. Eventually, the shadows resolved into people, ragged and injured, being pulled from the wreckage.

One person, a woman, was helping passengers out through a hole in the hull, redirecting any help the emergency workers tried to offer. She wore a ruined dress, torn raggedly off at the knees, her face smeared with dirt and blood, her dirty, red hair chopped off just below her ears. Then her blue eyes found him and he saw through the layers of dirt and trauma the woman he had so longed to see.

Attempting in vain to smooth her dress, she marched towards him.

~ * ~

William stood his ground as she approached. She knew it was him from the moment she saw his face. The brown suit of a gentleman. His mustache, long and elegant, was unmistakable. What troubled her was the look of astonishment on his face. Agnes stopped half a meter from him, hoping, *praying* his shock was not for her ragged countenance. The dried blood on her face itched. She ignored it and made a perfect curtsey.

"Mister Denefore." She folded her hands before her. "William."

William said nothing, his brown eyes fixed on her. Agnes fidgeted, not meeting his gaze.

"I must apologize for my state of dress." She attempted in vain to smooth her mussed hair. "I assure you I am not normally like this. Battling pirates is not a habit of mine."

She attempted a nervous laugh, but it died away in the face of his silence. Why wouldn't he speak? She'd disappointed him. She must appear counter to everything she had told him of herself. He would reject her. She would be creditless again and a stranger on a strange world. No. It was more than that. She couldn't stand the thought of losing his love. She *did* love him and she wanted to be loved *by* him. Tears wetted her eyes as panic and despair set-in.

"William, please forgive me," she burst out, her voice soft and timid, tears trickling down her dirty cheeks. "I've ruined your dress. I butchered my hair. I wanted to be the kind of woman you wanted. I didn't want to disappoint you. If...if you no longer want me, I...I—"

With movements both swift and gentle, he stepped to her, leaned down, and laid his lips upon hers. His kiss, warm and soft, told her he still wanted her. Still loved her. She melted into him, her tension fleeing. He pulled away and stared into her eyes, gentle hands on her smattered face.

"You are an amazing woman." His voice, like a warm pool, buoyed her soul. "You are brave, selfless, and I would be a fool not to take you as my wife. More than that."

Releasing her, he retrieved a long case from his hover car and bent down on one knee before her. He pressed a button and the lid retracted, revealing a brass telescope, obviously old, and well maintained. A gold ring lay atop mounted with a diamond glittering more beautifully in the Martian air than any jewelry Agnes had ever owned. For it was full of his love for her.

"I would be *honored* to take your hand in marriage."

Agnes burst out with a brief laugh, delirious with joy. Covering her mouth with one hand, she offered the other, gaining back enough control to say, "And I would be honored to be yours."

William laid aside the telescope and fit the ring on her finger. It slid on smooth, a promise made and kept, a moment signifying the end of an interminable heartache. William stood and she embraced him, her tears of joy flowing freely.

She found in the warmth of his embrace she could hold herself together no longer. The strength that helped her survive for the past year at last failed. Her body shook, her legs buckling. But then William's arm was beneath her legs, lifting her into his arms. She wept into his shoulder, grateful, so very grateful, as he carried her away towards her new home.

~ * ~ * ~

**Luke T. Barnett** grew up on a steady diet of Sci-Fi. As an awkward kid with ADD, good stories, and deep characters were his great escape, be they in movie, TV show, book, or video game. Star Wars, Star Trek, Firefly, and Cowboy Bebop are among his favorite space adventures.

With all these good stories rolling around inside his brain, he longed to tell his own stories and began writing fanfictions and original works in grade school.

His first works, which were school assignments, were praised by his teachers. By adulthood, he had discovered anime and the world of pen & paper role-playing games. He wrote several short works based on his characters and fanfictions based on the video games and tabletop games he played.

His first publication was in a local gaming newsletter which featured an early version of his Cryos & Jade series.

In 2021 he began work on a sweeping sci-fi epic called Galactic Core. It is inspired by the many sci-fi and anime movies and TV shows he has enjoyed over the years.

Luke currently lives in Mentor, Ohio where he spends his days working a day job and caring for his family while writing at night and on the weekends. He has a beautiful, no-nonsense, Star Wars loving, writer wife, two slow-motion loving, story-telling-addict boys, and one dragon-slaying, unicorn-loving daughter. He regularly reads his stories to his boys who are constantly begging for more. He is happy to provide.

# HAD MY REASONS

## Dana Bell

*I must be out of my mind*, Abram decided even as he stepped through the door of Space Brides, LLC. The company only had one office in the asteroids. How many of the other miners used their services he had no way of knowing. There were what, he mused, several hundred rock scroungers seeking their fortune, like he'd read about during the historic gold rushes of long ago.

When he glanced around the office and noticed the lack of clients, it came as a huge shock. Most of the men where single and in need of feminine company and not just those in the saloons or brothels.

"You're Abram Labronno," the gray-haired woman sitting behind the metal desk greeted him. She wore a blue jumpsuit with the SBLLC branded in silver on the left side.

He nodded, not surprised she knew him. Back on Earth he'd been a well-known actor clawing his way up the stardom ladder. Would have had a good shot too, if he'd not learned about the back room deals and roles directors cast before agents could approach them. He'd lost too many opportunities due to their antics. He cringed. Plus, a foolish decision that had consigned him to darkness.

So, he'd sold everything and migrated out to the asteroids on a slow freighter. Abram scrapped by like everyone else.

"Quite the profile you have," the woman continued, her voice firm and warm. "I'm Liz," she introduced herself.

"Pleasure," he returned. He pointed at the empty benches attached to the rock floor. "This place ever busy?"

"Only when the supply ship docks." She smiled, the lines around her blue eyes crinkled.

Abram knew how busy the main complex could be when the supply ships came in and how quickly everything ran out.

"I have a couple of contractors who come in to help out," she continued.

Contractor was a way of life. Many worked odd jobs filling in as needed. Harsh way to survive, yet he'd done so himself when he'd first arrived. Made enough to stake his own claim.

"Any prospects?" Abram inquired, doubtful the answer would be any different than it had over the past year or so. Brides migrated to the planets and moons, not the asteroids.

Liz pulled up her screen which shimmered in the air. "Hmm." Her gaze studied the information. "Maybe."

"Maybe?" He refused to get excited or get his hopes up.

"Looks like we may have a query from a transferee on Io."

Io. Biggest mining operation in the solar system. Rumor had it they'd had some problems a few years back. Local law enforcement had cleaned it up. Company changed hands afterward and expanded operations.

"Profession?" His nose itched and he scratched it. Could be a night lady wanting out and a new start. Not an ideal match.

"Cook," Liz answered.

He blinked. Cook? The woman had one of the most in demand skills. She could get a job anywhere and be paid well. Why would she choose to come to the asteroids?

"There's a hitch." Liz studied the info.

Just his luck. "Someone already hired her."

"No." She sent him a stern look. "The prospective bride has guardianship of her younger siblings and—" She chuckled. "A cat." Liz became all business. "As you know, children and pets must be disclosed and agreed upon beforehand."

"She in route?" He felt a moment of panic.

Liz checked. "Leaves next week. Ship will come through dropping off new miners, supplies, and any passengers before continuing to Mars."

"Picture?" Long shot. Seeing what she looked like wouldn't matter.

"Surprising, yes." A 3-D image wavered.

His gray eyes darted to the image. A woman with shoulder length black hair, her features plain, but not unattractive, and eyes the color of sapphires. Looked to be a bit older than most brides who migrated out. Forties maybe. She wore a brown jumpsuit and in her arms an orange cat glared with yellow eyes.

Beside her stood a young boy and girl, who didn't look anything like her. Step siblings perhaps or adopted. Both wore colorful pants and tops, with brown hair and eyes.

"They seem young to be siblings." He waited for a response.

"Adopted according to the file."

"Am I allowed to read it?"

"As long as the prospective bride has permission to do the same."

"Granted."

Liz held out a disc. "If possible, I'd like a decision in two days."

"You'll have my answer within a day."

~ * ~

Narissa Lawrence couldn't believe her good fortune. The disc she'd received didn't have a lot of information on her perspective spouse, yet enough for her to know she wanted to meet him. The first perspective husband she'd heard from. Several others had come in later from interested potential partners on Mars. She didn't want to live on the red planet. Too much of a chance of running into her father's old business associates, who would make demands she wouldn't agree to.

Her father's second wife had assigned guardianship to Narissa in the event something happened. Unfortunately, an incident had occurred and they'd both been killed. If she'd been there, she could have warned him, although she doubted he would have listened. He made a stupid tactical mistake.

With a sigh she put the past behind her and studied what little had been provided. Abram Labronno. Forty-two. Strong, determined face. Long pale brown hair, sad gray eyes. Stubble on his chin. Ex actor. She didn't care about his old profession. Quit the business and migrated out. Owned his own mining operation.

Included were a few photos of his home. Lights along the ceiling of a chiseled-out cave. The rock walls red and black with some white splotches. Had its own water supply, which impressed Narissa. How had he managed that feat?

"He lives in a cave?" Bruce asked, gazing over her shoulder. He'd just turned ten.

"Seems to."

"Dazzling!" The boy grinned. "Better than the box we're living in."

He referred to their current soon to be former home. When the kids had arrived, her employers had emptied a storage room, put up bunk beds, plus a single for her. Crowded for her, two children and a cat.

Susan frowned. "Won't it be cold?"

"We'll have to ask." She thought she'd read somewhere caves kept a constant temperature back on Earth. Couldn't be sure the same applied to the asteroids. "At least you'll have some room to run and play."

The nine-year-old girl thought about it. "Guess that'll be okay."

Tibs, her orange tabby, yawned and closed his eyes. The affairs of humans never seemed to concern him. Or so Narissa assumed.

"He okay with us?" Susan gave her a worried expression.

The note her potential mate had thoughtfully included read, "I'd never considered children, but am willing to try to be a father or at the very least a friend they can rely upon."

"Yes," she told the girl.

"Guess that's good." Bruce seemed uncertain.

Her father and his second wife had adopted the siblings when they'd been very young. The couple had lost their lives about three years later. The children had become her responsibility and the joy of her life.

"We have a trial period to see if it'll work out. Whatever happens, we'll be together as a family," she promised.

Her answer seemed to satisfy Bruce and Susan. They both grinned.

"It's an adventure!" Bruce bounced over to his bunk to finish packing.

"You packed, Susan?" The girl nodded.

"Good." She stifled a yawn. "We leave early in the morning." Her eyes traveled the cramped space. Narissa wasn't sorry to leave. Granted most barely scrapped by in the asteroids. She hoped their living conditions would be much better.

She could also find work as a cook. Had to be plenty of hungry men.

"Where's my doll?" Susan asked, her expression frantic. The doll had been the last gift she'd gotten from her mother.

"Look under your bed," her brother suggested.

"There you are." She pulled the cloth doll out and tucked it in her suitcase.

Heart aching, Narissa wished the two had more. Her salary

though generous, didn't go far with the price of shipping supplies out from Earth. Wouldn't change with moving, yet it was the only way out she could think of to change their circumstances.

Living off Mars kept her away from her father's profession she'd refused to be a part of. Although his compatriots still tried to recruit her. Finding her on Io had been easy. Searching for her among the hundreds of asteroids would make locating her much more difficult.

She could live with not being found.

~ * ~

Waiting for his perspective bride to arrive, Abram paced the Space Brides office stone floor. Being the only one there, since Liz had gone to meet the woman's ship, he had no one to talk to. When they returned, his first meeting with his prospective bride would be supervised.

Before coming, he'd taken care of his needs, including using the bath house to clean up, putting on clean clothes, shaving and brushing his long hair, secured at the base of his neck. After waiting for so long, he wanted to be as presentable as possible.

He hoped they clicked instantly. Realistically he knew it would take time. She'd opted for waiting the two weeks allowed to decide. Given the circumstances he could understand why. His lifestyle could be challenging. In more ways than one.

"Here we are," he heard Liz say.

He straightened and smiled.

Her eyes widened when she saw him. She shook herself as if distracted and smiled. Two children followed behind, each carrying small bags. His bride put down the cat carrier. The creature yowled loudly in protest.

"You're fine, Tibs," she gently told the cat.

Liz made quick introductions. "I'll be in the back if you need anything." She disappeared to give them time to get acquainted.

"How was your flight?" He couldn't think of anything else to say.

"Fine. Tiring."

The children sat down on the bench. The little girl hugged a doll. The boy looked bored.

"I'm surprised you agreed to meet," she continued, her eyes

uncertain.

"Been waiting a long time," he honestly answered. "Not many women come here."

"I'd heard it wasn't a desirable place to live. Still." She frankly looked him over. "I don't understand why any woman wouldn't want to meet you." Her cheeks turned pink.

"Can get lonely here," he agreed. She only carried a backpack. They'd come with so little.

"I have no desire to live on Mars or Earth."

He frowned, not sure why she'd shared the information. "Are you from either?"

"Mars." She glanced down. "Let's just say my father and I had a falling out."

He sensed that was all she'd share for now. "My home is about an hour away. Is there anything you need before we head out?"

"I'm hungry," Bruce griped.

He smiled. "I think we can find you a good meal." Rubbing his chin he regarded the small family. "Suspect I need to buy a few groceries and a number of other items for your comfort." Quite a bit. He had the funds to cover. He'd learned to live with little and saved his profits.

"We wouldn't want to—" the woman began.

He held up his hand. "If we are to become a family, it's the least I can do. Liz!" he called.

The older woman popped out, her eyes darting between the couple.

"You had mentioned you wanted the two-week trial, is that still your wish?" Never hurt to double check. He waited for her answer.

She nibbled on her lower lip. "If you don't mind."

"I agree." He glanced at Liz. "We're leaving now."

Liz smiled broadly. "Good luck!"

~ * ~

How much had their shopping spree cost him? Narissa wondered, gazing at the huge pile on the counter.

Abram haggled with the keeper like an expert and took a small wagon to load the supplies.

"It's too much," she protested.

"Better to have too much than not enough," he countered. His tone told her it wouldn't do any good to argue.

Walking though the main hub, she got stares from many of the miners. Some looked envious.

When they reached the docking area, he started loading his transport. Bruce gave his bag to his sister and picked up smaller items, handing them to Abram. The man gave the boy a smile. When they finished, he complimented her brother, "You did a fine job of helping. Thank you."

Bruce grinned proudly.

She felt a smile tug at her lips. If his words and actions were an indication of the man, he'd make a great father figure.

He tossed a coin to a young boy who hovered in the background. "Take it back for me?"

The kid nodded, pocketing the money, grabbed the cart and vanished in the direction they'd come.

"Saves me a trip," he explained. He motioned. "We'd best be going."

"Of course." She and the children entered the transport. The size of the craft surprised her. They weren't cramped.

"These are called hoppers." He started it up and it darted out through a rock tunnel into the blackness of space. Stars twinkled around them dominated by Jupiter.

"It's dark," Susan whispered, cuddling closer to Narissa.

"Always is in space." Abram glanced back. "Beautiful too."

"How long before we arrive?" Narissa thought he'd told them earlier, but her tired mind couldn't remember.

"We'll be there in under an hour."

"Ever see pirates?" Bruce asked, his eyes shining.

"Heard stories. They mostly go after supply ships or luxury liners. Usually the latter because there's a higher profit to be made."

"How do you know?" Bruce eased up to look over Abram's shoulder.

"Another day. If you don't mind, I need to make sure we don't hit anything."

"Bruce, sit back and let—" she hesitated, not sure if she should use his name. "Abram get us home safely."

"Okay." He sat back and crossed his arms over his chest.

They completed the rest of the trip in silence. Narissa kept sneaking glances at Abram, marveling how handsome he looked.

How had he not had any women take an interest? Granted his face seemed a bit pale. Living in space with little sunshine easily explained his complexion. His body, under the jumpsuit he wore, looked trim and muscled, normal for a miner.

She had noticed he hadn't eaten any food. Crisp fries with a spicey vinegar dip and a veggie platter with a creamy sauce had been their meal. The simplicity made her mouth water just thinking about it.

"Aren't you hungry?" she'd asked him.

His lip twitched. "I ate earlier."

Explained his lack of an appetite. Narissa shrugged off her suspicions. Her father had taught her to watch for unusual behavior and why. Not eating food had been one of them.

The hopper slid into a tunnel and a metal door opened. They waited several minutes before the second door slid back.

"We're equalized," Abram explained.

"So we can get out." Bruce glanced around, his face reflecting his disappointment. "Don't look like much."

"Better than most," Abram returned, not seeming upset by the boy's comment.

"Bruce," Narissa warned.

"It's fine," Abram assured her. "Bruce, want to help me carry everything to where you'll be sleeping."

"Sure!"

They all pitched in carrying the supplies through the metal doors opening to a large cavern. She noticed the ceiling lights did a good job of lighting the area. A few spots held shadows and Narissa took a deep breath. Nothing lurked there.

"This area should be safe for all of you. I have a door which seals off the main mine." The huge box of groceries he set down on a smooth rock counter. "The cooker is new. Haven't had a chance to use it."

The small silver appliance sat against one wall. She ran her fingers over it, planning dishes to cook for them. "What do you eat?"

"Mostly rations." He shrugged. "I had it shipped in when I started looking for a bride."

Having lived on Mars most of her life, she knew how costly the appliance must have been. "I'm impressed."

"Least I could do."

"Where we gonna sleep?" Susan glanced between the two adults.

"I'll show you," Abram offered.

They left the alcove, went down a short hall, until he reached three carved out areas. "You can pick which one you want. I created niches for beds and put mats in. They should be comfortable."

"There's no door." Susan hugged her doll.

"We can fix that." Narissa could jury rig some blankets as doors, or at least she hoped she could.

"Bathroom is down the hall on the left."

"Where's your room?" Bruce asked.

Abram chuckled. "I have a niche upstairs, there on the right." His eyes sought out hers. "I know it isn't much." She sensed he offered an apology.

"It's more than we had," she assured him.

~ * ~

Abram left them to settle in and went back to the kitchen. Putting away the groceries on the shelves he'd built, he marveled his bride had finally arrived. For so long he'd waited for her. Part of his mind still couldn't believe his good fortune.

Granted, he needed to show them around and go through several emergency procedures and how to handle them. He suspected coming from Io they probably would be familiar with similar drills. Most mining operations had them every week, from what he'd heard.

A bump rubbed against his leg. Startled he gazed into the yellow eyes of the cat. "Hello."

"He's probably hungry." Narissa stood in the doorway.

"I have plates, glasses are there." He pointed to the wooden box he used as a cupboard. "Utensils are there." Another box held them.

"You're well prepared."

"Had time." More than she realized, he added to himself.

"I'm guessing you had your reasons for migrating." She picked a bowl and opened a canister, pouring dry smelly food. The cat followed as she placed it on the ground, nibbling at the meal.

"We all do." A good general answer and hopefully one, which would prevent further questions. He had no desire to share his secrets. Not yet.

"We do, yes," she agreed. "I'm going to put the kids to bed and retire myself."

"Pleasant dreams."

"Thank you." She left, her sweet scent lingering.

The cat finished its meal and sat cleaning itself.

"I'll bet you sleep with her." Ignoring him, the cat continued washing itself. "I envy you."

Not feeling like working, Abram double checked the airlock, before climbing the stairs to his sleeping chamber. Laying down on the mat, he closed his eyes. He'd become used to being alone. No doubt it would take time to become comfortable with others close by.

Vaguely he heard the four heart beats, even though the rock, before he dropped into a sleep where he never dreamed.

~ * ~

Rising before the children, Narissa took a quick shower and put on water for tea. Tibs sat beside his bowl not understanding why it had become empty. She chuckled and fed him, before putting oatmeal on the stove. Slicing up some apples, fresh ones, from what she could tell and put them on a plate. Where had Abram found those?

She left them on the counter and wandered down the hall. Noting the opening to his room she resisted the urge to take a look. If he slept, she didn't want to wake him. At the end she found a metal door. Probably the mine. Another short tunnel led to an open area and she stopped, amazed at what she'd found.

A huge garden filled the space. Fruit trees scattered about with rock piled rock containers and others full of plants. A well-tended herb garden. She took a whiff noting basil, peppermint and catnip? Tibs would love the treat.

"I see you found my garden."

Narissa jumped. "I thought you were sleeping." She turned to face Abram.

"I only require a few hours of rest." He smiled. "Didn't mean to scare you."

"I see where the apples came from." She pointed to the tree.

"There's granny smiths, galas, goldens, pears, peaches, lemon, several nuts, potatoes, carrots, spinach, lettuce, radishes and much more."

With a garden they wouldn't be dependent on off world shipments. Plus, it would all be fresh. A rarity in most of the colonies.

"Gardening's a hobby," he explained.

She heard a buzz and instinctively ducked.

"Just a bee." He pointed toward the back. "I have a hive. They pollinate and I harvest the honey."

"I'm impressed."

He glanced down. "There's a door which seals the room in case of a breech. Safest place if anything happens."

A chill traveled down her spine. "Has anything ever happened?"

"No." His facial expression reassured her. "I need to go to work. When I finish there are several safety protocols I need to walk you and the children through."

"We're familiar. Io did the same."

"Figured you would be. I'll see you in a few hours." He left her.

Returning to the kitchen, she finished making breakfast and woke the children. They ate around a small table in the back corner and washed the dishes afterward.

"What are we going to do all day?" Susan hugged her doll.

"There's a garden. I think we should see what's there and decide what to pick for lunch."

"A garden?" Bruce stared at her. "Here?"

"Yes." Afterward she'd get Bruce and Susan set up with their school homework. She'd allowed them to take a break while traveling. While they studied, she wanted to explore the cavern they'd come through when they'd arrived.

Tibs ambled behind them, sniffing at the walls. When they entered the garden, he found a spot to his liking and laid down, stretching his full length. His eyes closed.

"What do you think we should have for lunch?" She waited for the children to decide. At least she'd grabbed a bowl to fill.

"Any oranges?" Susan loved the fruit.

"Let's find out."

They explored and found some. Bruce picked lettuce and tomatoes for a salad. Susan added carrots. Narissa plucked radishes plus basil and spinach. They'd have salad and she'd figure out how to make a dressing.

Taking their food to the kitchen, she set up the children's lap coms so they could do lessons and left them in their rooms studying.

Entering the main area, she surveyed the large cavern. Lots of open space. Nothing done to make it cozy or homey. Panels had been installed on the far wall next to the main entrance. No doubt Abram would teach them what they were and how to use them.

In a cubby she discovered suits, enough for all of them and even a special box for the cat. Abram had thought of everything and been ready for them.

Returning to the kitchen she began making lunch. For dinner she was thinking about a nice hot soup and maybe some bread. When Abram finished working, she'd talk with him about what he liked to eat. Surely he didn't eat rations all the time. Not with the garden available.

Tibs bumped against her. She rubbed along his muzzle. "Have a nice nap?"

He purred and wandered out. No doubt he'd end up on her bed.

Making herself another cup of tea, she sat at the table and sipped the brew. She'd wanted to wait two weeks so she could get to know Abram. He'd left his acting career and she wondered why. His reasons might be private so she might never know.

Just as she couldn't explain about her family. Their profession had been passed down through the generations, starting on Earth and carried on as they settled further out.

She'd gotten tired of chasing legends.

~ * ~

Abram took a quick shower after he'd finished working. The new vein he'd found held promise and he'd kept at it for as long as he could. It would cover many expenses and allow him to provide for his new family. Provided Narissa decided to stay.

As he dressed in fresh clothes, he knew eventually he'd have to share his secret with her. Only fair for her to know before their marriage. He wanted her to have a choice. He'd just have to make sure he covered his tracks in the event she couldn't accept him.

Sighing, he left the bathroom and caught the scent of potatoes cooking along with other delicious smells. Meat, a luxury item, rarely available. He couldn't remember the last time he'd eaten any. Not that he'd be able to digest it.

He entered the kitchen. Soup bubbled on the stove. Narissa sat at the table lost in thought.

"Everything all right?" He leaned on the counter.

"Fine." She offered a shy smile. "Bruce and Susan are doing their homework."

He hadn't thought about the children having schoolwork. As a child he'd hated it. "Willingly?"

"They don't argue."

Tibs sauntered in sitting in front of his dish. Narissa rose, gave him food and smiled. "This place needs a few things to make it a home."

"I'll leave the choices up to you."

"We never had much." She glanced away. "Importing from Earth is expensive. Guess I'll have to get creative."

Part of him relaxed. Narissa's thoughts were to make the caverns a home. Perhaps she'd stay. Question was, would she want to when she learned the truth?

~ * ~

Over the next few days, Abram taught them how to put their suits on. Narissa and the children already had learned on Io so it wasn't much of a learning curve. The box for Tibs was new and they each took a turn putting the cat into it. He yowled the entire time.

Her prospective husband also taught them about the various doors and how to reach the garden before the auto seal. She learned to care for each plant and even had a quick lesson on bee keeping. A chore she'd leave for Abram. The insects weren't dangerous as they were a hybrid breed with no stinger.

She'd even had a few lessons on driving the hopper. He'd taken her around the asteroid and back inside. How she'd ever be able to navigate through the field she had no idea and wasn't certain she wanted to find out.

Only one thing frustrated her. He never ate with them. Either he was in the mine working or performing maintenance on the equipment. He went to bed after she did and rose long before she woke. Not a good combination for building a marriage and partnership.

A couple of days remained before the trial period ended. Narissa hesitated making the commitment to Abram while at the same time not wanting to travel to Mars; back to a past she wanted no part of.

"You look troubled."

She glanced up from her mug, her eyes meeting Abram's. "Having a difficult time making up my mind."

He nodded. "There's only a couple of days left." Rubbing his neck, his expression reflected his doubt. "I need to share something with you before you decide."

Her heart sped up. What could he be keeping a secret? "Oh?" Like she wasn't keeping one herself.

Abram sat down across from her. He took a deep breath. "I'm not exactly what you think I am."

"Did you murder someone?" She slapped her hand over her mouth. She hadn't meant to say those words.

"Not intentionally."

Took her a moment for his words to register. "How did it happen?"

"I," he paused as if searching for the words. "Hard to explain."

"Suppose you try." She knew she sounded cold.

"Not what you think."

"I know from reading the scandal rags you left your career suddenly." She took a sip of tea. "Lot of speculation as to why."

"Behind the scenes stuff I couldn't deal with. Not important."

"Have a disagreement with director or producer?"

"No. That would have been easy to fix." He leaned forward slightly. "I was a bit wild in my younger years."

"Womanizer?" She hated men who used women.

"I went out with many hopeful actresses. Not proud of myself." He drew a pattern on the tabletop with his finger. "New club opened. Heard good things. Went to see for myself." He shook his head. "Wish I hadn't."

She waited for him to continue, glad she'd held onto the tickets to take her and the children to Mars, even if she didn't want to return.

"I met a woman. A dark beauty with a sultry voice and eyes I couldn't break free from."

Narissa blinked, a chill filling her. Surely not!

"I woke the next night not sure what had happened and a dead body beside me. She told me I killed the man."

Barely able to get the words out she asked, "Killed. How?"

He squirmed. "You won't believe me."

"Try me."

"I had a taste in my mouth. One I didn't know and craved." He swallowed. "She turned me into a creature who hunted humans in the night." With a shudder he told her, "I'm a vampire."

All of her instincts rushed back. Without thought she grabbed a knife and raised it over her head ready to strike. Abram made no move to defend himself. His nonaction caused her to pause. Instead of taking his head, she stared at him, trembling.

"You're a hunter." His statement so matter of fact, she almost found it amusing.

Lowering the knife she tossed it on the counter. "No. My father was."

"He taught you."

"He did." Shaking, she sat back down. Abram had shared the one thing she'd never even thought about. Her father had been good at hiding the bodies so she had no idea if his claims had even been true.

"I know there's a colony of us on Mars," Abram told her. "Hunters too, from the warnings I got."

"My father had a strong following. I'd been living on Io when he died so I don't know any details." She covered her eyes. "I never wanted to."

"Wouldn't blame you if you wanted to leave." His voice conveyed his sadness.

"It's a shock." She dared to look at him. "Have you?" Narissa couldn't ask.

"No," he answered. "I only need to feed once a month. Gift from my creator."

"Is that why you wanted a wife?" She couldn't imagine needing one for any other reason.

"I want a wife for the same reason any man does. Companionship and other things."

"Not blood?"

"I have a rat population in the mine I use."

She blinked. "Rats?"

"They're not bad."

Confused. Narissa needed time to think.

"I'd understand if you wanted to leave. I can check the ship schedule if you like." He looked like a lost little boy.

"I'll let you know." Dazed, she wandered into the garden glad the children were doing their lessons. Her father's training and warnings warred in her mind. How could Abram be a vampire? He'd taken such care to make certain she and her siblings would be safe.

No matter what.

~ * ~

As Abram worked in the mine, he feared what Narissa would decide. As a hunter she'd be perfectly justified in killing him. She knew how. Her training had been obvious when she'd grabbed the knife. Yet, she hadn't killed him. Instead, she talked with him.

If she decided to leave, he'd wipe her memory, the children's and Liz's. Leave no tracks leading back to him. He'd suspend his Space Bride's contract and try again in a couple of years. Only course of action available to him.

When he finished the vein he'd been working on, he cleaned up and went to find Narissa. He found her in the garden, sitting under the apple tree. She didn't look at him as he sat beside her.

"You're leaving." He knew she had no choice.

"No."

"I can—" he stopped, not sure he'd heard her correctly. "What?"

"I'm not leaving." Her hand found his. "I left Mars because my father tried to marry me off to his second in command. They'd arranged it without me knowing and if anything happened, well, I think you get the picture."

"There'd be no question on who took command," he filled in.

"Exactly." A tear trickled down her cheek. "I said horrible things to my father and took the first ship off Mars. In some ways, I regret not ever reconciling with him. In others—" She shrugged. "I'm hoping I did the right thing."

"Were you ever a hunter?"

"Dad trained me to be. I chose another path. I like to cook."

"I'm sorry I can't sample your food."

"Now at least I understand why."

"Do you want to marry me?" He waited for her answer, afraid

of her response.

She laughed. "I think my father would be appalled."

"Is that a yes or no?"

"I've never been an obedient child. So yes, I'll marry you."

~ * ~

The trip back to the main hub and the Space Brides office Narissa enjoyed. She wore a simple dress and both Bruce and Susan bounced with excitement during the whole trip. Liz arranged for the traveling parson to be present and he married them with Liz and the children as witnesses.

Liz registered their marriage and wished them well.

Back in the mine, Narissa began to plan on how to turn the cavern into a home. It would take time and imagination. She felt up to the challenge. After a dinner of stuffed baked potatoes, Bruce and Susan went to bed, with Tibs electing to sleep with her sister.

Nervous, she mounted the stairs to Abram's room. He smiled at her, extending his hand.

"I never thought to ask," she began, not sure how to frame her question.

"There are many myths about us. I'm capable of being a true husband to you."

"Children?"

"Possible, if you wish it." He settled her beside him. "We have time. There is no rush."

"Good."

He kissed her and she forgot about everything except enjoying being with her new husband.

~ * ~

Owned by two cats, Taj and Esther, **Dana Bell** enjoys writing stories about her feline companions, places she's lived or visited, and allowing her mind to turn tales sideways. Currently she has four published books along with more short stories than she can count, one of which is in an award-winning anthology, and has won awards for her poetry.

Also an editor, she has lost count of how many anthologies she's done along with the number of new writers whose careers she has helped launch.

She works a day job to keep a roof over her head and food on her table. Her cats appreciate her efforts as they stay warm and fed.

Hobbies include doll houses, arranging silk flowers, and making candle holders.

# SHE'S A BIT GREEN

Bogna Jordan

## Voymir

"No mom, I didn't find a girl yet." Voymir rolled his eyes, thankful the camouflage shield of the mercenary ship interfered with holograms.

"You have to quit that silly business and settle down," his mother continued, as on all previous calls these past few years.

"Yeah, yeah." Obviously, his mother did not appreciate he'd completed the training on the Orly armour to become the elite warrior, and earned a comfortable living. Apparently he needed to be saved from his job. He added a few more drops of oil to the wing of his armour and tested the mobility of the joint. Satisfied, he moved to the next.

"When will you be back on that Io base? I want to send you something." She dropped the girl subject, which Voymir took with relief. He was way more comfortable talking about sun storms and asteroids than his love life, or lack thereof. He'd love to talk about the upgrades in his armour, but mom didn't really care. Even the crew members just laughed it off, shaking their heads at his craziness.

He shrugged. In the beginning being an Orly ended up in death more often than not. Things changed, armour improved, and flying on various missions through the atmospheres of planets was usually a repeat experience. Unless the armour failed. Then an Orly would be at the mercy of gravity or the enemy's weapons the armour could not protect them from anymore. The survival statistics were much better than when the first Orly flew, but the reputation remained. Possibly right so, because Voymir couldn't imagine himself doing anything else, even if it would still be a toss of a coin if he'd come back or not. Being an Orly let him have an impact. A single mission could save the lives of hundreds of men. Or destroy them. Thankfully, the captain only accepted jobs which aligned with both of their moral compasses.

"Yeah, we'll stop by next month or so." That was the most specific he was allowed to be, though they'd be there much faster;

their current mission was taking them to the mists of Jupiter.

His mom kept chattering about her complaints about the weather control system back on Earth, and why he wasn't visiting. Surely they didn't have quality food on Io. He certainly was skinny now and would get sick any moment. Voymir finished inspecting of his armour and leaned against the wall, letting her talk, dropping in a word or two.

The interference noise announced the end of the conversation.

He stared out the window, they were approaching Jupiter. With his usual breathing exercises he started to mentally prepare for the jump. Galactic Pirates kidnapped a five-year-old. They attempted to use the boy to enforce above-the-law status for their organisation. They were not known for treating their prisoners well. Especially when the blackmailed would not submit.

"Heads up, Voy," the Captain's voice came through the gauntlet.

"Got it," he answered and started pulling on other pieces of the armour.

Once again, he tested the armour's shield and sensors warning of malfunctions. Satisfied, he left his cabin.

He nodded at the members of the crew, lining up in the corridor. He hit his chest and they responded. Only two crew members and the Captain were actually needed for his takeoff. But he was an Orly.

Beating of the crew's fists against their uniforms accompanied him all the way to the hatch. Ned scanned his armour with a diagnostic machine. When it beeped happily, confirming the operational status of Voy's armour, the Captain came up to him.

"Ready?" he asked.

Voy confirmed with a nod.

"We'll be awaiting the call." The Captain nodded back at him and waved to Fax to let Voy out.

He stepped through the inside hatch door, which closed with a hiss after him. The panel beside the outer door beeped and the green light lit. The door slid open and he jumped into Jupiter's atmosphere, igniting the thrusters in the armour's boots to clear away from the ship.

After a few seconds of dropping down, he spread the wings of his armour. A jet threw him sideways. He adjusted the metal feathers and used the wind to carry him from the brighter coloured zone to the darker belt of descending gases.

Voy activated the scanner for solids. The pirate base was easy to find, as the only big mass staying afloat in the stratosphere.

The first lightning struck him.

He cursed, blinded by the light as the armour absorbed the power.

"I hate flying in Jupiter," he mumbled and transferred a portion of the energy into speed. Five flashes of lightning later, he saw the dome of the protective shield over the pirate base.

## Nimfa

Nimfa checked her face in the mirror. Again she thought about concealing her green skin.

*No. I won't lie. Won't pretend to be something I'm not. If he'll reject me because of my skin colour…then too bad, I'll just wait for another applicant. My life will be no worse than it was. And maybe he'll learn to be more precise than requesting someone with good cooking skills.* As much as a man caring only about his stomach displeased her, it became her best chance, because she did cook well. Life as a cook was still better than being a lab rat.

A gentle chime alerted her that they'd be landing on Io soon.

*Well, that was my last chance. Nothing to do now but smile.* She got up and gathered her things.

Photosynthesizing humans had not, to the company's dismay, become a hit. While she became less valuable as a failed product, the scientists kept experimenting, trying to regain some of the costs sunk in her production. Her so-called parents signed off her human rights at the donation of the reproductive cells. She belonged to the company since birth. But the company was no more.

She closed her eyes, recalling the image of the Orly, diving down from the sky, rescuing her from being contained in her cell at the lab and being subjected to the endless painful procedures. What his true purpose had been, she never found out. But by wiping out the owners, there was no one who could claim her.

Many of the other experiments decided to stay, but how could she stay when there was a whole world to explore?

She nervously flicked her wing, then folded it neatly against her back, hiding it between the folds of shawl she specifically draped to hide them. As much as she didn't want to lie or pretend, maybe one shock at a time would be wiser.

She looked uncertain at her cabin door. After so many rejections, it was hard to hope.

Thinking back to the Orly who had saved her, she straightened up. She'd be brave. With a heavy exhale she touched the panel beside the door and stepped through once they slid open.

There was one benefit of her indecision. She avoided the rushing crowd, fighting over exiting the ship the fastest.

She went down the empty corridor all the way to the ship's exit door and pulled out the description of her fiancé attached to the original request.

She skimmed through the flowery language and the many amazing features he supposedly had. *This guy has some serious problems.* She sighed. A narcissist was not optimal, yet she'd give this relationship her best. She gave her word by signing the contract. At least she knew she should look for a tall, and muscular, if you believe his self-advertisement, man with bright brown hair and hazel eyes.

When she didn't see anyone resembling the description, she just shrugged. If the description would be even half-true, he wouldn't need to use a Space Brides services after all.

She moved to the closest brown-haired man. Before she could reach him, he was surrounded by what looked like a family group and they left the terminal talking and laughing.

She looked around for another suspect, but everyone seemed to have already met up with whoever they came to pick up and soon she stood alone in the huge hall.

*What a great start to a breathtaking romantic adventure.* She took a deep breath, trying not to fall apart from disappointment. She knew she shouldn't expect a warm welcome once he saw what she looked like, but not even picking her up? She squeezed her eyes, determined not to cry. Not in public at least. *Maybe the company couldn't get a hold of him, there had been known to be some communication interruptions in the farther Solar System.* She put down her luggage and sorted through papers to find the address. She let her watch read it. The glasses slid over her eyes and a hologram overlay appeared, with bright orange arrows pointing her way.

# Captain

The Captain flicked through the holograms with job opportunities. They all required an Orly. Of course. A fully functional Orly.

He squeezed the bridge of his nose. It'd been a month. Voy hadn't died yet, but he hadn't woken either. Soon, decisions would need to be made.

Bio-recognition activated a hologram notice that his assistant was at the door. Dath still knocked, of course.

"Come in, come in." He waved his hand to open the doors.

His assistant looked…unsure. Embarrassed?

"What got you tied in a knot, Dath? Finally meet a girl?" He laughed.

"There…is a girl, sir."

The Captain snorted.

"She's here to see Voy," Dath finished.

The Captain narrowed his eyes. Voy wasn't exactly in shape for spontaneous dating at the moment.

"We know her?" he asked, frowning.

"No, sir. And…she's a bit green." Dath added.

Green, huh. That would leave two options. Either she was a thankful rescuee who somehow managed to track them, or she'd been sent to kill them.

"Any weapons?" he asked.

"Kitchen knives. Really nice, cladded." Dath nodded. "Should we confiscate?"

"No, send her in. Set Randy and Pat on standby. In the worst case, you'll get a promotion." He winked at Dath.

"Don't joke like that, Captain." He shook his head and left.

Dath came back, leading a lean, green, and visibly disturbed, lady.

"Hello." She tried to smile, a rosy-pink colouring her pale green cheeks. When he only nodded in response, she sighed and continued, "I'm looking for Voymir C…"

"Chruscik," he supplied with a sly smile. "You read 'ch' as 'k' and you get pretty close." He did not, of course, help her with the last part of the name. If she did indeed come here to blast them off the surface of Io, he would not deny himself the amusement of her stumbling over Voy's name.

"Um, yes. Thank you. So he does live here, correct? Didn't the company notify him about my arrival?"

If they had the same company in mind, they would definitely not warn them about her visit.

"I'm afraid not. What's the company?" He flicked on an empty hologram screen.

"Space Brides." She bit her lip, the pink of her cheeks turning darker.

A clash outside the side door informed him one of his body-guards dropped something heavy.

*So professional.* The Captain almost facepalmed himself.

"I wasn't aware he planned on getting hitched."

"That's the agreement." The girl passed him a file of actual paper. "I like paper." She added after he raised an eyebrow, then blushed again, probably realizing how silly it sounded.

The Captain checked the file, making sure to keep part of his attention on his green visitor. Voy's information was scary accurate, especially since the signature definitely wasn't his.

## Voymir

He heard footsteps and the deep rumble of the Captain's voice. A gentler, female voice joined in, asking about something. Pleasant voice, like the sound of a creek and the warmth of a fireplace.

Voy grew tired again, drifting off to nothingness before he could recognize who it belonged to.

## Nimfa

The Captain led her to Voymir's cabin. She plopped down, trying to process the situation.

"At least he didn't lie about his description much." She laughed, reaching to her boots. She swallowed. There was something wrong about seeing a strong man helpless, connected to pipes and wires.

She pulled her boots off and looked about the room. Startled, she noticed she sat on Voymir's bed. It surprised her to discover a homemade quilt, made with denim hexagons, covered the top. Behind it, a potted ivy plant covered almost the whole wall. A plain shelf with some gaming gear and a few old-fashioned books. She almost walked over to pick them up, but she stopped when she saw the armour.

Voymir What's-his-name was an Orly.

She took a step toward the armour. Nimfa hesitated and turned her head to look at the security camera the Captain pointed out to her, apologizing they needed that safety measure.

Will they storm in and arrest her if she came close to Orly's armour? Better not risk it.

She sighed and went over to her luggage to take out her nightgown. At least the washroom was supposed to be private. And surprisingly luxurious.

After a much-needed shower she was left with the dilemma of where to sleep. Or more, if she dared to sleep in a stranger's bed, even if that stranger were absent.

Finally she slid under the hexagon quilt and layed on her side, at the very edge of the bed.

## Voymir

The silence was mixed in with the Captain's visits, when he talked to his girl. He still couldn't tell the words apart. But the Captain's voice was, if not pleasant, familiar. And the girl's, if not familiar, definitely pleasant.

*Too bad she's taken.* A thought drifted in and out, unable to take hold in his unfocused mind.

"…Voymir…?" She'd said his name. He tried to open his eyes. Couldn't. Too hard.

## Nimfa

Almost a week had passed since Nimfa arrived. Her fiancé hadn't awakened yet. What would happen if the decision period would lapse before he'd be up?

She smiled and waved to the crew as she passed on her way to the kitchen. They bowed slightly. Shaking her head, she almost laughed. Was it because her fiancé was an Orly? Though she did see a great improvement in how they treated her after the Captain let her cook.

She arrived at the kitchen and got to work.

"Donuts?" the Captain asked, refilling his coffee mug.

"Uhm, with pudding filling." She placed the dough in and

clicked away at the cooking machine. Once it started frying the donuts, Nimfa clicked a few more buttons, allowing it to make the pudding by itself. It was one of the few meals where the machine had the upper hand, or, circuit boards. Most other foods when entrusted completely to it were edible at best. "We're running low on vanilla extract, should I switch to something else next time?"

"Use whatever you want, I got a local contact." He winked at her.

"A vanilla smuggler?" She lifted her eyebrow.

"Grower," he whispered, as if it would be a criminal secret.

"Aw, you're willing to risk your reputation for me?" She laughed. The machine beeped, announcing the first batch ready.

"If you keep cooking like this, I won't have a choice, under threat of mutiny." He poked her with an elbow on his way to snatch three donuts. "Are you ready to visit your fiancé?"

She nodded, taking a donut for herself.

"You may need to find yourself another cook, to avoid mutiny and all." She took a bite, trying to gather thoughts. "I don't know what will happen if Voymir doesn't wake up by the end of next week."

"If he's still in the hospital by the end of the month, I'm out of business anyway." The Captain scowled.

They came in for their daily check up on Voymir's health. She was glad for the Captain's company, otherwise she would have grown hopeless with no signs of his improvement.

The Captain greeted the nurse replacing the jug of water at Voymir's bed table.

"There had been heightened brain function yesterday," she responded with a smile. "Still, we shouldn't expect many changes yet." Sighing, she adjusted the cup and the paper napkins beside the jug.

"At least something." He sat on a chair beside her, starting his last donut.

"What will happen to him? If you'll..." she wrung her dress in her hands, not sure if she overstepped. But she needed to know. Even when she didn't know her fiancé yet, she saw the respect and care the crew had for him.

"He'll be all right." The Captain bit his lip.

"Voymir was...is your close friend, isn't he?" She leaned closer, trying to comfort him with a touch on his shoulder.

The Captain finished off his donut and got up.

"You outdid yourself. I'll need to grab some more before my locust of a crew descend on them." He winked at her and smiled, but that didn't cover the hurt and sadness in his eyes.

The doors closed after him and Nimfa was left alone with her unconscious fiancé.

"Voymir, your friends miss you," she told the Orly.

His head tilted slightly and a strand of hair fell across his closed eyes.

Without thinking, she reached out to tuck the hair behind his ear.

His eyes slowly opened. They were indeed hazel, and when he saw her, they lit up with a smile.

"I wondered…who the…beautiful voice…belonged to." His voice was hoarse and sounded like he had trouble speaking. Still, he somehow managed to sound charming. The man matched his flowery description even better now. Strangely, he did not seem narcissistic.

Nimfa noticed she still had her hand touching the side of his face. Before she could snap her hand back, the door opened.

"You won't believe it! Those scoundrels didn't leave a single one…" The Captain dropped his mug with coffee, which automatically produced a lid before hitting the ground, staring at his friend.

"You're not going to introduce us?" Voymir asked in his raspy voice.

"Oh, I'm sure you'll want some water." Nimfa got up and filled a cup.

"This lovely lady is Nimfa. She already knows who you are." The Captain nodded to Voymir.

She didn't know why they both insisted on calling her pretty. Goodness gracious, she was green! Probably mannerism from their past. She lifted the cup to Voymir's lips, giving him a moment to refuse if he somehow was not thirsty. He lifted his head and started taking small sips. He barely drank a quarter of the cup before his head collapsed back on the pillow. He started to strain to lift up his head again, but seemed to have run out of strength.

Nimfa slipped her hand under his head to help him drink.

He grinned and looked like he was about to say something, but looked at the Captain and changed his mind. Regardless, he drank the full cup.

"Are you hungry? I could go make some broth," she offered.

Voymir glanced at the Captain again.

"Yes, please." He nodded.

*I guess I am intruding.* She nodded with a smile and left.

# Voymir

When the pretty girl left, Voymir cleared his throat.

"Sorry, man. I didn't mean..." he tried to run his hand through his hair, but he didn't exactly have the strength. "I didn't expect your girl to be so keen on physical contact." He laughed anxiously. The Captain must have noticed that he did not mind being touched by Nimfa at all.

"She's not. Not with me anyway." The Captain cocked his head. "And she's not my girl. Technically, she's your fiancée."

Voymir frowned.

"Not that I mind..." he looked at the door through which Nimfa left. "But, did I hit my head or something?" He tried to force his memory to work. "I got to the pirate base with the normal amount of trouble, found the prisoner and was about to leave. Then that guy came with some kind of electric weapon..." He slowly lifted his hand to his head, fighting the weakness of his muscles and the tangle of cords pinned to him, and rubbed his aching forehead. "It felt like they compressed the lightning bolts, much stronger than even Jupiter's bigger ones. The boy...the boy! Is he all right?" He suddenly remembered the mission's objective. He had no memory of what happened after the weapon hit him.

"He's safe, back with his family. Your armour sent a distress signal. We were able to track you falling through Jupiter's atmosphere. The little guy clung to you, and your wings covered you both. Catching you was tricky, but..." The Captain shrugged "You both survived."

Voymir sank deeper into the pillows, relieved that the first information he received after waking was not one of failed mission and guilt.

"So, just to be sure, do you remember filing to Space Brides?" the Captain asked.

"The what?" Voymir lifted an eyebrow.

"I thought so." The Captain opened the hologram of the copied documents Nimfa had shown him, stopping at the last page, pointing to the signature.

Voymir frowned.

"Why..." he read through the application. He groaned when little details started adding up.

"You know who did it?"

"Yeah. My mother." He clenched his teeth. "How could she do that to me?" He swiped the hologram away and fell back on the pillow.

The Captain cleared his throat.

"I'm sure Nimfa would understand if you don't want to have anything to do with her..."

Voymir shot him a glare.

"Don't you dare use that I'm angry at my mother against me." Part of him did want to ask the girl to leave just to show his mother that she couldn't force her will at him like that. But from her gentle voice and the way she treated him, he knew Nimfa deserved better. He needed time to find a solution.

## Nimfa

Her fiancé was finally awake. Nimfa bit her lip, waiting for the broth to simmer. She didn't have to worry anymore what would happen if the contract lapsed with Voymir still in a coma. Now she had to face the possibility of rejection. When she came here, she knew it was probable, and felt prepared. Back then, she didn't have anything to lose.

She looked around the familiar kitchen. Some crew members passed by, nodding to her with a smile. It felt more like home than any place she'd stayed so far. Shaking her head, she settled on cutting up the vegetables and dropping them into the machine's pot compartment. She hand washed her knife and started nervously tapping the counter.

The machine chimed, informing her the broth was ready. With a sigh she poured some into a bowl. Time to face her destiny.

The closer she came to the med wing, the more her hands shook.

*It will be all right. Whatever comes, I can deal with it, and keep the pleasant memories of my stay here with me forever.* She took a deep breath and entered.

Both of the men were tense, tracking her steps with their eyes.

"Nimfa, I need to tell you something." Voymir bit his lip.

She grabbed the bowl tighter. It did not sound like good news.

"I did not fill out or sign the Space Brides contract." He swallowed.

She felt her body getting colder with shock. *A fraud? How? What will happen to me now?* Her fingers trembled against the hot bowl.

"I know you're close with the captain, so if you'd rather…" he cut off.

*Captain? What does the Captain have to do with any of that?* She frowned.

"If I'd rather what?" she asked when he didn't continue.

Voymir cleared his throat.

"If you'd rather have him as a potential fiancé." The Orly shrugged and reached for one of the paper napkins from the bed table. He rolled and unrolled it while he waited for her answer.

"We're just friends." She shook her head. What was happening? "I was waiting for you. I signed the contract to you, even if you didn't," she finished weakly. She wanted to hug herself, yet still held the bowl.

"Ouch." Voymir laughed, poking the Captain in the ribs.

"Like I would flirt with a girl who might possibly be your fiancée." The Captain rolled his eyes. He got up and approached her. "If that idiot fails to see what a treasure you are by the end of your contract, you know where to find me." He winked and patted her shoulder.

Voymir tossed a rolled-up napkin at the Captain's head.

The Captain laughed and left.

Nimfa sighed. She still didn't know what fate awaited her. The joke about switching fiancés did nothing to clarify her situation.

"I brought the broth." She tried to smile as she came closer.

Voymir took the bowl, scowling at his shaking hands. He put it on the bed table and grabbed her hand.

"Welcome to Io." He whispered with a charming smile, kissing her knuckles.

# Voymir

He forced himself to sit. His muscles shook at the effort. He took a few deep breaths and lowered his bare feet to the ground. The doctor told him he shouldn't try to get up yet. Time to find out who was right.

Holding tight to the rails of his medical bed, he straightened himself up. His legs felt like noodles, not used to supporting his body anymore. He locked his knees and straightened out, slowly releasing the hold on the rails.

*I am an Orly. My body will obey me,* he commanded himself.

He heard the door open, yet didn't look up, unwilling to sacrifice his focus.

"Looks like I won." The Captain laughed. "Doc said you won't be up till tomorrow."

Slowly, making sure to keep control of his muscles, Voymir turned to look at his friend.

"Did anyone even bet I'd follow Doc's advice?" he asked.

"And stay in bed another week?" The Captain snorted.

"In a week I plan to be out of here," Voymir forced through gritted teeth, angry at himself that he barely stood. He'd hate to show his weakness by sitting down, with the Captain present to witness it.

"Um, are you going to order a second cot or you're going to go with the 'one bed' trope?" the Captain teased.

"The what?" Voymir lost his focus and his legs buckled.

The Captain started to laugh, then swore.

"You're all right?" He crouched beside Voymir.

He shrugged. No, he was not all right, but the fall wasn't the biggest culprit.

"She's," he paused, catching his breath. "She's staying in my room?" He asked, pulling himself up on the bed. He didn't even bother forcing himself to sit. There was no pride to salvage.

"We don't exactly have spare rooms here." The Captain shrugged. Voymir could tell something bothered him. He didn't bother prying for the reason. Not when he was too tired to keep his eyes open.

"Don't die yet. We've got a business to run." The Captain punched him in the arm and left.

Voymir's last thoughts before he fell asleep were about the pretty woman with a kind voice staying in his room. Sleeping in his bed.

## Nimfa

She wasn't sure how Voymir would act now. He was pleasant and charming, but that could have been just his personality. Was he even interested in marriage? And, as an Orly, and with how he looked, he certainly didn't have to settle for her. A freak. A failed experiment.

Last night she almost packed up and left. She loved this place and the crew, who seemed not to notice her greenness, but all the names she's been called through her life rang loud in her mind. It seemed another rejection would make her collapse into despair.

But she signed the contract and intended to keep her word.

While she dared not hope Voymir would fall in love with her in the short time caused by his coma, she knew she'd forever torment herself with the 'what if'.

She took another determined, though slightly shaky step toward the medical wing. She braced herself against all of the reactions her appearance usually caused and opened the door.

The Orly caught her off guard.

When he saw her in the doorframe, his eyes lit up and he smiled like he actually wanted to see her. More, like he was waiting for her.

She stepped in and turned her gaze to the floor.

"You…don't have to do this, you know," she managed to say.

"Do what?" Confusion in his voice made her look up.

"Pretend that you want to see me. Nobody ever wants me. The only reason I even was matched with your application was that you…" she paused, catching herself. "I mean, it only specified that you'd like someone who cooks well." She swallowed, waiting for his reaction.

"Ah. I heard that you're starting a coup in the kitchen." He winked at her, still smiling.

She winced. Nobody ever joked *with* her. Only about.

Hearing the rustling of the fabric, she looked to Voymir again. And dropped her gaze to the floor again, for an entirely different reason.

The footsteps were slow, and uneven. She wondered if maybe she should come to him, as walking seemed to be hard for him. Before she decided, he stopped. A warm hand touched her cheek.

"Hey, now." He spoke gently, as if to a spooked animal. He moved his hand under her chin, and she had to close her eyes not to gape at his bare chest. Her face finally in a position that promised safety, she dared to look. "Who wouldn't want to be with someone able to start a riot with a handful of cupcakes?" He grinned at her.

## Voymir

Nimfa had so much pain in her voice. So much fear. He told her he wanted to get to know her better. Why didn't she believe him? Her whole posture showed she expected to be hurt, kicked like a stray dog. Anger boiled in his blood, but there was no way to track down those who caused that. So he covered his rage with jokes, trying to let her know he valued her.

When she winced, he barely stopped himself from swearing.

He was out of ideas. When he was a little boy, hugs helped him calm down. Not that he'd ever admit it now. He had a reputation to uphold. Maybe touch would help her too. Make her believe he really treasured that she came to visit him every day. That it was her voice that brought him out of the coma.

He breathed heavily, forcing his legs to move, having to think about how the muscles of his feet should behave to keep him upright. But he made it.

Now what? He doubted Nimfa would be happy with a forced hug. So he opted for touching her cheek. His hand looked terribly pale against her green skin. If he'd tan a bit more though, it'd look really nice. They'd need to move closer to the sun for that. And she'd have to be willing to move with him for any further comparisons to be made. She was still looking down. He tipped her chin so she'd look at him.

"Who wouldn't want to be with someone able to start a riot with a handful of cupcakes?" He smiled at her, trying to put warmth and humor into the expression. She didn't laugh. He thought he saw a corner of her mouth lift in amusement, but her body was stiff and mostly she looked…uncomfortable. What was he doing wrong?

"Um, would you mind…putting a shirt on?" she whispered

timidly.

"Oh." He felt his face burn. "Yeah, let me see." He glanced around the room. There was no sight of spare clothes anywhere. "I guess they're all in my room. I could cover up with a blanket?" he suggested.

She gave a little nod, her eyes fixed on the floor and not him.

Step by step, he managed to return to his bed. He sat, securing himself with both arms, then reached for a blanket to wrap around himself. Nimfa reluctantly followed, and sat at the edge of a chair beside his bed.

"So, what do you like to do, besides cooking?" he asked after a moment of awkward silence.

"Travelling?" she answered, although she sounded more like she was asking. "That's how I learned to cook, actually." She continued when she saw he expected her to tell him more. She talked about the different regions, and where what foods were the most popular. How sometimes within the same city there were multiple food factions. She told him about an old man in a small restaurant who took her in and showed her different meal modifications.

The more she talked, the more invested she became in her memories. When inevitably his stomach growled from all the descriptions of delicious food, she laughed.

"I'll go make you something." She smiled.

## Nimfa

She smiled at her reflection. It had been almost a week since Voymir awoke from his coma, and so far none of her fears came true. Not only did he tolerate her looks, strangely, he seemed to like it. Slowly, it made herself like her body more too.

She walked toward the door, when someone knocked. She opened and two men nodded hello, bringing in a mattress. Confused, she watched them place it on the floor and before she could ask why they brought it, they'd left.

She shrugged and headed to the med wing.

Voymir was doing push-ups.

Nimfa cleared her throat.

"Some men brought a mattress to my...well, yours...our? Room." She decided to omit she doubted the doc approved his exercises. She knew him well enough now to know that it would not, in fact, make him stop.

"That's great." He got up. "Let's go." He pulled her back to the door, stopping at the pad beside it.

"I'm signing myself out, Doc." He recorded the message and off he went, still holding her elbow.

As they walked, he glanced at her back, like he was…

She twitched her wings nervously. That didn't help to hide them of course, but not all her reactions followed logic. Very few of them did, if she had to be honest.

Will he ridicule them? It wouldn't match with Voymir's behaviour she'd seen so far, but her mind had no trouble imagining him saying cruel words like she had heard about her wings over and over. And, did she really deserve better? She was just a lab rat.

"Can you fly with them?" Voymir asked in a timid voice.

She shook her head.

"They were designed to increase sunlight exposure," she explained, still wondering when he'll degrade her for being an experiment.

"Still, flying on Io, outside the fake gravity zone…um, I promised Doc I'd take it easy, so that's where I'm going to check my armour." He ran his hand through his hair. "Would you like to come?"

## Voymir

The screwdriver fell from his clumsy fingers. He could blame his hospital stay, but he knew it was all because of his need to impress Nimfa.

Finally, he double-checked the armour, making sure his clumsiness did not cause an error. Then, satisfied, he put it on. Relaxing under the familiar weight, he followed his routine. He initiated connection. The armour pressed against his back between his shoulder blades.

Instead of awareness of the wings, a sharp pain exploded.

He gasped and kneeled over.

"Voymir! Is everything all right?" He heard Nimfa's panicked scream, but he didn't have strength to respond.

His head hurt like a super nova exploded. He shut his eyes. It didn't help. Couldn't open them again though.

He heard running. The door slid open.

"Captain!" Nimfa yelled.

More footsteps, rushing in. Someone pressed the armour release. The pieces fell away, like he'd shed his skin.

"Miss the med wing already, Voy?" He made out Captain's voice.

He felt the poke of a needle and a liquid being pressed into his veins. His blood seemed to turn sugary-thick and the pain started to fade. Hands grabbed him and placed him on something soft.

*They're counting on me. I need to be Orly. For them. I need to make it work,* he repeated as he drifted off to sleep.

## Nimfa

She tapped her fingers on the counter. The Captain had secured a specialist to check the damage.

The doctor had sadly shook his head and informed them Voymir would never fly again.

The once Orly had gotten back to walking and exercising, but ever since he heard the news, he'd been only a shell of himself. It had been even harder to watch than when he was in a coma.

"Smells great. Do you need any help?" Voymir popped into the kitchen and asked with a smile, which didn't reach his eyes.

"If you'd get the plates." She smiled back at him, trying to convey encouragement. Would it be all right if she'd touch him? He did touch her before, so...

She reached out, though Voymir already turned to the dishpenser, a handy machine that washed, sorted and stored the dishes. Her hand hovered over his shoulder, but the fear of rejection won out. She went back to the cooking station.

Voymir brought the dishes over. He held onto them instead of placing them on the counter.

"I'm sorry we had to meet like that. I wish..." he stopped.

"That's hardly your fault. I doubt you let that guy zap you on purpose." She winked at him.

"Even Orlys are not that reckless." He laughed and bumped her with his elbow, finally setting the plates down. Then all the good humor drained out of him, as if what he said caught up with him.

Not knowing how to cheer him up, she focused on food.

"Do you want to eat here or in the cafeteria?" she asked, serving the pork chops, beets and potatoes on the plates.

"Actually, I'd like to show you a place." Voymir smiled shyly.

He led her to the very top of the building, with only the dome containing the breathable air above them. She looked through the transparent panels, framed in golden alloy, at Jupiter. The swirling, rust-colored belts separated the beige parts, seemingly made of coffee with freshly poured milk. The storms moved in deceptively slow, mesmerizing pace.

She tore her gaze from the view and focused on Voymir.

"Why does it bother you that you can't fly? Most people can't. I even have my own wings and I can't. Somehow, we survive." She asked the question that had been bothering her.

"I…Being an Orly is who I am. It's the only thing I was ever good at. I miss flying. I miss feeling the armour. I miss how the air currents surrounded me, lifted me. How with a turn of few feathers I could manoeuvre, no matter what obstacles I met on the missions." A dreamy smile spread on his lips as he recalled the memories. "And, they were all counting on me. This whole company was based on me being the Orly. The Captain managed the business side. No Orly, no business. We'll have to lay off the entire crew, and I can't do anything about it." His voice broke.

Nimfa blushed, ashamed she hadn't thought about the repercussions herself. She'd seen how the whole crew was waiting for Voymir to wake up.

"If I'm not an Orly, I'm worthless," he whispered.

She snapped her attention to him. How could he think that?

"No, Voymir," she assured him with more conviction than she had about anything else. "You're kind, determined and caring. It doesn't change just because you can't be an Orly anymore. Whatever you decide to be now, you will succeed." She squeezed his hand.

He grasped her hand and started stroking it with his thumb.

"Thank you," his voice quiet and broken. "Would you…" he started but shook his head. "If you're not married yet when I do, I'd very much like to meet again."

She frowned, trying to figure out what he meant. He did want her, but didn't want to marry her? At least not right now. She couldn't understand how not being an Orly affected their relationship. No doubt he could find other work. Surely, life in between jobs wouldn't be nearly as rough as what she experienced after she'd left the lab?

"Would you mind if I'd stay?" she asked.

"Would you?" He gaped at her. "You'd marry me even now?"

"You didn't exactly propose," she teased. "But yes."

He pressed her hand against his lips.

"Oh, I'm sorry." He knelt before her. "Nimfa, my gentle voice who drew me out of my coma, my kind girl with the strength of an Orly, would you do me the honour of becoming my wife?"

Nimfa blushed from hearing the compliments. She smiled at him and nodded. "Yes."

Voymir stood up and stroked her jaw. He stepped closer and gently kissed her. Then kissed her again, like one kiss was not nearly enough. Nimfa agreed.

*I guess I can touch him now. Perhaps even ogle him when he takes off his shirt next time.* She'd scoff at her thought, but she didn't feel like explaining the reason, so she just grinned in a short break between the kisses and sneaked her hand up his chest.

~ * ~ * ~

**Bogna Jordan** grew up in a picturesque town of Łagów, located in western Poland. Surrounded by beech woods, lakes, and with a view of the castle from her bedroom window, it's no wonder she told fantastical stories for as long as she could remember.

Through the years spent studying organic chemistry in an effort to have a more predictable career than writing, her creative hobbies were pushed aside.

Now, as a stay-at-home mom of seven kids, she can freely commit to the frivolous path of a storyteller; it's not like you can mix up pharmaceuticals amidst unpredictable toddler interruptions. And while renovating with her husband the 100-year-old courthouse in the middle of Alberta, Canada, that is now their home.

After over a decade of writing mostly to keep her adult brain working, she's taking a critical look at the pile of works-in-progress. She's starting with the release of a middle grade book "Warning", the first in the Children of Sherwood series, and joining another anthology, "Holding out for a Healer".

If that was not quite enough of chaos, she's also making movies—only short films so far. The two she's most proud of are "Skipping Tomorrows" and "Wanted Dead" — this one used to be on Fantasy Network, but with the untimely demise of the platform, you can now only watch it on her YouTube channel, Mystic Forest.

# More Books from WolfSinger Publications

***The Dragon's Hoard*** – edited by Carol Hightshoe

Dragons are well known for their hoards—but not all hoards are created equal.

A young dragon starts his hoard with some very precious gifts.
One dragon shares her complaints about taxes with a friend as they wait for a lunch delivery.
Another dragon defends her most precious treasures against a group of greedy goblins.
And yet another may hold the solution to saving the Earth after a devastating apocalypse in his collection of bottled treasures.

In addition to the normal gold, silver and jewels here you will find dragons who collect many different treasures. 25 storytellers invite you to enter The Dragon's Hoard and share the treasures within.

***The Dark See*** – M.R. Williamson

As Helen Durkin's journey to find out about herself continues, she finally realizes she needs the help of someone with more knowledge than dwarves, elves, or even dragons. But, just how do you approach the old Wizard Andsell Phagan?

As she tries to solve that problem, yet another dangerous situation presents itself. This mysterious person is no friend of the Phagan family. And, Helen quickly finds herself on a collision course with a halfling who most refer to as Scar—one who dabbles in the dark side of magic.

With this added pressure, the effort to approach and perhaps train under Andsell Phagan intensifies. As time progresses, an old friend comes to her aid and presents the young girl's plight to Andsell. Now, the race is on and the old Dragon Pragamore takes the lead in Helen's plight.

Will Helen finally find out why the Faes are calling her Bright

Helen?

What of Pragamore? Will his years keep him from helping?

And who is Scar really after—Helen, the old wizard, or Pragamore?

## *The Steel Fist* – Rob Jackson

The survivors of Recon 9 are needed in the Ozarks where some home-grown autocrats have taken over parts of Arkansas and Missouri. They've looted National Guard armories and hoarded weapons, ammunition, and vital supplies, just waiting for the opportunity to take over the area. While most of their transport, armor, and aircraft are obsolete, they face people with no protection against such deadly equipment. And they're trying to get the local natural resources to gain control of weapons even the military have no defense against.

Recon 9 has gained four new members and formed an alliance with locals, many of them veterans, against a common enemy. The locals have some grasp of tactics, an excellent knowledge of the hilly, forested countryside and a burning desire to be rid of the terrorists, who call themselves: THE STEEL FIST

## *Crisis in Big-G City* – S.D. Matley

Olympus, Inc., is locked in battle with climate change!

Athena's Secret Ops program steps in when bad boy and technological genius Hermes can't come up with a carbon-curbing solution. Undercover agents Cleo Petra and Pan are deployed in the mortal world to vanquish the notorious East brothers, chthonic fossil fuel magnates who pass as human and eat humans, too…

Two-month-old Pablo, the one-quarter chthonic infant son of two fathers formerly known as P.B., employs his extraordinary abilities of adult speech and intellect in pursuit of climate justice!

Meanwhile, David Bernstein, whose hot romance with Cleo Petra meets a rocky end, recovers the memory of his century-old love affair with a beautiful Spanish nurse. He time travels to 1918 to find her and encounters love, loss, and the City of Mount Olympus —a dark and sinister place where every inhabitant lives in fear of volatile and destructive Zeus!

David's birth father and Hera's former fling, Saul Crispin, is outed as a mortal made immortal. Will Hera's high crime of granting Saul eternal life land her before a jury of her peers for judgment?

And what of baby-crazy Queen of the Underworld, Persephone, pregnant at last but not by Hades?

Intrigue, espionage, crimes of passion, secret babies and looming existential threats—everywhere you look there's a Crisis in Big-G City!

## *Tree of Bones – Book Two: A Familiar's Tale*
- Verna McKinnon

*Two Curses*

*A curse of Darkness…* Deep within the Thill forest, stands a tree made of human bones, crowned in black leaves and red thorns.

*A curse of Light…* Beneath the Wastelands of Skarros, a crystal imprisons a dark, immortal queen.

The Sorceress, Runa, is tormented by horrific images of this tree of bones in a distant, lifeless forest. Even as the visions debilitate her, Mellypip, her beloved familiar, also experiences these sinister dreams, bound by the same dream seer magic as his mistress. The tree of bones summons Runa, and she must risk madness and death as obsession drives her on. What she finds reveals a devastating truth.

Koll the Sorcerer awaits trial for his crimes. His familiar, Xabral, searches for allies to free him. Driven by his own dreams of dark prophecy, Koll seeks to free Obsydia, the Bloodstone Queen, from her prison. Determined to let nothing stop him, Koll will commit any evil to achieve his goal.

Runa and Mellypip's newest journey reveals truths behind ancient secrets, as Koll's obsessive hunt for a fallen queen threatens to doom the world forever. Runa and Koll, bound by opposing magical destinies of Light and Dark, will ultimately face frightening revelations and unimagined consequences.

## *Gate of Souls – Book One: A Familiar's Tale*
– Verna McKinnon

Familiars.
Magical animal companions of sorcerers.
Keepers of spells and secrets.
Most important, devoted friends for life.

When one such familiar, Mellypip, bonds with the young sorceress Runa, he shares in the wonders of magic. Together, Mellypip and Runa train under the tutelage of Runa's grandfather, Cathal, and his cantankerous mountain owl familiar, Belwyn. But secrets and spells do not make for good sorcery. Old friends begin to vanish even as enemies from Cathal's past return, threatening to reveal the truth of Runa's parents; a truth from which Cathal must protect his granddaughter at any cost. When Cathal is kidnapped, Runa and Mellypip rush against time to save their family and friends from dark sorcery that will not only destroy them, but shatter the Gate of Souls and release demonic creatures of The Otherworld into the mortal realms.

## *The Seven Exalted Orders* – Deby Fredericks

Arkanost has Seven Exalted Orders. No more, no less. When a magus goes renegade in a far-off province, the Mage Lords demand something be done.

Ryamon is bitter and frustrated. He longs to be a Fire magus; as a Stone magus, he's miserable. If he can bring the rogue back, he has a chance—his last chance—to fulfill his dream.

It's a great plan—until he actually meets Valdira.

## *Tails from the Front Lines 2: The Thin Blue Line*
– edited by Carol Hightshoe

Come meet some of the four-legged members of Law Enforcement who also serve and protect.

Here our authors will introduce you to the brave K9 officers who serve alongside their human partners. They are their eyes, ears, noses and sometimes when necessary they are their shield, protecting others.

Proceeds from this anthology will be donated to the El Paso County (Colorado) Sheriff's Office K9 program in memory of K9 Jinx who was killed in the line of duty on April 11, 2022.

## *Ring of Fire* – edited by Dana Bell

Enter the Ring of Fire, as unpredictable as the land masses shaking a city and volcanoes erupting covering the landscape. Could there be other reasons for these events? Or could these rings be more than a geological location.

They may be dragons playing tricks
or magic portals opened to mysterious realms
or sacrificing the best work of a lifetime.
Perhaps a rescue during a forest fire
or an attempt to raise the dead
or even while attending a high school reunion.

Journeys are taken to far off lands, another world, and through caves, each with their own unique twist.

Each tale presents a new idea on what the Ring of Fire could be. It is more than what many have been led to believe. Pull up a chair and warm yourself by our fires—just don't let yourself get burned.

## *Coyote* – Charles Combee

While camping in a remote canyon in Utah Jim accidently sees an ancient rite taking place with a coyote like creature presiding over it. Now this creature wants Jim dead.

Audrey and her family go hiking in Utah and are attacked by this creature. Audrey is the only survivor, but she is pulled into a strange world of darkness and glass. She is 'rescued' by Jim, but is still linked to the creature, whose hold on her will end in her death unless Jim can find a way to break that link.

In his dreams, or are they ancient memories, Jim begins to learn more about Coyote as well as the magics that previously bound him. But those dreams end without teaching him the full magics. Can he find a way to free Audrey and stop Coyote from once again terrorizing humankind?

**And more – check out our books at**

*www.wolfsingerpubs.com*